Kala

Kala

Colin Walsh

Atlantic Books
London

First published in hardback in Great Britain in 2023 by Atlantic Books,
an imprint of Atlantic Books Ltd.

Kala received financial assistance from the Arts Council of Ireland.

1 2 3 4 5 6 7 8 9

A CIP catalogue record for this book is available from the British Library.

Hardback ISBN: 978 1 83895 860 2
Trade Paperback ISBN: 978 1 83895 875 6
EBook ISBN: 978 1 83895 875 6

Printed and bound by CPI Group (UK) Ltd, Croydon, CR0 4YY

Atlantic Books
An Imprint of Atlantic Books Ltd
Ormond House
26–27 Boswell Street
London
WC1N 3JZ

www.atlantic-books.co.uk

For my parents

You don't look back along time but down through it,
like water. Sometimes this comes to the surface,
sometimes that, sometimes nothing.
Nothing goes away.

Margaret Atwood, *Cat's Eye*

In Kyoto,
hearing the cuckoo,
I long for Kyoto.

Bashō

Index of main characters

The place:

Kinlough, a tourist town on the West Coast of Ireland

The gang:

Joe Brennan

Katherine 'Kala' Lanann

Helen Laughlin

Aidan Lyons

Mush

Aoife Reynolds

The Brennans (Joe's family):

Dudley Brennan, Joe's father

Margaret Brennan, Joe's mother

The Lananns (Kala's family):

The Mammy Lanann, Kala's grandmother

The Laughlins (Helen's family):

Rossie Laughlin, Helen's father, soon to marry Pauline

Theresa Laughlin, Helen's younger sister

The Lyons (Aidan's family):

Ger Lyons, father of Aidan and the twins, Pauline's ex-husband

Pauline, mother of Aidan and the twins, soon to marry Rossie Laughlin

Donna and Marie Lyons, Aidan's younger sisters, 'the twins'

Teabag Lyons, Lee Lyons and Boomerang Lyons, Aidan's cousins, nephews of Ger

Lydia, Aidan's aunt, Pauline's sister, Mush's mother

Mush, cousin of Aidan, Donna and Marie, nephew of Pauline

Kala

Summer 2003

WE'RE PERCHED ON our bikes at the top of the hill. There's a turning melt of sky above us. The town's glittering below. We're fifteen and it's the summer of our lives so Kinlough is gathering itself up into the moment with us – the whole town's pure responsive to our energies. It races with us in the rhythms of the half-light, hums over the distant fields through the twisting flow of the River Purr, warms itself across the slated rooftops and ledges, climbs with us in the ticking turns of our bikes as we wheel them about the top of the hill, our sneakers scuffling the gravel as we turn to stare down the barrel of the evening, and tip our front wheels slowly, carefully, to the edge.

We are the girls: Kala, Aoife, Helen. We are the boys: Aidan, Joe, Mush.

Kala is between us. We're close enough to see the freckles at the frayed collar of her shirt. Her smell is shea butter and incense, tea tree oil and tobacco. Her crooked eye is already elsewhere. But her other eye is fixed on our target, below.

The target's a narrow gap at the bottom of the hill. It's the slip in the wall where the bicycle path gushes out into the main road. Cars blip and flash inside it, from left and right. The idea is to go cycling down the hill and then pedal blind through the gap, cutting clean and unscathed across the road. It'll be a test of ourselves, our willingness to meet the moment. It's difficult to know whose idea it was, cos by now our group's like a murmuration of birds, turning telepathically into ever new shapes. We all know that if we hit the bottom of the hill at the wrong time, the cars will come screaming at us from every direction.

Which is what makes it so exciting.

Kala wants to be the first to go. She's called it. There's an unspoken agreement that she won't actually ride alone, we'll all go together. This is how it works. We're a crew. Still. We watch her grip flex on the handlebars, waiting for a sign. Her teeth tug on her bottom lip and we straighten on our bikes. Ratty Converses rise to the upper pedals. The sky draws breath. Kala's front wheel noses its way over the edge and her bike tips into the fall and time dilates into something unstable once the rest of us pedal after her, turning the world beneath us, our bikes peeling off the top of the hill into the nothing, where immediately there's no need to pedal any more, gravity's taking care of everything now, coiling us through itself and tearing the path apart beneath our tyres as we go faster and faster, the cars growing louder, the gap getting larger, the lads yelping and shrieking, the bike chains beneath us screaming, when we see that Kala has begun to pedal furiously, all of us shouting and her leaning deeper and pulling out ahead of us, gathering herself into a surge, hair streaking back at us like dark lightning as the path suddenly runs into road, and the sounds become noise, and in the roar of that moment it feels like we're foam becoming ocean.

KATHERINE 'KALA' LANANN

Missing since 3 November 2003 from Kinlough

Born: 1988
Age: 15
Height: 5' 4
Hair: Black
Eyes: Brown
Build:

Last seen wearing large hunting coat over army reserve shirt and black jeans. She also had a distinctive shoulder bag with the logo 'RATM' on it.

Katherine 'Kala' Lanann was 15 years of age at the time of her disappearance. She left her house on the evening of 3 November 2003. It is thought that Kala left her home for a pre arranged meeting with an unknown person.

She made a phonecall from a phonebox in Carthy, a neighbouring town, near 8 o'clock that evening. A short time later a girl answering Kala's description was seen leaning in the back door of a dark coloured Hyundai Accent type car. There were further sightings of a girl similar to Kala in Kinlough at around mid night. When she did not return home, her grandmother became concerned and reported her missing to the Gardai.

Despite an extensive investigation by the Gardai and widespread publicity at the time, Kala has never been found.

If you know of her whereabouts or have any information to offer please contact any Garda Station or phone the Garda Confidential Phoneline on 1800 666111.

This information has been placed here with the permission of Kala's grandmother.

See the missingkids.ie website for an age progressed photo.

**For more photos please visit www.helpfindkala.bebo.com
Email: helpfindkala@gmail.com**

Summer 2018

Friday

Mush

I'M THE WRONG side of thirty and I still love it when summer bursts over this town. That school holiday vibe. First hint of suncream or cut grass hits the air, and I get the tingly bellyflut feeling. It's always a surprise, like. As if every year I forget those smells exist, and bam! The world's young again. Then it's the stretch in the evenings, the drone of the bees, all that good shite.

After close-up I sit by the window of the caf with a six-pack of Tuborg on the counter. I knock the cans back as I watch Kinlough melt into a glisten, parading itself up and down Fox Street, being pure fabulous. People look the most alive they've been all year, like. Their smiles that bit wider. This type of heat makes shite out of everyone – people are lobster red and delirious by the end of the first week of it – but no one gives a fuck, cos Kinlough's being a giddy carnival of itself, all saturated colours. Mams with prams, pizza-faced young bucks messing, young wans smoking, all shimmering and exaggerated movements. For a few weeks a year, Kinlough gets to be the place it really wants to be.

Last summer, when I still smoked, I used to duck out the caf every couple of hours, telling Mam I was out for a rollie. But what I really wanted was a few minutes' peace to let summer flow over myself, and I could linger and merge with it.

No chance of that this year. I glance out the window whenever I can, but there's no let-up. Town's surging. You can smell the money. People come into the caf and make their orders in hysterical voices, sweat beading off them the second they hit the air conditioning. It's a pain in the hoop. Mam loves it, of course. She has the chats with the punters, shouting over the scream of the bean grinder, handing out compliments with every coffee. I keep my back to her and the punters as I prepare the orders, throwing an eye to the madness of town outside. I'm like a dog in a hot car. Hard to even daydream when it's this busy.

All the while, the queue's getting longer, but Mam coos at babies, tells young fellas they're filling out nicely – 'Oh, you'll break a few hearts!' that sort of bollocks – and she knocks a bit of craic out of little kids too. Leans over the counter and they look up at her, all moon-eyed next to their mothers. Mam insists on calling me away from my jobs to offer them some of the crumbled bits of brownie that we keep in a little basket by the till. I hold the basket out like some sort of medieval beggar. Mam gets all excited about the exchange, like it's a real moment. She says, 'That's Mush's Brilliant Brownie! Mush makes that every week, for good girls and boys like you!' The kids just paw at their mouths with the cake, in a world of pure chocolate. Then the mothers say stuff like, 'What do you say to the nice man?' and the kids thank me in that vacant, haunted way kids have. I keep my face turned from them. Some mothers make a big hoo-ha of how grateful they are for Mush's Brilliant Brownie, eager to show that my face doesn't bother them. Others look uncomfortable, alarm in their eyes, despite themselves, and I can respect the honesty in that, even if it does send red blotches pattering up my neck. I mumble some thanks and get back to making the coffees with a towel thrown over my shoulder, head low, glancing out the window, counting down the hours till closing, when everyone will finally fuck off and I can crank up the sound system and have my few cans at the window, watch town do its thing for a bit, float into the beer buzz like a kite cutting its own strings.

It's not easy. People are hyped. You'd like to think it's cos of the Races, and the Festival with the parade, all that. Well, it's not. There was a body found down the woods last week. By the lake. Human remains, that's what they're calling it. No one knows who it is. Was. Punters look around as they mutter about it. *Human remains*, they go, whispering loud enough to be heard, desperate to appear like they might have secret information.

Mam's as bad as any of them. When Auntie Pauline came in earlier, I assumed it was to talk about her upcoming wedding. But the chat immediately swerved off the road into the ditch of human remains. *Human remains*, the pair of them said, eating each other's words, delighted something's happening, something you might read about in the paper.

People are as ghoulish, like.

Everyone's got a theory about it. Even me. Some dark part of me immediately thought it'd be Kala. I didn't want to think that, but sure you can spend your life wanting your brain to work one way and not another, walking around trying to control your thoughts like some fucking Rain Man. No use. The brain does what it wants. People mention human remains and a switch gets flicked in my skull and I see limbs lying in the mulch of the lake like the severed hands in *Jaws*, spilling with claw-clicking crabs. Only suddenly it's not limbs, it's Kala and she's my friend and we're still fifteen and she's looking at me like I can still help, and it's horrible.

So I kept quiet today, even as Mam and Auntie Pauline gossiped about it. Then they started going at me about getting my hair cut for the wedding. Mam said I'd a head on me like something dragged through a hedge. She wouldn't leave me alone till I agreed to get a clip, just so they'd give me a bit of peace. Turned away from them and focused on things to look forward to.

My few cans of Tuborg. I've had them cooling in the fridge all day.

And now it's only me and the sound system. I've counted the register, mopped the floor, wiped down the tables. I'm almost at the point where I can take my spot at the window.

I'm stacking the last of the chairs when the bell on the door tinkles and the twins come in doing their imperious little march to their favourite booth. Auntie Pauline named the twins Donna and Marie, after the Osmonds. Donna has her hair rowed into these knackery braids, and she's wearing her I'm-sixteen-and-this-world's-brutal puss face. Marie's hair is bunched up in two little balls on her head, like Minnie Mouse. She smiles and gives me the finger as they take a booth.

I give her the finger back.

They used to call in to me for a hot chocolate after closing when they were kids, but that's slacked off a fair bit since the eyeliner and fake tan came in.

I've already cleaned the machine, I tell them, and continue stacking the chairs. They don't even say hello, just murmur. Marie taps on her phone while Donna tears sachets of sugar onto the table I've only just wiped down. I hesitate. 'I'm only after wiping that down,' I say. Donna rolls her eyes so theatrically I have to dip my head or she'll catch me smiling.

I suck on my mouth a moment, tap on the counter. I can picture the beads of glisten on the cans, tucked in the back of the fridge. This is my little moment of the day, like. To myself. The twins are sitting in their booth, not paying any mind. This is the way it's been with them for a while. They impose themselves on you, this pure moody silence, and make you ask them questions just to break the silence they're after fucking creating. Teenagers.

'So, what have ye been at today, then?'

'Ah,' Marie shrugs, staring at her phone. 'Nothing, like.'

She holds the phone out to Donna, and Donna starts laughing, hand over her mouth.

'Oh my God,' Donna says, and they giggle together. 'Oh my God.'

I sigh. 'Hot chocolate, is it?'

Donna shrugs. 'Yeah, whatever.'

'Make mine a flat white, actually, Mush,' Marie says, yawning. I raise an eyebrow at that – flat white, is it? – and she raises one

back, big mocking shit-eater of a grin on her. Again, I've to dip
my head or I'll give the game away. Smile and it encourages them.

So I get to work, grinding the beans, frothing the milk,
and over my shoulder I hear them huddled and giggling at
whatever's happening on Marie's phone.

Some stupid part of me still thinks of them as kids. And
they'd been lovely kids. Always a bit of a handful, like, but
you wouldn't change them for anything. I'd been the cool
cousin they always wanted to sleep over. I used to build forts
for them, extending the duvets over the gap between their two
beds so they could pretend they were trapped in the dungeon
of a witch. I introduced them to movies every kid should see
– *Princess Bride*, *The Goonies*, stuff like that. Looking after
them made me feel useful, good for something other than
working in Mam's café. Donna and Marie both asked me to
be their sponsor when they made their Confirmation, and
made me escort them to the little party held for their class at
the Fitz Hotel. There was a disco with coloured lights and a
mirror ball. All these twelve-year-old girls on the dance floor
together, demented on sugar, on each other. Auntie Pauline
was still married to Uncle Ger at the time. I was sitting quietly
with them and Mam, nursing a pint, when the twins came
over and took me by both hands and insisted I get up and
dance with them. I was mortified. I had my head dipped the
whole time. But the girls were delighted – they whooped and
shouted, 'Mush! Mush!' – showing me off to their friends like
I was a trophy.

When I bring them their drinks, Marie's rolling two
cigarettes.

'Your mother was in earlier.'

Marie doesn't look up. 'Pauline,' she says. She sings her
mam's name like Dolly Parton's 'Jolene'.

'Was she crooning?' Donna says. 'Mam's always *crooning*
these days. Wedding jitters. Going about cleaning the house,
laughing to herself.'

'Sure that's nice, isn't it?' I say.

'She's being a dope,' Donna says.

'Ah,' I go. 'She's only happy.'

'She's. Being. A dope,' Donna says. Christ, she's got some sulk on her today. When she's on form like this, she gets this furrow between her eyes. It's always been lovely to me.

'Well,' I say, 'not long now till the big day and then everything'll be back to normal.'

There's an awkward pause. In fairness, it was a stupid thing to say. Obviously things won't be back to normal – their mother's getting married. Herself and Rossie Laughlin, making a go of it in the town hall on Monday. When they moved into Rossie's house last year, it was *Brady Bunch* style for a while, two families under one roof: Pauline and the twins along with Rossie and Rossie's daughter, Theresa. Mam and Auntie Pauline were talking about Theresa earlier: 'How old would she be now? Twenty-five? Twenty-six?' 'She's one of them vegans, so she is.' That's how Mam said it, 'One of them vegans,' like she was talking about something from outer space. Mam got me to help Theresa move into a flat of her own a few months ago. I was all antsy at first, being out of the caf and all that. But it ended up being really good craic hanging out with Theresa. Like, I'd still been thinking of her as Helen's baby sister, but here was this pure sound grown woman giving me hippie tea, telling me funny backpacking stories, talking about her art practice like I'd have a notion what that was. I couldn't resist asking Theresa if she thought Helen might come back for the wedding. Theresa just shrugged and made a 'who knows' flick of the hands.

'Are ye set for Auntie Pauline's shindig tomorrow?' I say.

'Can't wait,' Donna mumbles.

'She's calling it her *bachelorette* party,' Marie says.

'Her *hen* party,' Donna says.

'We're bringing *willy straws*,' Marie says.

Donna snorts. I hope they're not bringing willy straws.

'Still off the smokes?' Marie says.

'I am.'

'D'you not get bored, like? Maybe you should vape,' Marie says. The idea seems to excite her. 'Oh my God, he should vape.'

'Vapers are cunt wands,' Donna snaps.

Jesus. She's in such a mood, like.

Donna's always been more volatile than Marie. Less fluent with words, always confusing signals, getting it slightly wrong, getting angry at herself for getting it wrong, taking it out on whoever's there. This one evening, when the twins were only young, I was in their kitchen and they were stuffing their skulls with pepperoni pizza. They were giddy cos I was there to babysit. They kept shouting, 'Food in face! Food in faaaace!' as they ate. Auntie Pauline was doing Uncle Ger's tie and giving me pointers on bathtimes, bedtimes, all that, when Donna called out, 'Look at me!' She had a slice of pizza held next to her cheek like a monstrous melt of scar tissue. I knew she didn't mean any harm, but I still felt my stomach drop as she put on a deep voice and said, 'I'm Mush! I'm Mush!'

Auntie Pauline looked mortified. 'Love!' she said, her eyes glancing automatically at my scars. 'That's not very nice.'

Uncle Ger said nothing. He just walked over to Donna and wrenched her hair tight in his fist. She squealed. I didn't know where to look. It was awful. 'What do you say to your cousin?' Uncle Ger said in a calm voice. 'Sorrysorrysorrysorry,' Donna cried.

I shift in my seat. 'How's your dad getting on?'

'Oh, brilliant,' Marie says. 'Probably shitfaced in his kitchen right now.'

'Wish I was shitfaced right now,' Donna says.

'He's pathetic,' Marie says.

'He's just sad,' Donna says.

'He's *pathetic*,' Marie says in a firm voice. 'Sitting up on that farm, feeling sorry for himself. I wouldn't live up there if you paid me. State of him.'

I know it sounds bad, but I'm glad Marie talks about her father that way. Donna still has this kind of confused loyalty to him but, fact is, Uncle Ger's no one's idea of a good time.

He's been living with his nephew Teabag on the big farm out in the Warren ever since the divorce a few years back. Mam was delighted when Auntie Pauline finally left him.

'Sure ye'll be off to college soon enough,' I say, foot tapping. I'd murder a can. 'Only two more years. Then ye won't have to live with any of your stupid family ever again.'

'You're our family,' Donna says. 'You're not stupid.'

They both look at me now. There's a kind of brittle energy about them. Something's about to happen. I don't know what it is, but I suddenly see they've been working up to it.

Donna stands up – 'I'm bursting for a piss'– and climbs out the booth. This has been planned. Marie exchanges a look with Donna over my shoulder as she walks to the jacks.

'Yeah. It's funny you bring it up,' Marie says. 'Like, the whole where-we-live situation. I mean, it's sort of a thing right now. Cos, like, we wouldn't need to worry about Mam or Dad at all,' she says, 'if you gave us a loan and we moved into a flat of our own.'

I make a noise somewhere between a laugh and a cough. 'If what?'

'Exactly,' Marie nods, as though I'm the one who's just suggested something. 'We kind of thought we could talk to you about that. Like, wouldn't it be cool if me and Donna had our own place?'

She gives this expectant look. I should be skulling my second can by now.

'What's wrong with living with your mam and Rossie? Don't you like Rossie?'

'*Mam* likes Rossie,' Marie says. 'Mam likes Rossie so much it's as if no one else exists. Couldn't we arrange something with you and your mam? Just to cover a deposit?'

I tug at my mouth. 'What's Uncle Ger say about this?'

'Dad's got nothing to say about nothing. He's a pisshead.'

'Yeah, but—'

'And you know your mam will help out if you suggest it.'

'If *I* suggest it?'

'Yeah. I mean, why not? Don't you want to help us?'

'What? No, it's not... of course, like. It's not that I think it's a bad idea or anything.'

'Then what?'

I scramble around for a minute. 'Well... Ye're a bit young, like. How would ye cover rent? Groceries?'

'That's where your loan would help.'

I rub my forehead. 'Ah, now... think of the hassle it'd cause. Like, for your mam.'

Marie exhales sharply through her nose. 'Hassle for you, more like.'

'No, no. It's not like that. I just—'

'If you don't want to help, just say it.'

'No, you're not listening to me. I just think—'

'You know what?' Marie says, tucking her cigarettes behind her ears. 'Forget about it. We just thought maybe you would understand.' She begins to gather her things.

'Ah, Marie,' I say, as she stands up and Donna arrives back from the jacks.

'He said no,' Marie says.

'See?' Donna says. 'Told you he would. Can we go already?'

'Girls,' I say, trying to get out of the booth.

'Don't worry yourself, Mush,' Marie calls out as they walk to the door. 'We'll take care of ourselves. We always do.'

'Ah, Jaysus,' I say. 'Girls—'

The bell on the door chimes as Marie shoves her way out and shouts back through the glass, 'Enjoy your cans.'

I'm about to say something, I don't know what, even, when Donna looks back at me through the window as they walk off. And it shocks me. Her face in the glass. She isn't even angry. She just looks sad. I open my mouth to call after them, but it doesn't matter. They're already gone.

Helen

THE WINDOW OF the bus. My forehead, rattling against the window of the bus. Beyond the glass, the world already turning into Kinlough. I know this, because of the weird evening light threading the sky, the sudden strangeness of the trees, the hot churn in my viscera. Soon I will have to get off the bus. Soon I will arrive where I already am. Kinlough.

The bus veers off the motorway and we sink into the arterial maze of roads that fringe the town. Trees arc overhead and splinter the light across the sleeves of the other passengers. Bunched hedges seething about the windows as the road gets narrower and darker and thickens with branches. Witch's fingers scraping against the glass. I am already in the veins of the place. Kala was the first person I heard call this place, these roads, the Warren.

I take my phone.

just at the warren now

I add an exclamation mark and hit send before I can delete it.

Everyone else on the bus is sleeping. Pretending to be sleeping. They could be dead, for all I know. There is a woman drooling next to me. She looks drowned. I wonder if I should bother applying some make-up and decide I cannot be bothered. Though I am doing it, so I can be bothered.

Theresa has seen my message but she has not replied. I add some emojis of excitement. I messaged her a couple of days ago to confirm I was finally coming. There was no excuse good enough to miss our father's wedding, though I have not been back here for more than ten years. Facebook was how we kept in touch, for a while. Gradually the fake-casual online chats died down, and we politely liked one another's photos. This illusion of communication. People have always relied on certain excuses to explain why they lose contact – lost addresses, incorrect phone numbers. The internet simply removes those old justifications. Eventually I deleted my social media. Since then my relationship with Dad and Theresa has been a couple of emails per year. Which is fine by me. Last night Theresa and I arranged to meet at the bus station. She said she was looking forward to seeing me. That was kind of her. I said, **me too.** That was kind of me.

The Warren coils around the bus. Trees that have always been here. Twisted limbs and deformed faces, watching, waiting. The roads still stubbled with stones and potholes.

I have always avoided coming back.

I was fourteen when Dad first broke the news about moving to Kinlough. He got Theresa and me to sit side by side on the bed we shared in the Drogheda flat. He must have read somewhere that this is what you were supposed to do when you give your kids big news. Make them sit on a bed. I had been watching him for a while, nodding to himself, pacing about our flat and making decisions like a moron. There had been knocks on the door he would not answer and lots of phone calls late into the night. I knew he was planning another move. Theresa and I sat on the bed listening to him say how what we really needed was a change. Theresa kept trying to scoop Misty into her arms and Misty kept wriggling onto the floor. She lay like a sad-eyed rug at our feet. Every now and then I gave her a nudge with my foot and she glanced up at me, her tail drumming off the carpet. Misty's eyes were gorgeous wet black pools. They made me feel better about what was happening and I was glad she was there.

Dad was going through his greatest hits: Change of Scene. Lease of Life. New Beginning. I had heard it all before. But when he said, '...which is why... we're moving... to Kinlough,' his voice rising on the last syllable, stretching it out over us in a tightrope of mad optimism, I did not know how to respond. My eyes snapped up at him and he was already looking at me, waiting for my reaction. I mean, it was a ridiculous idea. Kinlough was a place for visiting, not for living. We used to go there for two weeks every summer when Mam was intact. Race Week, followed by Festival Week. Games of hide-and-seek in Caille Woods. Candyfloss on the edges of Fox Street, watching the parade. Mam called our yearly visits 'a nice little anchor' – which I think meant Kinlough was a place she could use to gather breath before moving on with real life, which was always elsewhere. No matter where we actually were, real life for Mam – as with all interesting people – was always elsewhere. But Dad was forever keen to get back to Kinlough. Despite the fact that both his parents were long dead, he was a home bird. Mam used to describe this as the symptom of a disordered brain. At the end of every trip, I would help Mam pack up the van, just so I did not have to see Dad sulk about leaving. Mam would chirp at me, 'Two weeks a year is more than enough, isn't it?'

But as Theresa and I sat on our bed, I could see that Dad was excited to be moving to Kinlough, and that he was convinced we would be, too. Even then I knew there was something depressing about the excitement of grown men. The expectation that the world is really meeting them halfway. I suppose it often is. He had sorted himself a job and he had sorted us a house, he said. A real actual house, where Theresa and I could have separate beds, in separate rooms. And he was delighted with himself. Proud as anything. 'It's all taken care of,' he said, rubbing the back of his neck, squinting, stammering. 'This will be a f-f-f-fresh start, like.'

Theresa squealed and leapt off the bed to hug him, which made Misty give nervous yaps, standing on her hind legs and pawing at Theresa, which changed the whole atmosphere of the moment into something of celebration, which was what Dad had wanted, of course – a big swell of violins – and he kissed Theresa on the head and took her up in his arms like she was a smaller child than she really was, and he ruffled Misty's ears with his free hand and they had their big Kodak moment. I stayed sitting on the bed, staring at them. I wanted to hit them both very hard in the face.

'What about my school?' I said. 'It's May. I literally have exams in a month.'

Theresa was swinging out of Dad's neck and he was smiling at her. 'Sure can't you do exams in your new s-s-school?' He ruffled my hair like I was the dog. 'A b-b-b-brain like yours? You'll dazzle them.'

Theresa said this was the best news ever, and Dad was happy because she was happy, but Theresa was only happy because she was still ten.

I was not happy about anything. I was fourteen.

The bus station has changed. It used to be a giant shed with rotten pigeons surveying everything from the rusted beams, shitting on the tiled floor. Young guys in hoodies phlegming into the puddles between their runners and a rickety kiosk where they would sell fags without asking how old you were.

Now it is a fluorescent dream of glass. Over every gate there are screens announcing the departure times. It is like any other terminus. The same benches you see everywhere, with spokes between the seats to stop homeless people from sleeping.

My roller case clickclacks at my heels, till I see a poster for an upcoming concert and stop. Jungle Heart: *Bringing It All Back Home*. It is a photo of Joe, still a wide-eyed teenager, looking up into the camera like Bob Dylan on the *Bringing It All Back Home* cover. I wonder if Kala took the picture. I check the date of the concert and realize it is this week. My first time back here in years, and Joe is back in town, too. Great. Fucking great.

Outside it is like an oven. Kinlough in summer. A thick feeling, a sweet note to the air.

I message Theresa: **just landed!**

Bus stations, unlike airports, are never happy places. Just down the street, on the corner that leads into town, there is a person wearing a heavy black hoodie with the hood pulled tight around his skull, despite the heat, or because of the heat. He is standing like he has been struck by lightning. A petrified shadow. This is the natural citizen of the bus station. A hovering lunatic.

Theresa messages me:

traffic brutal

can u walk to hogans sq?

To get to Hogan's Square from this side of the road, I need to walk past the hovering shadow man who, I have noticed, is looking at me. I hold his gaze for a moment and then look back at my phone. I cross the road so I do not have to walk around him.

My roller case claps its wheels, strained hinges nipping at the backs of my feet, people rushing into me, late for their buses.

I am gathering speed when I notice that the hovering shadow man has crossed the road too and is now standing on the corner to which I am walking. There is something wrong with how he is standing. He holds his arms rigid at his sides. Even at this distance I can see how his fingers are curled and tense. I check my phone.

will pick u up near the burrito place

its up the top of the square

I feel him looking at me again. I do the usual calculations. I tell myself I am being paranoid as I cross back to the other side. But then, at the edge of my vision, I see him mirror me. He is crossing the road, again.

More calculations. Are his hands in his pockets? No, they are by his sides, he is not masturbating. Is he holding anything?

A bottle? A knife? No. His hands are empty. Tensed, claw-like fingers.

I will walk past him. I will not let this place get to me so soon. Kala taught me this: always walk like you mean it. I hold my shoulders back and pick up speed, to show confidence, then slow down a little, to show I do not need to show confidence. I do not look at him. Not directly. He is a dark blur in my peripheral vision. A shadow. Nothing to be afraid of. I am getting closer. My nails teeth at my palms. White bones of my knuckles. I will have to lean in to the wall so I can pass without brushing against him. He is filling the path now. Close enough to touch me. Spit at me. I wait for the move. The muttered word. Bitch. Slut. Cunt.

But he says nothing.

I am around the corner and do not look back until I have reached the traffic lights, where I turn and see that he is looking at me from the corner, arms still out, and I rush into the road to get away from him and cars blow their horns because I do not have the right to move where my body needs to move, and I keep walking with my eyes to the ground to get away from the station and when I look up there are suddenly faces and noises twisting through the air around me, people are swarming on the grass, drinking cans, eating ice creams, a group of students are shouting and playing Frisbee and being loud near the tourists who huddle around one another looking at their phones, completely blind to the danger of the shirt-less lads with see-sawing shoulders who criss-cross Hogan's Square with medallions flashing in the sun past the dead-eyed office workers slouched with open shirt collars and loosened ties over cans of Dutch Gold on the benches and I am caught in it, I am in this now, Kinlough is a sudden sea foaming up around me, and I am islanded in the grinning churn of Hogan's Square.

Joe

HOGAN'S SQUARE IS pure buzz as you walk towards Flanagan's. It's Friday. People are coiled like a spring. They wanna dance, they wanna sweat, they wanna fuck. They want. You provide. The contours of the Square shape themselves towards you. You're a new focal point. Faces turn to you like flowers seeking the sun. Feel their energy, the rush of recognition. *Is that Joe Brennan?* Phones rise to take photos, and you pretend not to notice, gliding above the world, in the Other Place.

Tonight's your first night without your arm in the sling. Elbow was still tender as you cut off the cast in the kitchen, the skin around it a bruised corsage. But you'll be able to play guitar again by tomorrow, if you keep it rested. You're sure of it. Haven't been able to do any workouts with this elbow on you, but when you glance at a group of young wans you catch their eyes running over your chest, your tatts.

You catch the noise from Flanagan's before you cross the road – music throbbing under the sound of drills, nails being hammered. You wanted it this way. The venue officially launches next week, but you want to build the buzz already, so you've the doors wide open, allowing the music to pour out, giving people a glimpse behind the curtain into a magic you're bringing to Kinlough. There's a front-facing window with a small bar, already serving takeaway pints. Flanagan's was a legendary spot before the recession. Now you've swooped in with the money to relaunch the place. Home-town boy made good. Posters for your residency on the windows – solo acoustic shows starting tomorrow night. *Bringing It All Back Home*. You want people to know this is happening. Tonight's about making an appearance, meet and greet the staff, take a few pictures for their socials, your socials.

Pause for a second to let a gaggle of girls take a selfie with you. Ohmygod Ohmygod Ohmygod. Tell them to be good and cut through the road between stalled traffic, feeling eyes widen as they watch from their cars.

Inside Flanagan's it's a hive. Stand in the door frame. Inhale the moment. The sawdust scattered on the ground. The unvarnished wood tables. Lads with hipster beards are attaching an old bike high over the bar. Several projectors are in place, '70s exploitation movies patterning up the walls. Tattooed girls at the bar stuffing empty wine bottles with candles. Guys dressed like Oliver Twist painting a mural of Bosco and The Morbegs in the corner where the board games are kept. Someone's inside the photo booth, polishing the seat. Duggan is behind the bar with a notebook, taking stock. Chin your hello to him and walk to the stage, slip into the DJ booth by the PA. Slowly turn the volume down so people don't even notice it's happening. There's a microphone. Turn it on and the speakers groan. Every face turns to you. The ripple of recognition moving through the place. Laugh into the mic. 'Evening, guys. Just wanted to drop in and say hi. You're doing fantastic work. This is gonna be fucking awesome. I'm gonna spin a few tunes up here for a bit and say hello to each of you. I hope you're all as excited about this new adventure as I am. All right? All right.'

There's a scattered applause as you connect your laptop to the PA, open Spotify, and start the playlist you've been working on all afternoon.

Start things slow. Cook things up into a smoulder. 'Our Theme' by Barry White and Glodean. The synths ripple slow and the bottles on the bar quiver when Barry's vowels shudder through the speakers. People are working with more urgency now. The air's more charged. The place is a universe in the scoop of your palm. Feel the staff glancing over. Affect a faraway look, like you're seeing something on the horizon, like you're the music. Bob Dylan expression. Visionary, staring into the mystic. Early evening and it's a sweet one. The air crackling. Take a photo of the view from the DJ booth. A blur of bottles and bodies glows warm in the background. Fiddle with the filters then stick the photo on Instagram with the tag Our Theme x. Theresa likes it within about ten seconds. So does Mush. Stare at the phone till you hit 100 likes. Less than thirty seconds. Good.

'Lonely Disco Dancer' by Dee Dee Bridgewater. People are still at their tasks, but their heads are bopping. The tattooed girls are smiling at you as they move their hips. This is the vibe you want when the interviewer arrives next week. A *Rolling Stone* profile to mark the ten-year anniversary of *The Other Place*. You want the profile to happen in a variety of spots around Kinlough. Portrait of the Artist as a Local Man. You've lived in LA for five years, snatching visits back every six months or so. But you're on home turf now. Can feel it, in your gut. You've landed. You're here.

At the bar, Duggan's polishing glasses.

'Some talent in here tonight,' he goes, looking at the girls. 'What'll you be having? Still on the Granny beer?'

You nod and he takes a non-alcoholic Paulaner from the fridge, shaking his head to the cluck and gasp of the bottle as it opens. 'It's a sad day when a Kinlough man won't have himself a proper drink during Race Week.'

'I suppose you'll have to live with that.'

Duggan is one of these lads who's never left Kinlough and can only understand himself in terms of the town. He's a big deal here – he's managed several bars over the years – which makes him think he can talk to you as an equal. 'That stuff's like beer with a condom on,' he says.

Ignore him. You've already explained about your elbow, the bruising, the pain medication. Can't drink alcohol till you're healed up. That's not even a lie. But Kinlough isn't LA, people here see you not drinking and they get suspicious. Something behind their eyes closes up.

Tell him you're gonna nip out for some air. The 12-inch cut of Isaac Hayes's 'Walk On By' booms about the walls.

'Good man,' Duggan says, staring at a tattooed girl as she leans over the bar to adjust the frame of a photo by the mirror. The picture is of your first band. It's you and Mush and Aidan, skinny and ruddy-cheeked, guitar cases at your sides. Ye're trying to look cool, arms folded, squinting into the camera, engulfed by the sunlight blaring through the fountain at the top of Hogan's Square.

Someone had always put Fairy Liquid in the fountain by the time ye got there on Fridays after school. Ye'd stand about Hogan's Square, waiting for the bus, pretending not to notice all the girls. Ye were fourteen now, so ye'd gone half your lives without speaking to a girl your own age. Ye'd all been mixed together – fellas and girls – in the same primary school, until ye were seven and made your Communion. Then all the lads got turfed into St Jude's, which was the all-boys school down the road but might as well have been another planet. Boys' school was a new place with new rules and ye'd had to learn them all overnight. How to curse, and spit, and scrap. How to stare someone down, how to kick someone without them grabbing your foot, how to knock the shit out of someone on their birthday without hurting them. Ye got tighter then, yourself and Aidan and Mush, like sticks binding so none of ye would snap under pressure. In primary school you were a king. You didn't need to fight to prove yourself, like everyone else, cos you were the best at football and the smartest in the class. Now you were fourteen, and in St Simon's Secondary School for Boys, with hair around your dangly bits and a new voice after dropping on you. You'd heard that girls loved lads that went to St Simon's, cos it was the one secondary in Kinlough that made you take an entrance exam. 'Only the cream go to St Simon's,' Dad often said. Yourself and Mush had been shocked that all-boys secondary school was nothing like *Saved by the Bell* or *Buffy* or *Dawson's Creek*. It was just another load of smelly lads.

So after school on Fridays, ye'd walk up to Hogan's Square and try and look cool for the beors from St Anne's. Mam said you were handsome. And you knew Mush was handsome too – all the mams commented on it. He had curly hair and what Mam called 'boy-band features'. Ye'd be leaning against the railings at Hogan's Square trying to look cool and Aidan would catch scoops of foam from the fountain and try to mash it into Mush's hair, and Mush and him would get each other in headlocks and everyone in the Square would look at them, and you, and you'd laugh and pull them by their school-bags till they fell over, and if the girls from St Anne's were looking at ye then ye'd fight a bit louder, and knock each other about like that all the way onto the bus to your house where ye'd fling the schoolbags under the stairs and get out of your uniforms into your trackies, swallowing whatever snack Mam had made – scorching your tongues, fanning your mouths, panting like dogs – heading out to play headers and volleys at the old goalposts in Taylor's school yard. Until recently enough, ye'd still play the Gun Game, where ye'd run around the school grounds and duck behind prefabs, killing each other. Mush did a brilliant line in getting machine-gunned to death, he could make his body thunder about before he hit the ground. Ye were too old for that now, though. When ye got back to the house from playing football, the minute ye'd get in the door, Mam would be serving up the Friday Classic: chicken nuggets and chips drowned in her special sauce. 'How d'you always know the exact moment we're gonna be back?' Aidan would ask, and Mam would laugh and tell him it was a woman's intuition. 'And that's a wonderful thing, Margaret,' Aidan would say, arms folded like he was one of the grown-ups. He loved saying things like that to your mam, to annoy you. After the Classic, there'd be a giant mess-fight in the sitting room till ye felt sick, then multiplayer GoldenEye marathons on the Nintendo, eating Tayto and chocolate and shouting abuse at each other. Dad would come in from work with a box of almond Magnums and he'd fake arm-wrestle each of ye before handing them over. When he'd lose, he'd say, 'This is police brutality,' which the lads found funny, every week, cos Dad was still in his Garda uniform. Then he'd sit in his chair, crackling the newspaper and falling asleep. At around ten o'clock, he'd drop Aidan home.

This was when yourself and Mush would head upstairs and chat.

Whenever ye did this – chatting – there was something secretive to it. Unknown country. Chatting was a girl thing, something boys weren't supposed to do. But Mush was different. He liked conversation. He knew loads about films – way more than you. His mam let him watch anything. He'd tape mad stuff off the TV which ye'd watch at sleepovers above his mam's café. Stuff with boobs in it and everything. Half the time ye didn't understand the films at all. But ye'd watch them and know that ye were reaching out to something bigger than Kinlough – touching the Other Place, a world that was realer and more romantic than life – and sometimes the movie would linger in the room afterwards like an echo of the future and ye'd sit by the window of his mam's flat and stare out over Fox Street saying nothing.

That's where ye were sitting the first night you told him about the girl.

You'd first seen her at the bus stop in Hogan's Square. Spotted her the odd time on Fox Street, too. She stood and stared like she was being soundtracked. The thick storm of dark hair, the lazy shadow at her mouth. Her eyebrows – pure Hollywood. The Other Place. Mush knew who you were talking about straight away. Said she sometimes came into his mam's café with her friend, a loud blonde wan. You spent a whole Saturday sitting there pretending to read a book and she never showed.

The quivery feeling inside you after school every Friday as you walked to the bus stop, hoping she'd be there. The time you worked up the nerve to stand near her when she was leaning against the railings, listening to her Discman. The day you almost sat next to her on the bus.

You made her vivid in poems, lyrics, daydreamed scenarios copied off TV and music videos. You'd write things in your diary like, 'Everywhere I stand is a shore she is washing over', and then you'd read that to Mush and he'd close his eyes and shake his head with a pained look on his face and say, 'It's the thunderbolt, man. Like when Michael Corleone meets Apollonia in Sicily when he has to run away after killing McCluskey and Sollozzo but she gets blown up by the Barzini family and Michael never gets over it, but he becomes the Godfather.' Mush's brain was wired backwards. But that's why he was someone you could chat to – he had something of the Other Place in him too.

You'd tell him you'd written another song about her and he'd get excited and urge you to play it. After pretending you didn't want to, you always played it in the end. Ye were going to be famous together one day. Biographers would include photos of your handwritten lyrics and you and the girl would be one of them legendary couples that become synonymous with true love. John and Yoko, Sid and Nancy.

Mush started elbowing you every Friday to go up to her and ask what she was listening to. But you were too nervous. There was one time you thought she was looking your direction and you felt yourself burning up under her stare while Aidan ran about like a fool trying to nuggy Mush's skull. Mush was distracting Aidan on purpose, to keep him busy so you could just talk to her, pure casual. But you chickened out. No balls. Mush never slagged you for it – he just made eye contact to show he understood. That was one of the best things about Mush. Sometimes ye'd hear a particular tune, or see a scene in a particular movie, and ye'd look at each other and know that ye were both thinking the same thing. You only get one friend in life like that. And Mush was yours.

◎

well man
what's the craic?
you done at the caf?

yo man

busy busy lol

Fancy calling up to flanagans?
I'm out the front, it's very chill

Mush doesn't answer. Been trying to get him to meet up ever since you came back. Three weeks, now. Look at the message again. **Very chill**. You sound like someone who lives in LA. You can picture Mush rolling his eyes.

Usual craziness across the road in Hogan's Square. People drinking cans, relaxing in the grass, getting the last of the full sun. And you having a drink outside Flanagan's is nothing at all, it's no big deal. It's a non-alcoholic beer, so you're not even really drinking. You only do it because you choose to and if you ever did drink again and it was an alcoholic beer, so what? You're a grown man. It's Race Week. You don't need permission. You're working. You can have a drink when you're working, you're a rock star, for Christ's sake.

Take a picture of your pint and Instagram it when a voice shouts from the Square: 'Howya, sexy!' The twins are shouting at you as they cross the green. 'Any chance of a lush of your drink?' Marie calls. Donna walks next to her like a glum shadow.

Marie's a pure flirt. She was a chatty kid, but now her jokes have got a charge and she expects you to hit the ball back, hard. You're about to shout a comeback, the voice already in your throat, when a feeling like cold birds flutters from your heart and down through your arms. If you looked quickly you'd say it was Theresa, walking through Hogan's Square, past the twins. It could almost be her, something of her essence is there. But everything's slightly off. The posture, the haircut, the vibe. It's Theresa in a fun-house mirror. Her back is ramrod straight and she glares around herself, all forward energy, dragging a roller case.

It's Helen.

You almost duck back into Flanagan's in case she sees you.

Marie hugs you gently. 'Are you well?' She has been doing this every time she sees you, ever since you came back. Donna hangs back, as usual, looking suspicious. 'How's the elbow?'

'Grand.' Look over your shoulder, to the Square. Helen's still there. Phone in her hand, looking around. You need to get inside.

'Is it not difficult to play guitar like that?' Marie says, touching your bruises. She's standing close to you. 'It's like a gorgeous armband, isn't it? It could be one of your tattoos.'

She looks up at you with dangerous eyes, and you hear Donna snort behind her: 'God.'

Mush once told you he was convinced that, one day, Donna would literally be bored to death.

Marie takes a selfie with you for her Instagram. You smile reflexively. Your head's full of noise. The Square, the brassy blare of Isaac Hayes from inside Flanagan's, the loud chatter of the people around you.

Helen's still there, standing. Helen in Kinlough.

Helen

HOGAN'S SQUARE IS somehow larger and smaller than I remember. The green is better kept. The path that slashes diagonally through the grass is now that rubbery playground surface instead of gravelled dust. I pull my case past the bust of JFK, walking towards the fountain as it sprays its fan of rainbow-fringed light skywards. Someone has put Fairy Liquid into the fountain, a monster of foam sending torn suds gliding across the pavement. Everyone is laughing.

I walk through the Square, spine straight, eyes forward. This place will not get to me.

I am sweaty from the bus. This will make hugging Theresa more awkward. I go through the list of things we can talk about. How her art is going. How her life is going. How is everything going? I practise the words quietly to myself. How is everything *going*? How is *everything* going? How *is* everything going?

There are two girls walking towards me, and I do not want to embarrass myself because they look sulky and cool in that effortless teenage way that everyone ends up losing. Their scowls are sharp enough to tear my face off. It is oddly exciting. Their swagger. A sudden burst of pigeons from the grass next to them and they both shriek and laugh, their hands instinctively reaching for one another, and there is a sweetness there till one of them catches me looking and a hardness comes over her eyes, and I look away. As we pass one another on the path, I expect a comment. But their attention is already elsewhere. I hear one of them shouting, 'Howya, sexy! Any chance of a lush of your drink?' The other one mutters, 'D'you've the photos on you?' 'What?' 'The photos, we have the photos.' When they stride across the green towards Flanagan's, I am relieved. I am old enough to stop being afraid of many things. I will never stop being afraid of teenage girls.

On my first day in St Anne's I was boiling. The sun ran in scorching belts off the dark pinafore, the itchy shirt, the navy cardigan. Damp around my collar, under my arms. When I touched my hair, it felt like my skull was melting. The varnished wood gleamed from below and the white sun poured from above, and I was caught between two bright-nesses, squinting. You have very little time in a new school to become whoever you are going to be for that place; I was already drifting into the role of the sweaty, squinty sap that people do not talk to.

The chats flowed about the classroom along well-estab-lished arteries. I was an obstacle around which they moved.

At the beginning of the first class, the English teacher made me stand and introduce myself.

'Where are you from?' she said. They always want to situate you. Where you are from. What your parents do. I never had neat answers to their questions.

'Um, kind of all over,' I said. 'We sort of move around a lot.'

A scatter of giggles from the other girls. A voice whisper-ing, 'Fucking knacker.'

'Well, where were you born?'

'Um, France, actually. My mam was half French, so sometimes—'

'Where d'you live in Kinlough?' the teacher said.

I could not remember the name of the estate. We had moved in a few days ago. Dad's friends had been leaning against the house, waiting to help us carry things.

'Rossieeee!'

'Rossie feckin' Laughliiiin!'

One of the men awkwardly extended a hand for me to shake. Silvery stubble, sun-raw skin. I could not remember his name. 'Welcome, welcome!' he smiled. He was missing teeth in his upper mouth. 'Christ, you've grown, girl, hah? I thought your sister was you!' He nodded over at Theresa, who was doing cartwheels in the front garden, like anyone could give a shit. 'Last time I saw you,' Silvery Face said, 'you were only a whelp.' He squinted and squeezed his eyes shut, smiling at me as if this was some joke we were sharing. I gave a nervous sort of nod. I hated this role play. The shy kid, the friendly uncle type.

'You don't remember me, do you?' he said. 'I'm Blinkie.' He squinted and squeezed his eyes shut again. A tic. This must have been where the Blinkie name came from.

He extended an arm to the dark-haired man behind him. 'Maybe you remember Dodo, hah?'

Blinkie. Dodo. What kind of grown adults had names like that?

'Helen,' Dodo said. He looked as jittery as I sometimes felt, which made me approve of him, even though I did not want to.

'We're the bad influence your daddy's warned you about,' Dodo laughed. He slapped Dad on the arm. 'That right, Rossie?'

Blinkie squinted and nodded.

Dad was pepped to see them.

'Well, would you look,' another man said. He had a cudgelled face, like a heap of salted meat. Forehead ridged and folded like a brain. He was rolling a cigarette in giant shovel hands. 'You've gotten very mature, Helen.'

'You remember Ger, don't you?' Dad said.

I did. I remembered the tightness in Mam's face whenever Ger's name came up.

Later, when we ordered Chinese for dinner, Ger presented Dad with a large bottle of vodka. Dad avoided my eye as Blinkie poured the vodka into Styrofoam cups.

'To the future,' Ger said.

The men raised their Styrofoam cups together. Theresa raised her can of Coke with them. I watched them do this. I watched them smile and laugh like something from an ad. The way Blinkie pretended to twist Dad's arm into going down to the local shop for more drink. I watched how Dad adjusted his body language with them, spread himself wider. They all deferred to Ger whenever he decided to speak. Blinkie and Dodo rolled their cigarettes with stained fingers, dirt that had become skin. Dad, after the first two vodkas, told them they did not need to go out the back garden any more to smoke. 'Just light up, lads. Mi casa is y-y-you casa.'

The teacher raised her eyebrows impatiently. 'I asked you where you live in Kinlough.'

'Oh,' I stammered. A smatter of giggles from the class. I could feel the skin getting hot in my face. 'I can't remember our estate. It's not far from the Coast Road. We live in number forty-seven.'

The giggles from the class were more confident this time. They were finding a place for me. It was pretty near the bottom. There were mocking whispers of 'number forty-seven'.

The teacher gave a thin smile. 'What does your father do?'

I did not have an answer for this either. Dad was a bouncer, a taxi driver, a bricklayer, a roadie, a barman, whatever you wanted him to be.

'He's an engineer,' I said.

This pleased the teacher. 'Very good. You may sit down.'

They never asked what Mam did. Though this was for the best.

In between classes, the popular queens colonized the radiators and laughed theatrically. The other girls did what the other girls were supposed to do. They muttered amongst themselves and stared with longing and hate at the queens. I made an effort to smile at what the girls in the next row were saying to one another, giving little laughs whenever any of them made a joke, as though that was the secret to making friends. They pretended not to notice my efforts.

The French teacher was a sweet lady named Mrs Mulkerns. She made me stand up and introduce myself to the class, again. Some girls said, 'Do it in French, forty-seven, do it in French.'

Mrs Mulkerns's eyes brightened.

'Parlez-vous français?'

I responded in fluent French. The teacher loved it. She kept the chat going for a while. There was laughter and bored sighs and 'ooh-la-la's as we talked. When I was allowed to sit down, the teacher gave me a big smile. I kept my head down after that.

In the yard at small break, some people muttered 'forty-seven' or snorted 'ooh-la-la' as I walked through the crowd. The school yard was dense with uniforms, a clustered maze of tightly packed islands, each populated by a different tribe of girls: loud girls, GAA girls, murderously quiet girls, quietly murderous girls, crow-faced what-ya-looking-at? girls, popular queens orbited by their sad consorts.

It was like this every time I started a new school. I walked around, trying to look like there was a place I was supposed to be.

Eventually I found a spot in the shade, away from the crowd. Old packets of Tayto and sweets covered the tarmac. The walls, spackled in chewing gum. Nearby, I could see some other girls standing together, looking as if they were part of the shadows. These were the plain girls, girls so invisible that no one could even be bothered to bully them. At least I had already earned the distinction of being 'ooh-la-la'. I pulled at my sleeves, hoping the plain girls would not invite me over. They would not do this in any overt way. That was not how plain girls operated. They would initiate you into their pack with a servile, defeated glance of complicity through a drab fringe. I had been a plain girl before, in other schools. I was not interested in becoming one again.

This is when I first see them.

Two girls, walking through the yard together, arms linked. They stand out in the school yard. Way out. The blonde

one is a head taller than most of us but she does not hunch
her shoulders the way tall girls do. She walks with her back
straight, looking vaguely amused at everything. Her smile is
loud and wide. She leans in to the other girl and then fans
open with a laugh that booms over the crowd. The other girl
is dark, almost foreign-looking, with hair that is thick and
knotted in a black storm. She is gesticulating with her free
hand while speaking through a smile, like she knows a great
secret. They are walking like they mean it. They move with
the confidence of the popular queens but, unlike them, they
seem indifferent to who might be watching. And they know
people are watching. They mutter to each other and laugh and
I can see that they are each other's spectator and spectacle.
When they turn their attention elsewhere, it is with sceptical
eyebrows. They drift through the uniformed scraps of chat
and laughter, and the air is charged with the electric distance
that separates performers on a stage from an audience whose
only purpose on earth is to watch them. I do not know what
they have. I can feel it reaching up through my belly, to my
chest, and closing tight, like a fist.

I found out the blonde one with the big laugh was Aoife
Reynolds. The dark one with the knotty hair was Kala Lanann.
They were in the same year as me, but a different class.

    I started to watch out for them every morning. They always
came into school together, arms linked, with their schoolbags
loose and low off one shoulder. The uniform looked dishev-
elled on them. The nicotine glamour of an unmade bed.
They tied their cardigans about their waists and wore the
shirtsleeves open and rolled up on their forearms. Kala played
with her hair a lot. It was so thick that, when she ran a hand
through it, the fringe remained fanned out, suspended mid-air.
Aoife sometimes wore a choker. Slashes of eyeshadow beneath
the lash line. On the first weekend in Kinlough, I walked the
Prom into town and bought eyeshadow from Boots on Fox
Street. I poured small drops of Dad's vodka into a glass and

sipped as I experimented in the mirror. I painted dashes of dark beneath my eyes and held the drink aloft. I tilted my head and tried to be melancholic, haunted. I caught sight of Theresa in my mirror, giggling at me through a crack in the door, and chased her into her room, pinned her to her bed and punched her on the arm till she screamed while Dad shouted from downstairs, 'Jesus! Would ye give it a f-fucking rest!'

I followed them up town during lunchbreak.

I watched them traipse through Dunne's Stores to sit in the sunned grass of Hogan's Square, near the stone bust of JFK. Kala sat Buddha-style, legs crossed. This pulled her skirt taut across her lap to make a tabletop on which she rolled their fags. Aoife looked about them, saying things that made Kala laugh. I sat far enough to be aloof, worried they would notice me, hoping they would notice me.

One day in Hogan's Square, a week before school finished for the summer, Aoife was lying in the grass, stretching luxuriously, talking and talking, and Kala had her head down towards her lap, concentrating on rolling their cigarettes, and I noticed that her hair had a bit of dye in it now, a rumour of dark wine, and the sun brought out the tint and made her hair a bloody incandescence, and I was admiring how it sprayed about her head like a dark halo when Kala's eyes snapped up from her lap and looked straight at me. I got such a fright that I did not even look away. A hot rush of tingles down my back. Kala gave me a half-smile, like this moment was a private joke we were sharing. I turned my head away and scratched at a stain on my pinafore.

When they got up to leave Hogan's Square, they walked with shoulders touching, each holding a rollie aloft on either side, teapot style. The light glanced off them as they got smaller, and I stayed where I was, wondering what they would get up to during the summer, picturing scenes of night magic, shared secrets, interesting regrets. Then Aoife suddenly spun around and looked right at me. I looked away, but I was almost sure she smirked and gave me a little wave. When I looked again, they were already reaching the top of the Square, passing the fan of the fountain spray, walking through the road to make cars blare. They entered the mouth of Fox Street, and then they were gone.

Traffic is at a standstill, ringing the entire Square, and it sounds as though every driver is leaning on their horn. I am trying to see where this burrito place is. Through the blare I can hear a familiar sound, blowing about in the chaos. It sounds like my name.

It *is* my name.

One car, the head of all the snaking traffic, has stopped in the road. The driver is waving at me. It is Theresa. My stomach jumps as I rush towards her, military clicks of the roller case behind me, I stumble into the passenger seat, clapping my knee off the dashboard, taking the case onto my lap, and before I even shut the door she lurches the car forward and we are driving.

The car has a homely, sweet incense smell. Over the dashboard is a picture of a Vedic saint and a card with the handwritten words, 'Take your time and be wherever you are.' Theresa's eyes do not leave the road, which allows me to gaze at her without embarrassment. She looks well. Really well, like one of those people whose parents did not let them watch TV as a child. An open face, meeting the world full on. She is wearing a cheesecloth shirt and baggy, paint-spattered dungarees. A single dreadlock in the back of her hair and the rest of it all matted and purple-tinged, a strip shaved by her temple. She still has her nose piercing, she wears no make-up, her hands leave the wheel to gesticulate wildly when she talks, and she never stops talking. From the moment we start driving, she is a torrent of words. It is like she does not draw breath. She begins, 'This traffic, my fucking gaaawd,' and interrupts herself to shout in the rear-view mirror at the car behind her to 'get out of my arse' and continues like this, telling me she forgot just how bad the roads get during the Races, how she was stuck for fifteen minutes – fifteen minutes! – on the Prom, how honestly she can't remember when she last came into town during Race Week, how Kinlough degrades itself by becoming a seven-day playground for overpaid arseholes with more cash than taste, how herself and Dad were opening the bike shop just that morning and some KPMG fuckhead in a shirt with a tie around his head was pissing against the wall of the shop and how Dad tried to get him to move on and he got up in Dad's face and Dad is a nice man but like he could've put this Goldman Sachs fuck in the hospital if he wanted to and believe me, Helen, I wanted to, I wanted to.

We glide across Toner's Bridge, past the Widow's Arch, where people freckle the banks of the Purr. The river gallops out towards Kinlough Bay, and Theresa takes us along its course. We stop at traffic lights near the Prom. Power walkers talk breathlessly in their fluorescent summer jackets and runners glisten in the light. Kids skip to keep up with their parents. At the traffic lights, there's a toddler crossing the road, holding his mother's hand, trying to manage a 99. The wind slices the ice cream off the cone and it splats onto the road in front of us. The toddler begins to wail.

'Ah, the lamb,' Theresa half-laughs, as the toddler is scooped up and carried off, purple face arched skyward, bawling.

I clear my throat. 'How is Rossie?'

'Dad?' Theresa says, correcting me. She keeps her gaze forward. 'He's good. You know. Bit jittery. He's been trying to write his vows all week, the dote.'

'He's probably more nervous about reading them out loud than anything else, no? With his stammer.'

'Dad hasn't stammered in years,' Theresa mutters. Her voice is flat.

Neither of us says anything for a while. She checks her phone.

'Right,' she says. 'So tomorrow night's this hen party thing at the gaff. D'you have a gift yet?'

I do not know about any party.

'No,' I say. 'What should I bring?'

'Don't worry, I'll have something,' Theresa says. 'We can just say it's from the two of us. Pauline's not fussy. You'll like her.'

'I remember Pauline,' I say. 'She was Aidan's mam.'

Theresa nods. 'She was.'

The last time I saw Pauline was at Aidan's funeral. She could barely lift her face to all of us as we filed past to shake her hand.

Another silence. Theresa checks her phone again.

'So what is the plan for the hen?'

'Nothing too wild,' Theresa says. 'Pauline doesn't really drink much, y'know. With Dad and all. So there'll be, like, cocktails, mocktails. Maybe a bit of silly dancing in the kitchen, I dunno. We should prepare like an appetizer or something.'

'Who will be there?' I can already imagine the same ten-minute interrogation, repeated with rotating partners for hours.

Theresa is on her phone, glancing up at the road only half the time. 'There's me,' she says. 'And you. Pauline, obviously. Pauline's sister, you remember Lydia, Mush's mam? And Pauline's youngest, Donna and Marie, of course. They'll be the ones looking for cocktails instead of mocktails, if you know what— Dickhead! Get out of my arse!' She gives the finger to the driver behind us.

'How old are they now?'

'The twins? Sixteen.'

'Jesus. How did that happen?'

Theresa shrugs. 'It's not like you've been around so much.'

We do not say anything else till we get to the house.

Joe

'KINLOUGH MUST SEEM tiny to you now,' Marie says as she takes your photo. 'I'd say you've loads of mad stories from LA, do you?'

Can't locate Helen in the Square at all now. She could be anywhere.

A message on your phone. Theresa.

What's with the photo of the beer on IG? Thought you're off the drink...

Fuck sake. Put the phone away.

'You must be so *bored* being back in this kip,' Marie says. She's tilting her head and staring at you. 'We must all seem, like, so boring to you.'

'Not at all.'

'Ah, yeah?' Donna calls in a monotone. 'You think we're interesting, Joe, do you?'

'I think your braids are interesting.'

'They're not braids,' she says. 'They're cornrows.'

'Right.' You could make a quip about cultural appropriation but you don't actually give a shit.

'Joe's a man of the world,' Donna says to Marie. 'A man of mystery.'

Marie laughs. 'He is! He's so mysterious! I bet Joe knows secrets about Kinlough.'

Donna nods. 'Did you know Joe was down the woods earlier?'

Marie makes her eyes go wide. 'Was he, Donna?'

'He was. Down at the lake. Walking about near the building site where all the Garda tape is.'

'Ye following me around?'

'Kinlough's fairly boring, Joe,' Marie says. She touches your chest and Donna's eyes follow her hand as she does it. 'You never get bored?'

'The body in the woods,' Donna says. 'They're saying it was, like, a ritual killing.'

'Who's saying that?'

'A little bird told us,' Marie says.

Donna stares. 'There were photos and bones arranged around the body. Like, pure culty.'

'I hadn't heard that.'

'What *have* you heard?' Marie says. 'Your dad's a cop. He must tell you things.'

'What you think he tells me? It's a murder.'

'A *murder*,' Marie says. She and Donna share an excited look. 'Some people were saying it might have been a drowning. But Joe says it's a *murder*.'

You need to get out of this conversation. 'Forget I said anything.'

'God, I bet you there was a pentagram drawn in the soil, like,' Donna says.

'Satanists,' Marie says.

'Definitely Satanists,' Donna says.

'Girls.' They look at you, waiting for you to say something responsible. But you don't know what that would be. 'I'll chat to ye later.'

'Ah, don't be dry, Joe. You could be cool if you wanted. Here, check this out. You'll think this is good.'

She takes a photo from her pocket and hands it over.

It's a picture of you, white in the flash. Gel in your hair. Clean pink jaw. Thin neck. A can of Dutchie in your hand.

'Where did you get this?' you say.

Kala's forehead, resting on your shoulder. Sweep of her dark hair down your chest. Her fingers in a V-sign, behind

44

your ears. You remember the electric current that exact moment sent through your spine, right into the riverbank. The night of the Sisco, when life began for real.

It wasn't a normal Friday. You and the lads had gone your separate ways after school. Soon they were gonna come over for Mam's Friday Classic, but the Nintendo wasn't gonna be switched on after. There'd be no Tayto or Magnums. Outside your window the sky looked like a normal sky, but the cars in the driveways were only pretending to be cars in driveways; the whole world was magic dressed as matter. The bellyfluts happened as you did your hair in the mirror, coiling your fringe in gelly fingers. You put on the wine-coloured shirt Mam had bought you and she said, 'Who's that handsome man? Have you seen my son at all?' More bellyfluts as the doorbell rang and Mam answered, all excited. 'Who are these handsome men? Have ye seen Mush and Aidan at all?'

As the lads came upstairs you caught your reflection in the mirror. You looked like a lad who'd been holding in a cough for years.

Yourself and Mush shared nervous smiles while Aidan was in the jacks. Ye talked about *Buffy*. Ye only did this when Aidan wasn't in the room, cos he didn't watch *Buffy* cos it was gay. Ye talked about random stuff like what ye might do for the summer. Ye talked about anything except the Sisco, and the girl. She might be there.

Mush asked if he'd used too much Brylcreem in his hair. He might have, but you told him he looked pure decent. He was wearing the fanciest shirt out of all of ye – it came from River Island and had a cool dragon pattern with Chinese letters down the side. Aidan took one look at it when he came in and said, 'You bender.' Mush told him to piss off but he kept touching the shirt after, looking at himself in your mirror, big puppy eyes on him.

By the time ye sat down for the Classic, no one was talking. Eye contact non-existent.

Aidan broke the silence by taking the tickets for the Sisco from the centre of the table and reading in an old radio-announcer voice:

ST SIMON'S DISCO (THE SISCO!)

DOORS 8PM

FINISHES 1AM

<u>STRICTLY NO ALCOHOL</u>

THE LAST PARTY OF THE SCHOOL YEAR!

THE BIGGEST! AND THE BEST!

'Biggest pile of shite is what it is,' you muttered.

Mam blew tusks of smoke and sighed, 'No girl wants to dance with a sulker, Joe.'

Aidan kicked you under the table. He nodded over at Mush, who was staring into his Classic with a sort of insane look in his eyes. He hadn't eaten a thing. Normally he wolfed the Classic, swallowed it without chewing. In the chip-fat glow of the kitchen, his shirt had already darkened under his arms. Just looking at him made you feel worse. You pulled a mocking face at Aidan, like you were above it all. But your knees were doing ninety under the table.

Not a bother on Aidan, of course. Munching away, keyed up to the gills. He'd been to the Sisco before and he'd been wearing the glory of it like a satisfied god ever since. He'd got the shift off three or four beors. You and Mush met him down at QuazerDome the day after. He drip-fed ye the details while ye gave him all your 50-cent pieces so he could finish Time Crisis 2. His eyes glowed as he laid out the scene: who'd got the shift, who'd had to get their stomach pumped, who'd been grounded for the rest of time. He wove it into a symphony, an X-rated montage of short skirts and squirty flesh and sliding tongues and things so vivid they made you lie on your belly in bed and now had you primed to puke all over your Friday Classic.

'Aren't they very smart-looking tonight, Aidan?' Mam said. She had her quiet smile on her, the one she used whenever she was having a private joke with herself at the world.

Aidan jabbed at the air with his fork. 'Oh, they're *fierce* smart-looking tonight.'

Mam licked her thumb and started scratching at something on your cheek. You jerked your head. She tutted as she stood.

'D'you know who ye're like?' she said. 'Ye're like Westlife.'

Aidan coughed on his chips. 'You're exactly right there, Margaret. They could be straight out of Westlife.'

Mam smiled and stuck on the kettle. Mush was glaring at Aidan. You stabbed at your chicken nuggets. Aidan's shoulders bounced as he ate.

'The lovely boys from Westlife,' he grinned.

Mam dropped ye off near the cathedral, far enough from the school so no one would see ye and think ye were losers. You told her to make sure Dad knew to collect ye *here*, at the cathedral. *Not* at the school. You didn't want Dad making a mong of you by showing up in the middle of the yard in a squad car.

Ye walked in the usual formation, yourself and Aidan up front, Mush behind. You were pure nervous. Aidan asked if you were on your period. You told Aidan to get fucked. Aidan smirked and grabbed his balls. 'That's the intention, my good man. I swear, the horn on me tonight, lads. I don't think the shift's gonna do it. I'm serious – I'm gonna have to do some fuckin' damage. Get me fingers filthy.'

'Bollocks,' you mumbled.

Aidan said your hair looked like dog shit left in the rain and ye shoved each other in the path. Mush told ye not to make shite of each other's hair or shirt.

That's when ye started to see them.

Sisco folk. People your age, from other schools. Loads of them, filling the street, drifting towards St Simon's. People were all done up. The lads were dressed like ye were – jeans, shirts, hair gel. But the women. They were unreal. They were wearing loads of make-up and hugging their arms against the breeze. There was something stilt-walkerish about the way they moved, like they were still figuring out the high heels, but somehow that looked sophisticated too. The clickclack of their shoes skittering across the tarmac made the pavement feel new. You watched them laughing with their swirly hair and their fake tan and their glittery cheeks and their boobs and their eyeliner and their chokers and the whole lot of it.

'Lads,' Mush whispered. 'It's like *Night of the Living Dead.*'

Your eyes flitted across them, looking for the girl. You didn't want to shift anyone else. You wanted her to be your first, like in a movie.

Theresa keeps messaging you, asking if she can come and keep you company in Flanagan's. Message her, tell her you're still on the dry, the beer's non-alcoholic, don't be worrying. Tell her you saw Helen. Don't mention the uneasy feeling beginning to claw at your guts. A weird feeling to everything now. Human remains in the woods. Helen striding through the park. The twins, making you feel your age. And this photo from the Sisco. They must've got it off Mush. You wish they hadn't given it to you.

Look up and see one of the bar staff with her back to you. Nice tilt to her hips. She runs a hand through her hair and shakes it out, and something about the gesture carries a weird echo. From the back, she isn't a million miles from Kala. It takes a moment before you notice her eyes in the mirror behind the bar. You thought you were watching her. But she was already watching you.

Helen

MY BLOOD IS hot as Theresa turns the car into the estate. It all looks more or less the same as when we first moved in. Two rows of small gardens separated by tiny walls. Gates on some driveways. People still differentiate themselves with the colour of their front doors. My heart is thrumming when we pull up at the house, which is when Theresa turns and looks at me for the first time, takes me in. Her eyes are like Mam. Her expression is like Mam. It frightens me. She waves her phone. 'Something's after coming up here. I gotta go take care of someone.'

She pulls her keys from the ignition and wriggles one off the ring. 'Will you be all right letting yourself in?'

I force a smile. 'No problem.' I look at the front door.

'Don't worry, Smellen,' she says. 'Dad has his meeting this evening. He won't be back for a bit. Pauline and the twins will keep you busy.'

We sit for a moment, till I realize she is waiting for me to get out.

'Oh,' I say. I fumble at the door handle, struggling with the case. 'Thanks for coming to collect me.'

'Yeah, no bother,' Theresa says distractedly. She is looking at her phone. 'Leave the key under the pot, yeah?'

I go to the door and hear Theresa calling, 'And help yourself to whatever! It's your house too, you know.'

I wave her off. The estate is quiet. The purr of a distant lawn-mower, the smell of cut grass, oily tarmac. A drowsy sky hovers above the roofs, a heatwave setting in. They said so on the radio.

I turn Theresa's key in the lock. The weight of the door gives, the house opens its mouth, my eyes go blind in the sudden shade. I see blurred blue spots against the black. The smell of the house hits and I see Kala sucking on her bottom lip, concentration worming her eyebrows, during our eyeliner experiments. I see her sitting with Aoife at the foot of my bed with little points of sunlight dappling their bunched-up faces as they lip-sync to Jeff Buckley. I see a half-eaten sheep, a body hanging from a tree, shapes screaming in the dark.

We first spoke on the morning of the Sisco. I had been walking the Coast Road when I should have been in school. Misty had run away in the night, because Dad and his friends had left the gate open when they came tumbling in the door at stupid o'clock. I hid all the bottles that were left around the kitchen and got Theresa ready for school. I brought her to her bus and set off to find the dog.

I did not see them sitting on the wall along the Coast Road till it was too late. They were in their uniforms. They were looking right at me. As I got closer, I felt my face beginning to burn. They were smiling.

'Hiya,' Kala said.

'Why aren't ye in school today?' I blurted. Their body language subtly altered. A wire of tension in the slackness. I immediately deciphered it: part of what makes mitching cool is not even acknowledging that you are mitching.

Aoife snorted. Kala said, 'No one gives a shit if we're there on the last day. Right?'

'Sure,' I said. I pursed my lips, looking away with a studied bored face. Trying to just hang out.

A few seconds went by when no one said anything. It was excruciating.

Aoife shifted on the wall and said, 'You're not wearing your *Mighty Ducks* hoodie today.'

'No,' I said. I folded my arms. 'It's kind of warm.'

Aoife and Kala smiled at this. Kala had a turn in her left eye. One eye was looking at me. The other was just a little bit elsewhere. I had not noticed this before. I had never been this close to her.

'Why d'you wear a *Mighty Ducks* hoodie?' Aoife said.

Because Mam got it for me. 'I liked the movies when I was a kid.'

'Oh,' Kala said. 'D'you watch *Dawson's Creek*, so?'

'Sure,' I lied.

'Yer man Charlie, from the *Mighty Ducks* films,' Kala nodded thoughtfully. 'He's in *Dawson's Creek*. He plays Pacey. Paceyyyy Witterrrrr.'

'Fucking ride,' Aoife said. 'What's his name in real life?'

'Joshua Jackson,' I said immediately. I knew this from the TV guide.

'*Yeah*,' Kala moaned. She closed her eyes. 'Joshua Jackson.'

'*Joshuaaah*,' Aoife whispered.

'*Joshuaaaaaah*,' Kala whispered.

'God, I actually shlide off the sofa when he's on the telly,' Aoife said. I had never heard a girl say anything this vulgar before. I half laughed but my hand was at my throat. Kala giggled.

'So,' Aoife said. She was looking at me but talking to Kala. 'What about her, then? Is she a Jen or a Joey?'

'Well,' Kala said, smiling at me, 'she's new in town... so that makes her a Jen, I guess.'

'Are you a Jen?' Aoife said. 'Cos Jen is kind of shitty.'

I blinked.

'Yeah,' Kala nodded. 'She's sorta cool, though. Shitty, but, like, cool.'

'She looks like she's about to cry the whole time,' Aoife said, tipping ash from her cigarette. I did not know if she was talking about Jen any more, or me.

'Who's Jen?' I said in a quiet voice.

'Uh, Jen and Joey?' Aoife opened her hands. 'The girls? From *Dawson's Creek*?' She rolled her eyes and, suddenly bored, said, 'You seem more like a Joey to me.'

Kala winked. 'We won't hold that against you.'

I smiled, but I did not really know what I was smiling about. Aoife was looking down the road, swinging her heels against the wall. The sound sent echoes through the silence. Kala was staring along a knotty rope of her hair, curling it with a finger. They were bored with me. I was being dismissed. I needed to say something. Entertain them in some way.

'What are you doing here?' Aoife said.

I took a step back. My hand reflexively went to my throat again. 'Oh, sorry.'

Kala tutted and nudged Aoife.

'She means, "What are you *doing* here?" Not, "What are *you* doing here?"'

I did not look at Aoife to see if she agreed. Kala felt safer. There was an openness to how she was looking at me – like she was lowering a drawbridge for me to cross.

'So?' she said, fluttering her lashes in an exaggerated way. 'What *are* you doing here?'

'My dog's gone missing.'

'Oh, that sucks,' Aoife muttered.

'You need to be careful with dogs around here,' Kala said. 'It's not safe to leave them out.'

'Really?'

'Yeah. Like, sometimes dogs get murdered and stuff,' Kala said. 'It's totally messed up.'

I smiled and rolled my eyes, to show I was in on the joke. Neither she nor Aoife reciprocated.

'My mam said it was Devil worshippers,' Aoife said. 'They torture animals for black Masses, like. Burn them with cigarettes and hang them off trees and cut their tummies open while they're still alive. Fucked. Up.'

I was not sure if they were making fun of me. I searched both their faces. They seemed serious.

'Where d'you think your dog's gone?' Kala said, hopping off the wall.

'Somewhere out this way. Maybe in the woods. This is where we walk her. Where I walk her.'

'We'll find her with you,' Kala said. 'Won't we?'

Aoife lowered herself to the ground. 'Sure there's fuck all else happening. What's your dog's name?'

We walked together along the Coast Road. The sky was a tumble above us. The girls scuffed their shoes in the gravel. There were wild bushes and fields of jungle green. Weeds searching out from the broken gums of the stone walls. Sometimes Aoife hummed to herself. I kept quiet.

They asked me where I was from. I told them I was born in France, and I could see it impressed them. When I told them Mam was half French, I blurred over the 'was', so I was not really lying about anything. I told them I'd already had sixteen addresses in my life. This was true. Kala smiled and said, 'That's so cool.' When she rolled the next cigarettes, she offered to roll one for me. I told her I was trying to quit and she said, 'Oh my God, me too.'

After searching for a while, the girls said they needed a break. We climbed through a patch of grass leading off the Coast Road. We sat on a large mound overlooking an empty school yard. The grey-black gravel glowed in the sun and the vacant goalposts gaped at us like shocked mouths. The girls told me this had been their primary school. They told stories about their favourite teachers, conjuring this intact past together, picking up each other's threads, weaving them for me. Sitting this close to the girls, I noticed little details. The downy fuzz on Aoife's arms. A mole on Kala's neck. A garish heart-shaped ring on Kala's left hand. Traces of glitter in Aoife's eyeshadow. The scatter of freckles across both their noses. The way their bodies fit themselves so well. How they closed their eyes to the sun and did not worry I might be watching. What it looked like to be seen.

The girls talked about the disco they were going to that night in a boys' school. I nodded along when they talked about shifting – French kissing – and told me about a boy called the Ride. The Ride and his friends sometimes played football in this school yard on Friday evenings. The girls sometimes spied on them. But they did not say 'we spy', they said 'we perve'. They did not say 'good-looking lads', they said 'the talent'. We perve on the talent. Kinlough slang. The Ride would probably be at the disco that evening and Kala said she was determined to get the shift off him. Aoife slagged Kala about how much she fancied the Ride. Kala laughed at herself. I laughed along, pretending I knew all about it.

There were ants in the grass and I let them run over my hands, then brushed them off and reached out to Kala. 'Actually,' I said, 'd'you mind if I have a drag off your smoke?'

Kala handed me her rollie without hesitation. It felt like something we had done before. Something unspoken, telepathic. The filter was damp and familiar with her mouth as I put it in mine.

Aoife's eyes were not closed any more. She was giving me a funny sort of smile. She sparked up her own rollie and inhaled very deeply. The tip of her cigarette flared like a molten bud, blooming.

We were sitting like that when Misty just appeared, as if by magic, looking happy. Without thinking, I rushed forward and hugged her. It was only as I had my face buried in her warm fur, my eyes closed, that I realized how lame I must look. I kept my eyes closed tight, afraid that once I looked back at the girls I would see that I had ruined everything, condemned myself to uncoolness for ever.

But that is not what happened. The girls were both happy to see my dog. Excited, like Misty was something we all shared now. Even Aoife was smiling as she ruffled Misty behind the ears.

Walking home along the Coast Road later, I saw everything refracted in the light of the girls. It was still the road Theresa and I went down when we walked Misty, but it was something else now, too. Everything – the arc and beam of the sun through the trees, the shadow of pebbles in the dirt, the tufts of grass in the road – was fused with a kind of drowsy glamour. It was as though the whole world had been torn and rethreaded in a way that felt different, even if it looked the same. I was looking at things from a place in myself that was more observant than my eyes. My stomach, perhaps. And this new type of looking changed the nature of what I was seeing. Misty, for example. She seemed more *there*. The Misty-ness of her little trot walk, the rolling muscle of her shoulders, the hints of colour in her dark pelt. The world had become more vivid. It tingled beneath my clothes. I wanted to crouch down and hug Misty. I wanted to thank her, kiss her.

Before I left them, the girls were talking about how to get drink for the disco. I made my offer without thinking. I had a bottle of Dad's vodka hidden in the bottom of my wardrobe. I knew he would be too ashamed to ask where it had gone. Aoife said that vodka was the best because it left no smell and our parents would never find out. I nodded enthusiastically, my body ringing to the word 'our'.

I heard the disco from around the corner and now, as I saw the school building hulked and slouched and gushing noise at the end of the street, I folded my arms instinctively. All the other girls looked fabulous. My dress was a simple black thing, the only dress I owned. I had bought it for myself in New Look as a Christmas gift from Dad last year. Now I was too big for it. Girls passed by with arched eyebrows and some boys made crude noises. I kept pulling the top up and the bottom down. I had not been able to get my hair right, so I had tied it up and let loose strands fall from my fringe. I had given up on elegant eyeliner after nearly an hour before the mirror trying to achieve something cool. In a panic, I drew garish slashes of dark about my lashes. Now I wished I had brought a hand mirror so I could wipe them off.

I kept hoping to see them emerge from the crowd. 'Be at the gates at nine, yeah?' That's what they had said. Maybe they were already inside?

The school building was large and it was grumbling in the dark. Tearing and straining at the seams of itself. From inside I could hear a chaos of voices in the air, gathering and plunging in surges.

I took another sip from the bottle of vodka as people milled by. It was horrible, like metal fire. It hit my stomach hard and spread down my arms. It made me think of tidal flows of lava that course beneath the earth, pushing continents about. I went to take another sip, when I heard their voices. Hyper, excited.

Kala's, shouting to me.

'Howya, sexy! Give us a lush of your drink!'

Aoife: 'Where is she?'

'There. *There.* Hello, *you*!' Kala said. 'Sweet dress!'

'Ya slutty bitch, ya.'

'Oh my God, I love your eyeshadow.'

'Fair fucks, you actually brought the vodka, did you?'

'Aoife, I think she might be my hero.'

'Yeah, you're a bit of a hero.'

'*Such* a fucking hero. Helen the Heroine.'

I smiled and took another drink, deeper this time.

I foam mouthfuls of water from the bathroom sink. My pinched eyes in the stutter of the fluorescent bulb above me. There is no one else in the house.

I enter my old room. It belongs to one of the twins now. In the disorienting weeks after Kala went missing, this room took on its own nausea. I had the idea that, if I did not touch anything at all, if I left everything just as it was, she would come back. The haunted voltage of that feeling coursed through the colourless hours we spent wading through criss-crossed beams of torchlight, looking for Kala in the brush and the mud all around Kinlough. Her name echoing across the sky. Voices along the train tracks, shadows under every bridge. Answering the same questions from the Guards, over and over. No sleep or tears, just coffee, sandwiches and cigarettes. Those days were the first time any of us smoked openly in front of parents. No one cared. CCTV checks, knocking on doors, posters on lamp posts. Guards with sympathetic smiles, telling us to please go home and rest. But the only place I could come back to was this room. Its nightmare weather rolling around my bed. I knew I was being marked with it. The guilt.

I lower myself onto the bed and lie there, holding my breath, surrounded by the watchful silence of every object. Birthmark stains still blotch the wall next to the pillow. They look like icebergs at night, waiting for ships.

Mush

WHEN TERRENCE MALICK made *Days of Heaven*, he filmed
the day scenes during magic hour, that pocket of time when
the light gets all thick and pure dreamy. It's like that outside
right now. Fox Street gliding through its magic hour. Muffled
colour. The crowd, moving in honey. I watch it from behind
the glass. There's buskers with African drums after setting up
near the window. One of them's soaking juggling pins in paraf-
fin. Fecking class. Soon enough it'll be dusky and there'll be a
fire show going on right outside my window. People all dolled
up to make a night of it, gathered to watch, passing naggins
around. And I've got a front-row seat right here at the window.
The summer spectacle. I drain can number four, crush it, pluck
number five out of the plastic wrapping. I do this pure dainty,
like. Pinkie up. I take my pointy finger and give a tap-tap-tap
along the seal of number five, then crack it open.

But I can't shift the knot in my guts. I don't like things not
sitting right with the twins. Been telling myself, just give them
a bit to simmer down, like. But I keep seeing the look Donna
gave me through the window and can't resist sending them a
message. The soft touch, that's what Mam calls me.

I WhatsApp Marie:

come on

lets not fight

The two grey ticks appear, which means it's after sending,
delivering. After a moment, the ticks go blue, so Marie's read
the message. I watch for 'Marie is typing...' to appear.

But d'you think she responds to me? Does she fuck. Them twins are as stubborn, like. They're going to leave me stewing. So I check out Marie's Instagram. If I throw enough likes her direction she might come round. Twenty minutes since her last post. A selfie of herself and Joe, at Hogan's Square. I swear, Marie gets some queer notions. Ever since Joe came back to Kinlough, he's been like her pet project. She keeps pestering Theresa about him. The other day she asked if I'd any photos of Joe from back in the day. I asked what she wanted old pictures for, and she used the phrase 'wank bank' more than once. I think Marie has this fantasy parallel universe relationship with Joe. She hints at that type of thing all the time on Instagram, posing like they're a couple.

Fuck it. I give the picture an auld like anyway.

Donna's pure immune to all that Instagram shit. She dropped her phone down the jacks a while back and I'm half sure she did it on purpose. She's gas. There she is in the background of Marie's selfie, not looking at the camera, scowling out at Hogan's Square like the place has let off a fart. Big sulky stare on her. I get a bit of a sore tug on my belly looking at her, sometimes. The older she gets, the more Donna has these looks about her eyebrows, and I'd swear her big brother was actually in her eyes. Aidan, still here, looking out at Kinlough from beyond the grave.

You'd only ever know Aidan thought something was funny by the way his eyes would smile. The rest of him gave nothing away. Pure cool. He was five weeks older than me. When we were toddlers he'd eat apples down to the core and I'd sit in front of him with my hand out, waiting to take the core off him to put it in the bin. He was my cousin, and I tried to be as cool as him. Sometimes, when I brushed my teeth, I tried to affect his kind of 'Ah, yeah?' vibe about my face. I could pull it off in the mirror, like. But I could never hold that pose in real life.

Whenever Aidan hocked up a clot of phlegm and sent it arching out ahead of us, I tried to do it too. My phlegm always gave up and got caught on my chin. He was better at stuff like that, cos he had the Lyons to show him how to do it properly.

The Lyons were Aidan's cousins on Uncle Ger's side. They lived on a farm out the Warren, they all had nicknames – Teabag, Boomerang, Lee – and they were older. There was nothing familiar or warm about them. I mean, Joe's dad liked Aidan well enough – but he'd explicitly told Joe he never ever wanted him hanging around the Lyons. And I knew Auntie Pauline and Mam were afraid of them.

But that's where Aidan wanted to get our drink from, the night of the Sisco. His cousins. I thought it was a bad idea, but sure no one ever listened to me, like.

I saw the Lyons as we got closer to the school. They were in trackies and baseball caps, gathered in the door frame of a shuttered shop. They had bags of cans shucked on the ground before them. Crushed empties strewn like victims about their feet.

Aidan and Joe were walking up front, me trailing behind. Aidan had his new stroll on him, feet pointing outwards, thumbs tucked into the waistband, shoulders rolling like waves. No fear.

The Lyons were flaking leftover Supermacs at a crew of fellas from the year above us. A half-eaten burger left a bird shit splatter on Eamon Phelan's black shirt. The Lyons cackled in the door frame. Phelan's crew walked away from the Lyons like nothing had happened, because they were sensible. Not like us. Aidan was marching us right towards them.

'Well, lads,' he said.

The Lyons' body language remained lazy even as beady eyes clicked to attention.

Aidan had a cigarette – where'd that come from? – tucked in his mouth. 'Any of ye have a light?'

None of them moved. It was like Aidan's words hadn't even happened. Teabag slowly straightened and took a step towards us. Teabag was nineteen. He'd a face on him like a toolbox.

He wasn't the tallest or the oldest of the Lyons – Boomerang was twenty-one and Lee was twenty – but he'd always been the leader. He spoke to the others. 'Are ye cunts deaf or something?' he said. 'Big man's after asking ye for a light.'

A flutter of lighters at Teabag's command and Aidan sparked up. Boomerang and Lee were fanning out so they stood to either side of me and Joe. I knew if I looked directly at them I'd get a slap.

'Good night so far?' Aidan said. He was speaking with that sort of sighing voice that auld lads have as they squint over gates. Like the world is a sum they could do in their heads if they were bothered.

Teabag hocked up a load of phlegm and let the spit snake down and dangle from his mouth, like a rope. He looked up at Joe through his eyebrows. Joe didn't know how to respond, so he just looked away. After a moment Joe looked back, and Teabag was still staring him out of it. Teabag sucked up the long thread of spit and swallowed it. His eyes didn't leave Joe.

'Ye wouldn't have any cans for sale, would ye?' Aidan said.

Teabag was still gawking at Joe. 'D'you've any fags, feen?'

Joe shook his head.

'Does this cunt have a voice?' Teabag said.

'Yeah,' Joe said.

'*Yeah*,' Teabag said.

Aidan handed out a pack of cigarettes he had tucked in his back pocket. 'Here,' he said.

'*Yeah*,' Teabag repeated, nodding to himself as he turned to Aidan, took the pack of fags, crushed it in his fist and pinged it off Aidan's chest. 'How's little Mush?' he said, turning to me. He was like a general, inspecting recruits.

'Oh, I'm grand,' I said.

'*I'm grand*,' Teabag said. He turned back to Joe. 'Fancy a lush of Buckie, do you?'

He took a bottle in a paper bag and held it out to Joe. I knew about Buckfast. Tonic wine, full of caffeine. Some Saturday mornings Mam made me clean puddles of purple Bucky puke left outside the caf. A madman's drink, she called it.

Joe went for the bottle but before he could touch it Teabag jerked it out of his reach, then held it out again and let Joe have it.

Boomerang muttered, 'Don't backwash it, you faggot.'

Joe swallowed, then he coughed and spluttered and a dark clot of the stuff splashed at his feet.

Teabag took the bottle back and smirked at the others. 'See? This is what happens when you give a man's drink to a fucking piglet,' he said. He stepped to Joe again. 'Your auld lad's a cop, isn't he? That makes him a pig. Which makes you... a piglet.'

He squealed like a pig in Joe's face. We all jolted. Aidan cleared his throat and Teabag snapped at him, like a snake lunging. 'You saying something?'

Teabag had us wherever he wanted us. He spoke to the others. 'What ye think, lads? Should we give the big man a few cans?'

'We have money,' I said. 'We'll all pay you, like.'

Teabag rolled his eyes. 'Are you innocent?' he said. He jabbed me in the chest, right under my right shoulder. A short, sharp thud. I knew straight away I'd have a bruise in the morning. I tried not to flinch. Teabag was looking at me. A smile in the ink of his eyes. He jabbed me again in the exact same spot, harder. Heat in my cheeks. 'Don't be a fucking *innocent* feen,' Teabag said, jabbing me in the same spot again.

I was going to say something when a hand came out of the dark behind me and gave me a hard slap around the back of the head. It messed up my hair, but I didn't reach to fix it. If I did anything now, it'd only be a provocation. They'd kick the shit out of us.

Then a new colour cut the air. A girl's voice. 'Howye gettin' on, lads?'

There were three girls at the entrance to the door frame behind us. Cheeks shimmering, sculpted curls. The one who'd spoken was taller than all of us. She was blonde. This half-bored look on her face, letting a lazy furl of smoke roll from her mouth. There was another one, with scary-sexy eyeshadow and a tiny black dress.

And – fuck. Joe's girl. His Apollonia. She was speaking now. Her voice was pure smoky. 'Are ye selling cans or what?'

She slipped her hand into mine. She was holding my hand.

'Who's asking?' Teabag said.

'Me,' she said. 'How much per can?'

'Fiver,' Teabag said.

'Five euro? For a can of mouldy Dutchie?' She laughed. 'Get real, I'll give you three.'

'Three fifty.'

'Nah,' she said in a bored way. 'Three euro should do it.'

Teabag snorted. He let his tongue lie like a dead fish over his bottom lip while he stared her down. 'How many?'

'Ten.'

Teabag pondered this for a moment, then made a quick movement with a finger. Boomerang and Lee moved to sort ten cans in a plastic bag.

Apollonia gave a quick look around and we all hurried to get out cash. Joe had a 20-euro note straight away – he always had loads on him – and the rest of us threw in a couple of quid each. Apollonia handed over all the cash and took the bag. Then she looked at me.

'Come on, babe,' she said, and gave me a kiss on the cheek. 'We're all gasping for a drink, like.'

I could feel the rake of glares flaying us from the doorway as we walked away. Teabag was making squealing sounds after us, but I made like a sensible young fella and copied Aidan and Joe, who didn't look back.

Joe WhatsApps me again. Keeps asking if I want to come join him at Flanagan's. I don't know why he does this – he knows full well I'm going to say no. I'd nearly invite him to join me here in the caf, but sure I'm almost out of cans and I don't want to seem more of a loser than I am. Anyway, he's probably got loads of cool people to be hanging out with up there. He's just being polite, trying to take care of me, like we're still kids. The pity pints.

Joe says:

dude

guess who I saw in Hogans sq earlier?

I can't believe it when he tells me it was Helen. I stare at my phone for so long I end up spilling some of my can down my chin.

Me and Helen still email a couple of times a year. Big long emails too, like. You'd put an effort into writing them. She's the only person I do anything like that with. Maybe it's just the drink. Whatever. But my belly's all tingling, like.

Joe doesn't say if he chatted to her, which means he didn't. Figures. Way too much static there. Still, push comes to shove, we can at least pretend to be civilized adults. I open my last can and type back to Joe:

Wud love to be there man bt busy doing stock inventory here. my exciting life lol

I hesitate and then delete the message without sending. No point in lying to people when you can say nothing.

Joe

NO ANSWER FROM Mush, as usual. Any time you're back in Kinlough, he only ever wants to sit in the caf, and you can't do that because that means drinking. You'll talk about this with Theresa later, when she's less stressed. You can tell from her messages that she's flustered about Helen being here.

You don't know what Helen does. Lives in... Canada now? Or somewhere. Theresa mentioned something about freelance journalism, once. Or teaching. One of those worthy jobs that pay fuck-all. That'd be Helen, all right.

Theresa messages that she's stuck in traffic again, so you sit under a tree and try and watch the Square. The streetlamps have come on, and people are sitting in the dusk, eating chips and bushing. It's nice. You were once like that. You still carry that in you. Kinlough.

Sip your non-alcoholic Paulaner, listen to the kids sitting nearby. It's mad how Irish kids' accents have slipped in the past few years. You feel old even noticing how American they sound. That's why you want to spend time with Mush again. To touch something unchangingly real. Mush is one of those lads whose accent will never take on an American edge. He'll never pronounce 'water' the way these kids do. The way you do. A mid-Atlantic 'waadder.' It'll always be 'wawsher' for Mush.

You're about to message him again when you spot him across the Square, with Donna and Marie by the bus stop. Mush towering over them, big hoodie on as usual, with the hood pulled up to hide his scars. The light is gorgeous on

65

the three of them, they look cinematic. The Other Place. You take a photo and decide not to post it. You'll keep this one for yourself. Show it to Mush in person. You're about to walk over to them when the bus arrives, and they get on board. You wave, but Mush doesn't wave back.

The waadder kids all start to cheer. They've managed to convince some students to sell them two cans. They pass the cans between them in a round, one gulp each, all eager to drink, to be seen drinking. The giddiness in their faces. You remember that. The first taste of beer, the fluttering feeling of no longer being a kid stuck in the mucky sludge of the world, but a drop of tingling water, soaring into the blue deep of the Other Place.

The first can you ever tasted was like cat piss and the second was only less pissy because of how much mankier the vodka tasted. Ye were sharing the cans ye'd got from the Lyons, sitting down by the river behind the rowing club with the sounds of the Sisco throbbing in the distance. There were clusters of other lads and beors all about the riverbank, drinking, laughing. Everyone having a class time. You were trying to put a smile on things but it felt like you were sinking through the earth, watching the world climb higher around you. You couldn't believe what was happening. Bad enough that the girl – Kala was her name, even her *name* was cool – had taken Mush by the hand. But kissing him on the cheek? This wasn't meant to happen. Not to you. You were Joe Brennan.

The tall blonde girl, Aoife, made sure everyone kept drinking. The vampy girl with the vodka bottle was called Helen, but she said very little. Her eyes were beginning to swim with vodka.

Every time Mush took a sip from his can he smacked his lips and let out a sigh like the lad from the Diet Coke ad. Kala's dark lipstick was still smudged on his perfect fucking boy-band cheek.

And Aidan was chatting away, not giving anyone a chance to talk, pulling reams of shite from his hole. He'd been slagging Mush the whole time, only Mush was too innocent to realize it. Soon enough, you knew, Aidan would get bored slagging Mush and turn the focus onto you. The drink was making a prick of him.

He stood and patted his crotch. 'Christ, I'm bursting for a piss, like. You coming, Josephine?'

You didn't even look up.

'I'll come!' Mush said, beaming. 'These beers are going through me!'

He said this like it was the greatest thing ever.

Himself and Aidan walked off. It was just you and the girls now.

'Here, Helen,' Kala said. 'Take a photo of me and Joe.'

She handed Helen a disposable camera and leaned her head on your shoulder. Her hair tickled the side of your face, your neck. She smelled amazing, like incense. Her hand touched the back of your head and it sent an electric shiver right through you, as she said, 'Bunny ears!' and the camera flashed.

'I don't know if I did that right,' Helen said, waving the camera. She was slurring her words.

Kala nudged her. 'Hey. I think you're getting a bit pissed, babes.'

Helen shrugged and sipped at the bottle.

Kala whispered something in Aoife's ear and got up, brushed the back of her skirt with her hands, and left without looking at any of ye.

After a moment, Aoife crawled over and sat next to you. 'You having a good night?'

You shrugged. Kala had probably gone to shag Mush before he came back from the jacks.

'Your friend's fairly intense,' Aoife said.

'Who, Aidan?'

'If that lad was a bar of chocolate he'd eat himself.' Aoife grinned. 'Sooo... Joooe. What you think of us girls then?'

She had this smile on her like she was making fun of you in her head.

You didn't know if it was a trick question.

'How about Kala?' she said. 'D'you like her?'

'She's sound,' you said.

'*She's sound.*' Aoife grunted. 'I know she's *sound*. Don't be getting clever on me. D'you think she fancies any of ye?'

You shrugged again. You couldn't look at Aoife. You almost told her to fuck off.

'Have you been to the Sisco before?' Aoife said.

You shook your head.

'You don't know how this is supposed to work?' she said.

'What?'

'Oh, fuck sake, Joe. You're going to make me say it?' She rolled her eyes and put on a stupid voice. '*Will you shift my friend?*'

'Sorry?'

'Just give us a yes or no. She's waiting.'

Everything began to happen very quickly. Like the world had sped up. Your thoughts were whirring super-fast and the world was too, but it was also going slow.

Aoife led you by the hand through the crowd. You looked back at Helen, who was sitting alone like a crooked monk in the dark, staring at the grass, then the crowd closed over her like waves and you were being brought to another end of the riverbank, where there were people shifting everywhere, eating the faces off each other. They gnawed with noses wrinkled, as if confused, or pained, like they were trying to erase each other, get themselves erased. People walking about with mouths and noses blunted raw.

Kala was standing there. You opened your mouth to say something but Aoife almost swung you right into her and laughed and walked away. Kala flicked her hair back, and put her arms over your shoulders. She was almost as tall as you in her heels.

'Have you done this before?' you said.

She laughed. 'You're as cute,' she said. She flicked her hair out of her eyes again and looked into yours as you put your hands on her waist. Then her tongue was in your mouth and yours was in hers. You were getting the shift. Ye were shifting.

Her hand played with the back of your hair. Her tongue was pushing yours and you were pushing back. She tasted like strawberry bubblegum. Some unspoken signal and ye both knew when to tilt your heads in the opposite directions, when to go softer, when to be more hungry. You moved a hand in her hair cos you remembered the girls in *Friends* talked about that feeling nice.

It was like being made of caramel.

In the distance, the Sisco was playing 'Maniac 2000.' The song played three whole times and ye were still shifting.

She pulled her mouth from yours for a moment and whispered, 'You can give us a squeeze if you like,' and then her mouth was on yours again and she gave a small moan.

So you moved your hands, very slowly, from her hips to her ribs. Then you squeezed her ribs gently, like she was a music box. She giggled at that and you felt her laughter skittering all ticklish across your upper lip, and you laughed too, catching her breath in yours, and you could feel her smile on your mouth as ye kept on kissing and it was absolutely fucking brilliant.

Ye sat with feet dangling over the river. Her hand was soft in yours. Her head on your shoulder. Her thumb making little circles on the heel of your thumb. The light bounced off the water in slow ribbons. The phone was vibrating in your pocket but you ignored it. You had the sort of happiness that spreads out and covers everything. You were thinking about how many good things there were in the world and how everyone should have all of them. Even the way your tongue hurt was good.

Kala was telling you how she and Aoife had been best friends since for ever. She said they were the only sane people in their school. You were beginning to tell her that Aidan and

Mush were the two soundest lads in Kinlough, that it was just the drink that had Aidan acting the prick – and you'd always wanted to use that phrase, 'Don't mind him, it's the drink', cos it felt pure grown-up – when a great wave of cheering blew through the crowd.

'Oh my God,' Kala said.

Mush and Aidan were following Aoife and they had Helen suspended between them. Helen had her arms out and her head dipped. She looked like one of them people in the Middle Ages, in the stocks, about to get pelted by fruit.

Ye ran to them.

'What happened?' Kala said. She had to shout because the crowd around ye were making so much noise. 'Is she all right?'

'Does she look all right?' Aidan snapped. There were all these lads from your year shouting your names at ye. Everyone was laughing.

Helen's head hung down, a long string of puke threading her face to her chest. She was whimpering the same thing again and again. 'I'm sorry.'

Ye got out to the front of the rowing club to even more cheers and laughter. In the street light, Aidan's face was almost beetroot.

Kala took your hand as ye walked. Mush saw that – you were holding *actual hands* with Kala, in front of them all, like this was normal, like this was the world ye lived in – and he gave you a big grin.

Ye shuffled to the end of the street and leaned Helen on the stone wall of Toner's Bridge. Her hair was a mess, all slicked and webbed on her cheeks. She kept saying how sorry she was and Kala was rubbing her back and saying it was all right.

The Purr gargled beneath ye and your phone was vibrating in your pocket again. You took it out. Fuck. Dad. It was ten past midnight and ye weren't at the cathedral.

'We have to go,' you said to Kala.

'Thank Christ for that,' Aidan said.

'Where will we meet ye tomorrow?' Kala said, brushing

strands of hair behind her ear. The giddy quiver in your stomach at this. At how routine she made this sound.

'QuazerDome?' Aidan said.

'QuazerDome?' she said. 'What are you, twelve? What about Java's? Do ye know it? Just off Fox Street, near the Old Gate.'

You smiled and agreed on a time. Kala pulled her cardigan sleeves over her hands and said, 'Bye,' and then – in front of everyone – she gave you a big hug. She buried her head in your neck and took your hair gently in both her fists and kissed you quickly on your neck.

As ye crossed the road you had the dizzy feeling of being on a ship riding the shrug of a sea. The flat pavement beneath you lurching and bobbing and the stars whirring in the sky with the echoes of the Sisco music and you swinging wildly somewhere up there in the sweet blast of all that noise. Your skin was raw, tongue still sore with a delicious ache. The feeling of joy about something so simple as the anticipation of the cool gleam of the door handle on your dad's car, soon in your hand, the quick click of it opening into the safety and radio and clean smell of the journey home. Aidan was handing out chewing gum to cover the smell of the cans. He was ranting about how the night had turned, but Mush had a look of quiet happiness on his face. He clapped you on the arm and whispered, 'Apollonia, man.'

Been back in your parents' house a month and still haven't gotten the hang of this fucking key. Every night the same stupid ritual when you get back from Flanagan's, pushing and pulling at the latch, watching your face frown back at you in the door's gauzy glass spines, trying to get into your own home. Your parents' home.

It was Dad who suggested you stay here while the final touches are put to the apartment you're doing up over

Flanagan's. He'd been unreal over the past year, putting you in contact with all the relevant architects and contractors, sorting out all the licences for Flanagan's. You've never had a head for those sorts of details. Of course, Dad found a way to flip that on itself, turn it into a point of pride. 'Joe Brennan wasn't put on this earth to sweat the small stuff,' he said. 'Leave the admin to the rest of us.' You sent him a photo earlier, from inside the apartment. The sun was warm in the deep window ledges. You took pictures of the panoramic view of Hogan's Square, the seagulls arcing above, plunging for chips.

Get in the house and the light clicks on upstairs. It's like being a teenager again. Night after night, you'd come home to find Dad blinking in his boxers on the landing outside his room, to make sure you were okay. He'd smile and give a little wave of the hand before going back into his room. It always made you feel like you had something to hide. Maybe that's what makes him a good cop. The ability to make you feel guilty.

But when you enter the kitchen, Dad's already there, sitting at the kitchen table. He looks wrecked. Sometimes you look at your parents and think you can see them getting old in real time. He has a cup of tea on the table in front of him and the small glass he likes to take his whiskey in.

'What are you doing still up?' you whisper, leaning against the counter.

'Ach,' he says and waves a hand at the air. 'How's the prep going?'

'It's going.' You go to the kettle. 'Fancy another cuppa?'

Dad doesn't answer. The whole room feels heavy. A creaking from upstairs and you hear Mam making her way from her bedroom, down the stairs. She comes into the kitchen in her dressing gown but she doesn't look like she's been sleeping. Her face is all tension. She gives your arm a little squeeze and sighs.

You look over to Dad but he avoids your eye.

'Jesus,' you laugh. 'Who died, like?'

Dad tells you to sit down with him.

When you do so, he reaches across the table and takes your hand in his. Can't remember the last time he did this. His big bear paw cradling your fingers. The hairs silvering his knuckles. All the hours you spend in the gym building your arms, you'll never have hands like this.

'Son...' He doesn't say anything else, just sits there squeezing your hand. Look behind you at Mam, but she's leaning over the counter with her hands against it as though to support herself. She's watching the kettle boil, her face turned away.

'What is it?' you say. 'Are ye okay?'

Dad pulls at his bottom lip for a moment and looks around the room as though the words he's looking for might be lying about somewhere. Are they are going to get a divorce? Jesus. That'd be fine. You've almost wanted them to do that for years. They've lived their lives around one another long enough.

'Joe, they've been running some tests, okay? Sending things to labs.'

Christ. Cancer. Must be cancer.

'The results aren't public yet,' he says. 'But it's going to be all over the news by tomorrow afternoon.' He sighs. 'Margaret. Can you maybe...?'

The kettle's beginning to wail. Mam's eyes are raw.

'Fuck sake, spit it out,' you say.

Dad's hand is almost crushing your fingers.

'In the woods,' he says. Fierce look in his eyes. 'The body. Son. It's Kala. It's really her, I'm sorry. It's Kala.'

Mam lets out a childish sort of whimper. The shriek of the kettle behind her is excruciating.

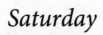

Saturday

Helen

SUDDENLY, SUN. THE gentle burn of morning through red linen. Birdsong like pinpricks of sound. I lie inside the noises of the estate gathering itself. Arms heavy at my sides.

The sound of the radio in the kitchen, beneath me. Muffled voices like rumours, cutlery clinking. Dad. Pauline.

Pauline's hen party is tonight.

I get up and open the curtains. The fields are no longer there. All buried beneath rows of unfinished houses. Window casements in the brickwork, like the hollows of skulls. Last night I half expected to see Kala amongst the building work, watching for me, waving for me. *Hello, you.* Three clicks on her torchlight. Then three on mine.

The room is full of Donna's things, of course. I do not know what else I was expecting. Some part of me wanted it to be untouched, to find the shelves still stuffed with my old mixtapes and CDs, my corkboard on the wall, pinned with Polaroids and the drawing of Leonardo DiCaprio screaming and crying on his knees – the scene where Romeo finds out Juliet is dead. Aoife loved the folds of Leo's belly as he kneeled, wailing. I wanted to see how well each artefact measured up to the emotional charge I expected it to hold, but the room is disappointingly real and ordinary.

I am checking my reflection, about to go downstairs, when I notice a set of old Polaroid photos, scattered on the chest. A crooked feeling as I take them in my hand, with a frown. These Polaroids are not mine, but I am in them. They are pictures of our gang. In one, we are all bunched together on the beanbags in Kala's room. In another, it is the boys at the Widow's Arch. Mush, with his hoodie piled like a turban on his head, crossing his eyes. His cheekbones are crescents carved in light. I check the Polaroids for captions or dates.

Where did Donna get these?

On the back of the third picture, I find Kala's spidery scrawl. *To Here Knows When! xxx* Blotches from where she leaned too hard on the pen. In the picture, Kala and I are down at Lough Caille. Kala took this photo. A selfie from a time before the word 'selfie' existed. She was always one step ahead. I blink back some twitch of an emotion and look closer. We are younger and thinner than I remember ever feeling. We look so clean. As if we mean no harm. As if we are not harm itself.

Pauline is all fizzling energy. Nervousness scuttles about her features like a spider in a sink. I had barely opened the kitchen door when she came surging towards me – 'Oh, there she is! Looking fabulous first thing in the morning, wouldn't you know it!' – and gripped me in a warm hug like we are old friends, like we actually know one another.

'There you are,' Dad says, looking up from the paper.

'Here I am,' I say. We did the awkward catch-up last night over dinner, talking about how busy the airport was, how handy the motorway is. Pauline did all the conversational heavy lifting, asking about my life in Canada. I nodded along to her chatter, watching Dad's knee bounce under the table, realizing that my knee was doing the same. My brain was like a TV, switching channels at a frenzied speed. Dad's hairline is higher, the skin tauter about the forehead, wires of silver in his eyebrows. Time archived in the lines of his skin. He has reading glasses now. He takes them off and squeezes my arm. 'There you are,' he repeats.

'Anyone like a cup of tea?' I say.

'That'd be mighty,' Dad says, sitting back.

'Doesn't she look great, Rossie?' Pauline says, hovering behind me. One hand on my shoulder, as though to hold me to the ground. 'Oh, you look great.'

'She does,' Dad says. 'There she is.'

Pauline tells me there is porridge. All I need to do is heat it up on the stove. I smile and do so, while she talks about how much the twins are looking forward to seeing me. For a moment I see Aidan's features in Pauline's face, and it feels like I am full of hot oil.

I look for the teabags. Nothing in the kitchen is where it used to be.

Dad is trying to catch my eye. Occasionally Pauline puts a hand to his knee to stop it jittering, but there is an ease to him which I do not recognize. His shoulders are lower. Arms still solid muscle but his waist has thickened; it bulges over his belt each time he tilts towards Pauline, which he does often, eyes softening and the edges of his mouth rising whenever she approaches a punchline he knows is coming. Pauline is explaining that the porridge is part of a vegan diet that Theresa has written for them. 'So we're trim and photo-fit for Monday,' she says. She reminds Dad not to forget to collect his wedding suit from the tailor's today. She tells him to double-check with the caterers if they will be able to deliver by tomorrow evening, or if Theresa will have to collect the food before the registry office on Monday.

I find it hard to focus, with all the voices on the radio. So many Irish accents at once. They sound like Americans in bars, trying to do my accent back at me. Exaggerated, stage Irish. Only they are real. As real as Dad's fingers tapping along to the jingles.

'You free this afternoon?' Pauline says. 'We're booked into the nail place at three. It'll be yourself, meself, Theresa and the twins. Just a bit of bonding time for us women before the hen.'

'That sounds fun,' I say, and Pauline looks at Dad like this is some great triumph.

'Prepare yourself for the twins,' Dad says.

They did not show up for dinner last night. Pauline was constantly checking her phone, and eventually got a message from Marie to say they were staying out with friends.

'Don't be minding him,' Pauline says. 'They can't wait to meet you. You're awful glamorous to them, you know? Freelance writer, living abroad.'

I almost laugh. Not at Pauline, but at myself. The idea that my life is anything but a struggle to make the rent.

I am about to say I am sure that the twins have grown up gorgeous – I know this is what I am supposed to do: ask questions, pay compliments – when the words on the radio begin to register. '...was initially reported missing by her grandmother on the fourth of November 2003. As you know, Seán, Gardaí engaged in an intensive search at the time. This included activities by the specialist units, including the underwater unit, which extensively searched both the River Purr and Lough Caille, where the grim discovery was made by a worker on a construction site in Caille Woods on the morning of July the seventh, one week ago.'

Pauline's eyes widen and she looks to Dad.

'...scene remained sealed off while the state pathologist conducted a preliminary examination on the remains. The remains were then removed for further examination by the Garda Technical Unit, who yesterday concluded, and today publicly confirmed, that they were those of the missing teenager. In 2003, Kala Lanann's disappearance was the subject of great concern to her family and the Gardaí, who issued numerous pleas for information. This morning, Gardaí have said that that Missing Person's inquiry is now a criminal investigation.'

A thick Kinlough voice comes on the radio: 'We are appealing to the public for their assistance at this time. We're appealing to anybody who was in Caille Woods or the Coast Road on July the seventh, and might have seen any suspicious activity, to please contact the Garda Incident Room on Bishop's Street.'

The first voice takes over: 'Gardaí have not announced the cause of death, Seán, but it is believed that the remains displayed signs of severe injury. Now, when I spoke earlier to—'

'Oh good God,' Pauline says. 'Oh good Lord.'

Her phone rattles on the table. She answers. 'Jesus, I *know*,' she says, standing. 'I'm only after hearing—'

She rushes out of the kitchen, taking all the conversation with her, leaving me and Dad alone. He has a startled look. His voice stirs in his throat. He hesitates. My legs are weak. The voices on the radio are still talking. Kala, circling us. Dad blinks at me. I realize he has been doing exactly what I have been doing: going through a set of questions in his mind, topics to talk about, safe coordinates to guide our conversation. I stand with the pot of porridge in one hand and the kettle in the other, and hear myself suddenly talking about the weather. Dad's eyes are frantic, trying to reach mine, even as he nods along to what I say. We both know what we are doing. I do not stop speaking. And he does not stop me. Because we know if I do this for long enough – just stand here, talking without interruption, hands fully occupied – this awful moment will retreat, and I will not have to hug or be hugged.

Mush

THE PUNTERS ARE relentless, the chatter of plates is relentless, but the way Mam keeps looking over at me with the big puppy eyes on her is an absolute dose. Once I got the news I just wanted to pull the noise of the caf over myself like a cloak and hide inside it for a while. But Mam insists on climbing under the cloak with me, making herself part of it. I wish she'd leave me alone. She told me to take the day off but fuck sake, I need to be busy. So that put Mam in a twist, cos her left hand wants to be kind and gentle and her right wants to smack me about the ear for not doing what I'm told like a good little boy. Outside, a bunch of Korean tourists are getting their photo taken with a lad painted like a silver statue. They have nice smiles. People who've never even heard of Kala.

Kala and me were friendly from the get-go, like. Even when Joe wasn't around I'd call over to hers to hang out, watch films. Girls were pure different from fellas. They lit the room with candles, got extra pillows and cushions from upstairs. Big bags of M&M's and Maltesers. Popcorn with lashings of butter.

There was one night they were all holding blankets to themselves on Kala's bed, watching the film. If Aidan knew I was doing this – alone with women, watching *Romeo + Juliet* – I'd never hear the end of it. Joe was off to Disneyland, as usual. He went there every year with his parents, for two weeks. I still couldn't believe there was an actual America, out there in the world and not onscreen. Every year he'd bring back stuff you could only get there. Posters of Spielberg movies. A photo frame where it's the shark from the *Jaws* poster and you put your picture between the shark teeth. I'd a photo of me and Joe and Aidan in it, in my room, which Aidan said was gay as fuck. But I liked it.

Joe'd given me a special package for Kala before he left: a letter with a poem, and five packs of Rolos – one 'last Rolo' for every week since their first kiss. The girls made a big chorus of ohmygods and Kala happy-cried. I'd never seen anyone do that in real life. Aidan would've rolled his eyes at that too, but Aidan wasn't there, he was busy with the Lyons doing odd jobs for Uncle Ger, and Joe was away on holidays with his auld pair, so I was basically stuck with the girls. That's how I'd have said it to Aidan if he'd burst in on us in Kala's room. 'Ah, man,' I'd say to him, raising my hands. 'Sure I'm stuck with them, like.'

But that wasn't how it was. I liked hanging out with the girls. They hugged me every time we said hello and goodbye. Girls did stuff like that. Hug, touch. Be soft, give compliments. It was great. Aoife was a delicate hugger, trying you on for size like she wasn't sure she'd take you. Kala sort of sank in, letting out snuggly sounds, the dark fuzz of her hair pure tickly. Helen was always a bit shy, but once she did hug you it was like she was squeezing for juice. Strong, warm. Being in their hugs was like going into a perfume cloud, and one evening I came out of it and saw Mam in the door frame of the caf, watching us. She took ages brewing up the joke as we made dinner, a smile working its way up to her face. Eventually she looked up from her spuds and blurted, 'So, how are all your *wives*?' She thought this was the funniest thing anyone's ever said.

I sat on a beanbag in Kala's room, flicking through her sketchbook while the women bet into snacks and murmured how much of a ride Leonardo DiCaprio was. The paper of Kala's sketchbook was thick and made mouth-opening sounds as I turned the sheets. Her drawings were class. The recent pages were all scattered fragments, sketches patchworked about the pages. Tree branches, the moon behind clouds, isolated floating bits of a face that I recognized as Joe. Joe's kind eyes drifting in a sea of white. Joe's mouth and jaw. Joe's silhouette. You felt how handsome he was to her. It was cool, seeing him through her eyes, made into a kind of artefact, like he was famous.

As the notebook went backwards, to earlier drawings, things got weirder. Busy pages. Some were almost black with scribbles. A whole rake of pages where giant branches moved through one another like eels. When you looked closely, there was a girl between the branches, being crushed. Pages full of drawings of little girls and nuns. Some figures stood with hands on hips, but most were slumped and sad. Thing was, they had long branches slithering out of their eyes and mouths. Some of the branches had eyes caught between them, and they looked right off the page into me. They were Kala's eyes: one straight, one crooked. I looked at Kala giggling with the girls and she was cheerful, weightless, slapping her knee as she laughed. Aoife was wondering whether or not Leo DiCaprio would be a ride if he spoke like a muck savage from some farm out the Warren. Helen put on a thick Kinlough accent and quoted Shakespeare lines from the film. Kala was laughing as she looked over at me. She clocked the pages open in my lap. She kept laughing, but her eyes changed, like she was telling me a secret. It made me feel weird and I looked away.

'It's Leo's hair, isn't it?' Aoife said. 'That's what makes him such a ride.'

'It's his way of smoking a cigarette,' Kala said.

'It's his androgyny,' Helen said and we looked at her. Helen knew loads of mad words, she was pure smart like that and we were always slagging her for it.

'Oh, suck my dictionary,' Aoife groaned.

'What's an androgyny?' I said.

Aoife said, 'Sounds like a type of deodorant. *Androgyny, from Calvin Klein.*'

Helen explained it was when a dude sort of looks like a girl, and he's delicate and pretty.

'Like David Bowie,' Kala said.

'Yeah,' Helen said.

'Or... yer man from Placebo,' Kala said, crossing the room to crouch down next to me and the notebook.

'Wait, that's a *fella*?' Aoife said.

'Or...' Kala said, putting an arm over my shoulders. 'Like Mush.'

'What?'

'Oh my God,' Aoife said. She put her hands over her mouth and giggled.

Kala pulled at my hair and said, 'Look at his lovely curls, hah? Sure he's only gorgeous. Isn't he?'

Next thing I knew they'd me plonked in front of Kala's mirror, all three of them pulling at me, shouting excited instructions to each other. They ran their fingers through my hair and it sent these hot shivers down the back of my neck and shoulders. Kala got some sort of tongs and told me to hold still – 'Don't move or I'll burn you.' The others whooped. 'Straighten it, babe, straighten it!' 'Put mascara on him!' 'Where's your black nail varnish gone to?' 'No, don't move your fingers, Mush, let it dry!'

I felt this great galloping panic. They were doing some sort of dark magic. With every minor addition – some shade here, a pinning of my hair there – I was becoming someone else in the mirror.

'He's like uh... what's-his-face,' Aoife said, turning my head in Kala's mirror to accentuate my cheekbones.

'Edward Scissorhands,' Helen said.

Kala was putting eyeliner on me. 'Touch of Marc Bolan about you, Mush. Only you're prettier.' She was sucking her mouth, concentrating. Her good eye looked into mine and there was a smile in there. 'Mush,' she whispered. 'There's women who'd literally murder to have your lashes.'

The girls cooed over me like I was their doll. They laughed, but they weren't making fun of me or nothing. It was more like they were having fun with me. It wasn't like laughing with lads: they weren't going to attack me, or put me down. There was something soft inside the laughs, even as they got hyper.

I started laughing too, cos laughter catches that way, maybe, but it was like I was opening to the whole room, and the room – with the girls, the laughter, the candles, all of it – was swelling me up, making me bigger than I was. And it was weird, but. I don't know. I was in serious danger of enjoying myself.

The sky that night was a deep blue sheet folding over itself. Strands of Helen's hair snatched at my face as she held herself on my crossbar. Kala's bike wobbled under the weight of herself and Aoife. We were gliding from one pool of street-lamp light to another, turning through the laneways of the girls' estate.

Aoife lived three streets from Helen's, and we parked the bikes outside her house. As we gave the goodnight hugs we all said what we were going to do next. This was something we always did. It was like, if we knew what the other person was going to do, somehow we'd still be hanging out even when we were apart.

Kala and me pedalled away, drifting past the rows of sleepy cars. The silence of the estate was thick and we whispered in it over the ticks of our bikes.

'Ever lived somewhere like this?' Kala said.

'No, always in town.'

'Always over the caf?'

'Nah. That's only recent-ish. Mam took it over a while ago. It's her big dream.'

Kala said that was cute, and it was funny to hear my mam described like that. Mam was a total headwreck, like. Barking at me to speed up on the coffees then putting on this big cosy smile for the punters. She could be different people, depending who she was chatting to. The most interesting Mam, for me, was the one she became every time the Lyons came in to collect rent for Uncle Ger.

Earlier that day, they'd hovered over her in a grunty triangle and she wordlessly handed over the envelope. Lee and Boomerang loomed behind Teabag, staring at me, daring me to have an opinion. Teabag liked to get into character on rent day, playing the heavy. He'd started dragging his leg like he was a rapper or something. He always had some fuckhead remark he'd picked up from a gangster movie. Guy Ritchie, never Scorsese. Today he'd looked into the envelope and announced, 'Business could be busier, Lydia.' He smiled an ugly smile, all bared upper teeth.

Aidan was standing with the Lyons. I watched him adjust his stance to mirror them, tucking his thumbs into his waistband, scissoring his feet. It didn't feel nice, seeing him with his cousins like that. We caught each other by the eye and both looked away.

Mam muttered to me, 'There's punters outside that need serving, love. Hop to it.'

I took a tray and bounced off the jab of Boomerang's elbow as I ducked out into the open flare of the day.

Aidan followed me out and said, 'You should hang out with us some time, man. You'd need to lose the Nirvana T-shirt and baggy jeans but... the lads are actually decent craic, you know?'

The Lyons shouldered their way between us, muttering about Mam being a stuck-up bitch as they swaggered up Fox Street. Aidan drifted off in their current. I stood with the tray in my hands watching them go till Mam barked from inside that the apple tarts needed taking out of the oven.

'Must be cool living there,' Kala said. 'In town, like?'

'It's grand,' I said. I tried to say something sophisticated. 'I mean, it's noisy and stuff. You can't gather your thoughts. Sometimes I'd like to live out in a place like this, you know? Bit peaceful.'

Kala laughed. 'Quiet's *not* peaceful, man. Quiet is when the monsters come out.'

Neither of us said anything for a bit.

Then Kala added, 'I've seen shit to give you nightmares.'

'Yeah?'

At first Kala said nothing. She was hesitating. Then she said, 'Here, what time d'you need to be home tonight?'

I said I could stay out pretty much as late as I wanted. Mam was back on the sleeping tablets so there was no way for her to know if I was coming or going.

Kala turned to me and her face was very young. 'Can I go with you into town? For a while?'

'What,' I said. 'Now? Sure it's nearly eleven.'

'I don't wanna go home,' she said. 'Anyway, Nana doesn't even know I'm out of the house. She's well in bed.'

It was already weird to be hanging out with her like this, without Joe. But going into town together, at night, in secret, would be a whole other thing. It'd be like I was doing something wrong.

Kala rolled her eyes and punched my arm. 'Don't be worrying, fuck sake. We're only hanging out. I want to see what the city looks like in the dark.'

She turned away from me, already pedalling ahead into the gold halo of another street light.

'Come on,' she said. She looked over her shoulder, fixing her stare on me. Later, when I would think my way back through all of it – the secrecy, the thrills, the Crawley House, the nightmares – I'd always come back to this moment. 'Be sound, Mush,' she said. She laughed and cycled ahead. The night was bright over her hair and when she turned she gave a smile of pure mischief. 'Be nice to me.'

A jolt of energy moves through the caf when Joe's dad comes in, flanked by two uniformed Guards. The whole place adjusts to the heft of their belts, batons, walkie-talkies. Eyes following the fluorescent jackets, noting details for anecdotes they'll reel off later about human remains.

'Mush,' Mam says. I pretend not to hear her.

When the twins were very small, they used to hide behind their hands and think they'd disappeared. Get to my age and that sort of carry-on is pure foolishness, but here I am, polishing latte glasses, acting like the cops won't be there if I pretend not to see them.

'Mush,' Mam says.

Not everybody's like this. There are people who respond to things as they happen, right in the moment. They're the people you end up reading about, in books. People who do things.

'Mush,' Mam says softly. Her hand on my arm. She beckons over to Joe's dad.

'Dudley wants a quick word with you.'

I can hear the careful look she's giving Dudley as she says this. People think I don't notice how they act around me, but I do. Just cos I don't react doesn't mean I don't notice. I hear the edge in Mam's friendliness as she says, 'Don't keep him long now, Dud, d'you hear me?'

Eyes of the punters on me as Dudley steers me into the booth by the window where I had my blowout with the twins last night.

Dudley sits opposite. He's searching my face, my body language. Looking for whatever it is Guards are always looking for. The two uniforms hang back at the counter, getting coffee, pretending not to watch.

I scratch at a bubble of paint on the table.

'Thought you might've taken a day off for once,' Dudley says. Weak smile. He knows it's a shite joke. 'Anyone else been in to see you yet? No other Guards? Journalists?'

'People from the radio. Looking for local reactions. They asked Mam if she'd known Kala.'

'What did she tell them?' Dudley says.

I snort. '*Can ye not see that queue of customers behind ye?*'

Dudley gives a little laugh. 'Your mam is your mam.'

I grunt. Outside the window, people are going on like it's just another day. I keep expecting to see Kala winking at me from the spaces between them.

'The press will want to speak to you,' Dudley says. 'Once they find out she worked here. And who you are.'

Far as anyone knows, I'm the final person to see Kala. I dunno how many times I had to recite that night to the cops. Every couple of days they'd show up, asking me to go through it all again. It was hard, saying how she'd been. Her face a pure scatter of emotions, like. Panic, fear. Wet eyes. I told the story so many times it stopped being something that had really happened. I lost something in that. Like that moment wasn't mine any more, it was theirs.

'It makes no sense,' I say. 'In the *woods*? Under our noses, like? She's been there the whole time?'

'I'm not here on police business, son. I wanted to see how you were.'

'Yeah, not fucking brilliant, like.'

The tremble in my voice is a surprise to me. Like there's a bird in my chest, flapping its wings. Fucking Dudley. He's got this way of softly carving through you. Sliding his hands between your ribs and opening you up. When Joe and me were kids, he used to take us out the Warren in his squad car and let us mess with the siren in the passenger seat. I'd lie in bed at night, imagining what it'd be like if I was Joe's brother, and lived with Joe up in his big house, cos then Dudley would be my dad. Dudley always told me to call him *Dud*: not Mr Brennan; not Dudley; *Dud*. I liked that. One day I slurred his name, accidentally on purpose, so it sounded like I was calling him Dad. I just wanted to see what it felt like, to call someone that. Aidan slagged me about it and I wanted to hit him right on the nose, but I just cried and Aidan and Joe looked at the ground till I stopped. I've always been fucking weak, like.

I hold my breath till the tremble goes away.

'It's all right to be upset, son,' Dudley says. 'I know how close ye were. She was a good kid.' He sits back and lets out a long sigh, rubs at his eyes. He looks exhausted. 'Fucking disaster. You been on to Joe?'

I shake my head. Joe was my first thought when I heard the news. But I put off ringing him for a good hour, like. Cos

I knew once I talked to him, it'd make it real. So when Joe didn't pick up I felt this pathetic relief. I leaned against the drying rack in the kitchen with the warp of my face gawking at me in the stainless steel of the washers. Sent him a message: **Are you okay.**

'When I think of the phone bills Joe used to run up talking to you,' Dudley says with a smile. 'Christ. Talking, talking. Ye were such great pals.'

'Did she drown or what?' I say.

'Mush—'

'Okay, she didn't drown. What happened her, so?'

'You know Joe has these gigs happening in Flanagan's? The first one is meant to be tonight. He's been working towards this for a long time.'

At the counter, a queue is forming.

'I should get back and help Mam.'

Dudley chews this over for a moment. He's thinking of something to say. 'See, this is what I'm talking about,' he says. He smiles at me. 'D'you know who I see sitting in front of me today? I see a proper grown man. Someone solid, and responsible, and – don't be rolling the eyes, Mush. I'm serious. Shit's hit the fan today but you still showed up. You knew your mam would need help, so you sucked it up and did the right thing. That's what a man does. And I'm proud of you. Hey. Don't be pulling a face. I'm proud of the man you've grown into, Mush. So I want you to listen very carefully, right?' He jabs a finger at me. 'Do not go retreating into yourself over this. It's shocking news. It's awful news. But you can't be carrying the load alone. Ye were only kids when all that madness happened. Christ, no one could've handled it any better than ye did. But you're a man now. And retreating from life is no way for a man to handle things. You need to reach out to the world. To your friends.'

'I don't have any friends.'

'Joe is still your friend. And you're still Joe's friend. Ye can help one another.'

I dig my nails into my hand to get a grip. 'I can't stop thinking… Like, what if there was something I could've done to—'

'You have to push those thoughts back.'

I want to roar at him that it doesn't fucking work that way. I want to tell him how my brain just remembers what it remembers. That I can still watch a movie with a crowd scene and think I see Kala in the background, about to shout her *Hello, you!* That there are parts of Kinlough I haven't been to in fucking years. Caille Woods. The lake. Kinlough's too small a place to carry so much haunting.

Christ, it's like my insides are on fire.

'Focusing on what you could've or should've done yesterday helps no one,' Dudley says. 'It only makes it more difficult to do something constructive today. Best thing you could do this evening is meet Joe. Few cans. Reminisce. Put the world to right.'

'We're not kids any more.'

'I know. But circumstances like these have a way of bringing people together.'

'That been your experience, has it?'

Dudley sighs. He's getting impatient. 'Mush. Can you just do it for me? Look, I know ye're not pals the way ye were. I know ye're not kids. But Joe's always needed you. And it's hard for fellas to say things like that to each other. But he needs a friend. A real friend. Someone who's known him since before all the fame business.'

I just want to switch myself off. Disconnect from everything.

'Look,' Dudley says. 'I'll tell you what I know. About what was found in the woods. Stuff you're not gonna hear in the press. But you have to promise me you'll keep an eye on Joe tonight. Will you?'

I hesitate. Then I nod. He knows he has the measure of me.

He leans forward and lowers his voice. 'Okay. But this does not leave this table. You understand me?'

Helen

GRIEF IS LIKE falling in love; it is always narcissistic. Some catastrophe cuts through your life and immediately you reshape the world to make this disaster the secret heartbeat of all things, the buried truth of the universe. Everything is enchanted with her now. The sun, the breeze. When I sit in the mucky mess of the garden, swiping between newspapers on my phone, Kala is in the birds in the hedge. The distant sound of children, laughing and screaming. Misty used to paw about this grass, investigating, marking her territory. But Misty is long dead, too.

Everything inside me is trembling. The carsick feeling that comes when you realize the world is not what you thought. I need to know what happened.

Theresa messages me again.

thinking of u

The tears trying to fill my eyes. All these years, life has been playing a trick on me. This frightened rabbit feeling every time I picture Kala's face, her head arched back to laugh. Or the last time I saw her. The broken-up look in her eyes.

I begin to reply, but Theresa sends a chain of heart emojis and I close WhatsApp in irritation. I cling to the feeling as I swipe between news pages. Anger might keep me intact.

There is very little information online. Human remains found last week on a Kinlough Associates building site in the woods. The site, sealed by the guards. Testing has concluded the remains belong to Kala Lanann. Nothing about how she got there, how long she has been there. How she died. Nothing beyond the tired facts. Kala, reduced again to regurgitated snippets, dates, times. Last seen here. Reported sighting there. The RATM sticker. The final call from the phone booth. A still from the CCTV footage of her walking over Toner's Bridge, her body a dark blur levitating in grey light.

Every article leads with the photo from the missing posters. I took this photo. Kala's eyes, flared at what was happening beyond the camera. Her bloodpunch mouth opening into the start of a laugh. The giddiness. I once loved this photo, before it acquired its eeriness. Another sudden wobble inside, a stack of plates about to crash. I bite down on my cheeks. This frozen image is the way the world knows Kala, and it is the way it will always know her.

The anger I feel at this. That is what will get me through it.

There is a betting shop next to the newsagent's on the Coast Road. Three men in the doorway, the kind found outside every bookie's. The exhausted denim, the glaze of permanent disappointment. I ignore the tired eyes that drink in my body as I enter the newsagent's to buy tobacco, papers, filters, a lighter. I need a cigarette before I set foot in Kala's house. Which is where I am going. I leave the shop with sleeves bunched in my fists like I am a teenager again. Though I am not, I know I am not. I am not young. I will never be young again, and Kala will never be old.

But I used to love the walk to her house. Aoife or Kala always rang an hour beforehand and I loved having someone call the house phone specifically for me. A delicious feeling when Theresa watched me from upstairs while I stood in the hall, laughing into the phone, turning my jaw in the mirror, twirling the curly wire in my finger like a real girl. Then Kala's house rising up on the horizon, a bungalow hunched in the mouth of Caille Woods. Trees fanned over it like waves. Aoife once told me that the house used to be a police barracks, back in the day. She told me that Kala's room, in the basement, was where people used to be locked up during rebellions. I liked this, the feeling that we were part of some chain of freedom. I liked everything about Kala's house. The ritual of reaching her. First Aoife and I would knock on the door, then we would hear the crease of the floorboards as the wheelchair moved towards us. Then we had to talk with Kala's granny. Kala called her Nana. Everyone else referred to her as the Mammy. The Mammy's face was mapped by crow's feet and it was beautiful. Her eyes had a bird-like alertness and they shone up at us through the cigarette smoke. The hint of a smile seemed to hover at the corner of her mouth, all the time. She liked to tease us about what we were wearing, often making us stand at the fireplace in the sitting room. 'Let me have a proper gawk at ye.' She looked us up and down, taking long silent tugs on her cigarette. A serious expression of silent appraisal. 'Back in my day,' she once said, 'they would have burned ye as witches for looking like that.' I blinked, but Aoife laughed. I realized this was intended as a compliment. Later, I would realize this was a great compliment.

Once the Mammy had wrong-footed us like this, she'd give a subtle wave of a thin porcelain hand and turn back to her talk shows.

To reach Kala's room we had to pull open a heavy door through which daylight carried dimly over the top steps. The smell of cold earth and moist dark rose up and we descended, hands on the cool stubble of the brick walls for balance. Slivers of light at the bottom of the stone steps. A thick door marked the threshold into Kala's room. We pushed it open and suddenly Kala was all around us. Her room was huge, as wide and long as the house, and it felt like Kala, it smelled like Kala. Lavender, incense, soap. An elegant mess of clothes on the deep red carpet, cheesecloth shirts over wicker chairs. Everything ruined and regal. Guitar leads snaked across the floor. An electric heater thickening the air with warmth. An actual real-life lava lamp billowing in the corner. Photos of Kala and Aoife grinned out from the walls, next to cut-out magazine pics and drawings of singers I did not recognize. Clusters of beads, blank cassettes. Lots of lamps, always on, with thin veils draped over them, daubing everything in gauzy colours.

One afternoon we broke blank CDs with a hammer and Blu-Tacked their shards along the upper walls. The next day, the shards bent the stabs of light that came in through the slitted windows near the ceiling, giving off rainbow-coloured auras in which Kala's fag smoke rolled and furled. Kala was beneath them when we arrived, kneeling in front of a tall mirror that leaned against her wall, doing her eyeshadow. Her eyes snapped to us in the mirror, startled. One looking directly at me, the other elsewhere. 'Hello, *you*!' she said, springing up to dole out the hugs.

I loved getting her *Hello, you.*

There was an occult twist to the intimacy of us – me, Aoife, Kala – hanging out in the deafening noise beneath the house. Kala cranked her music to earthquake levels and the sound was a turning element in which we moved around one another, taking turns with lipsticks in the foggy mirror as the bass drilled through the ornamental jewellery boxes Kala kept on the floor. The noise never carried upstairs to the Mammy. It was one of the advantages of being in a former cell beneath the house. Here, down below the world, was our space.

'These would look great on you, Helen!' Kala yelled through the blare, passing earrings over her shoulder without looking, like an afterthought. I tried them on and leaned my head over her shoulder at the mirror. She was always right.

Aoife lay across a beanbag and told Kala to roll some cigarettes before we all died.

Branches were thudding to the ground at the slitted windows. Between songs, I could hear a chainsaw rattling. The crack-snap of branches, the chatter of leaves rushing together into a fall.

The girls talked about songs they wanted Joe and the boys to learn. They had started a band, and had a long list of potential names. Bueno Peach. Pariah Carey. Jungle Heart.

I was listening carefully to the girls' discussion of these names, trying to figure out what was cool and why, when I was put on CD duty. Every day I made mental notes of every musical choice the girls made. I paid attention to everything they said about individual songs. I went to the CD player and tried not to embarrass myself. I chose a CD with a drawing of a banana on the cover. When I pressed play, Kala made a murmur of approval at the opening notes.

A man's tattered boots and jeaned ankles were moving about in the slitted windows by the ceiling. Gloved hands, bundling up the branches. 'Who's that?' I said.

Kala was rolling the cigarettes. 'Nana's handyman.'

Aoife began to pull gormless faces, squeezing her eyes tight. She spoke in a low voice: 'Howya, girls. Ye wouldn't be able to fish a few coins out of me pocket there for me, would ya?'

Kala laughed despite herself. 'You're bad.'

Aoife squinted and winked a bit longer, then she smirked. 'You should see him, Vomitron.' She had been calling me that since the Sisco. 'Big creepy stare on him.'

Kala passed out the cigarettes and looked at me. 'He's harmless,' she said.

As we smoked, the girls talked about things they had seen in town last night with Mush, sneaking out. I had been at home, minding Theresa. I smiled to their stories, laughed in the right places.

The CD was very good. I said I recognized one of the songs from Dave Fanning's radio show. Aoife scoffed at that. She said Donal Dineen was the Dave Fanning for people who give a shit. I nodded and said, 'Oh my God. Totally.' I did not know who Donal Dineen was.

'Actual music,' Kala said, 'for actual people.'

The fourth track started and Kala turned the music up louder. It was a droning, hypnotic thing. Narcotic, vampiric. She shouted that this tune was brilliant. Not brilliant; *class*. Not just class; *pure class*. This was how they talked in Kinlough. The cigarette was giving me the best ever headache.

We lounged like this in a triangle for a while, in the moan and throb of the music, the thud of branches raining down. I imagined a coven of witches in the woods, moving around the flames of a fire. That probably felt as good as this.

The cigarette from the newsagent's makes me feel sick, instantly. There is a picnic bench next to the Coast Road, its feet buried in concrete, and I lean against it, head swimming. Nausea, weak legs. Kala would have laughed at me. Aoife, too.

I inhale deeply. I want to feel the char in my chest.

Kala is no longer the most-read story on the *Irish Times*. She has been bumped down by two headlines. 'Branch out on rustic Blackrock mansion for just €1.25m' and 'What tourists really think about Ireland'.

This fucking country.

Heart gathering speed as I stub the cigarette. The shadow of Caille Woods beginning to reach over the road. I know Kala's house is around the next turn in the road, waiting for me. I will be strong. I will hug the Mammy.

But when I round the bend in the Coast Road, there is someone already there, in front of Kala's house. A tall figure with his back to me. Even from this distance, I can see something strange about his breathing. He gathers his shoulders back, holds them tense, then lets them drop. He does this, again and again. For an insane moment I think he might be the hooded figure from the bus station last night. But this man is muscular, in skinny jeans and a tight T-shirt. He walks back and forth before the house, doing his strange breathing, talking to himself. I pull back for a moment, climb onto the verge at the road's turn. I stand behind a tree, watching him. After a moment, he squats down and begins to trace a finger in the dust before the house. His wrist moves as though he is writing in the dirt. Then he stops, turns, looks over his shoulder. He does not see me, but I see him.

Joe.

I should have known he would get here first.

He looks up for a moment, like an animal sniffing at the air. Then he returns to tracing patterns in the dust. Marking territory.

Joe

YOU'VE COME TO this house thousands of times over the years, in your mind. Whenever you need to believe there's a secret goodness to the world, a warmth beneath the white noise. Your life's a cocoon of air-conditioned spaces, every surface thumbed smooth and frictionless as a flatscreen. But this house is where your mind drifts when you're caught inside the hollow hours between soundcheck and show, or in some immaculate suite, lonely for the warmth of human imperfection.

First time you stepped in here, you fell in love with the handmade feel of the place. The Mammy had opened the door for ye that day. Sitting in her wheelchair. When the Mammy clocked yourself with Mush and Aidan, standing with guitars on your backs behind Aoife and Helen, there was a smirk in her eyes.

She glanced at Aoife and Helen. 'Ladies,' she said.

Then she eyed the three of ye. 'Who's this?'

'Aidan,' Aidan said, hands on hips. 'This is me cousin, Mush.'

'*Mush?*' the Mammy bark-laughed. 'What sort of name is that? And you. Which one are you?'

'I'm Joe, Mrs Lanann,' you said, extending your hand.

She looked at your hand for a moment, then took it. Her hand was slender but her grip was strong. She shook your hand and did not let go.

'So this is Joe, then. Famous Joe. Haven't you got lovely manners on you, Joe?'

'Nana,' Kala's voice warned, down the hall.

'What's your surname, Joe?' she said.

'Brennan.'

'The Famous Joe Brennan,' the Mammy said. She was still shaking your hand. 'And what, might I ask, are the intentions of Famous Joe Brennan with my beautiful granddaughter?'

Kala came stalking into view. 'Nana!' she growled. 'Will you leave him alone.'

The Mammy laughed. 'Ara, I'm only codding with the boy. Do I know your family, Famous Joe Brennan?'

'His dad's a Guard,' Kala muttered as she put things in her bag.

'Is Dudley Brennan your father?' she said. 'I haven't seen him since he was a whippersnapper. He would've worked with Kala's granddad. Did Kala tell you her granddad was a Guard?'

'Oh my God, Nana, no one cares,' Kala said.

'I'm trying to talk to Famous Joe Brennan here, love,' she said. She was examining you. 'I can see a resemblance in the face now. You're not stocky like him, though, are you? I don't know what they're feeding young fellas these days.' She turned to Kala. 'Jaysus, he's awful fragile-looking.'

'Nana, will you shut up, please.' She bowed down to give the Mammy a kiss. 'Be back later,' she said.

The Mammy whispered to Kala, 'He's awfully handsome.' Then she turned her face up to you and roared, 'I'm just after saying you're awfully handsome, Famous Joe Brennan.'

Famous Joe Brennan. Ever since the Sisco, that's who you'd become. You could feel it. Solid flesh and muscle. Inside your body, all the volume cranked up. You loved this feeling, a gliding inside yourself as you cycled into town with Mush and Aidan every other day after band practice, light blitzing your face through the trees on Blake's Road, the reds and yellows rioting in your skull. The world was suddenly your place. Food tasted better, colours burned brighter. The softness of Kala's hand in yours, the tickle of her bracelets against your wrist, the fact that you were the one whose hand she wanted to hold, whose mouth she wanted on hers, whose marks she wanted on her neck. That happened last week. The neck thing. Mad storm in your guts as ye sneaked away from the others down a lane behind the Widow's Arch, whole body booming like loud music as she sank her teeth into your bottom lip and you crushed her against the wall that was crushing her into you and ye kissed till the skin around her mouth was pink, and her hair was a mess, and you felt dizzy and blinked at her and she got the heavy look in her eyes, a swimming deep look, and she tilted her jaw to expose her neck and closed her fingers about the back of your skull and pulled your face down so the silver thread of her necklace got stuck in your lips as you dug into the space between her neck and shoulder and her breaths grew ragged in your ear, and she grabbed fistfuls of your hair and held your head against herself, heart juddering inside you because she was letting you do this, because she wanted you to do this, and then ye were kissing again, harder now, till it hurt so much it felt good, till it felt so much that it was beyond feeling good, beyond hurting, like when all colours come together to make pure white.

'Well,' Kala said whenever she saluted someone in town. All the eyes of Fox Street, turning on ye, cos Kala wanted your arm around her wherever ye went. Kneading the soft skin over her hips with one hand while lads from St Simon's stared and you carried yourself tall, spine stretching to heaven. The coolest-looking beors in Kinlough were your friends and the most gorgeous girl on the planet was your actual girlfriend. You loved how *girlfriend* was something you could say and still be talking about your own life. Going to the cinema with your *girlfriend*. Making a mixtape at night for your *girlfriend*. You got the bellyfluts every single time you saw her, which is how you knew this was true love.

Tunes pouring out of you cos of her. You could barely keep up. Mush would rehearse them with you in your room and shake his head, 'You're a genius, man.' You'd laugh it off, but deep down you were pretty sure that, yeah, you were a genius. You'd moved galaxies beyond yourself in a matter of weeks. Every night, you listened back to your tunes on a tape recorder, tweaking the lyrics as you ran your fingertips back and forth over a tealight to harden your callouses so you could dig deeper into your guitar the next day. Sometimes you'd see yourself doing this, as if you were floating outside the window, watching your life from afar. You saw yourself sitting on your bed, lit by the candle, staring out at the night, and you'd smile to yourself. You were the sort of guy that lived like that now; pure Other Place.

So whenever Mam and Dad asked about Kala, you rolled your eyes and said, 'Whatever.' You never told them anything about her, not even her name. Parents hadn't a clue. They still thought you were just a boy. But you knew, from the look Kala would give you whenever she wanted to go wandering off, that you were already the man you hoped to one day become.

The evening Kala finally met Mam and Dad, right in the middle of summer, was when she came to your house for dinner. Mam was excited to meet her, pacing about while you sat in Dad's armchair by the front window. There was a nice smoky light outside and your belly was somewhere above the house in all that summer sky, waiting for Kala to come strutting down your road. Mam's food smelled amazing. She'd made the French dinner, which she only ever made for special occasions. Garlic cheese potatoes with green sprinkles. She'd bought steaks and put out the good glasses. Fancy ice cream in the freezer. She was wearing her Christmas earrings, even though it was summer. Mam said she might change her earrings and you said she looked good. It was nice to see her on edge. It meant tonight was important. Kala and you were something real, a force in the world that people had to move around, take notice of. Dad was opening a bottle of wine for him and Mam. They were even talking to each other, deciding which music to put on. They knew the importance of appearances.

Earlier that day you'd been down the Widow's Arch with Kala's legs tangled in yours. Her hair smelled amazing. She was running her thumb slowly over the heel of your hand, her weight leaning against you. She was nervous about meeting your parents. You nearly told her about how Mam and Dad don't talk. How they sleep in separate rooms. How, each time ye go to Disneyland, ye have a room with two double beds and you share a bed with Dad while Mam sleeps alone. But you didn't say that, cos you were Joe Brennan, and you were in the thick of the world now, and suddenly Kala was walking down your road with the bounce in her feet, shoulders slowly rolling, ready to meet your parents. You stood at the window and waved. She had a little bunch of flowers in her hands.

'Hiya,' she said as she came up the driveway, past Dad's BMW. She'd straightened her hair, which you'd never seen before. She looked like something from a L'Oréal ad. You loved how she could change her appearance like this. A different lipstick, or way of tying her hair, and she could be all these other girls – the goth girl, the magazine cover girl, the sexy witch girl, the straightforward glitter-on-the-cheeks girl. She held all these girls inside herself and all of them were yours.

'You look unreal,' you whispered.

'Yeah?' Kala said. She bit on her bottom lip nervously and held up her flowers. 'I brought these for your—'

'Well, hello there, missus,' Mam said, opening the front door wide. She gave Kala two air kisses and Kala blinked at the suddenness of it. You'd never seen her stutter in her movements before. 'Let me look at you,' Mam said. She looked at Kala for one second. Two seconds. Three. Her smile was bright. Her eyes were busy.

Kala held out the flowers. 'These are for you.'

'Isn't that precious,' Mam said. 'Where did you get these from?'

'I picked them. On my way here.'

'How unusual,' Mam said. She stood back. 'Go into the sitting room while I put them in a vase.'

Dad was already standing by his chair. He reached out a hand and pretended to stumble forward when Kala shook it. 'Jesus, that's some handshake on you, girl,' he said. He smiled to show he was joking and you laughed to make sure Kala knew it was a joke too. But you weren't sure she did know. Her face had gone red.

Mam came in with a tray with small bowls of olives, red peppers stuffed with crème fraiche, pesto and crackers.

'Posh!' Kala said, like she didn't even notice herself saying it out loud.

'We'll be eating in the new extension tonight,' Mam said. 'You're our first guest since we had it finished.'

Mam talked about the new extension for ages. About how she decided on the paint job, the wood finish, all of that. But she was doing the thing she always did – talking with her mouth while doing lots of other things behind her eyes. You saw this any time she met someone in the supermarket. She could talk effortlessly to people, like you, but there was always another conversation happening inside her head and she would mutter its outcome to you once ye were alone again.

Now she was doing it to Kala. The cream sofa was huge and it made Kala look small. There was something weird about seeing her inside your house. Two realities overlapping.

Kala kept clearing her throat. When ye moved to the extension, you saw Mam check the sofa for any crumbs or olive stains.

At dinner, Kala laughed at Dad's lame jokes. He told funny stories about yourself and Mush and Aidan when ye were small. He told her about the time ye watched a Freddy Krueger movie at Mush's house when ye were ten and you'd been so scared that Dad had to take a day off work to stay home with you.

'That's adorable,' Kala said and you said, 'Yeah, yeah.'

'So Kala,' Mam said. 'Did you walk all the way here?'

'Yeah. Nana can't drive, so... I have to make my own way about the place. Usually I cycle but I didn't want to mess up my hair for tonight, like.' She gave a little giggle. She was more relaxed now.

'What about your parents?' Mam said. 'Do they not drive?'

Kala opened her mouth but said nothing. It was like when someone gets asked to read in class but they've not been following and they don't know where the sentence is on the page.

'Would anyone like anything from the kitchen?' you said, standing. 'Kala? Fancy another Coke?'

Kala nodded.

When you came back, Mam was asking about where Kala lived.

'Just down the Coast Road,' Kala said. 'You know, the old place near the woods? I think I'm, like, the third generation of our family to live in that house.'

Mam stopped cutting her meat. 'And which family is that?'

Kala put a hand over her mouth as she finished some potatoes. She made a laughing sound and rolled her eyes at herself, embarrassed at the delay. Finally, she said, 'The Lananns?'

And like that, something changed. The rain pattering over the extension seemed louder. Something was in the room. You could feel it, circling the table, pushing things around.

'This is the nicest dinner I've ever had in my life,' Kala said. Mam gave a pinched smile. But she didn't look up from her plate. Dad did his best to make up for the silences. Mam said nothing for the rest of the meal.

After dinner, Kala tried to help clear the table but Mam said, 'It's fine.' She stacked the plates noisily and took them to the kitchen. A few minutes passed. When she didn't come back with the fancy ice cream, you went and got it yourself. On your way to the freezer, you saw Mam through the door to the TV room. She was on the sofa, with the light of the screen flittering over her face.

*

As ye dropped Kala home, Dad joked about the rain, trying to get a bit of conversation going. But Kala wasn't chatting. She was next to you in the back seat, but she felt very far away. You squeezed her hand every few seconds. After a while she squeezed back. Ye did this, passing a slow pulse between yourselves, all the way down the darkness of the Coast Road.

When you reached Kala's you got out of the car and held the door for her. She thanked your dad, again and again.

'No bother, sweetie,' he said in a warm voice. 'Sure we couldn't have you walking home in this weather.'

The rain was like hot nails. It flashed like sparks in Dad's headlights. Kala's hair was already drenched, raindrops rolling down her cheeks. It was pure Hollywood and you wanted to kiss her, but you were too embarrassed with Dad right next to you. Ye hugged. Normally Kala's hugs were hungry, like she was crushing you. But tonight she felt limp in your arms.

'I don't know what I did wrong,' she said.

'It was great,' you lied. 'You were great.'

Kala didn't meet your eyes. 'I'm sorry,' she said. Her voice was dull, sunken.

On the drive back, you kept seeing how Kala had stood in her doorway. How alone she looked.

'All right there, chief?' Dad said. You were leaning against the window, the night glass rattling your skull.

'What was all that about?'

'Ara...' he said. 'Sometimes there's no understanding women, is there?'

You stared, waiting for him to say more.

'Son... you didn't tell us she was the Lanann girl.'

'So fucking what?'

You never talked to Dad like this. But you were annoyed, and knew you were right to be annoyed.

Dad sighed. 'Don't go flying off the handle, or getting into a mood. You're bigger than that. I'm just going to tell you the facts. How you respond to them is up to you. Deal?'

You shrugged.

'Your mother and I don't see eye to eye on a lot of things, Joe. But we know you're one of these lads that could do anything. Go anywhere. Be anything. You've it all going for you, the whole package. Brains. Talent. We're proud of you.'

You didn't know what this had to do with anything. But you felt yourself softening. Anger leaving your body.

'Myself and your mother were young when we had you. We had to set a lot of things aside to give you the life you deserve. I'm not saying this to make you feel guilty. Just stating facts. You with me?'

He'd never spoken like this to you before. Man to man.

'We're a good family, Joe. And it's not like that's the beginning and ending of everything, but... it's a good start.'

Dad turned off the Coast Road.

'Because by and large, it's people who come from good families who tend to go on to good things.'

He was making sense so far.

'But the Lananns...' Dad said. 'They're not a good family.'

'What d'you mean?'

'I mean your mother wouldn't want you getting mixed up in something like that.'

You frowned. 'Is it cos Kala's parents aren't around?'

Dad raised a hand and laughed. 'You want to know what's wrong with your mother, and that's what it is. I'm only telling you facts, chief.'

'How can they *not* be a good family? Her granddad was a Guard, like. Her granny said you even knew him.'

'Yeah, I knew him.'

'And?'

He turned the car into the estate. 'Everyone knew who Mick Lanann was.'

When he pulled into the driveway, he paused for a moment before cutting the engine. He looked at you with soft eyes. You couldn't stand the idea of Mam and Dad thinking badly of Kala. You had this sudden urge to jump out of the car and run in the rain to her house. The cosiness of its walls. The modesty of the tea-stained sofa. The knick-knacks and trinkets. In your mind, Kala's house would remain pure, and true.

An ashtray full of stubs, mounds of faded paper, and a filthy glass that looks like it's filled with smoke, the bottom thick with greenish grime and a smear of dusty lipstick on the rim. Kala's photo album, her stickers on the cover. Then the bottle of whiskey and two glasses that the Mammy has put on the table. One for her. One for you. When she offers you whiskey, say no.

'You won't have a drink with me?' the Mammy says.

Shake your head. You're here to do good. Told yourself last night as you sank into the bed, this would be the first thing you'd do: go to Kala's house.

It's like every room has been knocked out of time. The Mammy has all the curtains closed, but keyholes of daylight stab through the cloth where the moths have been at it. The air almost solid with staleness. The mirror over the range is nothing but a greasy blur.

The drag of the Mammy's movements as she wheels herself across the creaking boards of the kitchen. She groans herself out of her wheelchair, leans over the counter. The bottom of her long skirt rises to show pale legs, a mess of veins. She struggles to take the kettle from its cradle.

Stand up to help her. Tell her you'll take care of the tea. She touches your hand with cold fingers. Put a hand to her back as she turns, in case she falls. It's instinct that makes you do this. And when you feel the brittle ridges of bone slide like hinges beneath her cardigan, it's instinct that makes you pull your hand away.

'You always had manners,' she mutters as she lowers herself into the wheelchair. The shake in her hands is new, along with this constant nodding, like she's agreeing to a voice far beyond your hearing. Tell yourself this is just shock, working its way through her.

'You probably want a drop of milk with your tea,' the Mammy says, wheezing to get up again.

Tell her to rest herself. You'll get the milk.

Such a nice boy. So polite.

Clink open the fridge. Flinch at the sickly body smell. The shelves are sour.

The Mammy's head dip-dips as she takes her cigarettes from her cardigan.

'Famous Joe Brennan,' she says as you pull up a chair. 'You were famous in this house long before everyone else caught on, hah?'

There is no smile to her voice when she says this.

Give her the smile you use for selfies. Your head is full of borrowed language. Phrases of condolence that have passed through a million mouths.

'I still can't believe it,' you say.

'Can't you,' the Mammy says. There's no question mark in her voice.

She puts her hands on Kala's photo album. 'Was going through this, so I was. The little slogans she used to write under all her Polaroids, you remember that? Used to put hearts on the "i"s, instead of dots. Half the pictures are missing.'

When you pour the milk it hits the tea and bursts into a flurry, like maggots. The Mammy is distracted by the plastic wrapping on her cigarette pack, struggling to open it. 'I suppose,' she mutters, 'you'll want to go down to her room again.'

No warmth to these words, either. She's talking about the last time you were here. Couple of years ago, now. Even the thought of that night. You were a fucking disgrace. You'd spent the whole evening trying to feel normal, drinking in the caf with Mush. Found yourself alone outside Kala's house at some awful hour, shouting at the place. 'Ms Lanann!' you roared. 'Ms Lanann! Mammy!' Then, 'Nana! Nana! Want to be inside!' The world was coming at you in flashes. The light clicked on in the house and the Mammy looked terrified in her nightgown. She said, 'I didn't recognize you with your beard,' as you shoved past her into the house, slurring that you wanted to see Kala's room as your shoulders pinballed off the hallway walls. By the time Dad arrived to get you, you were passed out on the floor next to Kala's bed. He found you drenched in piss.

Take the cigarette pack from the Mammy's hands. Tear the plastic open. Hand her a cigarette. 'I half hoped you might've forgotten that night.'

The ashtray rattles across the table when the Mammy pulls it to herself, spills ashes and old stubs. She makes no effort to clear the mess. 'When I think of the years I spent tidying up after that girl,' she says. 'D'you know I used to fold up her washing and leave it at the door to her room? Just to see would she pick up the clothes by herself, without needing to be told to.'

'How'd that one work out?'

The Mammy sniffs. 'Let's say it was an ongoing experiment.'

There's the ghost of a smile there. Like Kala is briefly in the room.

The Mammy nods at the clutter on the table. The ashtray full of stubs, the old newspapers. Her whiskey glass, yours. And next to them, between ye, the filthy grey glass.

'See that yoke? I was watching TV and she came blustering through the house, poured herself a glass of milk and knocked it back. And she stood there, looking at me in that mirror.' The Mammy does an eerily good impersonation of how Kala used to flick her head as she combed her hands through her hair. Then the Mammy kisses her hand and flashes her fingers out, to send her goodbye. 'And then she stomped down that hall in them bloody clodhopper boots, the Doc Martens. *Back in a bit!* she said. And I was about to call after her when I saw she was after leaving that fecking glass of milk behind her on the counter without rinsing it out. I let out a roar: *I'm not going to be the one to clean that glass up, missie.* And she shouted something back from the door, but I never heard it. So I left the glass out, as part of the experiment.'

The Mammy exhales heavily through her nose. Twists her mouth. The glass stands on the table. The rind at the bottom is nearly black. A dirty lipstick stain on the rim.

'So, there we have it,' she mutters.

This fucking tightness in your chest.

'Watching *Emmerdale*,' the Mammy mutters. 'That's what I was doing. Fecking *Emmerdale*. It's memories like that which come at you from the walls. Nothing ever goes away.'

The sound of a clock ticking. The light hovering in the whiskey on the table.

Your voice is quiet when you finally speak.

'Do the Guards know what happened?'

The Mammy shakes her head.

'But it makes no sense that she'd be right here. We looked. Everywhere.'

The Mammy's eyes begin to brim. 'I've had more people to this house in the past twenty-four hours,' she says, 'than in the past fifteen years.'

You don't know how to respond to this.

'They say moments like these bring people—'

'Christ,' the Mammy says. '*They* say this. Who the hell are *they*? Wait and see now. The do-gooders all coming out of the woodwork, to have a gawk. Talking about how lovely Kala was, how lovely I am. There's nothing people love more than closing the book on you. *They. Them.*' Her mouth twists. For a moment, she looks like someone else. '*Cunts,*' she whispers.

It's horrible. But you remember how she looked in the days after Kala went missing. You'd never seen an adult look like that before. A terrible noisy rawness always on the verge of another rawness. Every time someone suggested Kala had run away, the Mammy spat, 'She wouldn't do that to me.' But her eyes were wet. Rage, coiled in fear, coiled in rage. The gut wound of that feeling, saturating the strange, shapeless hours as you and the others searched together, or sat in silence, nodding in and out of sleep on each other's sofas. After weeks of searching, with no sign of a body, the Guards had no choice but to step down the investigation. There were rumours of sightings in Cork. A blurry CCTV video of someone boarding a ferry in Dublin, which turned out to be an Italian backpacker.

'I always knew she didn't run away,' the Mammy says. 'I knew this town was after doing what it always does. Eating my poor girl.'

She pours another glass of whiskey. When she motions for you to drink yours, you hesitate. See Kala's face, how she looked, the last time you saw her.

Have a drink. Just take the fucking drink.

'But...' you say. 'Who'd have wanted to hurt Kala?'

The Mammy points to the drawn curtains. Pinpoints of light rush over her trembling fingers.

'*They*,' she says. '*Them*.'

Helen

IN HER NOTEBOOKS, Mam used to write that people were like trees. Whenever I read this, I pretended to understand what she meant. But now, walking through Caille Woods, steeped in the heat and smell of twisted tree branches, I see: a growing tree, upon meeting an obstacle, does not stop, or reflect. It pushes itself blindly on, a surge of dumb life eager to continue itself, and it does this, again and again, till it becomes a warp of limbs, and this is how people are like trees; live long enough, and your life becomes a tangle of trajectories, a crooked monument to its own mutilations.

So I walk with my head down.

I will let Joe have his time with the Mammy. In the meantime, I can smoke on the chipped wood of the jetty at Lough Caille, where Kala taught me how to roll. I remember Kala's feet were bare and so were mine. The legs of our jeans, rolled up around our calves. I had the sleeves of my T-shirt folded over my shoulders so it looked more like Kala's sleeveless top. The tips of Kala's shoulders were tanned. Bruised peaches. I could feel my shoulders going pink in the sun-glare. It hurt like something good.

The island in the lake trembled upside down in the water, rings cresting out from Aoife and the boys as they splashed and screamed. Their voices boomeranged about the woods climbing above us. When I asked Kala why she was not swimming, she ran a hand through her curls and giggled over a yawn. 'My vagina's spitting today.' I must have looked taken aback, because she gave me a mocking shove.

I was trying to keep up with all the different Kalas. She shapeshifted constantly. When it was her and Joe, huddled and whispering, she went full girl; her voice got soft, her movements defensive and feline. But with Aoife and me, she could be dirty. Imperious. Herself. I knew she was being herself now, tipping ash from her cigarette into the reflections which hovered beneath us like ghosts in the pebbled shallows. She told me about the island at the centre of Lough Caille. It used to be a source of rivalry between Kinlough and Carthy, the town on the other side of the woods. Fellas from Kinlough and Carthy used to have a competition every summer to lay claim to the island.

'*The Big Race*,' Kala announced in an accent that sounded like Dad.

It made me laugh, hearing his voice come from her mouth. That someone like Kala and my dad could exist in the same universe seemed absurd. By now the gang and I were sneaking out two, even three nights a week. On those nights I lay awake, listening out for when Dad would slip into his beer snores. Each time, as I shushed Misty, slipping out the door to cycle to my friends, I felt giddy with the shifts in gravity, barrelling upwards from some obscure ocean depth towards sunlight, air, the fresh elevation of some clean thing.

The previous night I'd woken to the feeling of Theresa in my bed, hot against my back, her hand over my heart. She always crept into my bed on the nights when Dad was working. I shrugged from under her and watched her suck on her bottom lip, deep in dreaming. I was about to punch her awake, send her back to her room, when I heard the floorboards creaking downstairs. Voices whispering to one another.

I do not know what I was expecting, but my stomach sank when I crept to the top of the stairs and saw who it was. Dad, slumped at the front door, at the feet of the others. Dodo and Blinkie were holding him beneath the arms, shaking their heads, laughing. Ger watched vacantly.

The men's faces acquired the pantomime seriousness of drunk people as I walked downstairs, rubbing my arms.

Dodo hissed – 'Ach, he's fine, girl' – like I had made an accusation.

'Knackered, is all,' Blinkie slurred. Dad gave a low moan. 'Rossie rips the arse out of it again, what?'

'Stop clowning,' Ger said. 'Bring the man to the sofa.'

Blinkie and Dodo dragged Dad into the sitting room. I stood in the doorway, watching them scoot Misty off the sofa and lay Dad down. Blinkie giggled as he struggled with Dad's boots.

Ger stood in the door frame next to me.

'That man was a beast, once,' he said. 'No better cunt in Kinlough.'

I cleared my throat and said, 'He's not supposed to drink.' I wanted to sound angry, accusing. But my voice came out quiet. There was even a shake in my words.

Ger looked at me. He reached out and clutched me by the jaw. It was not rough, but the intimacy frightened me. He turned my head this way, then that, like a farmer inspecting a horse's teeth. His eyes were searching my face for something. When he found it, he let go. 'You're like both of them,' he said.

I was suddenly very aware that I was naked under my pyjamas. Ger reached out to my face again and I flinched. He paused and a hint of a smile passed over his features. 'We'll be off, so,' he said.

Blinkie and Dodo were smiles, floating in the dark. They both touched my arm as they brushed past me. I double-locked the door behind them. Mam had always told me men were dangerous. Boys.

I watched the boys now – our boys, Kala called them – messing with Aoife in the shine of the lake. They barked everything they said, like their conversations were for our benefit. That was our role as girls: sit back, be impressed. The boys were the show, we were the canned laughter.

They came from the water and descended on us like birds squawking, shadows blocking the sun. Everything about them was thud and noise. More voltage than they knew what to do with. Joe crouched over Kala and shook out his hair like a dog. She squealed. Aidan told us we were being boring for not getting in the water. Without hesitation, Kala said she was worried Aidan might tug himself asunder if he saw us in our swimsuits. Mush roared laughing.

Joe laid his head in Kala's lap and she combed her fingertips on his scalp. She caught me staring and asked if I wanted to try rolling again. My cigarettes were always too loose.

'Helen's about to roll another tampon, lads,' Aidan said.

Joe asked me how to say 'Fuck off, Aidan' in French and I said it.

'So cool,' Kala said.

Aoife sighed from the water.

'Can't believe you lived in France,' Kala said. 'Must've been better than this kip.'

'Speak for yourself,' Aidan said. 'Kinlough's class. Everyone loves Kinlough.'

'I don't,' Kala said. 'The minute I turn eighteen, I'm gone. If it wasn't for Nana, I'd have run away years ago.'

'*Run away*,' Joe scoffed. 'Sure where'd you go?'

'London,' Kala said. 'Ever been there?'

The boys shook their heads. I said, 'I lived there once.'

This was true. Mam and Dad had spent several months in a squat in Brixton. I had no memory of it. But there was a photo of me from that time, a toddler in Mam's lap. I kept the photo in my wallet. Mam had matted hair, a single dreadlock, and hooped Gypsy earrings. She was laughing at something beyond the camera.

'Isn't it *amazing*?' Kala said, touching my knee. She told us she visited her mother there a couple of times a year.

'Is your mam a Brit, like?' Aidan said.

Kala laughed. 'No. She's a singer in the West End.'

'Really?' Mush perched up on his elbows. 'That's class.'

Kala got excited. 'Ye haven't lived till you've been backstage there. Soho, man. All these mad characters.' She looked at me. 'When were you in London?'

I took the photo of Mam from my wallet and handed it to Kala. 'We used to live in a squat.'

'What's a squat?' Aidan said. 'Like, when you take a shit?'

Kala looked at me admiringly as she handed back the photo. 'Your mam looks like the coolest person ever.'

'Let me guess,' Joe muttered. 'She thinks Kinlough's a shithole too.'

Mush pinched up his face like he was about to sneeze and spoke in an exaggerated French voice. 'Is zat troo, Ell-ehn? Duz yer meeuhm zink Kinlough izz a sheet-ole?'

'No,' I said. And before I even thought about it, I added, 'My mam's dead.'

No one said anything. It was like that feeling where you are going over a bump in a road and your stomach vaults. The moment stretched.

'Oh,' Kala said.

I looked down at the rough wood of the jetty. I did not know why I had said that.

'Jesus, Helen,' Joe said. 'I'm sorry. I didn't... like...'

'Yeah, sorry, Helen,' Mush said.

I could feel the weight of their eyes. When I looked up, the boys turned away. Kala had a thoughtful expression, like I was a sum she was trying to figure out. After a moment she shuffled towards me.

'Come on,' she said, taking her tobacco from her satchel. 'Let's get you rolling properly.'

We sat cross-legged, facing each other, knee to knee. She took a paper and showed me how to hold it. She rubbed her thumbs against her forefingers. The paper slid and rolled. As she lined my paper with tobacco, I felt the boys watch us. Kala gave me a secretive smile. She shook her hair back and winked with her crooked eye. I adjusted my posture to look like her, holding my shoulders back to accentuate the curve of my spine. Something had slipped. In this moment the boys were the audience, and we were the show.

Aoife sighed in the water. 'Bored,' she sang.

The boys pushed themselves off the jetty. Aoife giggled and threw handfuls of lake at them when they swam out to her. She pointed to the island and asked if they thought they could swim out that far. The boys shouted about how they could. Boys were so obvious they ended up looking mysterious.

'I'd love to go to London again,' I said quietly. 'I always think about running away.'

'Ha, totally,' Kala said.

'Maybe we'll run away there together, some day.'

For a moment I worried that Kala would make me feel stupid for saying such a thing. But her eyes went wide. 'Look at that!'

I looked at my hands and saw. Without thinking, I had rolled a perfect cigarette. Kala raised her hands and made a whispered cheering sound, like the noise of a stadium. She reached into the shallows, scooped water onto the back of her neck and shoulders, then scooted next to me and held her Polaroid camera out, turning it around to point at us. There was a shock of wet against my skin and I yelped. Kala laughed. The water on my skin was flashing relief and there was a shudder of pleasure down my back as it grew warm in the sun. It was like when you slowly push a grape against the roof of your mouth with your tongue and the juice explodes. The camera clicked and wheezed. The Polaroid emerged like a square tongue. Kala fanned herself with it as it developed. I smiled, leaned across her, and cupped the flame of her lighter as I lit the cigarette. I inhaled deeply and, as I leaned back, Kala took another picture of us together. 'That's one for you,' she said, 'and one for me.'

We sat on the jetty like that, waiting for the photographs to develop. Out in the water, Aoife was looking at us now, but from so far away it was impossible to make out her face.

I am clutching the Polaroid of Kala and me as I approach the lake. I will sit on our jetty. I will roll cigarettes. One for her, one for me.

But when I get there, the wooden jetty is gone. The lake is now ringed by an ugly, rubberized path. Tourists in paddle boats drift on the water's surface. Picnic benches every few steps, with street lamps positioned at pentagram points about the shore.

A Garda van and two squad cars are parked next to a monstrous building site on the water's edge. Several diggers standing dormant, like muck-spattered dinosaurs, their jaws waiting to gouge our lakeside even further. As I approach the ugly mesh of wire fencing, I make out the foundations of several large houses, their cavities like open wounds, strewn with trash. I read the promo side-boarding. 'Caille Cottages, coming soon from Kinlough Associates.'

Holiday homes. Fucking holiday homes, all over the lakeside. There is nothing this country won't sell off for a few quid.

The site is fenced off. Uniformed officers stand on the other side of the chain-link wires, squinting in the sun, batting away questions from local eccentrics. I overhear the Guards explain that all construction has ceased. Ongoing scene of investigation.

And there, in the middle of it all, is a white tent, erected to preserve the integrity of the crime scene. The white canvas stirs in the breeze. This is where they found her. My Kala.

Mush

PUNTERS ONLY COMING in dribs and drabs by now. Last hours before close-up. Few huddled heads reading their phones at the odd table, some toddlers on the floor next to their mothers' chairs, gawping at their hands.

Mam comes downstairs in a new blouse. She's after getting ready for Pauline's hen. All done up for the evening out. She does a girlish curtsey. 'Amn't I fab?' Talking to herself more than to me. She empties her handbag onto the counter, pores her hands through the contents, hands me her compact mirror and I hold it up before her face. She stares into the mirror in my palm, combing fingers through her fringe. 'Had to talk Pauline off a bloody ledge there. She's after getting herself into a tizzy about whether or not they should go ahead with the hen party.'

'What? Why?'

'Ara,' Mam says. 'You know Pauline. Got it into her head that it'd be in poor taste to be celebrating, given the news. About Kala, like.'

Her eyes flit between the mirror and me, eyebrows wig-wammed in concern. 'You're sure it's all right if I go to this party? You'll be all right by yourself here?'

'Would you stop asking me that?'

She asks what I'm gonna do with myself all evening, doesn't wait for an answer, plucks at something in my hair and tells me I should get out and about, fine summer evening blah blah. Asks if there's anyone I can meet up with. Tells me not to stay in the caf. And the recycling bins need changing. And don't forget to take that batch of brownies out of the freezer. And which of these lipsticks should she wear?

I pick the darker shade and she unscrews the cap.

'You could always join me, if you like,' she says. 'I'm sure the twins would love to have you there.'

'I'm not going to a fecking hen, are you joking me.'

'You heard from them today?' Mam says. 'The quare pair?'

'No.'

'Strange.'

I haven't told Mam about my bust-up with the twins. Last thing I need today is more fucking headaches. I just want to be left alone. Even so, I've been trying to justify to myself why the twins haven't been in touch. I know we're fighting, but still. It's unlike them not to send me some stupid Snapchat or memes. Or to be gentle. I know they'd be gentle with me today, if they knew about Kala. Probably haven't heard the news yet.

'They slept at a friend's yesterday,' Mam says. She's pure rough with how she applies the lipstick. 'Didn't think to clear that with their mother before, of course. That old trick.'

She leaves a moment for me to protest, but I don't have the energy. Mam and the twins have always had a prickly vibe, like a party that's constantly on the verge of getting out of hand. She loves their spunk, but hates how Donna and Marie slag her for using words like 'spunk'. And yeah, maybe Mam's a bit less patient with the twins cos of everything Auntie Pauline went through with Aidan back in the day. But to be honest, I reckon Mam has a push-pull vibe with the twins mostly cos they remind her of herself.

'Them girls would want to get a grip,' she says, touching up her foundation, almost jabbing herself in the cheeks. 'Sent Pauline a text last night to say they wouldn't be home. Missed the dinner with Helen and everything. I'd Pauline and Theresa both ringing me this afternoon... from the nail salon... Twins hadn't bothered showing up for the appointment there either. So what you make of that? I ask you.'

Mam shites on and on but I'm not listening any more. I'm almost smiling at the thought of Helen, being fussed over by everyone. How much she'd hate it.

Helen was fucking cool, like. She didn't give a fuck. Every time we went sneaking out, Helen and me would set each other challenges like swiping pints off a table outside a pub on Fox Street. I was pretty good at that, but sure it was easy – Fox Street was mental every night, a huge tunnel of noise and people. Different music poured out every door and I'd go running up to a terrace, mace two pints, run back to the cheers of my friends with a drink in each hand, and Helen would always say, 'One of them have my name on it?' and just start drinking it. We were like daredevils, egging each other on. We called ourselves the Two Ninjas.

One night Helen tried to get served in a bar. We were all across the road, watching, waiting. I was nervous for her, for all of us. I had visions of us getting arrested, Mam having to come and bail me out, me getting grounded and never seeing the girls again ever. I recognized the bouncers outside the place – they were all Uncle Ger's men. Uncle Ger and the Lyons ran the security on all the nightclubs and pubs in Kinlough. These lads were fucking huge, arms like tree trunks. I was busy worrying about Helen inside when I saw this dude striding down Fox Street, swigging from a huge bottle of champagne or some shite. His arms were pure covered in tattoos, just this maze of them slithering all the way down to his wrists like leaves. Thing was, the dude was *surrounded* by people, this huge gaggle of young wans and tourists all swarming about him, taking photos, following him down Fox Street like the trail on his comet, like he was the Pied fecking Piper. Something about his face made me feel weird. Like, something about it made my stomach actually flip. I was gonna point the dude out to the girls when we saw Helen being escorted outside the bar with the bouncer holding on to her arm. The guy held on to Helen, towering over her, roaring into her face.

'What a fucker,' Kala said.

But Helen was looking the bouncer guy right in the eye, with a sort of 'And what?' expression on her. When he eventually let go of her arm and told her to fuck off, Helen didn't move for a moment. She stood there, staring at him.

'She's so badass,' Kala whispered. And she was right – Helen had come across as pure shy when I first met her, but more and more I could see she was actually a total legend, not giving a fuck what anyone thought.

As she made her way through the tables on the terrace, the bouncer was watching her, so she moved deliberately slowly. Then, just before she was out of the terrace, she grabbed a drink off one of the tables – I don't know what it was, it was in a tall thin glass – and knocked it back in one go.

'Oh my God,' the girls shouted, and Helen turned back to the bouncer with the empty glass in her hand, raised it like she was making a toast, and dropped it to the ground, and as the glass shattered she ran to us and we ran to her and then we were all running together down Fox Street, and it felt savage, like the whole town was ours, in the palm of our hands.

We cycled out of town, past the Prom, out to the golf course, and when we left our bikes by a stone wall I cupped my hands and the girls took turns putting a foot in them and I hoisted upwards as they jumped to catch the top of the wall and pull themselves up, and we did all this without speaking or anything. Telepathic stuff. I was pure lanky so it was no bother on me scaling the wall myself. The girls thought it was cool how I could do that. That made me feel cool, too.

We jumped down into the golf course. Something about the dark there felt like wet dog. The grass was pure smooth, all these rolling hills in the moonlight, perfect and fake, straight out of *The Sims*. I ran ahead on to the green and threw myself rolling down one of the hills. The girls came walking after me, huddled together with their arms linked against the salty breeze. Sometimes I wished I could be one of them, cocooned and warm. But I couldn't, cos I was a lad.

We got to the far end of the golf course, where huge stones – boulders, more like – heaped over one another in a slope to make a long barrier wall to protect against the sea. I climbed them and started walking the length of the golf course from up there, arms out.

The girls were in the grass below, chatting about freaky stuff. Kala was saying how she hadn't always slept in the basement of her house, but had to move there because of weirdness.

'My room used to be upstairs,' she said. 'But I started to hear this voice outside every night, calling. *Ms Lanann! Ms Lanann! Mammy! Nana!* I told Nana about it – she said it was all in my head. But one night she hears it too. So we look outside the window of my room, and there's this man there. This thin dude with a beard. Only... it's weird, right. It's like he's shitfaced or something, he keeps swaying back and forth. And he's going, *Ms Lanann! Mammy! Wwwant to be inside!* Nana said she didn't know him. But she told me I'd have to start sleeping downstairs, where I could lock the door. That's why my room's in the dungeon.'

'You serious?' I said.

'Swear on my mother's life,' Kala said.

On the other side of the boulders was a drop into a deserted country road. It was pitch black. Anything could be lurking in it and you'd never know till a claw reached out of that dark and grabbed you by the ankle. I made big leaps from boulder to boulder to show I wasn't afraid of nothing.

'We should go to the Crawley House some night,' Kala said.

'What's the Crawley House?' Helen said.

'It's in Caille Woods,' Aoife said.

'Some people say it was a witch's house,' Kala said.

'My dad told me a load of people were hanged there by Cromwell,' Aoife said.

'I'd say it's haunted, either way,' Kala said. 'It's got a spooky vibe, even on a sunny day. Like, you can feel it when you're there.'

'You couldn't pay me to go there at night,' Aoife laughed.

'Why not?' Helen said. 'Are you superstitious?'

'Feck off, Vomitron.'

'My Nana's not superstitious, and even she's afraid of the place,' Kala said. *That's a place of evil, girl.*

I was turning back to them, about to say, 'I'm not scared of any of that auld shite,' when a blast of light screamed from the road, tearing into my eyes with all these blue blotches. I nearly shat myself, legs half buckling on me as I scrambled down the boulders and back to the green. 'Suss!' I whispered. 'Someone's there!'

'What is it?' Kala whispered.

'A van,' I said. 'Parked down the road, like. I think it's been there the whole time.'

'Is it a security man?' Aoife said.

'Why would a *security man* be parked out in the middle of the road?' Helen snapped.

Kala shushed us all. I heard the waves in the distance, then, in the murk, the sound of the van door clicking open. A pinging tone from inside it. Shoes, scuffling onto the road.

I looked at the girls, like I wanted them to show me how to feel. Kala stayed still, head tilted, listening. The noises weren't coming any closer. She whispered, 'He doesn't know we're here.' She had a look of mischief on her. Like this was exciting. Not frightening.

She put a finger to her lips and began to walk alongside the wall, her hands against the boulders, towards the pinging sound of the open door. A drumming hiss began on the other side of the boulders, turning to slosh. The man was pissing on the road. Kala had her hand over her mouth to stop herself giggling.

She whispered, 'Will I give him a fright?'

The girls began to argue in whispers but Kala was already climbing the stack of boulders. She crawled quietly above, like a panther. When she looked back over her shoulder, with a cheeky smile on her, I smiled to show I was brave. But I didn't like the feeling. We were doing something we shouldn't.

Kala was lying across the top boulder. All I could see were her Doc Martens, her laces hanging between all the stars.

I waited for her to do whatever she was going to do – scream, shout 'Enjoy your piss!', whatever. My legs were already tensed, waiting to burst into an escape.

Above us we saw Kala's hand. She was waving furiously, gesturing at us to come up.

I didn't want to. But the girls were already climbing.

We stayed low to the boulders, like cats that don't wanna be seen. The rocks were cold and gritty on my palms, raw against my knees. Kala's face was looking back at us, a finger to her lips. We dragged ourselves to the edge on our bellies, like snipers.

Below, the road was still pitch black, except for the glare of the van's headlights in the dark. The van was dark red, and there was a man standing before it, in the light. His shadow was huge over the road. He was wearing jeans and a hoodie. But his head was all wrong. At first I didn't know what I was looking at. The pointed ears. The thick long snout. Then I realized it was a mask. A werewolf mask.

Aoife went to say something and Kala held her hand up, finger against her lips.

Werewolf was walking back and forth in the light, waiting for something. There was something off about Werewolf's walk. The right foot, dragging a bit. Something about it was familiar. Every now and then he'd look back at the cab of the van where there was a dark shape in the driver's seat. An arm resting lazily on the window.

My belly was pushed against the cool knuckles of the stone and the heart was thudding through me so it felt like the stone was throbbing.

Then things happened pure fast. Werewolf had his back all flared up by the headlights, facing down the length of the road into the dark with his shadow stretched before him, when he raised a hand in signal to someone else. I heard it before I saw it. Another vehicle, in the distance. Coming from the direction of town. I saw its lights snake through the hedges from far away, heard its motor get louder. Werewolf motioned with a finger. His driver turned the keys. The van grumbled awake and suddenly the air was being pummelled apart by deafening techno. The music was pure aggressive, too fast to dance to, too busy to let you think.

Werewolf limped back to the dark van and yanked the side door open.

The other vehicle rounded the corner. It was another van, a white one. Werewolf walked towards it, one hand raised, and the van came to a stop but the engine kept going. The two vans growled at each other, the red one snarling at the white, with Werewolf walking in the bright pool their headlights made in the road.

The white van opened and the driver stepped out, wearing a motorcycle helmet. The moon glinted off it in shards. Himself and Werewolf spoke, Motorcycle with his hands on his hips, gesturing back at his van.

'What the fuck's he wearing a helmet for in a van?' I said.

Kala said, 'Same reason the other guy's in a mask.'

Werewolf and Motorcycle walked to the side door of the white van. It was only then that it clicked with me. The way Werewolf was dragging his foot, like a rapper.

Teabag.

I was about to say this to the others when Motorcycle peeled back the door of the white van and we saw what was inside. It was men. Loads of them, all wearing masks of celebrities you'd get out a joke shop. One by one they got out the van, these cartoonish faces with exaggerated cheeks, hollow gaps for eyes. Teabag was speaking, gesturing with his arms like giving instructions, but we couldn't hear a word of it over the techno. The masked men stood before him like a weird army. Then Teabag took a Tesco shopping bag out his pocket and handed it to the first masked fella, who took something out his pocket and put it in the bag, then passed the bag on to the next masked man, who did the same. This went on.

'It's their phones,' Helen said. 'They're handing over their phones.'

Teabag waved his arms about some more, then walked across the ring of noise to the red van. The masked men all followed him. One by one, they piled into the back of the red van.

There were fucking loads of them, like. Easily twenty.

Teabag closed up the van and locked the door. Motorcycle was standing in the middle of the ring of noise, in this giant sea of headlight gold, watching. He raised a hand and Teabag, still wearing his mask, did the same. Then he got into the red van and it reversed into the dark, turned, then sped into the Warren, taking most of the noise with it.

I turned my head to look at the girls. I wanted to get the fuck out of there. But all three of them were staring at Motorcycle.

As he walked back to his van I said, 'What in the name of fuck was—' and Kala grabbed my arm tight, her eyes going pure wide.

Motorcycle stopped walking. He turned. He was looking in our direction. The lights of his van broke around him in weird winged shadows. He didn't move. We didn't move. The night bounced off his visor. I was holding my breath, as though that'd somehow make us invisible.

Then he turned, walked back to his van, and drove off.

None of us said anything till the sound of the engine had faded.

Then Kala rolled over on her back and shouted, 'What the fuuuck was that?'

Aoife was laughing, but it was forced. Her eyes were scared. And Helen's face had gone pure tight, like she'd seen a ghost or something.

'Lads,' I said. 'That was Teabag, like. In the wolf mask.'

'You sure?' Kala said.

'Hundred per cent.'

'What about the guy in the helmet?' Aoife said. 'Was that one of your cousins too?'

'No,' Helen said. Even in the dark, I could see the little wrinkle between her eyes. Her voice was pure quiet. 'That was my dad.'

Mam's still ranting on about Donna and Marie, stabbing her mouth with lipstick.

'I didn't realize Helen was going to come to the wedding,' I say.

'Sure no one did,' Mam says. 'She only sent word a couple of days ago. Always the dark horse, that wan. Christ, and don't you know the twins will be all over her. Bit of foreign glitter. Well, if they try and turn this evening into one of their little Donna and Marie dramas I'll knock their feckin' heads together.'

'They told me they're bringing willy straws,' I say.

Mam tuts and rolls her eyes. But she's smiling too, despite herself. She loves the twins, obviously. She has to, they're family. But the thing is, she *likes* the twins, too. More than she lets on.

'Here, Mam.' I hesitate. I decide to broach the topic. 'You know how the twins will be living in Rossie's house till they finish school?'

'Well, they're hardly going to live with Uncle Ger, are they?' Mam says. She unscrews the brush for her eyeliner.

'I dunno if they're so keen to stay in Rossie's either.'

Mam gives a snort. 'When they're paying their own rent they can pick and choose where they live.'

'They're kids.'

'Exactly,' she says, breath held in concentration. 'And... kids... can be childish.'

'Must be tough on them, no? All these big changes.'

Mam stops doing her lashes and fixes me with a stare. 'Right. Out with it. What have they said to you?'

'Nothing.'

'Can Pauline not come first, just once? After all she's been through?'

'I was just making conversation, like.'

Mam mutters under her breath, glaring into the mirror. 'Mr Conversation... Are you going to tell me what Dudley Brennan wanted earlier, or do I have to drag that out of you too?'

'Nothing.'

I don't want to think of what Dudley told me. I don't want to think about anything. I want to have about ten fucking cans and pass out. Dudley didn't put me at ease at all.

Mam's shovelling her things into her handbag. 'He had you at that table long enough,' she says. 'Seemed ye were talking about more than nothing.'

Dudley said Kala's bones had been moved there. Like, they weren't uncovered on the building site. Someone had deliberately left them there, in a sports bag. A sort of reluctance came over Dud's face. Then he leaned across the table to me and whispered. 'Mush... her skull was left on top of the bag.'

The idea of this. Kala's skull.

'Whoever put it there wanted it to be found,' Dudley said. 'It was fractured. Very badly fractured.' My whole body went cold. Dud cleared his throat and said, 'There was something else, son.' For a moment I didn't recognize the expression on his face. Fear. He leaned close and whispered, 'They found something tucked inside the skull.'

'Christ, it's like pulling teeth,' Mam says. 'What did Dudley want from you?'

I start wiping down a countertop. 'Just wants me to keep an eye on Joe.'

Mam brightens. 'Sure haven't I been on to you to meet up with him for ages? Are ye getting together tonight? Ye should.'

I wring out the cloth and start stacking latte cups.

'Mush,' she says.

I grunt.

'Mush, did you call Joe or not? You—'

'Fuck sake, can you not leave me be for five minutes?'

Some of the punters look over. I dip my head and continue stacking.

'It's not good to be alone, love,' she says. 'I think you—'

'*Mam.*' I grab a tray of mugs and stop to give her a kiss on the cheek. 'Just go, will you? Get out of here. Enjoy the hen.'

I walk away from her before she can try another angle.

'You'll be okay?' she calls after me.

'Say hello to Helen,' I say. 'And go easy on the twins for once.' I walk into the kitchen and set the tray down. I stay there till I can be sure she's left. My head's pounding, like.

When I finally close up and open a can, I don't sit by the window as usual. I stay back in the pantry, hunched between the dishwashers, listening to their guts churning. Just want to drift off. But I fucking can't. I keep seeing the agitation of Dudley's face. Keep feeling it inside me, like he was after passing it on to me.

I go out to the fridge for another can and nearly let out a roar when I see someone standing at the window of the caf, waving in.

'Well,' Joe says through the glass. He has a bottle of something expensive in his hand and he raises it. 'Are we drinking?'

I unlock the door. Me and Joe hug quickly, two claps on the back, we know not to linger.

Joe heads straight to the booth I sat in with his dad. Sits in the same seat. Like the world's trying to rub my face in it, in Dudley's fear, when he was looking at me. Pure cold fingers sinking into my belly as he whispered, 'Inside the skull, Mush. There was a picture. A photograph.'

'Of what?'

'You. Joe. Kala. The whole bloody gang of ye.'

Helen

THE PERFUMES OF all the women in the kitchen, their laughter and noise merging with the sweetness of the curries and pasta bakes bubbling in the oven. The air, thick with the sound of laughter. I do not know where to stand, so I linger in the doorway to the sitting room. It is like being back in the school yard at St Anne's. I have never been able for large groups. I always fail to mirror other women, or else I mirror them too much.

Over the years, I have imagined Kala watching me at such moments. She comes strobing into my life like this whenever she likes, pulling back the curtain of the years between us to whisper in my ear, pass comment on how I am doing my hair, who I am doing it for. 'Are you for fucking real?' she giggles at me now, and I clear my throat like that makes a difference.

There is a woman in the kitchen who has been staring at me. Fifties, with violently bright red hair in an eighties power-ballad style. Her eye make-up is thick. She is staring without smiles, without apology. I am waiting for her to approach me. I look away and pretend to be at ease. A frenzied joy in the kitchen because Pauline has put on an eighties playlist. Whitney Houston's 'I Wanna Dance With Somebody' peals out of the speakers, pushing the voices higher. I watch Theresa, perfectly at home in the thick of limbs. The kitchen shapes itself around her and she conducts it like an orchestra. She reaches for glasses without looking and they hop eagerly into her hands. She opens and closes the presses with her elbows, throws together ingredients while chatting over her shoulder, making the other women laugh. She puts salad bowls on the table without breaking her stride to the fridge to get more bottles of Prosecco, and when she sees me standing in the doorway, she beckons me to join everyone.

On the other side of the room, the red-haired lunatic keeps staring.

Theresa arrived at the house after lunch, a silhouette of Mam, standing eerily against the sunlight at the front door. She was wearing a wraparound Indian-style dress, the colour of flames, and she had already done her make-up for the hen party. Subtle lipstick, light foundation. Hair pineappled into an elegant mess, with brightly coloured slides to hold the strays in place.

'Oh, Helen,' she said. I was brittle in her arms. 'I'm so sorry. You must be gutted.'

She leaned back to look at me. Behind her eyes, the shutter movement of a camera. I was still in my jeans and shirt. I had not washed my hair. I was not in any state for the hen.

Now Pauline is in the party's furnace of approval, and there is something rabid about the need to have a good time. The twins have not arrived. Everyone in the kitchen knows it. But they all mirror the positivity in Pauline's eyes. I know this look. I have worn this look. A deranged commitment to rising above circumstances. I pull back from the kitchen to the sitting room. Pauline's touch is everywhere. Every surface has its own infuser or basket of pot-pourri. Pastel colours. There are track shadows across the carpet where I hoovered. Framed photos and angel ornaments fill almost all the available space. Pictures of me and Theresa. Pictures of the twins as babies, toddlers, teens. Pictures of Dad and Pauline sunburned in Rome, standing with their arms around each other outside the Colosseum. At the Cliffs of Moher, squinting. A life about which I really know nothing.

At the centre of the mantelpiece, a recent picture of all of them – Dad and Theresa, Pauline and the twins – at a restaurant. The flash is too bright. Theresa is sitting between the twins and they both have an arm over her shoulders. A 'Sweet 16' birthday cake before them, with sparklers in it. They all look happy.

There are pictures of Aidan, on a small table surrounded by angel ornaments. A shrine. I wonder what he would have made of this. Aidan as a baby, in a cot with baby Mush. Aidan and Mush on their first day of school, tiny in their shirt collars. Aidan looking pale and embarrassed, cradling the twins in his lap. Aidan holding a cigarette, wearing a '21 Today' badge, smirking at the camera. A Mass card with the same image of Aidan's face.

Through the bodies of the kitchen, the lunatic is still staring. She even leans slightly to the side to keep her eye on me.

I need to get away. But when I open the door to the hallway there is someone there, whispering furiously into their phone.

'...bloody disappointed in the pair of ye. Ye're not feckin' kids any more, d'ye hear me? This is the last fecking voicemail I'm leaving so...'

She turns to face me and I retreat to the sitting room. There is a half-full bottle of Prosecco on the coffee table and I refill my glass. The woman who was arguing on the phone comes through the hall door. Her face is familiar. She puts the phone back in her bag, looks up, and sees me. Her nostrils flare. Her eyes dart to the bottle of Prosecco. 'Give us them bubbles, name of Christ,' she says. She grabs the bottle and drinks straight from it, then hands it back. She takes a packet of cigarettes from her handbag and offers me one. 'Helen, isn't it?' she says. 'Welcome back. Come on.'

I follow her through the kitchen, through the patio doors, into the back garden. I do this without thinking. There is something unquestionable about this woman's authority. An effortless gravity.

'Saw you looking at all the pictures in the sitting room,' she says. 'Auld Aidan. God love him. He'd have liked all this. Family celebrations and all that.'

I look at her again. Suddenly it clicks. Lorraine? Olivia?

'Mush's mam,' I say.

'Lydia,' she says.

'You gave Kala a job,' I blurt. 'She always liked you.'

'God help her,' Lydia says.

She takes out her phone and begins to tap out a WhatsApp. I remember her now. An earthy, aggressive sort of humour. Kala always said she could imagine Lydia living many past lives, a Russian farmer with a brassy laugh, wringing chicken necks and striding past tragedies.

'How is Mush?' I say.

'Still Mush.' She hunches her shoulders and puts on a deep voice. *'I'm grand, leave me alone, would ya.* Next thing you know he's half ripping the door off me dishwasher. But he's not going to talk to me about it. Sure I'm only his mother.'

I smile at this. Mush, still living on his own planet.

'Apparently he's going to a gig in Flanagan's tonight. First night he's gone out in years.' She hands me her lighter. 'He was asking after you earlier. Sends his regards. Mush isn't exactly one of life's big talkers, but he always speaks highly of you.'

It's probably the alcohol – I haven't eaten enough today – but these words spread like a warm smile in my stomach. 'Really?'

'Don't act surprised,' Lydia says. 'You were always a good friend to him, throughout all of it.'

I don't know if she is referring to Kala here, or Aidan. Both. I remember getting the phone call about Aidan. I was in Dublin, on Grafton Street, on my way to my final university exams. I remember Mush's voice, so small on the phone. He could not even bring himself to say the word 'suicide'.

'You were like someone in an art gallery, in there,' Lydia says. 'Looking at all the photos.' She ashes her cigarette. 'No need to be staying by yourself all evening.'

'I've never been good at parties,' I say.

'Ach, sure everyone thinks that about themselves.' She says this in such a straightforward way – no suggestion of doubt or discussion – that I find it oddly comforting.

I pour myself another glass, watch the foam as it rises to the rim, almost spilling.

'Christ, here we go,' Lydia mutters. There is a migration of women coming out to the garden. They swarm us. It is already that part of the evening when non-smokers want to have a cheeky cigarette. The women are girlish now, excited, like they are getting away with something naughty.

'Excuse me?' An excited voice, next to me. 'Excuse me.' A hand on my arm.

It is the lunatic. She is standing much too close. I can see the cracks caked in her eyeshadow. 'I hope you don't mind me saying this, but you have the most incredible aura.'

'What?'

'It's remarkable,' she says. She looks around my shoulders. 'It takes up so much space! You must have lived a thousand lives.'

'It feels that way some days, doesn't it?' Lydia says. She takes me by the elbow and steers me back towards the house.

'Who is that?' I say.

Lydia opens the fridge.

'Moira,' she says. 'Pauline goes to her for tarot readings, that sort of thing. Thinks it keeps her in touch with Aidan.'

Lydia pops one bottle of Prosecco, then another. 'Listen, can you do the rounds out there?' she says. 'Just top up the glasses. I need to check on Pauline. Keep this show on the road.' She looks out at the garden, then back at me. 'The best way to get through these things, Helen, is to give yourself a job and keep doing it. Okay?'

The bottles are cool in my hands. I am drunker than I realized. My balance is slightly crooked as I wind my way through the voices in the garden, my ear snagging on caught snatches of conversation, like tuning through stations on a radio.

A cluster of women talking about Lydia.

'No, no, that's the sister. The caf on Fox Street.'

'With the simple fella? The lanky lad with the face?'

'I don't mean to be rude, but really. It's unsightly. Those marks on him.'

'You're so bad.'

'There's something sinister about him.'

'He's harmless, really.'

I do not pour for them.

I approach a pair of women standing apart from the others, absorbed in one another. They extend their glasses without looking.

'Damaged goods,' one of the woman says as I pour. 'Sure wasn't it written all over her. But what chance could she have, growing up in that house?'

'D'you know, I always had it in me head she was older,' the other woman says. 'Only fifteen, she was. Barely a child, when you think of it.'

My skin goes hot, then cold.

The first woman scoffs. 'That wan was no more a child than you or me. Sure wasn't Siobhán's youngest in St Anne's with her? Oh yeah. Says she was up to all sorts.'

The other woman leans in, enjoying the hint of scandal. 'She wasn't, Bernie. Was she?'

I pull back. I bring the bottles inside and drink two glasses quickly.

Through the double doors I see Lydia standing with Pauline and Theresa. Lydia is combing a slow hand through her sister's hair, speaking to her. Pauline traces a finger beneath her eyes, shakes her head. Her mascara is running. I know I should get involved. This moment of domestic drama with the twins. It could integrate me. Give me somewhere to stand. But the words of the women in the garden are burning through me. The relish in their voices. Luxuriating in their closeness to disaster, safe in their distance from it.

I turn to pour another glass and suddenly the lunatic is there, filling my entire field of vision. Moira. She is so close I feel her breath on me as she speaks. Sour wine.

'There's someone absolutely insisting I pass on a message to you, dear.'

She grips my wrist tight. When she smiles, her teeth are wine-stained.

'She's been following you around all night.'

Mush

SEA OF FLANAGAN'S faces everywhere, the crowd's thick with bodies all around me, knocking against me, backing into me, moving to whatever Joe's putting through them from the stage and Joe's guitar is clear and clean and thrashes when he wants it to and weeps when he wants things pure quiet. All around me, everyone shouts to Joe in the quiet parts and sings back to him in the choruses and sends him drinks from the bar and whenever he raises a glass it's like being in the middle of a lake and I'm slipping under, drowning in people, the way they raise their arms. The closeness. The surface is just above me, I can see it, like, at my fingertips, but I can't push through it and I'm sinking.

I've drained my pint and without it I feel useless so I grip my phone and look to it every minute or so, as though that's gonna save me. I go on Mam's Facebook to see how the hen's going. There's a photo of herself and Pauline, all done up. They're in the kitchen, standing by the fridge back to back like Charlie's Angels, fingers pointing up like guns. I recognize a few of the women at the edges, laughing and holding their own phones at Mam and Pauline. The picture has twenty-three likes already. All the women who are at the hen party have commented on it. **Looking fab!**

Mam's written, **Sisters doing it for themselves** and Pauline's after commenting, saying, **When u look good, u look good**, and lots of people have liked that too. I begin to type a comment, **have a blast!**, but I delete it without sending. Don't want to be a complete sadcase.

I'm a fucking eejit for letting Joe bring me here. I should've gone to the hen, I know that now. I'd have hated it, but at least I'd have some notion what to do with myself. I could just sit on the sofa and talk shit in the corner with the twins.

I take a photo of Joe onstage and it helps. Taking pictures of a situation keeps the situation at bay. Being in my phone gives me somewhere to stand, a little island of my own. I send the photo to Marie:

guess where i am :-)

The message gets the blue ticks, seen. Marie doesn't write back.

Joe tilts his face into the burn of the light and he's like one of them blurred photos you'd see of someone in the nineties, frozen in the flash of live magic, in his element.

I don't know what the fuck I'm doing here.

I need another pint. The place is a wall of bodies and when I say, 'Excuse me' and 'Sorry' no one hears so I have to push against people, and I don't like that cos I never touch people and people never touch me. Most of them move when I nudge, but they're slow about it.

I try to get through a group of young wans on their phones. One of them looks up and her eyes go wide before she even knows it and then she's giving me the Look, the 'I-don't-even-see-your-scars' look, and by the time she's got polite about it the Look is rippling through all her buddies, all clocking me for that second too long, practically leaping out of my way.

I keep my head turned so's not to see myself in the mirror behind the bottles, so's not to get the Look from the bar staff. They're pure cocky, the fuckers working here. The girls all have studs in their faces. Lads with those tunnel sort of earrings, ears like someone who'd sacrifice you on a pyramid in Mexico. I wish I was any of them.

One of the lads points a finger at me. Big Taliban beard on him and all these tattoos but when he speaks it's this fucking Wall Street baritone coming out of him.

'What can I do for you, buddy?'

'Could I have a Jameson, please?'

He leans forward. 'Hmm?' One of the barmaids passes behind him and he turns and mutters something to her and she laughs and says something back.

'I said, could I have a Jameson, please?'

He takes his time turning back to me and sort of blinks, like his brain's after resetting and he needs me to remind him where the fuck we are.

'Can I have a Jameson?' I say. 'And a pint too.'

He smiles like we're friends, knocks a knuckle on a blackboard behind him and starts reeling off a spiel about some artisanal beer he's got in from Prague, special offer, nice and hoppy.

'Yeah whatever man, just give us a pint.'

'You got it, dude.'

'Here,' I shout after him. 'Make that two pints, will you?'

I don't want to speak to this fucker for a while.

Outside, it's just as busy. The crowd's like foam brimming out of Flanagan's over the path and onto the road. They're all too close, everything's too sharp. High-definition Dolby surround sound. Cars beep at people as they scarper with pints across the road to Hogan's Square. Hot echo of the Jameson rattling through me as I try and carry the two pints to a windowsill away from all the noise. I could do with a puke. Not cos of the drink, cos of the people. I'm not used to this. I want to go home, back to my booth. But Joe would be thick with me if I leave without saying bye. Knowing my luck I'd bump into Mam and she'd eat the head off me for being home so early.

Phone buzzes in my pocket. I hope it's the twins. Even if they're ringing to bitch about the hen party, that'd be nice, just to hear from them.

But it's not the twins. It's Mam.

'I'm out, Mam,' I say. I hold the phone out towards the crowd so she can hear the noise. 'You happy now?'

I'm smiling as I put the phone to my ear but that gets

washed off pronto cos there's a tirade of words coming down the line. The crowd's too loud, I can only hear the edges of what Mam's saying, but her tone's unmistakable. I catch her saying, 'Donna and Marie'. She's on some warpath.

'Mam,' I shout in the phone. 'Mam, I can't—'

People are looking over at me on my windowsill so I turn my back on them. My reflection's a dark silhouette in the glass and I press the phone against my skull. Mam's ranting.

'I can't hear a word of... Mam, will you listen to me, I can't... Mam. *Mam*.'

I hang up and tap into my phone.

too loud here

whats up

I'm already thinking three steps ahead. Maybe I left something on the cooker in the caf and there's been a fire. Maybe I forgot to do all the windows and the alarm's after going. Some sort of excuse to get the fuck out of here.

Mam's typing. I'm looking at the phone when, for a split-second, I see a shadow lurk behind my reflection and suddenly there are hands over my eyes.

A voice close to my ear says, 'Guess who?' and I get this sudden heartcatch in my chest and I turn around and it's a jolt in my blood. Couple of faint lines next to her eyes and her hair's dyed a sorta warm dark but it's definitely her. Fucking hell, it's her.

'Helen,' I say.

She nods at the two pints on the windowsill.

'One of them have my name on it?' she says. She's smiling.

'Of course,' I say, and I can hear the jangled note in my voice as I say it, grabbing one of the glasses and holding it out to her.

'Shouldn't you be at the hen party?'

'Shouldn't you be at the gig?' she says. 'With the rest of Joe's adoring public?'

'Plenty in there without me.' Big stupid smile on me.

'So you're out here with me instead,' Helen says. She flicks her hair back. A secretive sort of thing at the corners of her mouth. 'The Two Ninjas.'

I laugh and shake my head. 'Fuck me, Helen. It's good to see you.'

I go to give her a sort of friendly bump on the shoulder and she dives in to me with a hug that sends half the pint sloshing over my fingers. Her grip is tight, warm. She muffles my name into my chest, and I put my arms around her. Her hair tickles at my nose, and I can hear how clotted my voice is as I say, 'I'm so glad you're here.'

Saturday Night

Joe

MUSH AND HELEN are deep into the chats when you see them across the road at Hogan's Square, sipping cheap auld cans. You duck inside to get a bottle of champagne from behind the bar, to bring it over. Something pricey. Need to get this right. Needed Mush tonight at the gig, he was taller than most of the crowd, a rock around which they were all breaking, your anchor point, the place you looked to when the stage was bending under you like a ship over a wave and some muscle memory twitch of your early gigs as Jungle Heart where Mush was always there in the crowd to smile at you and anchor you and keep you grounded and you often performed those shows directly to him cos it was like being back in your room when ye were kids and you'd play him your ideas and he'd give you the nod or the suggestion that'd nudge your songs and the years of your life in the right direction even though it led you here, to this, to drinking shots now with Duggan at the bar cos you can't face Helen and Mush, to— No, you led yourself here, fucking idiot, how could you ever let a friendship like Mush's wither so much, how— No, fuck that, why let yourself be so close to someone in the first place, why be close to anyone, the second you love someone you start losing them – fuck that – no one loves anyone cos no one knows anyone, people just know their ideas of each other (another shot), best just to be an idea, be the idea people want you to be, the Joe they want, and let them love that, let someone love something at least, just take the bottle of champagne out to Mush, fuck sake, touch solid ground, anything to tie you to the planet, find something to say yes to inside the noise of yourself.

Your elbow's throbbing with pain as you cross the road to the Square. Maybe you shouldn't have thrashed the guitar so much, so soon after cutting off the cast. Fuck it, you're Joe fucking Bre—

Mush jumps up as you approach. None of that quick-clap-on-the-back nervous-men-bullshit-hugging like earlier, in the caf. It's brothers-for-life hugging now. Yourself and Helen do the peck-on-the-cheek thing, like real grown-ups, and Mush laughs, cracking open three cans, one for each of ye.

Try to slip into their chats, but fame spreads its fingers between people. Turns them towards you, the way the sun turns the flowers. Irish people love to pretend they're oblivious to celebrity. Fucking bullshit. Hogan's Square's buckling towards your gravity. Eyes softening with expectation. Meet a girl's stare and it reverberates through her entire group. Giggles behind cupped mouths. Someone once told you fame's like when a frog gets stuffed into a glass bottle, and the frog gets all twisted out of shape. But that's just half the story. If you're the frog, you can still see out, through the glass. Helen and Mush are on the other side, some other place.

Mush

BEST THING ABOUT getting slowly pissed is how you don't notice it's happening till you need to get up for a slash and you miss a step. I nearly topple into Helen and Joe as I sit back next to them in the Square but it's all good, I'm with my friends, we're getting sloshed and it's lovely. Everything's rowdier around us – vibe in the Square's like a ride at a fairground that's all the better cos it mightn't be safe. Whole town's keeling into shitfaced and I'm right on that dip. First time not drinking alone in I dunno how long, and with Helen it feels good – her fire makes me feel strong. First few pints went down like water, like a tap was after being opened in the world, making everything gush. No awkwardness – just me and Helen on that windowsill, finishing sentences for one another, laughing at the bits between what we were saying. She rolled a smoke and handed it to me without looking up, just like the old days, and the hot crackle in my lungs made the sky swim and I looked at the rollie and went, 'I quit a year ago.' 'Me too, obviously,' Helen said, in her flat dry voice. I've missed how she talks. Joe always bitched how Helen had no sense of humour, but it wasn't true, like. Even Aidan thought she was funny, she just hid her jokes inside a poker face. It was one of the things I liked most about her. That and her don't-give-a-fuck vibe. When we went into Flanagan's to get more pints, the place was wedged, a wall of bodies, but Helen took me by the hand and led me like she always did, same Kala-style confidence, cutting through fuckheads like butter. At the bar she got Taliban's attention right away. I nodded towards Joe onstage, working his magic, but Helen pretended not to notice him. Whatever, I was just happy to be out drinking.

Joe's busy chatting to the fans that keep coming up asking for autographs and selfies. Dunno how he does it, like.

Mam's been sending messages the whole time, telling me to get on to the twins. So I message Marie. **Why arent ye at the hen? Pauline will be gutted if ye dont show**

'So, how's work and stuff?' I say to Helen. 'Any big stories these days?'

She flinches and shakes her head. She pauses before taking a sip on her pint. 'Long story.'

I used to keep up with all Helen's articles, back in the day. Now I don't read the news much at all. Pure pointless, like. Still, I read this one series Helen done ages ago, on how there's an epidemic of murdered and missing indigenous women in Canada. It was fucking mad, like. Once you got into the weeds of it, you realized that loads of the stuff that happened over there was like what happened here: women and kids getting locked up in places run by the Church, abuse all over the place, kids vanishing without a trace, women being disappeared, government not giving half a fuck and ordinary folk looking the other way. Helen got a fair bit of notice for them articles, like. Not just your usual reporting, either – she gave all this space to real human stories but then put them in this whole big-picture way of looking at things. Big Helen phrases like 'logic of carceral regimes', 'organs of the state apparatus'. Stuff read like a fecking symphony or something, when all the bits came together at the end and just fucking blew you open. Always knew she'd do something that mattered.

'*Freelance journalist...*' I say. 'Sounds pure class.'

Helen changes the subject back to the hen party. She says the twins never showed and I tell her how Donna and Marie are in a sulk with me and taking it out on Pauline. Helen says she can't believe they're sixteen already, and I laugh. 'Sure they've been sixteen since the age of five.'

Helen starts going on about some women at the hen who were saying snide shit about Kala. She pulls on my arm and squeezes it for emphasis. We're a few pints deep, but Helen's so smart that even when she rants it's like someone's written out her sentences beforehand. 'You see this fucking building site in the woods? Promising to show tourists *the real Ireland*? The real Ireland was back in that garden, standing back, casting judgement. As if they know anything about Kala. What she was really like.'

A WhatsApp pings through to me. It's Marie. Finally. But she isn't saying nothing, she's only after sending a photo. Takes a sec to recognize what I'm looking at. It's the caf, but the photo was taken from outside, on Fox Street. Two people are sitting in the booth by the front window. It's hard to make out who, cos of the flare off the glass. I zoom a little closer. It's me and Dudley, from earlier.

'Nothing's more crucial to the social order, Mush, than the sacrificial victim. The scapegoat. That's where the term "sacrifice" comes from, you know that? *Sacer-facere*, "to make sacred", and not in the banal way people understand the term—'

The 'Marie is typing...' yoke stop-starts on the screen. I feel myself getting proper pissed off. Not a word out of the twins all day – they *must* have heard about Kala by now – and... fuck it, like, I just want to be here with Helen, having my own life for once, listening to Helen talk to me, cos Helen looks right at me whenever she's talking, cos Helen's always seen me, not my scars, and—

The phone pings. Marie's message is two words: **NO POLICE**

I haven't a notion what the fuck to make of that. And to be honest I don't care. Not in the humour for this bollocks. So I type back:

stop fucking about

Give yer mam a break for once

And then I turn off my phone.

'Of course,' Helen goes on, 'it's convenient if the sacrificial victim's been elevated to the level of a Madonna, or condemned as a whore, either's sufficient. Just deprive the victim of their humanity, relieve the community of the burden, the human *burden*, of recognizing themselves in the scapegoat, of accepting any complicity in their fate, because psychologically, these people—'

'Helen,' I half laugh. 'I don't really know what you're talking about.'

'Those fucking plebs sipping Prosecco in the garden. What do those women do, Mush, once someone like Kala's been destroyed? I'll tell you what they do. They have a nice cup of tea and a biscuit and tut over the news, convinced they aren't part of the fucking problem. Have you ever read the theory—'

Helen's always talked about abstract stuff to avoid talking about her feelings. Or, she finds it easier to have feelings about abstract stuff than ordinary stuff. I don't mind. I've missed her fury. She's ranting away on my arm but I know this is her way of saying, 'I'm broken-hearted, Mush. I'm devastated.' It's just Helen can't come out and say that. She has to dress up her emotions in attitude, the way I dress up mine in quiet. But she knows I know that about her, and she knows that about me, too. So we're having this whole other, deeper conversation between us, right now, without needing to speak it, cos it's always been this way with us. Some people you can just know. I know the time will come when we have to talk about it, straight out. Ask ourselves if what happened to Kala was our fault. I'll have to tell her and Joe about the photo Dudley said they found. Kala's skull. But once I do this I'll have opened a door to something I can't walk back from, and I know what Helen's like, she'll start to obsess over it. So not yet. Not tonight. Tonight her arm feels good around mine, and she leans on me as we sit, and the soft part of me, the part that only ever makes me sad, feels happy.

Helen

JOE IS WALKING ahead like the Pied Piper, leading his public down the blare of Fox Street. Mostly tourist fans, hanging on his every word. He is bringing us to a traditional music pub, the Crannóg. I heard him tell his fans he wanted to show them 'authentic Irish culture'. Christ.

Whatever. I am glad he is distracted with his entourage. It means I have Mush to myself. We walk huddled together, our arms linked. It is nice, that we are old enough to do this. Such intimacy would have been strange at an earlier age. Mush is warmth. He smells like coffee beans and booze. He feels so safe. I ask him about Aoife. He has not seen her in years, but heard she's married and living in Carthy. He says he still has her on Facebook, if I want to reach out to her. I look up at him and smile, lean in to him more. Sometimes I wish people could touch all the time, that words only ever get in the way. Thoughts like this let me know I am drunk.

A glass smashes and I see a girl run from a terrace outside a bar, a bouncer shouting after her. The girl runs further down Fox Street where she's joined by two other girls and a curly-haired boy and they dart through the crowds up ahead, where Joe is swigging from a bottle of champagne, getting his photo taken by strangers. It is odd. I have my memories of Joe as an actual person, his distinct energy, all the idiosyncratic tonalities of movement and voice that make someone who they are in the flesh. Then I have the overblown image of him from music videos and billboards in different cities. And now both Joes are coiled about one another, twisting heads all the way down Fox Street.

He stands with his arm over a fan's shoulder, posing for a selfie, drinking from the bottle. Always trying to prove something to himself.

It was the exact same attitude, the night we went to the Crawley House. Mush and Aidan were supposed to meet us, but they had not showed up. Joe mumbled that they'd chickened out, and insisted on walking in the lead as we entered Caille Woods, chest out to the night, as though darkness did not frighten him.

The woods were still, but not calm. We were in the night-tree world. Tiny arteries of moonlight bled between branches. Our torches only caught glimpses. Twisted fingers, tortured limbs, trunks pushing up through the earth. Haunted, moss-bearded rocks with warped faces.

I glanced behind and saw the woods close itself in our wake, our trail disappearing behind us.

Ahead, the light from my torch was harsh on Joe's back. In the cold glare I watched the lazy way he draped his arm over Kala's shoulders. This was a place I did not belong. Kala was whispering in Joe's ear. Her thumb, pushing beneath the hem of his hoodie to touch his skin. I was willing her to turn and include me in whatever she and Joe were sharing.

I had been sitting on my bed for a long time, waiting. Anticipating the flashes of Kala's torch. One. Two. Three sudden lights, flashing in the dark distance outside my window. The third flash had held out for the longest, suspended mid-air, the smoky echo of its light lingering in the school yard. I could hear Theresa's shallow breathing in the blankets behind me. She had sneaked into my bed, again. I did not look back at her, because I did not like seeing this shape in the sheets. A grave-like mound under the blanket. It reminded me of the times when Mam became the Creature. The Creature wore Mam's face like a mask. The Creature had blank eyes and spent all day in bed with the curtains closed.

The Creature would not look at me. She was always thumbing at Mam's blanket like there was dirt there. But there was no dirt there.

I had been reading Mam's old notebook by the light of my torch. Misty was draped over my lap, warm on my knees. I had Mam's notebook poised on Misty's shining black pelt, turning the pages gently as Misty's hind leg twitched in dog dreams, collar tinkling. I do not think Mam wrote often, but when she did write, it was a lot. Run-on sentences, lasting for pages. She never wrote when she was the Creature. And she never wrote when she was at full voltage, either. Only in the times between. Sometimes I could tell, from how the ink looked on the page, if she was turning in either direction.

Kala's torch flared again. One. Two. Three. I flashed my torch back.

There was a loose floorboard in the corner of the room. Underneath was the dark gap in which I kept Mam's notebook. I tucked it back into place and carefully crossed the floor.

But as I opened the door, Theresa's voice whispered in the dark. 'Don't leave me.'

'Go to sleep,' I said.

'Please, Helen. I don't want to be on my own. I'll tell Dad.'

'Do you want me to tell Dad how you wet your bed last week?'

'No.'

'Then go back to sleep.'

I knew Aoife was frightened of the woods, because she was whispering to me so much. We were reaching the hill to the Crawley House, and her agitation was beginning to affect me. With every crackle of movement in the leaves, she pulled hard at my arm. She leaned in as we walked, so close that her bubblegum breath tickled my ear.

'You know it's all bullshit, right?' she said.

'What?'

She paused, enjoying my curiosity. 'All that stuff that Kala says about her mam. A singer in London? Please. No one knows who Kala's mam is. Or her dad. I don't even think Kala knows. It's like, so messed up.'

Blue shimmers of moonlight glittered in Kala's hair.

'You know Kala's not even her name?' Aoife said. 'If you ever want to see her properly pissed off, call her Katherine. Once in primary school—'

Joe and Kala shushed us from up ahead. They had stopped walking. We were at the bottom of the hill that led to the Crawley House. The path up the hill was like a tunnel of leaves and broken branches.

Something was wrong. Kala was staring into the leafy path, and I could see the tension in her shoulders. Joe fumbled to turn off his torch. Then he grabbed mine and turned it off too.

'I can do that myself,' I said.

'Quiet,' he hissed.

Aoife moved ahead and peered into the path. Whatever she saw made her grab Kala's sleeve. I do not know what I expected. Nothing would have surprised me. It is difficult not to be superstitious when you are in the woods at night.

And then I saw; it was not what was on the path, but what was beyond it, at the top of the hill. A warm glow of unnatural brightness. Candlelight. Unmistakably. Candles, up at the Crawley House.

Joe was already turning back. No fake bravery now. 'Let's go.'

But before Aoife and I could say anything, Kala stepped into the path and began to climb. And then the strangest feeling. I began to walk after Kala. She looked back and held out a hand for me and I walked towards it, reaching, only it felt like I was not walking towards her, I was being walked towards her, like something else was doing the walking through me, only I was not truly walking any more, either, because while I could feel the world around me – the sweet smell of rotting leaves and sour earth, the whispers of protest from Joe and Aoife, the ribs of the earth pushing through my runners – it was like being carried in a current, like the dark itself was lifting me, lifting Kala, and we were pedalling air, gliding together, towards the candle glow.

The Crawley House was a squat stone building with a tall tower at its centre. Six thick candles were arranged in a row outside it. There were cracks in the stonework, pulsing like veins, hot light coming from inside. The whole building looked alive, like its centre was thick with flame.

'We shouldn't be here,' Joe whispered behind us.

'What if it's a black Mass?' Aoife said. I remembered what Kala and Aoife had said, that first day on the Coast Road. Devil worshippers. Dead dogs in the woods.

I wanted to show Kala that I was not like Aoife and Joe. I was like her. And I wanted to see.

I crouched down and crept towards the house. The stone wall was damp against my hands. I peered through the cracks. Inside, it was glowing, golden with candlelight. Shadows were dancing up the walls. If I had been alone, I would have turned and run. But I was not alone. Kala was next to me. Her eyes, wild stars. I realized I could be brave for her, braver than I could be for myself. A moment's hesitation, each of us looking at each other for encouragement. Finding it. We took each other's hand and crept around the house, moving towards the open doorway. Then we stood before the entrance and looked inside. I see us now, how we must have looked. Our silhouettes against the candlelight. Trick-or-treating with the future.

The stone floor inside was scattered with leaves, muck. There were candles in each corner of the room. Towers of light and shadow twitched along the walls above them. The walls were moving, sliding away from themselves, as though the air were being stirred from above. At the centre was a carefully arranged mound of stones, ringed by tealight candles.

'I don't like this,' a voice whispered. Aoife. She and Joe were with us in the doorway. She pulled at Kala's sleeve and Kala shook her loose, stepped inside.

'Kala,' Joe hissed.

I held Joe's stare, and a silent argument happened in the space between us. I turned away from him to follow Kala in.

Kala crouched down at the mound of stones. Under the top stone I could see the corners of a square piece of paper. Kala removed the top stone. She took the paper and held it to the candlelight.

It was a photograph. We all gathered to see it.

I squinted hard at the picture, to be sure I was seeing what I thought I was seeing. But my body already knew. Noisy blood. Nausea.

Aoife's voice. 'Oh fuck. Oh fuck.'

It was a picture of us.

Joe began to speak when something thudded above us. Then a crash of footsteps rushing down a flight of stairs that we could not see.

'Fuck!' Aoife shouted.

'Let's go,' Joe said. 'Run!'

But when we turned there was a dark figure standing in the doorway behind us. None of us moved. The world tilted. The moment stretched. An ugly infinity. Then the figure at the door rushed in at us, and a huge voice screamed, and the walls of the Crawley House screamed, and we screamed, and there was no Helen in that moment, there was only all of us, dissolved in the screaming.

Joe

THE CRANNÓG'S PACKED. Never been here before, despite its legendary status. 'The best traditional music in Kinlough.' Warm shadows of cologne, sweat, perfume, the bar thick with chatter. Every night here there's a session. Musicians show up spontaneously, in dribs and drabs. They sit in a corner, one begins a tune, another joins in, another, and suddenly they're taking the room on a journey. They reach the end of one tune and the fiddler starts up a new melody, the others figure out the chords, the playing continues. You've spoken about these sessions in every long-form interview you've ever done – they lap this shit up abroad. You play up your accent, speak with a misty look in your eyes, as though you've wandered into the interview from some rain-sodden field, like you didn't grow up in the first house in Kinlough to have a flatscreen TV.

The mad alchemy as the musicians nod to one another, palpating the room with the bodhrán beat, the holy squeal of the uilleann pipes like laughter whistling the air between the bodies that are warm and tight as you pass through them, locals chatting with flushed faces, tourists filming every detail on their phones. Half a dozen musicians packed into the corner and the pub's purring to the pulse they have coursing through the place. Real musicians. Skinny-armed, soft-bellied, only interested in the music. You've more in common with some airbrushed cunt in a magazine than you do with them. Standing like a prick here with your stubble and tattoos. You've never been part of this world. Whenever you and the lads practised tunes in Aidan's shed, you always imagined ye were already before a huge crowd, playing the stadium gig that'd save the planet. You'd got it all mapped out – not just the setlist, but what you'd do at every point in every song. You got shivers picturing it: Aidan and Mush, your army behind you. You up front, in a hammering tide of chords, eyes closed, lost to the rhythm, the girls staring up at you, awestruck, till at some great peak you'd open your eyes towards Kala, her gaze lifting to meet yours across the noise, a secret moment passing between ye. The Other Place.

A sudden dip in the Crannóg and the pub tips for a moment. Stumble into someone. It's an auld lad, a local, wearing a moth-eaten jacket covered with badges. His face is bright pink. You go to apologize but he winks and grins.

Mush hands you a Guinness. Drink a third of the pint, half. Two large gulps. Drink yourself into the night so you can drink the night into yourself – get yourself swollen with the noise, the sweating sheen of the windows, the yelped cries of people as they barrel around every contour of the music. Close your eyes and get that good feeling, the proper drunk epiphany feeling of being lifted inside your skull while your belly drops from a great height. Wish you could just hit either end of this motion. Crash heavenward through the floor and never stop arriving. Pub's started to spiral. Another pint. Mush is next to you and this is real enough. If you could live like this all the time, you could really live.

Sky's gone grey over the small car park and ye push through the smokers. Helen's alone, sitting on a stone wall. You keep close to Mush, making sure he stays between you and Helen. She's barely looked at you tonight. You can tell she's drunk from the swim of her eyes as she tries some of Mush's pint.

Mush is sweating. 'You should take a look inside there, Helen. The music's amazing.'

'Are you serious?' she says. 'Trad?'

A few of the Flanagan's crowd are lingering nearby,

smoking, pretending not to listen. Adjust how you're sitting. They'll all remember the night they once saw Joe Brennan out drinking in Kinlough, like an ordinary guy.

Two blondes, psyching each other up to approach you. One of them puts a hand on your arm. The usual script. Huge fans. Been listening to your stuff for, oh my God, years. American accent, English learned as a second language. Scandinavian. Greek. Fuck it, they could be from anywhere.

'Did you grow up playing this sort of traditional music?' one of them says.

'We don't have this where we are from,' the other says. 'It must make you proud.'

You've had this conversation so many times it's autopilot. 'This music's who we are,' you say. 'It's in our blood.'

Helen snorts into her pint.

'What?' you say. 'You don't like trad?'

'No,' she laughs. 'And neither do you. Or has it become cool now?'

'Ah, now,' Mush says. 'Listen to them fiddles, Helen. Where's your priiiide?'

'Reactionary kitsch,' Helen says.

You frown. 'It's authentic. Romantic. It's—'

'There's a reason romantics always end up as fascists,' Helen says. 'Appeals to authenticity are always rooted in essentialist thinking.'

She has not changed.

One of the blondes touches your newest tattoo. In a quiet voice, she says, 'I think it's so beautiful.'

'Sentimental dog shit,' Helen mutters.

Mush nudges her. 'Nothing wrong with that every now and then, Helen. Bit of emotion.'

'Sentimentality is for people who want the luxury of an emotion without paying any price for it.'

'Oh, that's clever, Helen,' you say.

'That's Oscar Wilde, *Joe*.'

'Terrible to be cynical.'

'*I'm* cynical?' she says. 'This country invents a fake past, packages it for tourists as a product, and then cons itself into believing that somehow it's all real. When the reality of this place—'

'This is Helen,' you say to the blondes. 'She used to be fairly intense, but she's really mellowed o—'

'The reality of this place,' Helen says, leaning forward, 'is that people here will turn a blind eye to every sort of horror for the sake of a quiet life. And *this* is the music they use to tell themselves stories about how, actually, *they're* the great victims of history, when the truth is—'

'Helen,' Mush says.

'I mean, the hypocrisy,' she says. 'Frowning into your pint over some clichéd shit about the brutal Brits, congratulating yourself for your innocence, squeezing out a few cheap tears before staggering home to beat the wife.'

'Jesus, Helen, take it easy,' Mush says.

'I hate this music, and I hate this place,' Helen says. 'How can a country so self-absorbed never even come close to actual introspection?'

'Heleeen,' Mush drones playfully. '*Heleeeen.*'

Mush gets her in a headlock and she starts to punch him in the side. They squabble like that, like siblings, rolling over on their sides. Helen starts laughing.

'*Heeeeleeeeeen,*' Mush shouts.

The blondes are bewildered. More flustered by the happy violence between Helen and Mush than anything Helen has said.

Theresa's sending you screenshots of the selfies people are uploading with you on IG. You're wearing the same smile in each one, a drink in hand. Should never have told her you were on the dry. Message her.

Don't worry I'm good

Tho Helen's on form

should I be afraid lol

???

Helen

THE ATMOSPHERE ABOUT us is a shriek. People hover around Joe like vampires, and I sit holding my arms, waiting for Mush to come back. I am already hoarse – but I want to tell him about Mrs Mulkerns. I had shaken myself from Moira the Lunatic's grip and was making my way out of the garden to escape the hen, when a silver-haired woman put a hand on my arm and said how nice it was to see me, after all these years. She said this in French. *Vous vous souvenez de moi?* Of course I remembered her. Mrs Mulkerns. She was why girls at St Anne's called me 'ooh la la'.

She asked about my work, about life in Québec. She did this in that efficient, clean way teachers have of speaking, like everything can be highlighted, underlined, and arranged into neat parcels. She commented on how Québécois my French has become, but with none of the condescension this comment usually brings. Mrs Mulkerns was the only teacher Kala ever spoke well of. In the weeks before she disappeared, I often saw them speaking in the art room, faces tight with involved conversation. When I asked Kala what they were discussing, she gave a twist of her mouth, an irritable flutter of ringed fingers. Mrs Mulkerns told me she still had all of Kala's artwork at the school. 'A tremendously gifted girl,' she said. *Extrêmement douée.* 'Will you come into St Anne's tomorrow and see me? I'll be doing admin all day.' A flash of Kala's face in the yard, the last time I saw her. Part of me would rather do anything than enter St Anne's. But I agreed to visit Mrs Mulkerns. I wanted to know what she and Kala had talked about.

Mush approaches with more drinks. He smiles at me through the crowd, and I smile back, when Joe puts an arm around him and slurs to people, 'This is the guy. This fucking guy.' Mush looks uncomfortable, but Joe hands a fan his phone and asks her to take a picture of them. Mush turns, to hide his scars. 'One more,' Joe says, when Mush tries to leave. He claps Mush on the back. 'You good?'

'Yeah, man,' Mush says. His voice is hoarse from drunk-talk, like mine. 'It's mad seeing Helen. Haven't seen her since Aidan's funeral, like.'

Joe's smile falters. His face flushes and he lets Mush go. Always polite. Always a gent.

Mush

'MUSH,' HELEN SAYS. 'Do you remember the night at the Crawley House?'

'Of course.'

'D'you think that might be why?'

'Why what?'

She looks up at me for a moment. Her eyes are glassy. 'Kala,' she says in a quiet voice.

That's the big difference between Helen and everyone else, I reckon. No one likes to look under the rock and see what's wriggling there, but Helen can't help herself. She has to know. Always wants to see.

I've been avoiding asking myself about the Crawley House. Things turned on us that night. Aidan had convinced me, fuck knows how, to scare the bejesus out of Joe and the girls. He'd arranged Auntie Pauline's fat candles all about the Crawley House. He'd got me to put together a heap of stones and place one of Kala's Polaroids on top, like a cherry on a cake.

'Wait till you see their faces, man,' he said. 'Joe's gonna shit himself.'

Joe kept texting me:

we r w8ing what da fuck man

ok fine chat 2moro

Steam in the air between me and Aidan, from our mouths. I was shivering. It was fucking Baltic, like. Which made no sense. The night was lovely and warm outside. But inside the Crawley House it was pure cold. The place was weird as anything.

'Here, man,' Aidan said. He took a brown bottle with no label from his backpack, and a rag. 'This'll warm you up, like.' He unscrewed the lid, capped the mouth of the bottle with the rag, and held it upside down for a second. Then he handed me the rag and told me to hold it over my nose and mouth, like a gas mask. 'Just breathe pure deep.'

'What is it?'

'It'll warm you up,' Aidan said.

There was a dark stain in the rag. I cupped it in my hands and buried my nose and mouth in it. I breathed in deep and felt dizzy, but Aidan would slag me if I only inhaled once so I tried again. Aidan was laughing and his laugh fell through me like I was a well and it echoed in my body which was sinking down into the ground, my legs melting into the stone and Aidan speaking but the words were shapes, pearls of noise on a necklace, bells in my ears, the candles flashing in my eyes and the light was in my guts pushing itself hot from inside, and I wanted to look at Aidan but couldn't cos my head was gonna come loose and heart drilling me falling in myself floating over myself and Aidan was talking and I wanted to hug him but my arms were heavy like hammers, and Aidan laughed so I tried to laugh but the sound opened my head and the Crawley House crawled into my mouth and laughed into me like I was a ventriloquist's dummy and I began to move my jaw like 'argh argh argh' and Aidan's voice echoed, 'Jesus, you're shitfaced,' and he steered me to a doorway in the back of the Crawley House and pointed at steps that led up the tower and said I was supposed to hide up there and wait for the girls and Joe and when they came I was to call their names in a creepy voice and Aidan would come in the door behind them and scare them and it'd be hilarious but

suddenly he was gone, I was alone, up the stairs, on the landing, by a window,

with the walls of the Crawley House slipping about me and

next thing I knew I'd my head stuck out the window and the night was warm and I sucked air till I was dizzy with it and in the distance, way off in the dark, was this perfect bowl of light floating in the earth like a giant yellow eye, and I thought the eye might see me if I didn't hide so I sank down till I was lying on the ground which was gritty against the right side of my face, and I nuzzled myself into it and saw myself with half a face, like half my skull was ashes, and a wind blew those ashes inside me and in the wind I heard a baby cry and I was afraid for that baby when – like magic – the baby's voice changed and it was Kala below me saying, 'Oh Jesus,' and Aoife saying, 'Oh fuck. Oh fuck,' and I pushed myself off the ground and ran down the stairs and they were screaming and I got scared so I screamed too and

everything was pure woozy cos I'd run downstairs too fast and stumbled into the wall and Aidan was in the doorway with this look of triumph on his face, cos the others – even Joe – looked like they'd shat their jocks, and Kala was punching Aidan in the arm over and over, calling him a dirtbird, and

Joe looked at me like he was ready to bite the head off me, but then his face went concerned

'What's the matter? You okay?'

and I tried telling him about upstairs, the noise of the baby and the glowing eye, but it felt like the words were large and sticky in my mouth and

'Aidan, why's he talking like that?' Joe said

'Like what?'

'Like he's had a fucking brain injury,' Aoife said and

Aidan had the bottle and rag in his hand and said, 'Carbona. Teabag and the lads done it to me the other night, it's a laugh,' and

Joe started giving out to him about drugging me and Aidan told him to stop being such a cop and I tried to tell them I loved them – 'I think ye're all great, like' – but the words were gone weird and I sat on the ground with the head bowed between my legs and Joe hooked an arm under me to pull me up but I shook my head and the roof of the Crawley House was spinning around his head and I went

'I'm gonna puke'

and Kala snapped a Polaroid right in Aidan's face, 'Fierce gothic with the candles,' she said sarcastically, and she walked around taking photograph after photograph, crouching close to the candlelight, and I heard myself babbling about the golden eye in the earth outside and the crying baby and Aoife was laughing into her hand – 'He's literally tripping!' – so I got up

led them upstairs

and

they all stopped laughing once they looked through the broken glass, where Crawley Hill smeared down into a stretch of blue fields spreading far beyond Kinlough, out towards Carthy, cos there it was, away off in the distance, in the middle of a sea of blackness, only

it wasn't a golden eye,

but it was something all right,

an oval-shaped island of light in the dark, and

from inside it were distant shouts and screams, and the light was full of flickers, like giant shadows there, dancing, and

Kala said, 'Oh my God, you guys, let's check it out,' and

next thing I knew we were outside, legs pure wobbly under me, and I felt safe cos Helen and Kala were there and

we were on the other side of the woods, standing at the edge of a huge sea of long grass, grey in the moonlight, and on the other side of all the grass was a line of bright light, and the sky above was a billion stars itching like insects in my skull and

Helen and Kala stepped into the long grass and the ground dipped so the grass was up over their shoulders and

Aoife said

'Ugh, gross,' 'it's full of rats,' 'let's go back,' but

Aidan bounded right into the long grass and we were all in it and I was taller than the girls so the grass only came up to my armpits and it felt like swimming cos I had my elbows out, turning this way and that, picturing rivers of rats at my feet, hearing myself moan in

the grass making whooshing sounds as we went through

whoosh

and the earth felt soft and

I was above us, could see all of us from above, like I was dead and shattered about the sky with the stars looking down and I saw the way we fanned out to make a moving rope pushing itself through the grey grass

whoosh

and I was part of all my friends and they were part of me and I knew we'd always be friends and I'd never be alone

and

the ground shouldered upwards to the light, to the sound of voices boiling in music with

a constant clanging, like rain hammering a metal roof, and

I looked over at Aidan and he was not laughing, or smiling, and he caught me looking and smiled to show he was not scared but

I'd seen it

he was scared

and

we crept up the hill towards the noise till we were at the edges of the light and I saw that the oval of light we'd seen from the Crawley House was actually a large courtyard, ringed by a load of sheds, and there were

large generator-powered lamps in the courtyard giving off this pure marmalade-coloured light and

the courtyard was full of men, their shadows spidering along the ground up the walls and

they were all wearing masks

these fucking masks

and

Helen took Kala's hand and together they ran and hid behind the closest shed and when the rest of us hunched down and ran to join them

Aidan held his sleeve over his nose against the shed wall and said, 'Ugh. What the fuck's in there?' and there was a burst of movement from inside the shed, this furious noise of chains rattling, and high-pitched doggy shrieks and the girls screamed and

'Shut up!' Joe hissed

so we held still and

Aidan peeked around the corner of the shed

'The fuck...' he muttered and

I ducked my head under him to see

a cluster of masked men, their masks were straw bags with holes cut out for the mouth and eyes, and they were smoking and their clothes – sensible jeans, shirts – made them look like regular lads, out for a normal night in town and

'Man,' Aidan whispered to me, 'I think I know this place. I think I been here'

'Hm?' I slurred and

all the sheds around the yard were dark except for

one large barn

on the opposite side of the yard which was pure heaving with noise, like there could be a hundred people in it and

Helen was looking at Kala and she said she wanted to see what was going on inside that barn, and she said it like she was waiting to see what Kala might say, and Joe snapped

'Are you stupid? No way. I think we shou—'

But Kala grabbed Helen's hand and they ran away from us, out into the gap of light between the buildings, to the back of the next shed, and

Joe looked furious but Helen and Kala were already darting to the next shed again and I saw them run and they looked like held breath in the light, like freedom, slipping into the safety of the shadow behind the next shed, so

I ran after them and the others followed and when we reached them, they were holding each other, breathing heavily, their faces this riot of feelings, and I was about to tell the lads that Aidan thought he knew where we were when there was the sound of gravel crunching in the yard, the purr of a motor arriving and a scattering of applause to greet the new arrivals, and

it was a red van, I knew it before I even saw and

when it pulled up by the big barn the werewolf mask stepped out and I saw the foot-drag and I said, 'That's Teabag,' and

when I looked at Aidan I saw a face on him I'd never seen before, pure staring like a child, this wrinkle between his eyebrows, like he couldn't believe what he was seeing, he didn't even notice me looking and

the click and slide of Teabag peeling the van open and

all these lads came pouring out, masks over their heads, and Teabag pointed to the barn and led them to it and when he opened the barn door

the sound tore out at the night like an animal snapping its jaws like

the sound fellas make at school whenever there's a huge scrap and

we flocked from one shed to another, making our way around the edge of the yard, getting closer to the big barn, one more shed left, a squat little shed, and

we scattered in the run towards it like birds splitting and gathering together and

all checking on one another, making sure we're all safe when

fuck

oh fuck

he comes from the far corner of the shed,

first the shadow on the ground, then the gravel crackle,

everything freezes cos

it's a tall man, taller than me, he's come around the corner and stopped, right in front of us

it's too late to run away now into the dark of the fields

he's seen us

fuck

no one speaks

mind gone blank

as he stares

he's got no mask

but I can't see his face, just this silhouette staring, and his hair's a mess of curls, catching the light,

and he speaks to Kala

then he turns, bends his knees, and pukes,

strings of it hanging from his lips, and he wipes them away with a moan and I catch a glimpse of his cheeks, they're covered in all these scars like, and he straightens and looks over at us again, for a moment,

then staggers back the way he came, his steps pure crooked, and

'He's locked,' Kala said

'What'd he say to you?' I said, and

'*Is it really you? It can't be!*' she laughed. 'Then he spewed. He was polluted,' and

'Guys,' Aidan said, 'I know where we are. This is where me cousins live. Teabag and them. The Lyons.'

'What?' Joe said.

'I was here a few times when I was a kid,' Aidan said. 'I recognize the house at the far end of the yard. That's where they live, like.'

'What the fuck is going on at this place?' Aoife said and

we all knew the answer was in the barn and

there was this moment then, of hesitation like, we all looked at one another, we still had time to run back home, forget all about everything we'd seen, we'd nearly been caught by the curly pukey lad, we could just go like,

but Helen looked at Kala and said, 'I want to see'

and Kala said, 'Me too'

and none of the rest of us protested, so that's what we did.

A stack of pallets at the back of the barn so we stood on them, peered through the slit between the wall and the roof and

inside, it was packed with men in masks, all shouting, shouts surging around the walls to circle the centre of the barn where four sheets of corrugated metal formed a bright square like a vortex and

three men in the square, two of them stood in opposite corners wearing pig masks, and the pig men were hunched and pointing at one another, the skin of their necks was red, flushed cos they were shouting and

in the centre of the square, a big-bellied fucker wore a golden, grinning face, both his arms raised out, crucifixion style, like a conductor inside the sound, one hand held out towards each of the pig men and

then I saw

why the pig men were so hunched

why their outstretched arms kept juddering forward

dogs

they were each holding a dog and

the dogs were pure muscle, one had a coat of brown and white patches, his snout was smeared red, all bared teeth and

the other dog was black and white, breathing heavily, upper lip curled back, front paws pure frantic on the ground, clawing up dust, trying to get away from its corner, to attack the brown dog and

'The fuck...' Aidan whispered. 'I think that's Dad in that golden mask. That's me fucking Dad,' and

he was right, the push of Uncle Ger's belly, the cowboy stance and

Uncle Ger's mask turned from one side of the fighting ring to the other, shouting instructions at the men with the dogs, then

he gave a signal with his hands, stepped back,

and the dogs thundered across the square

into one another

and

Joe put an arm around Kala to turn her towards him, but she shook him off

'I want to see,' she said but

Aoife was looking away, like Joe, and Helen had a hand over her mouth as the crowd grew louder

Aidan's mouth turned downward like someone about to cry and

the dogs slammed into each other and

snapped with their jaws

rose up on their hind legs so

their bodies formed a peak of snouts snapping round each other as they tried to get a hold on flesh

then they were on the ground, each one locked deep in the neck of the other like a knot of muscle kicking as their heads burrowed and swerved, trying to chew the meat out

Uncle Ger was down with the dogs, slapping the ground, shouting at them

when the clinch went on too long and neither dog let go, Uncle Ger made a signal to the pig men to separate their dogs and bring them back to the corners

panting, eyes pure mental with the screams and the men around the square were all reaching in and slamming their hands on the metal fencing and

that's what the clanging sound was

the centre of the square all sprayed with blood and the pig men squirting water out of plastic bottles on their dogs and pointing opposite the square

Uncle Ger made another sign and they thudded into each other again, shrieking, yelping

this went on and on

clinch, break apart

clinch, break apart and

each time the dogs got bloodier and messier

their moves got more ragged and shapeless till they could barely stand, chests going, out, out, out, walking in small circles in their corners with the pig men shouting at them and

when Ger gave the signal to fight again, the two dogs didn't rush at one another

just stood staring across the ring and gasping and I knew the pig men were saying, *Fucking kill*, but the dogs weren't moving

Uncle Ger had his hands held open, like he was asking
Is this it? Are we done?
then the brown and white dog half limped, half ran across
the ring into the black dog's corner and got red jaws right in
under the black dog's belly and the black dog flailed with its
front paws on the brown dog's back but the brown dog wasn't
letting go
it began to thrash and
the whole barn felt like it was lifting off the ground, the
metal clanging louder as the screams got thicker
when the brown dog stepped back, the black dog didn't
even try and fight, it just stared with its head dipped
sad eyes
and the brown dog went at it again, and again, till the pig
men broke them up
the brown dog's snout looked like it was after being dunked
in red paint
Uncle Ger signalled to the brown dog's corner, telling the
pig man to join him at the centre of the ring
he took the pig man's wrist and hoisted it up and the whole
barn swelled and Teabag in the werewolf mask climbed into
the ring with a stick of rebar in his hand, this ribbed metal
stick, and he walked over to the corner where the black dog
was a bloody mess, only shallow sighs coming out of it now,
and Teabag prodded it with his toe, then kneeled on the
ground next to it, talking up to the black dog's pig man
then he raised the rebar over his head and swung it down
on the black dog and
Aoife was crying
but Helen was saying, 'We need proof of this,'
and Kala was nodding and already going through her bag
and
she took out her Polaroid and aimed it through the slit in
the roof and
'No!' Joe said but it was too late, the camera flashed and
Teabag's wolf mask snapped towards us and

we all shouted as we jumped off the pallets

'Maybe he didn't see us?' Kala said

but I could already hear footsteps coming around the corner, there was nowhere we could run without being seen, if we ran back towards the other sheds, they'd see us, if we tried to hide around the other side of the barn, we'd be in full view of the yard,

all we could do was hunch behind the stack of pallets

and that's what we did even though that only bought us a few seconds,

the footsteps getting louder, Helen grabbed my arm and

Aidan snatched Kala's camera, 'Don't any of ye fucking move,' he said,

and then he stepped out from behind the pallets, holding the camera up, 'How are the lads?' he said to the approaching footsteps, he set the flash off,

'The fuck you doing here?' a voice said

Teabag

other voices, too

we held silent

I didn't want Aidan to get it alone, he'd never let me get it alone, I peeked around the pallets and clocked Teabag slapping Aidan in the face while Boomerang wrenched him by the collar and grabbed the Polaroid camera and smashed it up and Kala pulled me back behind the pallets, and when I went to protest Aoife whispered, 'Shut up, please shut up,' and Helen was holding me tight, her hand on my heart

so that's what I did, and that's how it happened

I left Aidan to his cousins while I stayed safe with my friends.

Helen and me share a quiet look when I spot Theresa make a beeline for us through the crowd. I lean up on my elbows and reach out an arm. 'The Big T!' I shout. I can hear the booze sloshing in my voice.

She stands over us.

'How's Theresa?' I say.

'Yeah, hi,' she says. She looks at Joe, gestures to his pint. 'What's this?'

Joe shrugs. 'Nothing.'

'Thought you were on the dry.'

'Here, T,' I reach up and pull her sleeve. Theresa's great craic, always good for a laugh. 'Are you joining us? Fancy a pint?'

'No, Mush.'

Joe stands up, brushes the dirt off his jeans. 'I'll pop inside for you.'

'I said no,' Theresa says.

Joe points a finger between the rest of us, big handsome smile on him. 'You guys okay for everything?'

Theresa touches him on the arm and says, 'I want to talk to you,' but Joe pulls his arm free and leaves.

'How was the rest of the hen?' Helen says.

'Why, d'you care?' Theresa says. She fidgets with her keys, staring after Joe. 'It was mortifying. The twins never showed. Sometimes I don't get those girls at all.'

I pull on my rollie, hold the burn and breath in my chest. 'Two bulls in a china shop.'

'It's not like them to be unfeeling,' Theresa says. 'They been acting weird? Said anything to you?'

I should tell her about the argument, but I don't want to open that can of worms. 'It'll all be grand.'

'Not when Lydia gets her hands on them. I swear, Mush. Your mam can be so scary.'

'Get the crazy eyes on her, did she?'

Theresa makes her eyes bulge. I laugh. Theresa's great. Helen's great. Sure everyone's great. Kala's dead. Everyone's great.

Theresa crouches down with us, sighs, rubs at her temple.

'How's Joe holding up?' Theresa says. 'He must be heartbroken.'

Helen scoffs. 'He hasn't mentioned her once.' Her words are slurred. 'Too busy getting his ego massaged.'

'Ah, now,' I say.

Helen points in the direction of the pub, where Joe's stopped for another selfie with a guy wearing a Jungle Heart T-shirt. 'Are you telling me that behaviour is normal? On a day like today? It's like she meant nothing to him.'

'You don't know the first thing about Joe,' Theresa says.

'And you do?' Helen says.

'I'd say I know Joe intimately, yes.'

A beat passes between them as Helen stares her sister out, doing some telepathic girl thing.

'No,' Helen goes. '*Theresa?* No.'

Theresa shrugs. 'It was, like, two years ago. A little summer thing. No big deal. We email.'

'Joe *Brennan?*' Helen says, spine straightening. 'Joe *fucking* Brennan?'

'He's a good person,' Theresa says.

'He's a dick.'

'You're drunk,' Theresa says.

'I'm trying to be a good sister,' Helen says.

'Oh, spare me, you don't have the practice.'

Helen blinks at that.

'Your disappearing act tonight was noted, by the way,' Theresa says. 'Thanks for leaving me to deal with that.'

Helen pulls a sour expression, her face loosened with drink. Theresa's got her arms folded, looking over at the Crannóg. She says, 'He's not supposed to be drinking, you know,' when Helen reaches out and holds Theresa by the jaw. It's not rough, but it's weird. Theresa looks startled. Helen turns Theresa's face back to her, this way and that.

'You're like both of them,' she slurs.

Theresa pushes Helen's hand away. Ugly vibe to it. A few minutes ago everything felt pure sweet, like we were melting into each other. Now it's all this.

Theresa stands up. 'You could've helped, tonight.'

'How?' Helen says.

'You could've helped.'

Theresa turns and walks away. I push myself to my feet. I'm fairly drunk, fuck.

'Here, T. Wait.' I catch up with her. 'Why don't you stay for a bit? We're having a buzz.'

'I can see that,' she says. 'Christ, you're all so *drunk*.'

'We're just catching up.'

'For God's sake, Mush.' Her eyes do some inner search, like she's trying to decide on what to say. 'Mush, Joe shouldn't be drinking. He has a problem. A real problem.'

'What? No, he doesn't.'

Her phone rings. She answers and says, 'Enjoy your night, Joe,' and hangs up. 'I'm leaving.'

'Ah, Theresa,' I call after her. 'Stay. Sure what else are you gonna do?'

'I'm going to talk sense into Donna and Marie,' she says. 'One of us has to.'

When I return to the others, Joe's got another round of pints. He winks at me, and I smile, but Theresa's words are in my head now. Itching at my brain.

All around us, people are chatting. Groups everywhere, like scattered continents. I nod to the sound, trying to get back into the nice vibe from a few minutes ago. But when I go to finish my cigarette, it's after going out.

Helen

IT IS MY first time in Mush's flat. He has brought us here to show us something, whispering to us on the stairs to keep our voices down so as not to wake Lydia. Joe flings himself into an armchair and starts scrolling his phone. I do not sit down. I want to take everything in. *A home, darling, is a mirror to your inner life.* Mam would say things like that to me as she draped throws over a broken sofa, threadbare shawls over lampshades, trying to improve whatever shithole Dad had landed us in. Mam believed the world was an extension of the self. I have often thought of that on cold evenings in my bare apartment. Mush's flat is all handmade warmth. A well-stained carpet, magazines bent out of shape. It is as much Mush's place as Lydia's. It carries both their energy. Lived-in, unpretentious. The right level of messy. The sofa is strewn with cushions embroidered with lame jokes. 'Carp diem... Fish of the day!'

Mush and I move easily around one another in the kitchen, making tea and toast. We spend these minutes quietly, making small talk and murmured noises, our insides bleached tender by drink. I have been drinking water since Theresa's tantrum, sobering up. I will not be caught out like that again, lost for words.

Mush sets out three Cadbury's Creme Egg mugs. Tea stains etch their insides, like cave paintings. As the kettle boils, he hands me a plate of toast. His café finesse: knife arranged at a delicate angle across the plate, a perfect rectangle of butter and salt on the side, and a banana Mush has sliced into halves and drizzled with brown sugar. 'Get stuck into that,' he says, 'Bind the stomach.' He has taken care of me before preparing anything for himself. This urge to hug him. I am still drunk.

As I leave the kitchen he marks the day off a Cliff Richard calendar that must be a joke. We are one day away from the date marked in tiny capital letters: WHITE WEDDING.

Joe and I sit on opposite chairs, ignoring each other. He scrolls on his phone while I feel myself already getting more and more irritated by the fact that he got to speak to the Mammy today and I did not. I had stood by the lake for a while, staring at the fenced-off crime scene. The chit-chat of curious locals. The white tent stirring in the breeze. This ugly flutter feeling in my chest.

When I returned to the Mammy's house, there was a mud-spattered mobile home parked by the door. I lingered outside for a while, waiting till the visitor left. But this did not happen, and I was already running late for the stupid fucking nail salon.

Mush sets down the mugs of tea and Joe asks if he has anything stronger. Mush says he'll have a look, but I can tell by his face that he won't.

Eventually I ask Joe, 'Did you visit the Mammy today?'

He does not look up from his phone. 'I saw her, yeah.'

'Did she say anything about the funeral?' I say. 'Is there anything we can do to help?'

'We weren't exactly talking practicalities,' he says, turning in his seat towards the kitchen. 'Man,' he shouts to Mush. 'I said d'you not have anything stronger than tea?'

Mush comes in shushing us. He looks at Joe, hesitates, then runs off to get a bottle. Typical.

'How was she?' I say. 'The Mammy.'

Mush come in, hands Joe a bottle of whiskey, and kneels by the TV, messing around with an old video machine, connecting cables.

Joe shakes his head, pouring whiskey into his tea. 'The Mammy, yeah... I mean, Dad warned me she'd declined a lot but... She's convinced there's some sort of conspiracy. *Kinlough has always destroyed its women.*' He glances at me, draping one leg over the arm of his chair, holding the whiskey bottle in his hand, channelling Keith Richards or some bullshit. 'She sounded like you earlier at the Crannóg, ranting about trad. Paranoid.'

I open my mouth to savage him when Mush says, 'Guys, take a look.'

He turns off the lights and starts the video machine.

The screen is blue, then judders into a dark image. A figure, too close to the screen. The camera pulls back and Aidan comes into focus, crossing his eyes and twirling a drumstick between his fingers. Mush's voice, off-camera, whispering. *'Say what's happening, man,'* Aidan says. *'Tonight we're playing our first gig. An evening that's gonna live in the history books, baby. And Mush is a biteen nervous.'* Mush's voice, behind the camera, *'Fuckin' not, like.'*

Their voices are so young.

Then it's Kala's kitchen, warm light. Aoife, drinking a glass of milk. And me. My God, me. *'Say hi, girls,'* Kala's voice says. She is behind the camera, close to the microphone, so her voice is loud. Aoife starts to sing, holding a wooden spoon as a mic. I join in, with a spatula. Kala sings harmony behind the camera.

It is unsettling, the sight of us, trapped in the amber of a moment that I cannot remember. I look younger than I ever felt. My leg turned inward, adjusted for the camera.

The video cuts to Kala's basement. The boys are playing. It is the night of the Halloween party. Their gig. Joe is singing, but it is so loud that the microphone only picks up noise. Bodies thud about before the boys. The night is minutes, maybe seconds, from what happens.

Kala and me, together, showing off our costumes. Kala licks her fingertip and touches me. She pretends that her finger sizzles. She cups her hand and says something to me and I laugh.

Then she walks to the camera, filling the frame. Looking right down the lens. She is talking. Gesticulating. The video ends.

'Play it again,' Joe says.

Mush rewinds the tape. The light from the screen scrambles his features. With each replay, Mush points out details for us. He knows every nuance of the video. When Kala crosses the room towards us, her body filling up more and more of the screen, I feel my breath tighten.

Mush's hands imitate Kala's gestures on the video, like a pianist miming to a recording. He mouths along to Kala's inaudible words.

'How many times have you watched this?' I say.

He plays the video again. I cannot look at the screen any more. I need to know what happened to her, and why.

I look at Mush's sitting room, reflected in the glass cabinet behind the TV. Mush's eyes, lost in the screen. Joe's hands, clutching the bottle in his lap. Our faces floating in the dark, flickering with the borrowed light of the past.

Sunday

Joe

BIRDS WHEEL OVERHEAD. The sky shears at your eyes like a camera stuck in a permanent flash with your whole body freezing, face knotted tight. Shove the earth away from yourself. Damp of the grass in your hands.

Where the fuck?

Air's salty. Blurry dawn, bleeding into focus. Aches in parts you didn't know you had.

You're on the golf course, tangled in the long grass. You remember being at Mush's. He gave you a bottle. Shouldn't have done that. Did you take the bottle? Pat the damp grass around you. Feel at your crotch. No piss soak, thank fuck. So much of the night's vague. A film strip with half the frames missing. Check the phone. Your socials are mental. Pictures of you playing Flanagan's. A load of people with selfies. You standing behind the bar in the Crannóg. Fucking hell, the Crannóg. What did you do there? What did people see?

All the stuff is positive, in that hollow online way. Hundreds of likes. 'So down to earth!' 'Pure sound.' 'Absolute gent.' Someone says something about you buying pints for everyone in the pub.

You're gonna puke.

Veiny twigs beneath your hands. You retch. Nothing comes up. Eyes already gone watery. On all fours now, whole body shivering with heat.

Shove your fingers down your throat. Animal sounds over your knuckles. Don't pull them out till you feel the hot liquid. There's bread in the sick. Don't remember that. Mush's, maybe. Toast?

Puking again. A lot this time. Burning relief.

Vague memory of arguing with Helen. Can't remember what. Theresa too. Flash of her looking at you outside the Crannóg. Florence fucking Nightingale.

Feels like your bones have been in a fridge. Slap your cheeks. Take a selfie to check your reflection. Could be worse. Who cares.

Beyond the shore, the water stretching out. Beads of light shimmering. Open Instagram. Capture it. Caption it. 'Morning Glory. Home.' Post it. Fifty likes in twenty seconds.

Up ahead on the Coast Road there's a bunch of teenagers, guys and girls. You see them, but teenagers only see each other. You don't understand kids' clothes any more, what it all means. Back in the day things were tribal – clear lines. Your haircut and clothes said what music you liked, how smart you were, whether or not you were real, if you were reaching for the Other Place or stuck in the gutter. Internet's taken all of that, mangled the codes. People are mongrels of whatever the fuck now. Kurt Cobain shot himself for being a sell-out and these kids wouldn't even grasp the concept. You hate these kids. Wish you were these kids. Envy their obliviousness, like the world had just come into being, and existed only for you and your friends, and all you had was time.

'Fuck me, lads,' one of the boys says. 'Is that Joe Brennan?'

'It is,' you say. Mask on. Smile on. Joe on.

'Unreal,' one of the girls says.

'Can we get a picture?'

They gather around you, a hive of energy. Try to let their excitement in.

'Class,' one of the girls says. You're about to give her the charming smile and say, 'No bother, darling,' when she adds, 'My mam used to fancy you so much. You were, like, always on in the car when I was in primary school.'

They're not even looking at you any more.

'I'd better mosey on,' you say. You wink, turning away. 'Stay out of trouble, now.'

As you walk off, one of the lads shouts out the chorus of 'Faraway Stars'. It echoes down the road. Raise an arm and give a thumbs-up. This wobble in your chest. Don't know if these kids are mocking you. Don't turn to find out.

Ever since the night of the Crawley House, your place in the crew had been unsteady. Something had shifted the second Aidan stepped out and joined the Lyons. He'd made himself look like he was the big hero of the gang, the main character in the movie. But that was meant to be you.

It was obvious what ye needed to do about the dogfighting: tell Dad. But the others all said no. They had their reasons. Aoife said ye should just forget ye'd seen anything. 'It's none of our business,' she said. Mush pleaded with you to keep it secret. He said it'd fit too neatly: first the Lyons catch Aidan on the farm, next thing the Guards swoop down on the Lyons. There'd be consequences.

'Seriously?' you said. 'You're scared of Teabag?'

'Yeah, I am,' Mush said. 'And you should be too.'

'What's the worst that could happen to me?'

'It's not about you, man. It's about Aidan.'

That was the problem. Aidan could do no wrong in anyone's eyes now. The girls hung on his every word whenever he brought reports on his family's activities. Apparently the dogfighting had been going on for years. It was a year-round thing, and its peak was during the summer, when tourists got involved. The fights were going on one or two nights a week. There was serious money to be made on bets. Thousands, every night. 'Sometimes we have nine, ten Gs floating,' Aidan said, like he was a gangster. 'Lot of cash sloshing about.'

He was squatting in the grass at the edge of Hogan's Square. Helen was plaiting Aoife's hair while Mush ate his fourth ice cream of the day, rubbing Misty's belly, giving the dog licks off his cone. You were sitting on a small wall, next to Kala. You wanted Kala to be focused on you. After the night at the Crawley House, you'd given Kala a mobile phone with a camera in it, to replace her smashed-up Polaroid. You thought this would impress her, but she looked almost confused at being given something so expensive. And today she was all about Aidan. She wanted to know more about the operation, who does what, when, where. It was all the gang wanted to talk about these days. There was a pyramid in your group, and Aidan was going up. Which meant you were going down.

'We have pick-up points about town, right?' Aidan said. 'All the pubs where Dad runs security. Passwords and all that craic. Serious operation.'

Acting like he was a secret agent, feeding ye info about the underworld. When he was only another Lyons, someone from a fucked family, making a meal out of whatever edge he thought that gave him.

'Our drivers pick up punters at various points, pack them in the back of the vans. That's what your dad does,' he said, nodding at Helen. 'But he's tangled in the spaghetti, ya know.'

This pissed you off, too. How Aidan would mention something like 'spaghetti' without explaining it, doing it on purpose, cos he wanted the girls to ask him for more information, cos he loved being the authority on things, lording it over ye.

'What's the spaghetti?' Kala said.

'It's this system to stop anyone bringing the operation down. Teabag says it's how the IRA run things.'

'You're not the fucking IRA,' you said.

Aidan took a long drag on his cigarette, wincing in the distance.

'Spaghetti means the whole operation's pure tangled up, see? Everyone's got a piece in the jigsaw, but only the big boss has the full picture. So if someone gets caught, they can't squeal on everybody, cos they don't know how all the pieces connect. That's why the punters have to put on masks whenever they get in the back of the van. They gotta keep their masks on the whole time, in the van, and on the farm. Stops people being able to identify each other.'

'Is my dad... is he very involved?' Helen said.

'Ach, your auld lad's only a go-between. Not high up. He drives punters out to a meeting point in the middle of nowhere. Then there's a handover where he transfers his passengers to another driver, another van. That's what ye saw, out the back of the golf course. So, get this: the punters don't know where they are, cos they've been stuck in the back of one van, and then they all get moved into *another* van, and they don't know where *that's* going. They get taken out the Warren, and Teabag says he always does a few loops, so the punters are pure disoriented. And it's only then that they get dropped off at the farm. Pretty cool, right?'

'I wouldn't describe anything about this as cool,' Helen said.

'It's fairly fucking cool,' Aidan said, grinning. You wanted to slap him in the chops.

'So what do you do, then?' you said.

'Can't tell you that. Top secret.'

'You're full of shite. We should just tell the Guards.'

Aidan's mask slipped then. Worried eyes on him. 'No, you can't. It'd be bad for all of us.'

See? Aidan wasn't brave – he was afraid. But no one cared. If anything, it made the others respect him even more.

You were about to push Aidan further, make him squirm, when a voice called from across the Square. 'How are the queers?'

The Lyons were walking over to ye. Sunburned shoulders, golden chains flashing. Teabag up front, Boomerang and Lee behind him. A cluster of other fellas, too. Some of them crouched down on the grass, a bit too close to Aoife and Helen.

Teabag strode between Mush and the girls, cutting through them to reach you. 'You looking at something, Piglet?'

He stepped close to you. The hair around his pale stomach, the waist of his tracksuit bottoms. You knew you needed to meet his eye. But he was so close that you'd have to tilt your face up to do that, and then it'd be him looking down at you and you looking up at him. So you glanced at Mush and gave him a cheeky sort of smirk, like you didn't take any of this seriously.

'Know what I don't like about you, Piglet?' Teabag said. 'The way you look down your nose at everybody. The way you think you're better than Teabag Lyons. When all you are is a moshery faggot.'

Mush said, 'Ah, now—'

Boomerang grabbed Mush's wrist and shoved his ice cream into the side of his face. 'The fuck you think you're talking to, boy?'

Helen had her hand on Misty's collar but the dog was worked up, snorting.

Teabag looked at Misty. 'That bitch comes anywhere near me and I'll kick it asunder, d'you hear me?'

Before you could say anything, he stepped to you and his knees pinned yours to the wall. You couldn't move without a visible struggle. Which would be its own defeat.

'Think you're all big men, now, don't ye?' he said. 'Cos you're getting your hole from these sluts.'

'Fuck you,' you said.

Teabag wagged a finger before your face. Left to right. Right to left. You held his eyes, even with his fingertip slowly blurring through your field of vision.

'Piglet thinks he can talk to Teabag Lyons like that, does he? Just cos his dad's a cop?'

'Give it a rest, will you?' Kala said.

Teabag stopped moving his finger. He smiled.

'Letting your beor fight your battles for you now, hah? You a faggot or something?'

Your mouth was full of spit. You needed to swallow. You covered it with a mocking laugh. 'Well, she's my beor so... dunno if it makes much sense calling me a faggot, buddy.'

Teabag gave a grin. 'That right, *buddy*? You any idea, *buddy*, how many lads this wan's had in and out her cunt before you?'

Then it all happens very fast. He grabs you by your arms, pins them tight to your sides. You're shocked at how much stronger than you he is. You can't move your arms, or your legs. A quiver through the rest of the Lyons now, too. Coiled and ready.

'Ah-ah,' Teabag says.

He lurches you back so you have no balance. His legs still pinning yours to the wall, your entire upper body in a tilt, and only Teabag's grip keeping you from falling to the ground. A rush of blood to your face. Fuckheads in the Square watching. Humiliation.

'We were just leaving, Teabag,' Mush says. 'We don't want any hassle.'

Teabag's smiling face fills the sky above you. He straightens you up and flicks you in the forehead.

'Fuck off, so,' he says. He turns to Aidan. 'Not you. We've a job for you.'

Everything in you boiling as ye shuffled away from them.

'Here, Piglet!' Teabag shouted behind you. 'Decent tits on her, like.'

You pretended not to hear the clatter of laughs.

None of ye said anything as ye walked away from the Square. The girls were quiet.

'You okay, babe?' Kala said.

You gave a short nod. But you didn't look up, because your lip was trembling.

Mush started doing Teabag's voice. *'I'm fuckin' Teabag Lyons, living legend.'* The girls laughed. You were annoyed at how easily they shook off what had happened. Laughing along with Mush.

'You've still got ice cream all over you,' you said. It was smeared on the side of his face. Kala smiled and thumbed some off Mush's cheeks. 'Messy baby,' she said. You didn't like that. When Kala tried to take your hand, you acted like you hadn't noticed and tilted away from her, pretending to scratch your cheek. Ye walked side by side, not touching. Kala was looking at you now. Finally.

'That guy's, like, such a dickhead,' she said. She leaned in to you. 'You were great, though. Thank you.'

'For *what*?' You could hear the sulk in your voice.

'For sticking up for me.'

You didn't know what she was talking about. But she took your hand and went on her toes to kiss you on the neck. You saw some lads from school, noticing ye.

'No worries,' you said. When you kissed her on the mouth, you opened your eyes to check if the lads from school saw this too.

'My hero,' Kala said. For a second you thought she was mocking you, till you saw how she was smiling. Ye walked like that, hand in hand, in the turning faces of Fox Street, with a strange feeling inside. Like a stack of Jenga pieces had been wobbling inside you, but were settling into place.

Thoughts jangling about your skull as you sit at the kitchen island, trying to hold your head together. Thirty-one. By this age the Beatles had changed the course of music history several times, broken up, embarked on solo careers. Dylan had already been twenty different people. Hendrix, Morrison, Joplin and Cobain were well dead.

Dad comes into the kitchen with a tiny blot of tissue on his chin, thick with dark blood. A shaving cut. He looks you over and laughs. 'So we're both walking wounded this morning.'

Force a watery smile. Start scrolling your phone. Let the waterfall of bullshit clot your eyes till you see nothing, feel nothing.

'Good night, then?' Dad says, tapping the cut on his chin.

Watch him move about the kitchen. Slow easiness. He makes a bowl of bran flakes. Stands at his usual spot before the window, looking out at the garden as he eats. The marble on the windowsill, bleached pale in the spots where he rests his arms every morning during his two cups of tea. You will never have what he has. The contentment of a horizontal life, a world where there's no need to keep climbing. You wonder if he's ever felt this constant knot in the gut: the sense that life's a sheer cliff face and you're always on the verge of falling away from it.

'D'you ever worry?' you say. 'About whether or not you're a good man?'

'What?' He looks over at you, startled. 'Where's that coming from?'

'I just... sometimes I dunno if I'm a good man.'

He frowns. 'Sure you're a great man, Joe. There's thousands who'd say the same.'

But they don't know you. They know Jungle Heart. They know the mask. Sometimes you think you're not really a person. Just a composite of other people's opinions about you, a Frankenstein built of bullshit. You try and say that to Dad. But it's a struggle to find words that won't freak him out. Eventually you stop. There's a long silence.

Head's splitting.

'Did something happen last night, son? Someone say something to you about Kala?'

'I just... sometimes I get into these cul-de-sacs. In my head.'

He looks freaked.

'It's nothing, forget I said anything. I just need a shower.'

'Plenty of fresh towels up there,' he says, cheerful again. As you stand, he claps you on the shoulder. 'Hey. You're bigger than all of this. Remember that. Who are you?'

Force a smile. This old script.

'I'm Joe Brennan.'

'Damn right.'

He winks, like that solves anything.

When you climb the stairs, Dad's back leaning at his spot by the window, sure of his place in the world, and yours.

Helen

**Hello Helen this is Valerie Mulkerns from St Annes
we spoke last night**

Theresa gave me your number hope you don't mind

Looking forward to seeing you today

I will be in the art room come any time

My head is pounding. It takes a moment to remember where I
am. Mush's sheets smell of Lynx and old sleep, and I mash my
face deep into his pillows for a moment, inhaling him. I
cannot remember the last time I woke up to the feeling of
another presence. It makes me want to meet the day.

More messages come through.

I do hope you come

important things to discuss

about Kala

On the sofa, Mush's sleeping bag lies tangled like a question mark. There is a note written in thick red marker saying,
'Have a shower! Towels are there. Plenty of coffee waiting for
ya downstairs too.'

The café is a beehive. Noisy machines, the radio, the clatter
of conversation. Theresa is behind the counter with Lydia,
chatting. Mush is alone by the far window, a dish towel over
his shoulder, frothing milk in a metal jug, eyes cast to the
floor. He looks like an animal that has hunched to fit its cage.
When he sees me, he grins and raises a hand.

'And Lazarus arose and spoke to many,' Lydia shouts. 'How's the head, missus?'

She glances over at Mush and says, 'He's two foot taller since seeing you. Isn't he?' Theresa nods in agreement. They do this for a while; talk about Mush like he is not there. It irritates me. Lydia hands me a cup of violent-smelling espresso. 'Now. That'll blow those panda eyes off you.'

The coffee is like tar, but it works. Everything quickens, a dimmer switch brightening the world. My heart rising to meet it.

St Anne's looms ahead. Already from a distance, I see that the school yard is smaller than I remember. Life is like this: immense when you are inside it, but manageable from the outside, touched from a distance. I remind myself I am not part of Kinlough; I am outside this world, safe from its effects. I do this to paper over the churn in me as I approach the gates. I can already feel my heart quickening as I approach the yard. Theresa has insisted on accompanying me. It turns out that the twins work in the cubby shed at the corner of the yard, giving people tickets for parking spaces on Sundays; Theresa has come to give them shit about missing the hen party. I feel a sense of solidarity with them already. She asks about Joe, if I think he got home okay. Mush had been nodding off on the sofa last night, the video playing for the twentieth time, when Joe bolted out of his seat and staggered to the door. I heard him clattering down the stairs. She tells me to come and say hi to the twins when I am finished, and crosses the car park to the cubby shed.

The yard grows larger around me once I step inside it. I see the exact spot where Kala stood, the way she looked at me for the last time. I see her face, the pain in her eyes, and for a moment I think I cannot go any further. But my feet continue to walk me forward.

The corridor is dark, floor shining with threads of light. My footsteps echo in the church-like stillness. Girls' schools.

Cauldrons of yearning and cruelty. The walls are lined with framed pictures of classes dating back decades. Recent photographs, with their frictionless digital sheen, gradually fading to sepia blurs, then black-and-white.

Mrs Mulkerns said she would be in the art room.

I walk through the main hall, where the statue of the Virgin Mary still stands, the words 'Behold your mother' carved into heavy stone. Kala used to salute this statue whenever we passed it, feigning surprise. 'Ah, there you are, Mam!' she would say, and teachers would glare. In such moments I felt invincible. We had no idea how quickly time was running out.

Mrs Mulkerns prepares tea by the paint-spattered sink in the corner, dignified in her movements, a weightless grace. The art room is unchanged – the heavy chemical smell, underachieved sculptures, walls feathered with students' work, tabletops rainbow-speckled in paint. Ruined brushes, petrified like specimens in clouded jars. Whenever Aoife and I could not find Kala in the yard at lunchbreak, we always found her here, at Mrs Mulkerns's desk, discussing some art project. But things changed, sometime in October. The air in the art room was electric whenever Kala saw us hovering at the door. Mrs Mulkerns looking flustered, hot red in her cheeks. Kala noisily gathering her things and brushing past us. Something was happening between Kala and Mrs Mulkerns in this room, but Kala kept it behind walls, away from me.

'I've taught many talented artists in St Anne's,' Mrs Mulkerns says. She traces a fingertip along a grid of shelves labelled with students' names. 'None as good as your sister, of course. Theresa always had a great eye. But Donna Lyons? Tremendous potential.'

She plucks a folder from its slot, and hands it to me. On the cover, an ornately handwritten *Donna Lyons*. Beneath it, in graffiti font, *Donna'z Linez*.

'Her composition has improved remarkably,' Mulkerns says. 'Theresa's been helping her grow. I can tell.'

I look through Donna's work. It is good. Very good, actually. I stop on a charcoal profile of Mush, his neck corded with hollows. From this side, he is unscarred. It is like peering into a parallel world, looking at the man he might have become.

'Of course,' Mulkerns says, 'talent is widespread. Very few go the distance.' She hands me another folder, its colour faded. Kala's unmistakable scrawl on the cover. 'I think you'll agree there was plenty of raw talent here.'

As she makes the tea I look through the contents. Sketches of us, drawn in different styles, based on Kala's Polaroids. Aoife's mouth. Mush's hair. My nose. Constellations of facial features, swarming through one another.

'Aren't they wonderful?' Mulkerns says.

I stop on a pencil drawing of Kala and me, arms over one another's shoulders. This is copied from a photograph. In the drawing, Kala has straightened her crooked eye. I am wearing her earrings. The only colour is a sunlike-throb she has made, hovering between us.

'Get to my age,' Mulkerns says, 'and it's hard not to try and look for some sort of legacy. I take comfort knowing how many strong St Anne's girls are out in the world, making their mark. I read those articles you did a couple of years ago. About those poor women. Very impressive work. You might've been a detective.'

I flinch. I could tell her that the police were, at best, a source of facts designed to obscure the truth. Foot soldiers of the status quo. Instead, I ask her why she invited me here. It sounds more abrupt than I would like.

Mulkerns's eyes are busy. 'I've been wondering if what happened to Kala... if I had some role in it.'

'Sorry?'

She pulls on her fingers. Something in her eyes unnerves me. That feeling you get in a dream, when you are just about to fall.

'Helen, did Kala ever tell you about her mother?'

One morning, not long after the night of the Crawley House, Kala called to my house by herself. She had sent me a text the night before.

Hey babe pak a bag 4 2moro & cash... will explane in morning b ready!!! :-) xxx

Aoife was usually the organizer. This was new.

By now I had 30 euro in Mam's jewellery box. I had perfected my hair technique: if I showered the night before, went to bed with my hair wet, and got up early enough to shake the sleepiness out of it, my hair would find a rumpled turbulence by the time Kala arrived. Today was going to be a girls' day. The boys would be practising tunes in Joe's all afternoon – Mush joked that Joe was like the sergeant in *Full Metal Jacket*, drilling him and Aidan for hours till they got something right. Whenever we met the boys after practice, they would be flush-faced, a shout in their voices which I first thought was from excitement, before I realized it was because their ears were ringing.

I had my eyeliner slashes done and was wearing an aggressively red lipstick that Aoife claimed to have shoplifted from Brown Thomas, though I did not believe her. Misty barked when the doorbell rang. I saw Kala's blurred form through the fogged glass.

'Got your bits?' she said. She was wearing a choker and had her mouth painted wine red. She had done something with her lashes that I would need to learn. Her hair was sensational. It turned in a careless wave over her crooked eye. We allowed ourselves to be taken in by each other's gaze, catching ourselves in the act till it pushed at the edges of our mouths. Shy smiles. I thought of when a mirror faces another mirror, and they accordion outwards into two infinities.

Kala ruffled Misty behind the ears as I took my bag. She leaned in the door and peered upstairs. 'Hi there,' she said to

Theresa, who was sitting on the top step, watching us. 'I like your runners.'

Theresa opened her mouth to speak but her face went red and she pretended to be distracted by something on her sleeve.

'I used to have runners like them,' Kala said. 'With the flashing lights. Very cool.'

Theresa continued playing with her sleeve, mouthing the words to a song like she was unaware of us.

I rolled my eyes as I walked out the door. 'Later!' I shouted into the house. Dad was still in bed, so I gave the door a good slam.

We should have gone down the laneway to Aoife's, to collect her. But Kala had a plan for today, and there was an illicit thrill to realizing that Aoife was not part of it.

The horizon yawned open at the entrance of the estate, stretching itself towards the Prom. Kala got two rollies from her shirt pocket. I took mine wordlessly. We were cool like that. As I held it between my lips I thought of Kala rolling a cigarette for me in the quiet, earlier that morning, in the smoke-threads of her incense. How she had thought of me.

She would not tell me where we were going.

It was only as we moved through Hogan's Square towards the bus station that I realized we were leaving Kinlough.

There was a smile in Kala's voice.

'What ya reckon, babe? Wanna come with me to Dublin?'

I blinked. My first thought was about what time I was supposed to be back for dinner. Kala was looking at me, waiting for my response.

I grinned. 'Pure class.'

Dublin was a maze of gushing tributaries into which we weaved, talking non-stop through the frenzy of faces, splitting ourselves around clusters of people like a river pouring around stones just to merge once more into the link of each other's arm, admiring everything, mocking everything. We bought postcards of Patti Smith and Kim Gordon at a cool indoor market. Kala bought a Rage Against the Machine patch, a black square cloth with the letters RATM in white. 'I'm gonna get Nana to sew this onto my bag!' she said. We found an underground shop that sold bootleg CDs from concerts by people we had been born too late to see, people from the nineties like Nirvana, Jeff Buckley, Mary Margaret O'Hara. 'Everything was so real back then,' Kala said. She took a photo of the bootleg shelves on her camera-phone. I bought a tape of an early PJ Harvey gig. The cover was a home-made black-and-white photocopy of Polly Jean, her eyes smeared in long daubes of dark eyeshadow.

'My make-up is like hers,' I said.

'Babe, her make-up's like yours,' Kala said.

Grafton Street was huge, and the HMV on it was somehow even bigger. 'They've a whole room upstairs that's just for jazz,' Kala said. 'Fucking jazz, like!' I did not know anything about jazz, but I flicked through the CDs there anyway, to try it on, see how it felt. Kala was happy because she had tracked down a CD she had been trying to find for ages. The cover was a bombed-out photo of a blurry guitar in neon pink. 'According to *Hot Press* and *NME*,' Kala said, 'this is the pinnacle of sonic achievement.'

I turned the case over. *My Bloody Valentine*, by Loveless. Or *Loveless*, by My Bloody Valentine. I had never heard of it. Them.

'You can't find this type of thing in Kinlough, you know,' Kala said. She pursed her lips and nodded. 'This is old-school magic. Real stuff.'

The CD cost 20 euro. That was most of Kala's money. I offered to go halves on it with her but she said no, it was a gift for Joe.

'You know how he bought me an actual camera-phone after that night at the Crawley House?' she said. 'He's, like, so sweet.'

*

We ate at a canal, our feet dangling over the water. Kala had Nutella sandwiches wrapped in tinfoil and a couple of Capri-Suns. It showed how much forethought she had put into our day. It made me feel special. I watched her from the side of my eye, humming to herself as the world pivoted around her.

There was a looseness to both of us now, a sort of relaxed high.

Nutella crested out between the crusts with every bite. Kala got chocolate stains on the edges of her mouth and when I motioned to let her know, she slowly raised the full sandwich to her face and squished it flat against her cheek and smeared the ruined bread and Nutella all over her jaw. We stared at each other for a moment, then burst out laughing. People looked at us – hard-faced, Dublin looks – and it did not matter. No one beyond us mattered.

'I'm dying to know what this sounds like,' Kala said, taking the CD from her bag. 'I was talking to Luke, the guy who runs Cailleach Record & Book Shoppe? He told me this album *sounds* like what déjà vu *feels* like.'

I had no idea what that meant. Which meant it was cool.

Mam had had a theory about déjà vu. I had read about it, in one of her notebooks. It came in the middle of a six-page-long sentence about time. Her idea was that everything that happens only takes place in the present. There is no past or future: when we think of the past, our memories occur in the present; when we imagine the future, we only do so from the standpoint of the present. Everything is always happening simultaneously on this one plane of existence, but we experience it as a flux. 'The churning surface of an infinite ocean.' That was how Mam described it. 'We live in the churning surface of the infinite ocean,' Mam wrote, 'and each one of us is a churning surface of the infinite ocean.'

Mam thought that, because everything that happens only ever happens in The Now – that is how she always wrote it, The Now – this meant that all things that have happened and that will happen are always happening, simultaneously, in the permanent Now. I tried to explain this to Kala. I told her to imagine every film ever made, projected onto one silk screen in a riot of furious transparencies, playing out over one another in real time, for ever.

Because our minds are finite, Mam said, we can only experience one Now at a time – but déjà vu was what happens whenever two Nows slip through one another.

'That's some trippy shit,' Kala said.

'Yeah.'

'Where two Nows meet... Fuck. Your mam sounds like she was the best.'

Kala hesitated. I suddenly knew what was coming. The stone ledge of the canal was hot under me. The water, filled with sliced light. I swallowed.

'What... happened to her?' Kala said.

I never thought I would talk about Mam with anyone. But something strange happened there, sitting by the water. It was as though the words had been there in my mouth, waiting. Part of me was outside myself, watching as I spoke. I heard myself tell Kala about the stale air of the bedroom, whenever the Creature took hold. About the day when I was eleven and the Creature turned up barefoot at the school yard, calling for me. She was in Mam's dressing gown and nightie. Her feet were all cut up. She was wearing Mam's clothes, Mam's face. Kids were laughing at her. The Creature kept calling my name, but when I went to her, her eyes were blank. Like she did not know me. 'It's me, Mam,' I said. 'You're not my Helen,' she said.

Later that evening I watched the Creature fold herself into a mound under the blanket. A shaft of dusty light splitting the curtains. Dad humming downstairs because he was scared of the Creature. Theresa downstairs, playing by herself. They were useless to me. I was alone in this.

The Creature was blank eyes in a bed. A Mam shape, mocking me from the sheets.

I straightened and told the Creature, 'They're afraid of you, but I'm not. So you'd better give my mam back.'

I searched the Creature's face for some sign of Mam, calling to me from the dark inside. But the Creature turned away from me and began thumbing at the blanket.

The next day at school, the other kids teased me, calling out my name in the Creature's cracked voice. I spent the afternoon fidgeting in my desk, blood ringing in my skull, worried she would appear at the school gates again. But she did not.

When I got home, I saw that Dad had forgotten to leave the potatoes peeled and soaking for dinner. I was muttering to myself as I stalked to the bathroom to wash my hands. But the bathroom door was closed. There was a note on it.

Don't come in. Call an ambulance.

The canal water carved at my eyes. I was flexing my jaw now, over and over. Kala was looking at me.

'I remember thinking I should just go straight to the phone. But I wanted to see.'

My knees were bouncing. I could not stop them. I told myself to stop. Fucking stop shaking, idiot. 'I always want to see.'

Kala shuffled closer to me. When she tried to put an arm around me, I shook my head. Even though I wanted her there. 'Please don't,' I said. It felt as though there was a pillar of fire inside me, and I needed to hold still to stop it from tilting over and destroying things. I could see Kala's hands, in her lap. She turned one of them over, palm up to the sun, and let it rest like a bridge between her legs and mine.

I hesitated, then put my hand in hers. She closed her fingers and squeezed.

'Oh, babe,' she said.

The canal bank was full of people. We were the only ones there. When my hands trembled, Kala did not let go. Even when my hand became clammy, she was there, holding.

We sat like that in the sun for a long time.

*

On the bus back from Dublin, we listened to our favourite PJ Harvey song on repeat, one earphone each. 'We Float'. Biting our bottom lips and smiling every time the chorus hit. Ireland blurring past us in a rush of fields.

Kala leaned against the window, her face turned to the sun.

'He's special,' she said. 'Joe. He's like, so nice.' She pulled at a thick cord of her hair, staring at it. 'Now I need to, like, not fuck it up, you know?' She gave a nervous laugh, and I mirrored it, but I was not sure what she meant, or if I was supposed to ask her to explain.

'You ever been to Joe's house?' Kala said. 'It's huge. Like, ginormous. And his parents are... They're like something off telly, you know? This American sitcom family with a massive fridge. *Honey, I'm home!*'

She gestured to herself, waving her hands. The movement was odd. Uncontrolled.

'When I was up there I felt like I was this... *thing* that had managed to sneak into their lovely home... you know?'

The joy had faded from her face. Her voice was smaller. 'And I'm thinking, how long before he really sees me?'

She had dipped her head, so her hair hung like a curtain over her face. She pulled the frayed black rubber at the frame of her window, tearing it in pinches.

'I thought that was really cool, Helen. Not cool, that's not the right... It was brave. What you said to me earlier. About your mam. You're... you're so strong.'

It was the strangest feeling, hearing her say this. I knew something real had happened, sitting at the canal. I had felt it moving in Kala, in myself, as though some sort of knot had untied to open a space in my chest and that, even as I fell through it, that space within me was filling with a light that was growing fuller and brighter, and I knew that this light coming from inside me was not mine, that it was Kala's, it was my friend's, and I knew in that moment that we were friends, and that she was giving it to me, her light, so that it actually was mine. She was giving it to me because she wanted me to have it and all I wanted was to give it back to her too, so that even as I was falling into myself in that moment I was also soaring through myself, above myself, beyond myself, further into the everything that was not myself, into a world where there were no separations, only souls moving through one another, and she was giving that to me, my friend, giving me a world, and I loved it and I was scared of it and I loved how scared I was of it because that meant it was real. And I had never been more inside or outside myself than in that moment, and I wanted to tell Kala that. But when I looked over at her, she still had her head down, her fingers worrying at the black rubber. There was the strangest feeling coming off her. The way she held her shoulders. The drag of her breath. Her hair still obscured her face, but her mouth was moving. It took a moment to realize that she was whispering. I leaned closer. Her voice was almost all breath.

'I've never met my mam,' she said. 'I don't know her.'

A sudden patter of dark stains on her jeans. She looked up at me. Her eyes were shining. A face I had not seen before. It made me feel like I did when Theresa was a baby and I used to stare at the soft top of her head. The nausea of something so tender.

'Nana never lets me ask about her,' Kala said, taking my hand. *'Don't ask questions with answers you won't like.* There are no photos of my mam in the house.'

Kala was crushing my fingers in hers.

'She's never made any contact?'

Kala wiped at her nose and shook her head, made a whimpering noise.

'Like, what's so wrong with me?' she said. 'Why just leave me?'

I felt the rash rising on my neck and wanted to put a hand to my throat. I had asked myself the same question about Mam.

The fields were rushing outside.

'And your dad?' I said.

Kala shook her head. 'I've never told anyone this. They wouldn't get it, you know?'

I squeezed her hand quickly. A pulse, which she immediately returned.

She reached down into her bag and took out her sketchbook.

'I found this in my room ages ago. I'm sure it used to belong to my mam.'

The most recent drawings were Kala's fragments – a dog's snout, a white van, Joe's smile. But as Kala flipped the pages backwards, to earlier drawings, things got darker. The pages were almost black with ink. Drawings of girls, teenagers, grown women, nuns. They all had long branches coiling out of their eyes and mouths.

Kala pointed to a tiny signature at the bottom of these pages. 'Fiona L.'

'Have you shown this to the Mammy?' I said.

'No way. She'd flip the lid, like. But I deserve to know about my mother, don't I?'

'Of course.'

'I keep worrying cos... like, Joe's Mr Perfect Family and I don't want him to think I'm this... fucking weirdo, like.'

'You're not a weirdo, babe,' I said. 'You're a total goddess.' I did not even feel embarrassed saying that to her. We were inside something now, Kala and me. Cradled in the core of a thing that allowed us to say stuff like that. My heart was going like mad. 'Kala, you're like... you're the coolest person I've ever met.'

Kala wiped at her eyes and sighed. She took my hand in hers again and rested her head on my shoulder. Her smell was tea tree oil, shea butter.

'I know what I am,' she said.

Mush

HERE'S THE THING about working with someone: ye need to be telepathic, otherwise there's a stop-start vibe to everything. You can always tell when there's new staff in a place, cos the rhythm's off. One person turns and bumps into the colleague they didn't know was right behind them – they reach to the shelf for the same bottle and their arms stutter. But work long enough with anyone and ye combine into a Swiss Army knife. That's how Mam and me usually are in the caf.

But not today. An edge to her voice that'd tear the face off you. 'Two lattes, hop to it.'

She has us on the angry see-saw. One of us gets into a sulk and this pulls both of us into a sulk and then we're both sulking at being made to sulk and it's only a matter of time till one of us bites the head off the other.

Patches of damp under my arms.

Mam always gets like this during the Races. Kinloughers mostly stay home for Race Week while Fox Street gets swollen with fuckheads from all over. Money sloshing around, women with hats like bird's nests and men with stupid PowerPoint voices, yawping in salmon shirts. Some baldy fuck with a head on him like a thumb clicked his fingers in my face earlier when I took too long making his ristretto. I could see Mam's nostrils flare but I pretended it wasn't happening, cos this is how I always get by: zone the fuck out. We gotta keep the fuckheads happy, even when they come hammered into the caf, careering like lost atoms, looking to use our jacks without buying anything. Mam usually finds a way to schmooze them, plants a seed for them to call in the next day for a hungover breakfast. But today she's snapping. Some young wan hobbled in during the lunch rush, shitfaced – make-up pure smudgy, stilettos dangling over her wrist – and was making her way to use our jacks when Mam let such a roar at her that the girl nearly toppled backwards.

That was what I loved, back in the day, when Kala worked with us for Race Week; she took the edges off Mam. It was gas, Mam had been wary about taking Kala on for the busiest week of the year – 'A bit too cool for school, that wan' – but within Kala's first hour I saw Mam was impressed. Her work vibe was like Mam's, this boisterous, nudge-with-the-elbow style of joking with punters, knocking a bit of craic out of them. She'd shout, 'Ah, it's yourself!' whenever a regular came in, and her accent would go a bit more Kinlough as she chatted. I could see it was a role she was playing, but it suited her. This eager busy-bee buzz, sticking the orders up in the kitchen and reciting them to me with a military clip as she wheeled her way back out onto the floor. 'Two cappuccinos, babe, one with an extra shot, and a green tea to go.' Her notes were always underlined if there was anything special – skinny cappuccino, double shot mocha. She dotted all her 'i's with love hearts. If we could've afforded it beyond Race Week, Mam would've had Kala working the whole time.

Kala told Helen and Aoife stories about the caf during the sleepover we had that week. Joe didn't know about how I slept at Kala's, some nights. It wasn't my idea not to tell him, but Kala said Joe would get weird if he knew I was sharing a bed with her and the girls. I felt bad about lying, but she said feck it, what Joe doesn't know can't hurt him. So I'd tell Mam I was sleeping at Joe's, and I'd say nothing to Joe about sleeping at Kala's. I told myself it wasn't like I was betraying Joe, I was only being loyal to something else.

The secrecy meant there was something magic to Kala's room, even though it was just me and the girls chilling. Kala's room was pure massive like. Took up the whole bottom half of her house – you could fit fifty people in it, no bother. I was lying on a beanbag, cosy as anything, watching the stars appear and disappear in the windows along the tops of the walls, imagining we were in a submarine, gliding along the bottom of a secret ocean, like in *The Abyss* or *Das Boot*. Aoife was playing snake on her phone and the bleeps added to the submarine effect. Whenever she died she threw her phone down on the bed and shouted, 'Fucking bollocks.' Every time Aoife shouted, Helen's lips twitched and her fingers tapped on the book she was reading. Helen was pure contained, but I could tell when something was getting up her nose. I asked what she was reading and she held up the book – *How to Disappear Completely and Never Be Found*.

'Classic,' Kala said. She was arranging her Polaroids into a new photo album. 'That's another one Luke gave me. He says I'm his faaaavourite customer.'

Luke was this burly lad who owned Cailleach Record & Book Shoppe, the weird second-hand place around the corner from the caf. He'd a handlebar tache and frizzy hair, always wearing a *Swamp Thing* T-shirt. Mam called him harmless, which is one of the worst things you could say about a person. He'd call in to us for a takeaway cup of tea and Mam would wrinkle her nose. 'What'd possess someone to get a takeaway cup of tea? Surely he has a bloody kettle.' He'd started coming in daily, now that Kala was working with us. He chatted to Kala each time. Now she had stacks of ratty paperbacks from his shop, scattered about her room.

'I'm bored,' Aoife said. 'Vomitron, put some music on there.'

Helen didn't look up from her book.

Aoife looked at Kala. 'Vomitron's ears must be full of puke.'

I asked Kala why Luke gave her so much stuff.

'Because he's sound,' she said. 'I've had tea with him in his shop a few times. We talk about, like, philosophy and stuff. He wants to show me his personal library some time.'

Aoife sniffed. 'Wonder what Joe would say about that.'

We all knew Kala would never mention anything to Joe about hanging out with Luke. Joe'd get in a pure mood about it, like. I was noticing Joe's moodiness more and more, since the Crawley House.

And there was some amount of static between himself and Aidan. Feckin' edge to it these days. Last time we were practising in Joe's, they were like a gaggle of hens. Our big plan now was to get a solid set of fifteen tunes and play a gig in Kala's room around her birthday, during the Halloween holidays. Aidan had all these notions about charging people five quid on the door to come in, which Joe thought was stupid. I didn't care either way, I just wanted to fecking play, like. Sometimes I felt like knocking their heads together and telling them to agree on something for once. But no one listened to me.

Anyway, the three of us were having a break during practice, chatting shite, when Joe started bitching about Helen, saying she was no craic. And I remembered something Aidan once said to me: 'Joe's problem is, he's used to being the golden boy, the smartest fella in the classroom. But we don't live in a classroom.' I was thinking this was why Joe took against Helen so much. She didn't treat him like he was special, like he was the smartest. Joe was saying the night of the Crawley House had all been Helen's fault, that we'd never have been there if not for her. Which just wasn't true, like. But Joe didn't care about facts, he was making a point. He said that, if she'd been a fella, he'd have slapped her that night. I didn't like that. He must've felt it, cos he added it was stupid you can't hit a girl just cos they're a girl. 'A dickhead's a dickhead, right?' he said. 'Whether they're a girl or not. I mean… if women want to be equal and stuff.' I'd only opened my mouth when, out of nowhere, Aidan crossed the room and shoved Joe hard into the wall and grabbed him by the throat. 'You're nothing but a mong-child,' he said.

It gave me a fright. Grabbing Joe by the throat. That was Teabag-level behaviour. But Aidan wasn't Teabag – just before he stormed out of Joe's, I saw it was cos he was about to cry. That scared me more.

Aidan talked a big game in front of the others, but when it was just him and me I could tell he was miserable. Freaked out by his own family. The same details he told the others with his legs wide, hands behind his head, he'd say to me in whispers, hunched over, his bottom lip turning down between sentences. And there were things about his new job on the farm he only ever told me. The dogfights nearly always ended with one of the dogs too fucked to keep alive. Aidan hadn't had to finish one off yet, but he knew that day was coming. For now Uncle Ger had him working in disposal. This happened the day after the fights. Some lad named Blinkie had taught Aidan the process. First you'd to put what was left of the dog in a bag. Aidan said the smell got right under his nails. He'd asked for gloves and the lads had laughed at him. 'They've got this pure corrosive stuff, quicklime or acid or something. They keep it in a pink carton, like detergent. Once the dog's been bagged I gotta pour a load of that shite into the bag, enough to dissolve the thing. I tie the bag up and flake it into this pit in one of the sheds. Sometimes when you throw down a new bag, it bursts one of the older ones. You ever seen a skull, in real life? Wherever you move it feels like it's watching you. Like it's smiling.' There was no swagger in Aidan when he said this. He looked a foot smaller.

So I knew how, under all the shapes he threw, he wasn't doing great. I knew I should've been doing something to help. But it freaked me out. Even years later, when Aidan was gone off the rails – he'd vanish for days, mobile off, and end up calling from some hole in the middle of nowhere sounding awful asking for money to get back to Kinlough; or the time someone called Auntie Pauline to say they'd found him asleep on the golf course; or when he'd stay in his room for a week, not even playing Xbox, just lying there with the curtains closed – even then I still didn't get it. Auntie Pauline would ask me to talk to Aidan, but whenever I'd see how wobbly he was, I'd hear this weird irritation come into my voice, even though I didn't feel thick at him, not really. It's just I was meant to be the trembly one that wet the bed when we were kids. Aidan was meant to be the cool one, not giving a fuck. So whenever Aidan started seeming fragile, I automatically went kind of hard, to keep our see-saw in balance. I'd tell him he shouldn't spend so much time drinking alone, and he'd give me a big smile and say we could get a load of cans and sit by the window in the caf that night and get twisted, and just like that, he'd be back on top of the see-saw and I could slip back into my role, reacting meekly to anything he done. I'd squirm and say, 'I dunno man,' but deep down I'd be glad, cos it felt like we were ourselves again, and everything with Aidan would end up fine. Which was a mistake.

'Mush, are you after going deaf or something?'

Mam's glaring at me.

'For the tenth bloody time, two Americanos and one mocha.'

She gives an apologetic smile to a clatter of Dublin fuck-heads down for the races. They don't even look at her.

She stands next to me as I grind the beans. 'Will you wake up? I can't do this all by meself.'

I brush past her and squirt the chocolate gunk in the bottom of the mocha mug. Pour in the espresso, whisk it up. Froth the milk.

Jesus, I'm in a foul humour. More bloody journalists lurking about the caf, too, nosing around for any info they can get. Mam clears them out fairly lively, but still.

Whenever I get like this, all suffocated in my head, like, I remember a little card Theresa once made for the twins. 'We do not see things as they are, we see them as we are.' It's a quote from some wan with a name like mayonnaise. I've spent a lot of time turning that line over in my head. At first I hated it, cos it means there's no reality, only what we feel. And that's a load of bollocks. But there's something to it, all the same. Like, life's indifferent. It's got enough joy and shite in it to mirror whatever you're bringing to the table, day in, day out. So on days when I look out on Fox Street and I don't see any goodness to the world, I try and catch myself, cos I know it's there, and if I can't see it, it's my own fault. My brain's just focusing on reasons to feel depressed about shit. If you can't get one laugh out of every day, you're fucked.

Not a peep out of the twins since that weird photo of myself and Dudley in the booth. Normally they'd be the ones to cheer me up. Send me a Snapchat or a few memes during the day.

It's only when I check my phone I realize – sure I haven't turned the fecking thing on since last night. Eejit. Straight away I forgive the twins, apologize to them in my head for thinking badly of them.

Sure enough, I switch on my phone and it goes mental with messages. Theresa. Auntie Pauline. Marie. Marie. Marie. Marie. Marie.

Theresa:

Twins didn't show for work at the car park today

Can you do something about this

Situations getting stupid

Pauline:

Mush are you talking to D&M

They're sending strange messages

When I open Marie's messages, it's one photo after another. Always the same picture. It's them, as babies. They're sitting in Kala's lap. Someone's drawn an X through Kala's face, and theirs.

Helen

I HAVE BEEN walking about the Warren with my phone before me, trying to find my way. I am late. Walking all the way to Carthy was a mistake. I started on the Coast Road, squinting against the glare of the light, holding myself as the seagulls blew about above me. Tiny bodies clattering against the sky. I thought I heard my name whipping through noise. I held my arms tighter to myself and leaned into the roaring.

The first thing I did after speaking to Mrs Mulkerns was go to Kala's house. I knocked on the door, and waited.

'Ms Lanann? It's Helen Laughlin. Are you there?'

All the curtains were drawn. No sound from inside, like yesterday.

'Ms Lanann?' I said, knocking again. 'I'd love to speak with you, if you have time. I'm going to leave my details under the doormat, okay? Call me any time.'

Going deeper into the Warren, I put my earbuds in and listen again to the recording on my phone. I hold the buds tight, sharp enough to hurt. A noisy crackle, the thumbed sounds of static and a heart thump in the ears, and the recording comes to life.

Mrs Mulkerns's voice, echoing in the art room: *She came to me not long after the school year began. This would've been a few weeks before—*

My loud voice, too close to the recorder: *Can you say who, for the recording?*

Mrs Mulkerns's voice, still hollow in the art room: *Kala. Kala came to me. To talk about her mother. This was a couple of weeks before she went missing. She'd been doing her own—*

My voice interrupts again: *Sorry.* Here the recording muffles and cracks, and when I speak next my voice is quieter, the room cavernous around it, because I have slid the phone across the table to Mrs Mulkerns. *It's better to start at the beginning,* I say. *For the sake of clarity, we need to get the timeline clear. Talk about Fiona first.*

It is remarkable to hear the composure in my voice. The veneer of cool professionalism. How quickly the front comes up. I had been sitting down when Mrs Mulkerns first told me what she knew, but as she spoke it felt like I was falling, levers and handles breaking away in my hands as I tried to stop the plummet. There is nothing like real shock. The flash thud of the heart, the cold blood.

But on the recording, my voice sounds in control. Impervious.

Mrs Mulkerns: *When everything with Kala's mother happened I was only a young teacher – barely a couple of years into the job, very idealistic, all of it. Her situation wasn't something people talked about in the staffroom but… we all talked around it, if you get me. Stray sentences, a raised eyebrow here and there, you know? Tiny things to signal how we'd all noticed the changes in Fiona Lanann's behaviour. Constant trips to the bathroom, sick days, refusing to take part in PE. This is before the visible physical changes, once she was a few months along. It was very gradual, then very sudden. She stopped attending school. I tried to address this with some of my colleagues at the time. 'Surely we have a duty of care to the girl,' and so on. I was naive, perhaps.*

The Warren is an impossible maze of roads. Every stone-wall bend and split-artery road looks the same. The maps on my phone are no help, because nothing out here is named.

I drove out to the Lanann house one evening, full of ideas about how I could help. Convinced I would be welcomed with open arms. When the Mammy didn't invite me in, I

*asked if I could see Fiona. The Mammy refused. I should
have taken this as a sign that I wasn't welcome. Instead, I
thought to myself, well, she's just trying to maintain appearances, doesn't want me to see how Fiona looks at this stage.
So I decided the best thing would be to speak frankly. I told
her that Fiona's situation was an open secret in the school.
I said, I am not here to judge. But we're all aware that
Fiona has gotten herself into some trouble. Looking back, I
don't know what response I was expecting. I think… I must
have thought the Mammy would appreciate my honesty,
welcome my solidarity.*

(pause)

*I was a fool. The look that came over her face, Helen. It
was as if I'd slapped her.*

(pause)

I'd said something that simply could not be said.

The wind is howling in the Warren. I can see the rise of
the roads in the distance, and the clutter of Carthy buildings
nestled there. Two people walk ahead of me, leaning in to
one another, arms linked. I think of Mush and me, walking
like that down Fox Street last night. What Kala would have
thought of that sight. The man ahead is tall and has Mush's
curly hair. He walks slowly, his gait all crooked, supporting
himself with a cane. He looks too young for such a thing. The
woman clutches his arm as she looks up at him and laughs.
Her face is obscured by her hair blowing about.

I avert my gaze and pick up speed, passing them by.

– Mulkerns: *I remember the Mammy's exact words. 'If
you know what's good for you, you will never come to this
house again.'*

Me, dim in the background: *She threatened you?*

Mulkerns: *I can still see her face. Absolutely petrified that
I was there. I never saw Fiona after that. No one did.*

Me: *Why do you think that was?*

There is a long pause on the recording. I can see it now:
Mrs Mulkerns, staring at my phone, as though counting along

to the seconds on the recorder. When she speaks again, her voice is quieter. I have to struggle to hear it.

There was a way these situations used to be handled. Even in the eighties. A girl would get into trouble and, once the baggy clothes failed to hide the bump, she would be sent away for a few months before the baby was born. After the child arrived, mother and baby would quietly return home and the family would raise the baby like another sibling. The mother of the family would pretend it was her child, a late miracle, perhaps, a surprise gift, while the biological mother pretended to be an older sister. It was... far more common than you might think.

Me: *So why didn't the Lananns do this? Why not pretend that Fiona was Kala's sister?*

Another pause.

Mulkerns: *Because of me. I'd showed up on their door, blabbing about how everyone in the school knew Fiona was pregnant. A lie only works when you think other people will believe it. I made it impossible for them to put on the charade. And there I was, thinking I was helping the Lananns with my frankness. But I was making their situation impossible.*

When she speaks again, her voice is thick. *I carried that guilt for years.*

Me: *What about Fiona? Did no one make any noise over the fact that she had vanished?*

Mulkerns: *Girls didn't 'vanish'. They were just... sent away. Usually to family in England or some such. I mean, that was the done thing back then. I cannot overstate how commonplace it—*

Me: *For the sake of the recording, can you say how old Fiona was when all this happened?*

Mulkerns: *Thirteen? Fourteen, maybe.*

Me: *...And people knew this. Teachers knew this. A pregnant child.*

In the recording, I can hear the false calmness in my voice.

Mulkerns: *It was a different time, Helen. I'm not trying to justify anything but try to understand... it was possible to both 'know' and 'not know' these things.*

(pause)

Then one day, thirteen years later, I go into a room of new first years and Kala is sitting there.

Me: *You knew she was Fiona's daughter straight away?*

Mulkerns: *Oh, it was unmistakable. I didn't even need to look up the name. She was a Lanann, all right. Through and through. It was like you'd cut the head off her grand-father, her mother.*

Carthy rises on the horizon. I arrive on Main Street. I search for the coffeehouse, Googling for the exact address. Mrs Mulkerns's voice comes through clear.

Kala was a good student. Original. I liked her. I taught her for two full years.

Me: *When did she start asking about Fiona?*

Mulkerns: *She stayed after class one day in September and asked if I could give her old issues of the school magazine, from the seventies. She said it was for an art project. I believed her. Later I realized she had figured out her mother must once have been a student at St Anne's. Kala was doing her own little investigation, trying to learn about her mam.*

When Mrs Mulkerns said this, my mind started to race so much that I did not hear a lot of what followed.

Kala was doing her own little investigation, trying to learn about her mam.

This had been my idea. I was the one who started this.

After Dublin, Kala and I took several secret bus trips. Each time, the Warren was the threshold that let us know we had successfully escaped Kinlough. As our bus shrank into a new horizon, I imagined us running away together, vanishing into the fabric of the world, living at our private pitch for ever. It was a running joke between us, all the things we would do when we finally ran away for good. 'When we run away, we'll do *this*.' 'When we run away, we'll do *that*.' More and more, it felt like it was not a joke at all, but a promise being made, the sort you glimpse in the corner of your eye. We would disembark the bus at random and wander wherever we had landed. Sometimes it took hours to get back.

Our mams were always with us on those trips. Even if we never spoke of them, they were amongst us. We both knew it. It was on the last of the bus trips, at the very end of the summer holidays, that I first suggested to Kala that there might be some record of her mother at St Anne's. 'Maybe one of the older teachers would have taught her?' I said. Kala nodded thoughtfully. She said we could investigate once school started again the following week. Another plan. Another secret.

That evening, we arrived at Aidan's shed to help carry different parts of Aidan's drum kit to Kala's basement. From now on, the boys would be rehearsing in Kala's room. They could make as much noise there as they wanted. The guitars and amps were already there.

Aoife would not look at Kala and me when we arrived, pretending to listen as Mush told her how he boiled the strings of his bass every month to keep them fresh.

As we walked to Kala's, carrying the kit, Aoife asked Kala, 'Where were you today?' Her voice was striving for something between amusement and boredom. But I could hear her neediness. 'I called up to your house earlier. Your nana said you'd been out since the morning.'

'You should've texted me,' Kala said.

Aoife said that she had. Three times. Kala frowned and said she had not received any messages. This was a lie. I had seen her ignore the messages.

In Kala's room, I slumped on a beanbag and leafed through her photo album, looking at Kala's record of all our summer adventures. She had written cute captions for each one. At one point I yawned, and Aoife called across the room, 'Getting sleepy there, Vomitron?' She put on a baby voice. 'Need a widdle nappy-nap?'

I turned a page and sighed. 'I'm always so tired after our road trips,' I said. I could not resist glancing up. Watching the words carve their way in. I thought of how a paper cut happens, the delay between the incision and the blood rising to the skin. I saw it happen in Aoife's face. The tiniest, almost invisible flutter of feeling. I turned another page, pretending to read. It was delicious.

And the following Monday, when we all started school again, I walked with Kala and Aoife in the school yard. The tide of girls parted and curved around our line, geometric patterns swarming about our constellation. Aoife was still the loudest, gesticulating for her audience. But Kala and I were quieter, walking together, arms linked like a hot chain.

Carthy is unfamiliar, drab. Kinlough without the tourists, without their money. It feels like a place where nothing is celebrated, merely endured. I check my reflection in a shop window. I look terrible. A sheen on my forehead, my hair tired and windswept. I cross the road to the coffeehouse, still listening to Mrs Mulkerns.

...Kala had naturally started by looking for her mother in all the magazines from the seventies. She finally found what she was looking for in the magazines from the eighties. A picture labelled Fiona Lanann. Blurry, but the likeness was unmistakable. There was only one picture. The first year camogie team, from 1987. And I was the teacher in the picture.

Me: *Kala confronted you about this.*

Mulkerns: *Yes. After school, one day.*

Me: *When was this?*

Mulkerns: *October. A couple of weeks before she went missing. She was in this room every day after that, pressing me for information. At first I was reluctant to speak – it wasn't my place to tell her these things, this was a family matter. I didn't want to put my foot in the Lananns' business again. Kala was very upset. It was a lot to take in. The fact that her mother was so young.*

I enter the coffee shop and do a quick scan of the tables, face prepared for a smile. But she is not here yet. Good. I take a table by the window and tell the waitress that I am waiting for someone.

Kala told me she was afraid to confront the Mammy about it. But she was going to do it, during the Halloween holidays. I gave her my phone number, told her to call me any time. But she didn't.

I am touching up my make-up when two teenage girls walk by outside, laughing together. I recognize the summer flush of their faces, their moon-pooled eyes. A feeling you never get back. In my hand mirror I look old. I feel old.

I planned to speak with Kala, the Monday after the midterm holidays. But we both know what happened that day. Awful, horrible business. She was last seen that evening.

A uniformed Guard and a man in a suit enter the coffeehouse. The gravity of the place twists in their direction. I watch them move through the tables, out of my sight. I am jittery. Some insane part of me wants to rush to them and ask if they know anything that could help me.

Mulkerns: *They're saying now that Kala never even left Kinlough. That she's been here the entire time.*

Me: *I know.*

Mulkerns: *But who would have wanted to hurt that girl?*

I am checking my eyeliner, and this task – its simplicity – gives me a momentary sense of purpose. I am just realizing that, despite myself, I still have this urge to impress, when I look up and suddenly she is there, all of her, a long floral dress striding into the coffee shop and flooding my eyes, coming at me with open arms. A baby clings against her chest, wrapped in one of those African harnesses.

'Helen Laughlin!' she says. 'Well, hello, pet.'

I stand, rictus grin on my face.

'Aoife.'

Joe

SEARCH YOUR ROOM. No more sitting, pinging off the walls. Fuck that.

Go through the drawers. Boxes. Looking.

Three weeks ago, your first night back in the house, Mam took you for a walk around the estate. You waited till it got dark enough that no one would know you, though Mam was always glad if someone recognized you. She could live off the look on their faces for weeks. But there was no one around that night. Mam had her arm hooked in yours, telling you all the latest. The families living beyond their means. The couples who've split but can't afford to live separately. You didn't care about any of this. You just wanted the idea of people in their houses. Summer smell in the air. Heat in the tarmac. In the windows, all the lights on. A man in one house getting something from his fridge, a family in another, scattered about their sitting room, looking at separate screens. What kept snagging your eye were all the upstairs lights, the glowing bedrooms, where kids were being kids. Every bedroom, a laboratory of the self. Mam was talking, but you were thinking about how suburbs are perfect cradles for dreaming: they practically beg you to imagine another life, one lived at a burning voltage. The dreaming hidden in this place – murmuring beneath the comfort of the uniform gardens in their perfect rows, the mowed lawns, each driveway that bit too small for the two large cars – you couldn't have become what you are if you hadn't always been from this. You wished you could be back inside the womb of this dreaming, instead of having to live out its consequences.

Phone pinging the whole time now. The socials are busy. Could post a selfie of yourself and Mush, from last night. Mush is turned to the side to hide his scars, he looks normal, he wouldn't mind. 'Old friends – best friends.' Something like that. Could post that selfie of Mush, along with a photo of ye as kids. If you could find one. A post like that would do big numbers.

Hand feeling around the back of the bottom drawer till—
There it is.

The old biscuit tin. Kala's letters, her drawings. Logos she made for the band. That first envelope she gave you. White, with her lipstick mark on the seal. Nights you used to stare at the splinters of deep red in the blush of her lipstick, heat in your blood. Have a drink. Used to tuck that envelope under your pillow at night, thinking about her, her smell. The small black box she gave you, which she had scented with her perfume. A red paper heart inside it, and her handwriting. 'My heart.'

Sit on the bed, tin in your lap. Haven't looked at this stuff in years. Brace yourself.

When you open it, your own face stares up from your lap, warped in the box's metal. The biscuit tin is empty. Everything is gone.

Sun's scorching. Light blitzing your face through the trees on Blake's Road. Cars blow their horns at you, faces at windows – 'Is that Joe Brennan?'

Should've worn your baseball cap, your hoodie. Should've gone for a run.

That was Mam's suggestion, when you went out to the back garden, empty biscuit tin in hand. She was on a sun lounger, wearing sunglasses and a swimsuit.

Your shadow moved over her and she lowered her glasses. 'You look terrible. Go for a run or something.'

'This tin,' you said. 'I kept things in there. In my room.'

'Oh, I threw that stuff out years ago,' Mam said. She reclined back on the lounger. 'You know, I was watching BBC4 the other night, they always have these old rock stars on, sitting at a mixing desk, talking about their glory days. I wish they wouldn't show them playing their concerts *now*. There's something mortifying about a middle-aged man's body jumping about with a guitar.'

Another car beeps at you on the Coast Road. Plaster on a grin. Wave. Head splitting. Another round of the sweats coming on. Somewhere around thirty, hangovers become apocalyptic events. Every time a car blasts, you think it's going to be a journalist, catching up to you, someone who's connected the dots and realized that Jungle Heart and the Lanann Girl, the two most newsworthy things about Kinlough, are connected. Your name was never in the papers back when Kala went missing, and you were glad for that. Not because it protected your anonymity, but because it protected something intimate inside yourself, a place only Kala had reached, a part of you so vulnerable and real it could never survive the flashbulb violence of being public. You've spent years looking for that place. You thought you might find it in your box of Kala's letters and drawings.

And Mam's thrown them all out.

'Auld fellas with guitars, bellies like sacks of potatoes,' she said. 'Trying to pretend life's not behind them. You don't want to end up looking like all of them, do you?'

'No.'

'So go for a run.'

'Why did you throw out my things?'

'De-cluttering, Joe. It's good for the head.' She arched her eyebrows. 'You're not going to get all upset about that now, are you?'

One of the beeping cars has stopped and turned. It's crawling the kerb behind you. Fuck sake. Not now. But this person will make a story out of this moment – a story they tell in the pub for years about that time they met Joe Brennan and he was a total legend, or that time they met Joe Brennan and he was a piece of shit. There's never an in-between. So plaster on the smile and turn to the sound of the window winding down.

'Where you walking to?' Theresa says.

'Town. To meet Mush.'

She pauses. 'Going drinking again?'

Seriously? That's why she pulled over? To give you more shit?

Turn to walk away and she calls after you.

All you need to do is see Mush. That's what'll fix things. Him and Dad are the only people who see you. You know what you're gonna do when you land in town. There was an old trick yourself and Aidan used to play on Mush whenever he was at work. You'd ring him from out on Fox Street, hiding your caller ID. Whenever he'd pick up, Aidan or you would start talking in a hillbilly voice, breathing hard like a pervert. *Ah know whut yer wearing, boy. Ah wunna stroke yer curly hair.* Mush always looked scared. Then he'd look out the window and see ye laughing and, because he was Mush, he'd smile, everything forgiven and forgotten.

'I can give you a lift,' Theresa says. 'I'm not doing anything else.'

Mam would have said that this is the sort of thing that makes a good-looking woman unattractive. Sheer availability.

Fuck it. Get in the car.

Theresa has a picture of an Indian mystic over the passenger seat. A piece of paper that says, 'Take your time and be wherever you are.' Who in their right mind wants to be wherever they are? Theresa's like Dad; someone with a horizontal relation to things. She has the whole earth-goddess thing going on, a pure Kinlough hippie. On the surface, she could be from the Other Place. But she's not. She's just not. Theresa's the type of person who makes lists every day – totally embedded in a world of details, emptying and filling the dishwasher. Get to know anyone and that's what happens; they shed one layer of mystery after another, the dismal burlesque towards their inevitable ordinariness. There's a reason the surface of things is so appealing: it's the same reason we don't see what's going on inside us all the time. Organs squelching. All that blood. The things that keep us alive happen in the dark, because they're fucking ugly.

Kala never got old enough to learn this.

'Are you even listening?' Theresa says.

'No.'

'I was saying maybe you can get Mush to pull his finger out and do something.'

She starts going on about Donna and Marie. She says she doesn't get why they're acting out. 'I mean, they were excited to meet Helen. They must have asked a million questions about her in the past week. Not that I could answer half of them. They were asking about her, and you, and Aidan. And about Kala, too.'

Theresa glances over, as if she's worried even mentioning Kala will make you lose your mind. That's how fucking fragile she thinks you are.

'I liked Kala,' she says. 'I was just a kid but... She always made jokes with me. More than Helen, anyway. You know, having a big sister should prepare you for things. Like, getting your first period shouldn't come as such a shock, but the day I got mine, I literally thought I was dying.'

Why is she fucking talking about this?

'I'll never forget it. Helen and the girls were in her room, trying on Mam's old clothes, and I was on the toilet, bawling my eyes out. I screamed out for help. I was like, "I'm gonna diiie I'm gonna diiiie." Of course, Helen froze. But Aoife and Kala were so good. They cleaned me up and explained everything. Aoife made me hot chocolate and gave me one of her hair ties. A black band with a red butterfly on it. I'll always remember that. Helen looked embarrassed by the whole thing, but Aoife—'

'Fuck Aoife Reynolds,' you say.

Theresa sniffs. Pauses. 'Why do you always do that?'

'What?'

'Every time I try to make a connection, you throw it in my face.'

'No one's throwing anything in your face.'

'One of the things my dad told me about recovery—'

'Here we go—'

'He told me that alcoholism is a way to avoid intimacy.'

'Oh wow, Theresa. Wow. If your dad said it, it must be true. *Alcoholism is a way to avoid intimacy.* How deep.'

'See? You throw it in my—'

'Fuck sake, what do you want from me? Jesus. Talking to me in AA platitudes is a way to avoid intimacy. Treating me like I'm a fucking rescue dog is a way to avoid intimacy. If you—'

'I care about you, Joe.'

'Christ, T, I'm trying my best.'

'I know you are. I know it's hard.'

She touches your face. Pull your head back. She completely withdraws. Purses her lips and glares at the road. Rejected again.

Silence. She's upset now. Great. Just tell her what she wants to hear. You know how to do that.

'Look, I had two drinks last night. And I didn't even enjoy them. My body practically rejects the stuff by now.'

She gives you this sad, open face, like she wants to believe you. You wish she wouldn't keep doing that. Acting like things can be different. In the end, everyone's alone with everything.

'The whole reason I'm meeting up with Mush,' you say, 'is cos last night he was too busy with Helen to talk to me. I mean, we chatted but... nothing counts when you're drinking, does it? You can say anything and brush it off the next day. So I'm trying to reconnect with him tonight.'

You can't even pick apart the truth from the bullshit in what you're saying. It's all bullshit, in the end. Can't believe Mam threw out your letters from Kala. You should have a drink.

*

In town, you get a bag of cans. Tuborg. Dutchie. All the cheap shit Mush likes. The person working in the off-licence doesn't recognize you. This is almost as irritating as when they do.

But there's a sense of freedom now, walking down Fox Street, cans in a bag. The evening's coming in like a tide and it already has a shape: you and Mush, maybe in the caf, or down the Widow's Arch. One can, another, then another. A few laughs. A few chats. A world put briefly right.

You don't go into the caf right away. Linger outside, looking in. Mush in the window, working. He's at home in the world. Horizontal.

You call him. You'll put on the pervy voice. You'll say, *Turn araannd naah, boy*, and he'll see you out there on Fox Street, holding your bag of cans aloft. And he'll give you that smile, and you'll know that, even if just for a few hours, the world can be a home.

Mush takes his phone from his pocket. But when he sees you're calling, he hangs up.

Mush

MAM GIVING OUT. 'Was that cappuccino decaf? I said decaf.'

'Did you?'

'I know I did.'

'Maybe you didn't.'

'Are you telling me what I did or didn't say?'

Fucking headwreck.

'Are you making the decaf or what?' she says.

'What's wrong with you today?'

'There's nothing wrong with me,' she says as she nearly rips the door off the fridge getting the milk.

I mutter to myself. Who drinks a decaf cappuccino? Be honest with yourself and get a cup of warm milk.

When I take out my tobacco and make to head out for a smoke, Mam gives a sour look.

'What, I need to ask your permission?' I say.

'I've never stopped you doing anything you wanted,' Mam says. And then something happens. Her mouth does this little tremble, her eyes go all pooled. 'Maybe that's where meself and Pauline went wrong with the whole pack of ye.'

Her voice stumbles and gives out like an old knee. Fuck. She's going to cry.

My phone buzzes. It's Joe. I'll call him back. I swipe him away. Put the phone back in my pocket. Mam's already after disappearing into the back pantry.

Mam's not Auntie Pauline – she doesn't get emotional in that soft way. A while ago I was helping Rossie paint the walls

232

in the box flat Theresa uses as her home-slash-studio. Rossie and me have an easy vibe – he's like me, happy to be quiet if he's got nothing to say – but at one point I made a comment about Auntie Pauline's softness, and Rossie said, 'It only looks like softness from outside.' We kept working. But a few minutes later he piped up again and said, 'It takes strength to be that delicate.' I wasn't used to chat like that. Especially not about Auntie Pauline.

To be honest, I'd never really considered Auntie Pauline as an actual person before. Like, she'd always just been my Auntie Pauline. But Rossie's words got me to thinking about her, about everything she went through with Uncle Ger, and Aidan. And she'd always been a gentle sort, the first one to cry whenever we watched *E.T.* or whatever, but when Aidan died, it was like she'd gone into some sort of autopilot. Even when she left Uncle Ger, and the twins kept her busy, day in, day out, there was something hunched and numb about her the whole time. Going through life with the head down, like one of them horses that's gotta wear patches over its eyes so it can keep moving.

She was different now. She laughed more easily, tilted her head to the sky when she did it. Rossie was right, like. Auntie Pauline was like this flower slowly opening to get more sun, more life. I started paying more attention whenever she called in to the caf with Rossie. Thing was, I could see it in Rossie too. Both of them, these damaged people, curled up in hurt, slowly unknotting themselves to each other, to face the world. I'd talk about that with Aidan every second week when I'd visit his grave, tell him all about his mam, and how her and Rossie were good for each other.

And that got me thinking about my own mam, trying to think of her as a whole person and not as my mam. And with her, it's more like she has all the emotions that close a person off, the impatient blunt feelings that tell the world it can fuck right off cos you're going nowhere, you're not a flower opening to the sun, you're a thick, solid tree that stands in the rain with its arms folded and never flinches at anything ever. Which is why the sight of Mam now, sitting on a red crate by the dishwasher out the back pantry, all hunched with tears bubbling in her face, freaks me out a bit.

'Jesus, what's the matter?'

'I'm fine.' She scowls. 'When did you go back on the fags?'

'It's just for this week.'

Mam wipes her nose. 'Got one handy for me?'

I roll two smokes. Mam turns on an extractor fan over one of the grills and we lean under it, side by side, smoking.

'You were doing so well,' she says.

'Ara, I'll quit after the wedding.'

'The fecking wedding,' she says. I give a weak laugh and she echoes it, and we're on a different see-saw now, climbing towards some friendly place. 'Theresa says the twins didn't show up for work. You been on to them at all yet?'

I hesitate. Then I finally tell her about the bust-up with Donna and Marie two nights ago, how they wanted to move out and how they blew a gasket and stormed off cos I'd been less than enthusiastic. 'I've been texting them the whole time. I should tell Pauline a—'

'No,' Mam says firmly. 'Not a word to Pauline. I'll sort this out myself. It's my fault they're acting up.'

'How's that?'

'Last week I went to help them pick out a gift for Pauline and Rossie. Fecking disaster. They were the chattiest I'd seen them in a long time. None of the usual sulks. Full of questions, curiosities. Asking about you, me, the caf. But they were only buttering me up, to get me chatty. We were having a milkshake in Eddie Rocket's, and I'm banging on and they're asking about all the people who've worked here over the years. They start asking me about Kala. And this is before we know it's her in the woods. So I say all the usual. Lovely girl. Popular with the punters. Good handle of numbers, didn't need things explained twice, blah blah. But every time I change the subject, they keep bringing it back to Kala. It's Kala, Kala,

Kala. They want to know more about when she went missing. So I tell them what it was like. Guards, journalists, rumours, blah. But they want specifics. When did I last see her? How did she seem to me? What did I believe happened?'

Mam taps her fingers on the grill.

'And then they give each other that look. You know the one. Where they're putting some little plan into action. They both look at me, and Donna says, *Auntie Lydia. How exactly did Mush get his scars?*'

This cold feeling down my back.

'So I tell them the truth,' Mam says. 'I mean, like… a truth. It was an accident. Which isn't a lie. But they keep asking about Kala disappearing, your scars, Kala disappearing, your scars, back and forth like that, as if they're connected.'

This isn't good. Whatever it is, it isn't good. Mam looks at me, pure wary.

'They asked me how Aidan died.'

Fuck.

Fuck.

We've never told the twins the full story about Aidan. Auntie Pauline didn't want them to know it was suicide, not when they were kids. But it's like they've never quite got old enough for her to tell them. I've never liked how we dress it up in sentences – 'Oh, it was very sudden', 'No one expected it' – but Mam's always said it's not our place to say anything.

'What did you tell them?'

'I dodged the question, didn't I?' Mam says. 'Fed them all the usual lines. And they gave me that teenager look, like I was cheating them. And maybe I was cheating them. But… Mush, they *knew* I was lying.'

My phone buzzes and Mam's face brightens. 'Is that them?'

Joe, again. I hang up.

Mam has a forlorn look on her.

'Pet, you didn't see the way they kept looking at each other. They were putting me on trial, like. Insinuating terrible things. Paranoid nonsense. Implying some sort of connection between your accident, Aidan's death, Kala going missing. I said, "Who's been filling your heads with this tripe?" But I could feel me face going red, and they were looking at me like that proved them right. And Marie sat back and said, *A little bird has told us everything.* And I was aggravated, you know? My blood was up. They'd tricked me into this whole conversation, and now they were using it to attack me, and you, and Pauline, when... all we've ever done was to protect them. And... you have to understand, I was so annoyed.'

Christ. What did Mam say to them?

She pinches her front tooth and shakes it hard, like she could loosen it from her mouth. 'I let the truth slip, like. I said, *Your brother didn't kill himself over the bloody Lanann girl.* Mush... they didn't even look surprised.'

Mam sucks on her cigarette, hard. The extractor fan's roaring.

'They already *knew*,' she says.

'Sure who'd have told them?'

'Who d'you think?'

Uncle Ger.

'There's nothing that man wouldn't do, Mush. Not if it meant driving a wedge between the girls and Pauline right before the wedding. They kept saying, *A little bird told us this, a little bird told us that.* I could've slapped them, honestly. Then we find out that the body in the woods is Kala, and Pauline's getting in a tizzy because the twins are AWOL, and teenage girls go missing in this town, and—'

A voice from the entrance says, 'Hey,' and we both start.

It's Joe. 'Bit of a queue forming out there. Everything all right?'

Mam gets up immediately and claps her hands. She speaks in her full voice. 'Tip-top,' she goes. 'And how's Joe?'

'I'm grand,' he says. Hollywood smile. He raises a plastic bag of cans. 'I come bearing gifts. Thought we might hang out tonight.'

'Ah, sure that's lovely, isn't it?' Mam says. Her face has that shiny look of someone who's been crying. But she's smiling brightly at Joe, like she's turned off a tap in herself. Like if she closes herself up and waits, this'll all blow over. Maybe this is where I get it from.

'Won't ye make a nice evening of it?' she says to me.

Fuck that, like. I'm going up to Uncle Ger's farm and getting the twins.

Joe

TAP-TAP-TAP. MUSH'S HANDS on the steering wheel. He's churning ye through the Warren's blur of hedges and stone walls, staring at the road, but with his hands he's going tap-tap-tap. You want to ask why he didn't pick up earlier. But you don't want the answer you'll probably get. He doesn't want to hang out. Doesn't want you to be there. Fucking hates you. You're as far from life as you've ever been. You're something without gravity, all earthed chords severed, drifting silently out of orbit. Make a connection. A link. Gotta be something.

'Here, man,' Mush says. Tap-tap. 'I was checking Marie's Instagram earlier. Her last post is a selfie with you. Outside Flanagan's?'

You remember. How she leaned too close, how Donna looked through you with her Aidan eyebrows, past your tatts and smile into the desperate dwarf inside your skull, pulling all the levers.

'They seem weird to you that night?' Mush says.

Finally. Now you get it; this is how Mush wants to connect – not for you to elevate him to your place, the Other Place, the big life. No, he wants you to bring your large life into his small one. Thank Christ. You can do that. Speak like an ordinary dude. You tell him about the chat with the twins outside Flanagan's. About the photo they gave you, of you and Kala at the Sisco. Take it from your wallet and hold it up for him. He looks at it, does a double-take, then lingers on it for so long you have to warn him to look at the road.

He's distracted as he turns ye down a mucky trail, hemmed in by wild bushes. The ground's uneven, the car judders wildly. The bushes get thicker and wilder, the deeper ye go. Branches scrambling the light.

The bag of cans tinkles at your feet. Soon ye'll be in town again, knocking them back.

'Where'd they get that photo from?' Mush says.

'I figured they got if off you, man. No?'

Mush doesn't respond.

'So,' you say. 'Do they spend a lot of time out here at their dad's?'

After a moment he glances over and says, 'Who the hell would be giving them an old photo of you and Kala?'

'I dunno… It wasn't you? Marie said a little bird gave it to them.'

Something happens in Mush's face when you say that. He's never been good at hiding his feelings. He looks away from you. Tap-tap-tap.

Mush

OUT OF THE car. Heat's gone heavy now, like the sky's doing push-ups off me. Palms pure oily. Fecking T-shirt's lathered to me and all. At the end of the dirt road, the cattle grid and the gate. Gate lets a shriek as I open it. I'm the only one who dares visit this farm when needs be. Always this boiling in my guts, each time. I brace myself for Ger's dogs. Mongrels, mostly. There's usually one loose, running about, barking at me for the whole walk up to the house. A huge brown fucker. Ugly, coughing sounds, wild eyes, teeth designed for one thing.

Joe's following me. Our shadows stretch across the dirt as the trail opens to a flat, sandy yard with a giant sky and the yard yawns out for ages till it reaches the house. Bits of old cars, fridges, plastic sheeting, any amount of auld shite tangled up like broken artefacts amongst the weeds. Always looks like a junkyard's been blown through the place.

This feeling of pure unease about it all. It's as much about Uncle Ger as the farm itself. Even when I was a teenager, and himself and Auntie Pauline were still together and living back in Kinlough, I used to get that nauseous feeling whenever I'd call up to their house to jam with Aidan. I didn't know what it was, back then. But I remember this one time I cycled up there, soon after we all started back in school. This was after Aidan and Joe had had their weird bust-up during band practice. Joe was worried we wouldn't be ready for the gig if we didn't practise enough, but he was too stubborn to make the first move and smoothe things over with Aidan, so there I

was again, piggy-in-the-fecking-middle, pulling up on my bike
outside Aidan's gaff, and that's when I first heard the sounds
coming from inside. Like a heavy table screeching across a
floor. Shouting. Auntie Pauline. Her voice was pure high-
pitched, crying. Uncle Ger roaring, short sentences that rose
as they went on. Da-da-da-DAHDAH. Ba-ba-BAH. Ba-BAH.
Something smashed. Another scream. The babies were crying,
too. Donna and Marie. Not normal crying, like when they
were tired or hungry. More like wailing. There was another
voice in there too. Aidan's voice, a thin shout, a tone I hadn't
heard from him ever. He sounded small. Then something happened where all the voices in the house rose together into this
horrible peak and Auntie Pauline going, 'No,' and a clatter
and Uncle Ger going, 'Don't fucking think about getting up
again,' and Auntie Pauline saying, 'He's your son,' and a door
slamming so hard it made the front windows rattle. Then only
the sound of the twins crying. I was pure frozen on my bike.
Out the corner of my eye I saw a curtain twitch at the house
next door. An eye by the edge, looking at me.

'...Don't you think?' Joe says, behind me. He's been
talking non-stop, the whole way here. All the way through the
Warren. I can't be listening to it. He still doesn't know how to
drive. How does someone get to be this old without being able
to drive? I wonder what it'd be like to be him, gliding so high
above life, like someone riding over a jungle in a helicopter
while eejits like me are trapped on the ground, hacking at the
bush and getting nowhere fast.

'What?'

'I said, Kinlough was a great place to be young, wasn't it?'

I grunt.

Queasy feeling.

A little bird. That's what Marie told Joe. And what she
told Mam. A little bird told them about Aidan's suicide, and
a little bird spoke to them about my scars. A little bird's
been talking about Kala and a little bird gave them a photo
of her with Joe. And there's no way Uncle Ger would have

a photo like that. Find myself thinking about the photo the twins sent me, the one of me and Dudley talking in the caf. **NO POLICE**

My fucking head. It's like there are all these jigsaw pieces on the floor and I keep getting glimpses of the picture, but the jigsaw falls apart before I've time to clock it.

I'm so caught up in my thoughts that it takes a sec for me to notice how quiet it is. *Quiet*, like. I've never gotten this close to the house without at least one fucker of a dog snarling across the yard. No sign of any dogs, anywhere.

'You come out here often?' Joe goes. He's looking about the place, bit wary.

'Only if the twins are pulling a stunt like this.'

'Is this where you were going with them, the other night?'

I frown back at him.

'I saw you and the twins at the bus stop,' he says. 'At Hogan's Square. I took a photo of ye. Thought the light was nice.'

He holds out his phone. It's the twins, all right. Standing either side of some huge lad in a black hoodie. Arms out by his side at weird angles. I stop walking. 'That's not me, man.'

'It is you. Look at him.'

'It's not me, man. I fucking know it's not me.'

I zoom in on the photo with my fingers till the person in the hood is a blur of pixels. The agitated silence all around us, like it's waiting for me to spot something that's already right there.

I'm walking faster now. Moving quicker. My hand's gripping something tight. Joe's phone, in my fist. I'm trying not to run.

First thing I see is the powdered glass coating the ground around the house. The windows have all been bashed out. Every single one. Some are blown to pieces, others are intact but full of fractures, like white spiders. Splinters across the ground under every window and they crunch under us as we look inside.

'Jesus,' Joe says. 'What happened here?'

Front door's open and we step in. Immediately, none of it feels right. Uncle Ger and Teabag normally keep a neat house. Everything scrubbed, hoovered, all that. It's one of the things Marie jokes about: 'Everything about Dad's a mess except his house.'

But the place is a bomb site. Things knocked off the walls, sofa tipped over. Uncle Ger's little shrine to Aidan, in the corner – it's in bits. All the framed pictures have been stamped on.

Joe goes to speak and I raise a hand to stop him. The kitchen door's half open.

'Girls?' I say. 'Are ye there?'

I want the twins to jump out at me, give me a fright. This is still one of their favourite things to do. I brace for Donna to spring up from behind the sofa, Marie catching it on her phone. 'You jumped! We saw you, you jumped!'

But they don't.

I tap at the door, and it creaks open. Kitchen's been ransacked. Splintered plates on the floor. Chairs and table all on their sides. Couple of bluebottles tapping against a giant web-shaped fracture across the kitchen window.

I strain my ears for some sort of movement in the house. But the only sound is Joe, right behind me.

'Maybe we should leave,' he says.

Back out into the hall. Round the corner. There's a long corridor with no windows. Pure dark. I flick the light switch but the bulb's fucked and doesn't come on.

I peek into the first door. The bathroom. There's a spider in the bath, one of them dirty ones with the extra-long legs. Only two toothbrushes by the sink – Uncle Ger and Teabag. No extra toothbrushes. No sign the twins are sleeping here.

The last door in the corridor is the room the twins sleep in when they're here. I try and visualize it – Marie with earbuds in, on her phone. Donna on the floor, earbuds in, working on some sketch. I'll lean in the doorway and they'll both pretend not to see me. Eventually Marie will take an earbud out and, without taking her eyes off the screen, she'll start an argument. Donna will be stubborn and not acknowledge I'm there at all. Not till I've gone back and forth with Marie for a few minutes and we're friends again.

But the room is a war zone. The window's been entirely caved in. Glass shards like fangs about the frame. The drawers have all been ripped out and thrown aside, emptied onto the floor. Broken photo frames, heaps of jewellery, old cinema tickets, old teddies.

'Man,' Joe says.

Their beds. The duvets have been thrown back, and it's like someone's gone at the mattresses and the pillows with a knife. Great welts torn in the fabric, coughing out the stuffing.

'Man,' Joe says again. He's staring at the floor. His eyes are pure wide.

Vomit, in the carpet. A copper-red blotch next to it. Another, closer to my feet. And another, right under my runners. I step back out into the hall. Try and find another light switch. No joy.

I get out my phone, flick the torch on, hold it out before us.

It starts at the bedroom door. Snake-like smudges of slick copper-red, dragging down the corridor to the door out to the yard. Our red footprints are tattooed on the lino, cos we've been walking through the red, in the dark.

Neither of us asks what it is. We both know what blood looks like.

Helen

SOMETHING IS WRONG. The coffeehouse clatters about us and she is sitting opposite me – Aoife Reynolds, close enough for me to count her freckles, the hints of laughter lines; close enough for me to reach out and touch her straightened bleached hair – but something is wrong. I cannot find her. Even her accent slips from my grip. More Irish. More here, more now, waving at the waitress to bring a high chair for the baby, thanking the waitress by name, eyes busy while her hands expertly fetch a plastic bib and an arsenal of toys from her bag.

'Aren't you like your daddy, Otto? Another big Carthy man?'

The baby – Otto – stares between us, tiny fists held wide, as Aoife adjusts his pudgy legs in the high chair.

'Who's that?' she says. 'Is that Mammy's old friend? Is that Helen?'

The baby's face spreads in a giant gummy grin and Aoife mutters, 'You've a new fan.'

Something is wrong as we go through all the rituals. The excessive compliments. The self-deprecating responses. Shaping our orders to one another. Decaf latte for her, regular for me. I find myself mirroring her – the way we cross our legs, hold our coffees – trying to lock eyes and catch some shared moment to earth us in one another. But a frequency has been scrambled.

There is no sign of Kala's absence in Aoife's darting, efficient energy.

When I ask how she has been dealing with the news, she blinks, widens her eyes, and uses the sorts of stock phrases we once mocked in our parents.

'…It's just so shocking, isn't it? I mean. Like, this sort of thing happens in *other places*. You never think something like this will—'

I want to feel Kala conjured between us. I want Aoife to be cosmic, a violent star. But she is acting like she is just another bloody adult. Talking constantly and saying nothing.

She could be speaking to anybody as she opens a small Tupperware, unclips a plastic blue spoon from the lid for Otto, and asks how I have been keeping. When I say there is not much to tell, she immediately waves a hand. 'Don't be putting yourself down like that now, hon,' she says. 'One of the things I learned in therapy – this was years ago, no big deal, social anxiety, though I guess that's what being in your twenties is. You ever think that, about your twenties? Ever look back on that whole decade and be like, *Jesus*, what was that? – anyway, the thing I learned is that you really need to own your story, you know? Do I sound American, saying that? I suppose you know all about that, you live in America, right?'

'Canada.'

'Exactly,' she says, spooning half an avocado onto the table of Otto's high chair and dicing it up. 'Come on, pet. Tell me what's up with Helen in Canada. D'you know, I heard your dad's getting married. Isn't that adorable? Really goes to show, hah? Himself and Pauline. And them both after being through such trials. Sure now look at them. Life being life. Anyway, how about you? Any plans for Helen to get married?'

'What?'

'Boyfriend?' She makes a sympathetic face. '…Girlfriend?'

Christ. I put my phone on the table and prime the audio recorder.

'We should talk about Kala,' I say.

Aoife frowns at the phone. She gives an unsure smile. 'I thought we were going to catch up.'

'Could I ask you a bit about the time before Kala went missing?'

She adjusts her posture. Something about her retreats. 'Is this what you do, then? In Canada?'

I nod and tell her I write.

'So you're writing about Kala?'

No. Yes. I don't know.

''Cos I heard you were teaching?' Aoife says. 'Or am I getting my wires crossed? This munchkin has me up all hours, my head's—'

'Yeah, I do some teaching to pay the rent. Okay, so if we—'

'But journalism's something you can do on the side, is it?'

'No, I— It's freelance.'

Otto drops his plastic spoon and Aoife goes to pick it up. 'Freelance,' she says. '...But you're teaching journalism?'

'No. TEFL.'

'Oh my God, *TEFL*. I did that for a while. Australia. Thailand. The backpacking thing. I—'

'Aoife. Can we talk about the weeks just before Kala went missing?'

Aoife pauses. She taps her nails on the table.

'Honestly, Helen, everything around that Halloween is a blur by now. I mean, such craziness. It's actually hard to remember.'

I blink. She cannot be serious.

Her eyes are over my shoulder, vacant.

'What about the last time we saw Kala?' I say. An unexpected judder to my heart. An ugly bloodswell. 'You must remember that.'

Aoife considers me for a moment. She sits back.

'What exactly is this?' she says. 'I get a message from you out of the blue, asking to meet up. Such short notice. Only for my husband, I wouldn't have even come. But he thought it'd be good for me. *Reconnect, Aoife.* Bring Otto along. *You never know, it could have a heal—*'

'Do you remember how Kala looked that day?' I say. 'In the yard at St Anne's? You remember the way everyone was—'

'God,' she mutters. Something happens in her eyes. A glimpse of the real Aoife, flashing through the murk of adulthood. 'Sitting there with your recorder on your phone.'

I welcome the jab of it. The feeling that I am at least being met in some way.

Otto must notice the change in his mother, because he makes strange and begins to cry. I flinch – the baby is louder than I would have expected – and wait for Aoife to do something. But she keeps her eyes fixed on mine, long enough for the cries to become piercing. When she takes Otto from his chair, and undoes a hook on her dress to feed him, I look away. Across the coffeehouse a large man is sitting, staring over at us. A creepy grin behind a dirty grey beard. He raises one hand and slowly nods his fingers in my direction.

Aoife is looking at me. 'Want to know what I remember? I remember things no one else does. I remember me and Kala getting photos taken together in our Communion dresses. I remember the time we argued over who got to be Sporty Spice. I remember sleepovers from when we were ten. I—'

'But what about in those final weeks? Did Kala say anything to you about her mother?'

She snorts. 'Jesus, you haven't changed at all. Just want to barge right in and wriggle your finger in all these wounds I've spent years—'

'I want you to try and remember—'

'Jesus, Helen, *why*? *Why* would I want to do that? *Christ*. Kala was my best friend. And then she wasn't. And then she was gone.'

She takes a deep breath. Her eyes have a shine.

'It took years for me to process that,' she says. 'And you know what I learned, Helen? The past is not real. Like, it doesn't *mean* anything. The fifteen-year-old me I remember today isn't the fifteen-year-old me I remembered when I was twenty-five, and it won't be the fifteen-year-old I remember when I'm eighty. You know why? Because the past is just... random *stuff*, floating about the place.

None of it means anything at all until you make a story out of it.'

'But... but that's exactly what I'm trying to do,' I say. My face is growing hot. 'I'm try—'

'Helen—'

'Oh, for *fuck's* sake, Aoife,' I snap.

People at other tables glance over.

We sit in silence for a moment. My head is suddenly pounding. Aoife avoids my eyes, watching Otto feed.

'I'm not going back there, Helen. I'm just not.'

I am suddenly looking at Aoife from what feels like very far away. The café noise seems to get louder around us. She strokes Otto's face as she talks. She tells me life can be understood backwards but it must be lived forwards. She does this slowly, carefully, speaking in what sound like rehearsed sentences, comforting platitudes. At one point she says, 'I live for today,' and I want to reach across the table and shake her. Shout at her. Tell her to cut the fridge-magnet bullshit wisdom and remember who she is and fucking help me.

I am about to say this when Aoife suddenly adjusts Otto and reaches across the table and grips my hand.

'I live for today, Helen,' she repeats. 'Maybe you should too?'

She gives me a pleading look, like there is something only I can give her. I frown. I do not know what she is looking for. I shake my head, and a look passes over Aoife's face. It is brief, barely there for a moment, but I feel it carve its slow way through me.

Pity.

I thumb at my eyes, smudging my make-up in the mirror of the coffee-shop toilets. I splash water onto my flushed cheeks. Deep breaths. I can feel my heart thudding. I have spent my whole life in the aftermath of that summer. Every friendship, every passion, constantly measured to Kala. The older I get, the more incandescent Kala has become. A hidden sun, casting new shadows at unpredictable moments. I know Mush is the same. Even Joe, if his music is anything to go by, is frozen in some sort of crooked fidelity to adolescence. But Aoife acts like the past is just that: a collection of discrete events that she has carefully folded and tucked away.

Three slow knocks on the coffeehouse's toilet door.

I should never have come here. I am a fool for trying to reach out to her.

My fingers feel electric, not mine. A quiver in my blood. Aoife, rattling through me. Not only her words – everything about her. Her responsible-adult voice when she insisted on paying, making hollow invitations to visit her some time, meet her husband. The distance from which her eyes looked at me as we said goodbye.

I am a fucking fool. A stupid fucking—

The door thuds again. My voice breaks at the top as I say, 'All right.'

When I open it, it is the man with the silver beard, who nodded his fingers at me. He fills the door frame. I move to pass, but he does not give way.

'Ah, let me look at you for a bit,' he says in a low voice. He laughs. 'Don't you recognize me?'

I do not. Not at first. But something in his eyes is familiar. I know them, in an animal way.

He smiles. 'I recognize you, Helen.'

'Ger,' I say. Not now, Christ.

'Special prize for the brunette,' he says. 'Good girl.'

The silver beard is where I am confused. He did not have it, years ago. He is close enough for me to smell the chewed meat of his breath. The lingering note of alcohol.

'How have you been keeping?' I say.

His eyes are a murk. He raises an arm and I flinch. His hand rests on the door frame, by my face.

'Not great now, Helen. Not fucking brilliant.'

He leans close to me. His breath on my mouth.

'My cunt wife's about to marry your cunt father.' He barks a laugh. 'What's that make us, you reckon? Not that I hold it against you. I always had time for you, Helen.' He goes to touch my hair.

'Everything all right here?'

Ger turns. There is a man in a business suit standing behind him. He has the alert, suspicious eyes of a Guard.

'Everything's fantastic,' Ger says. 'Just old pals, catching up.'

The man steps towards us. I give him a sharp look to say, it's fine. Leave it.

'We can continue this later,' Ger says. 'You know where to find me, don't you, Helen?'

When I squeeze my way past him, Ger holds my arm and says, 'I know where to find you.'

I mutter thanks to the Guard as I pass him, but he keeps pace with me.

'Are you all right?' he mutters. 'Did that fucker say anything to you?'

'It's fine.' I fumble with my coins at the till. The girl working the register looks at me with tired eyes and reminds me that Aoife already paid for everything.

'Are you sure you're okay?' the Guard says. He glances back warily in the direction of the toilets. 'Let me walk out with you.'

Outside, he calls to a uniformed Guard, smoking against his squad car. 'I'll catch up.'

This man is middle-aged but boyish. Handsome, in a straightforward way. Something familiar about him, too. Everyone in this country looks like someone else.

'It's Helen, isn't it? You probably don't remember me. Joe's dad.'

He winces when I call him Mr Brennan. 'Call me Dudley, will you? Was that Aoife Reynolds I saw you chatting to there? I'd say ye have a lot of ground to cover.'

He is friendly but his eyes are alert. I realize he is trying to read me.

'When did you come back to Kinlough?'

'Two days ago,' I say.

'From where?'

'Is this an interview?'

He raises a shoulder. One of those men who are totally at ease in themselves. The world has always answered to him. He smiles, signalling I should respond.

'Look, I have to go. It's an hour's walk back to Kinlough, if I don't get lost again.'

He nods to a gleaming black car.

'I'm heading that way myself. If you can indulge me a few questions en route.'

The car is clean. Everything has been hoovered. He has air fresheners in the shapes of pine trees. Jaunty orchestration bashes at a low volume on the radio.

'I was in Canada myself once,' he says. 'Well, not really. The border. Lake Superior. Ever been there? Bigger than Switzerland. One lake.'

He drives with one hand on the wheel, the other resting on the edge of his window. He asks about the wedding, but when he sees I'm not interested, he doesn't push for more answers.

The light blitzes through the leaves into the car and he squints, adjusts the shade above the windscreen. 'You seemed uncomfortable back there.'

'Ger Lyons has that effect.'

'I meant uncomfortable with me, all my questions. Sorry about that. Joe's always telling me I ask too many. Says it makes him feel guilty. I just wanted to know if you were here before the remains were found.'

'Why?'

His eyes do not leave the road. 'Process of elimination.'

'You're leading the investigation?'

He shakes his head. 'Not allowed near it. On account of Joe.'

He slows the car at a T-junction. The engine purrs. The drip-drip of the indicator, ticking. He nods to the phone in my lap.

'Joe told me you were a journalist,' he says. 'I noticed you were recording your chat with Aoife. You interviewing people for a story or something? Spoken to any Guards yet?'

'No.'

'Why not?'

'No offence, but the Guards were useless when Kala went missing. I'm looking beyond the organs of the state apparatus—'

'The what of the what, now?' he laughs. 'Jesus, love.'

'I want to find out the truth behind the facts.'

'The truth behind the facts,' he says. He nods to himself, mulling it over. 'I'll remember that.'

He turns in to another artery of the Warren. 'Spoken to the Mammy?'

I tell him she will not answer her door.

'Aye,' he says. 'I heard as much from the liaison officers. She won't open up for anyone. She's a very confused woman.'

It makes my heart race, the matter-of-fact manner in which he says this.

'What d'you know about the Garda investigation into the disappearance?' he says.

'What I remember. What's in the papers.'

'And what's that?'

'Kala left her gran's house on Monday night to meet someone. She was still in her school uniform. She had her bag with the Rage Against the Machine logo on it. She was caught on CCTV walking over Toner's Bridge, out of town. There were several sightings of her talking to someone in a Hyundai. She never came home. A long search, everywhere. No body, or evidence of foul play, is found. The investigation slowly winds down. Then they find her remains on that ugly fucking building site.'

He frowns at me, confused.

I mutter, 'Butchering one of the most beautiful parts of Kinlough for the sake of a few tourist homes.'

Dudley raises a sceptical eyebrow. 'Kinlough Associates have done more for this town than any politician. Sponsoring the Races. The Festival. It's a tourist town, Helen. Relies on visitors' cash.'

'Not everything can be reduced to money.'

He smiles. 'In my experience, only people with plenty of it seem to think that way.'

I almost tell him I have not had more than a thousand quid to my name at any point over the past five years. That I live from one month to the next. But I do not need to prove anything to anyone. Least of all Joe Brennan's bloody father.

'D'you've a clear timeline, at least?' he says. 'What time did she leave her granny's house? Were there any phone exchanges between Kala and her grandmother? What time was she seen at the Hyundai? Was the driver of that car ever interviewed? How many Guards were assigned to the case? Why was the case suddenly stepped down? Who. What. When. Why. Tell me – have any Gardaí even interviewed you, since the remains were found?'

I shake my head.

Dudley gives a rueful laugh. 'Fuck sake... That whole investigation. They wouldn't let me near it like. Conflict of interest, blah blah. But I kept my finger on it. And there were things that never, ever fit. I'm not saying there was deliberate sloppiness but... there were things that should've been followed up. Leads. Details.'

I take my phone and open the recorder. 'Would you—'

'Leave that off. This isn't... We're not even talking, right now.'

His fingers drum on the wheel.

'Seamus Roche,' he says. 'That name mean anything to you?'

I tell him no, and he shakes his head with something like disgust.

'Are you saying the Garda investigation wasn't all above board?'

He does not answer.

'I'm sorry,' I say. 'What exactly are we doing?'

'A source close to the Gardaí. Call me that. Make me a she,

if you want. Whatever you think will fly, you're the writer. But there are things the public should know about this case.'

'I'll need to take notes.'

'Pen and paper's fine. But I don't want my name anywhere. Life's hard enough.'

'When could we do this?'

'We're already doing it.'

I glance at the time on the radio. 'How long can I keep you?'

He adjusts his wing mirror, checking to see if anyone is following us. He looks focused. He takes another turn in the Warren.

'How long have you got?'

Mush

I SHOVE PAST Joe, down the hall. My belly's a churn as I shout the twins' names, following the blood trail out the back door to the yard where I'm rushing across open space. 'Donna!' I scream. 'Marie!' My voice sounds far away. It echoes inside the walls of the first shed, the second, and I'm moving too fast to freak out about being where I am – I clock the broken hinges, the empty dog cages, everything stale with rust and animal piss – too fast to check if Joe's come with me, third shed, fourth, no sign of the twins, no signs of any struggle in the dust of the yard, like the blood trail dragged itself outside the house and vanished, and I've my hands to my head, the yard's almost spinning, Joe's at me, 'Dude, this is fucked,' and I can tell from the tint of his voice that he's gonna try and get us out of here but I'm already at the next shed, then another, now running to the barn where they used to host the dogfights.

'Donna! Marie!'

I open the door of the barn and there's only darkness. Smell's terrible, like a rotten mouth.

'Are ye here?'

Nothing.

I'm turning back out when I hear it. A long moan.

'Girls?'

A shuffling, deep in the dark.

I blink, waiting for my eyes to adjust. Dark blue shapes in the blackness. Barrels. Crates. Cages. I take out my phone and flick on the torch. The light's a white halo hovering on the ground. Flecks of mouse shit, bird shit, stone. There's a rustling above – pigeons, in long rows along the rafters. I see myself through their eyes, walking the path between torn-up cages, barrels full of rainwater. Heart thudding in me, cos this is where it happened, that night. Kala's was the last face I saw, before the dark ate me. I keep walking into the inky black. I wait for a glint of teeth in the torchlight. A flicker of oily eyes. Some dog bursting the shadows to crash into my face.

I round the corner, and stop.

I see the feet first. Tattered runners. Ankles bound with cable ties. Jeaned legs, outstretched flat on the ground. Sitting on the floor. I smell the piss and shit stains before I see them. Chest moving up and down. When I move the light up to the face, the torch catches a flare of white hair, forking out like straw. Silver stubble on his jaw looks about a day old. He's propped against a pillar, arms bound behind it. His mouth's stuffed with a dirty rag. His breathing's a frightened sound – short sharp squeaks into the gag – and he's trying to turn his face away but can't. There are cable ties around his throat, holding his neck to the pillar. The flesh has frayed along the seam of the ties. Friction burns, like rust.

'Oh, what the *fuck*,' Joe says behind me.

I don't know who this guy is. He's like a scarecrow.

'I'm out of here, man,' Joe says.

As I get closer the scarecrow flinches. One eye's shut and swollen purple. The other's bloodshot. He moans into the gag, trying to speak. I reach for him.

'Don't,' Joe hisses.

Scarecrow's silvery stubble is rough on my knuckles as I pull the gag down.

'Please,' he says. His breath is mank. Wrecked lips. There are deep purple lines beneath both his eyes. His nose looks broken. He squints and blinks hard. 'Me wrists are in shreds. Me neck. Please.'

Behind me, Joe's pacing. 'This is *not* happening, man. We haven't seen this.'

Scarecrow says, 'I know who you are.'

I look back at Joe. I can feel his panic at being recognized.

'I know all about you,' Scarecrow says. 'You'll help me because you're a good man. Donna and Marie told me, Mush is a good man.'

He's talking to *me*.

'What?'

'Let me go,' Scarecrow says. Slight sing-song to his accent. 'I know things. Things about your life even you don't know.'

Joe's voice, urgent behind me. 'Look, man, we get out of here, call the Guards, and—'

'No!' Scarecrow shouts. 'No police. Please. Let me go and I'll help you. I'll tell you fucking everything.'

He squints and licks his lips.

'Donna and Marie,' he whispers. 'I can tell you about them.'

'What?' I've done it before I even realize – grabbed his jaw with both hands. It's sudden, rough. 'What you saying about the twins?'

In the distance, there's the sound of an engine approaching.

Scarecrow's looking right in my face.

'I know,' he says. He enunciates his words slowly. 'I know how you got your scars.'

Outside, the engine noise is getting louder. Coming closer.

'We have to go,' Joe says.

'Please,' Scarecrow moans.

The sound of a car pulling up outside. The engine cutting. The door clicking open.

Joe's in a pure panic. 'Oh fuck, man.'

'*Please*,' Scarecrow says.

I grab Joe by the arm and we run into the darkness behind a stack of barrels and crates.

In the quiet I hear Scarecrow sobbing.

The air changes. Someone else is in the barn. Slow steps, scuffing the ground. I peer through the crates. A torch in a hand, approaching Scarecrow.

Then I hear Teabag's voice. 'Lose your gag, did you? What? You still don't want to talk to me?'

Teabag crouches over Scarecrow's legs. 'I'd say that nose is broken, ha? What you think?' He taps on Scarecrow's nose and Scarecrow lets out a high-pitched sound of pain. Spit dangles from his mouth in strings.

'That hurt, did it?' Teabag sighs. 'Yeah… Yeah.'

His hand snaps out and grabs Scarecrow's nose tight. The scream fills the barn. I feel it in my guts.

Teabag straightens up and turns in our direction. Then, in this pure cheerful voice, he calls out, 'I know you're hiding there.'

Teabag wrenches on a huge fluorescent light and the full sight of Scarecrow is brutal. His skin's like bashed fruit. I step out from behind the crates, all excuses, shoulders bunched up, hands out. 'I was only looking for the twins.'

'Seen what this cunt done up the house, did you?' Teabag says. 'Made shite of the place.'

I glance back to the crates, where Joe's still hiding, but Teabag follows my gaze.

'You alone?' he says.

'Yeah.'

Teabag's still staring at the crates. 'What's this fucker after saying to you, Mush?'

'Nothing.'

He prods Scarecrow with his foot. 'Doesn't sound like you, Blinkie, does it? Is Mush lying to me?'

'He asked me to let him go,' I say. 'Told me he knew things.'

'That right?' Teabag says. 'What you know about, Blinkie? Hah?'

'Please,' Scarecrow – Blinkie – whimpers. 'I'm gonna piss meself.'

'Sure you're drenched already. What's a bit more piss gonna do?'

A smile in Teabag's eyes, despite everything. He's enjoying this. Fully in character, now he's got me for an audience. 'Saw your car parked down by the gate, Mush. Were you poking around the house, hah?' He lights a cigarette and chins in

Scarecrow's direction. 'This fucker here done that mess. Oh yeah. Friend of the family, Blinkie fucking Roche.'

'Please, Teabag,' Blinkie says. 'I won't run. I... I need to piss.'

'Then *piss*, cunt,' Teabag says. He leans his boot on Blinkie's lower stomach and Blinkie groans. Teabag drags his boot along the floor. 'You're only an animal.'

Blinkie shouts up at me, 'I'll tell you what happened your friend! I'll tell you where—'

Teabag kicks him in the chest and shouts, 'Don't be filling his head with your shite, now. He's a liar, Mush. A snake. Looking for shit he's not owed. Isn't that it, Blinkie?'

Blinkie whispers a curse.

'Awful big words out of you,' Teabag says.

Blinkie looks at me. He hisses, 'I'll tell you the truth about this whole town.'

Teabag crouches before Blinkie. 'Give us a moment here, Mush.'

He takes Blinkie by the hair, twists his head, and digs his lit cigarette into Blinkie's earhole. Blinkie shrieks. His bound legs try to kick out, but can't. His scream turns to a wail. The sound is long.

Teabag straightens up. He claps his hands. 'Right, Mush. Let's go have a chat with Uncle Ger, hah?'

Uncle Ger's coming through the front door as we enter the sitting room. He stops when he sees me. Huge beard on him, like a cloud of greys.

'I was looking for the twins,' I say in a small voice.

'See them here, do ya?' he says.

'No.'

'So fuck off.'

'He's been out the barn,' Teabag says.

Uncle Ger darkens. 'Has he, now?'

Teabag nudges me. 'Tell him what Blinkie said to you before I got here.'

'I dunno, he was making no sense. He said he knew how I

got me scars. And that he knows things about me life even I don't. He... he said he knew things about the twins.'

Ger looks at me for a long moment. He scoffs. But from the way he looks at Teabag, I can see there's more to it than they're saying.

'Will one of ye please tell me what's going on.' My voice is quivering.

'You'd want to calm yourself,' Uncle Ger says.

'Don't be feeling sorry for Blinkie,' Teabag says. 'He's the one who started all this.'

He points to the broken windows, the upturned furniture.

'That's all him. Started a couple of weeks ago. Every night we'd wake up to the sound of another window smashing. We didn't know what the fuck was going on. Under siege, like.'

'Poisoned the fucking dogs and all, so he did,' Uncle Ger says.

'What? Why?'

'Business disagreement.'

I think of the swell and bloodshine of Blinkie's face. The way Teabag made him piss himself.

'A "business disagreement"?' I say. 'The guy's in bits.'

Uncle Ger steps to me and I step back.

'Think I enjoy having to discipline that stupid cunt out there just cos he's flaking his toys out the pram? The man's been a fool and he knows it. We gave him contracts to sign and the dumb fuck didn't bother reading them through. He knows it was all above board. He knows he cheated himself out of money. Hasn't got a leg to stand on. So he's been playing the hard man up here, smashing me fucking windows, doing in me dogs, trying to make a play.'

'But what he said about Donna and Marie—'

'He's *playing* you, Mush. A sly cunt like that, he'd say whatever the fuck it'd take for you to let him go. Blinkie knows fuck all about nothing.'

'The twins—'

'They're not. Fucking. *Here*. And if they were, you know what I'd do? I'd drag the pair of them out that fucking barn and give them a gawk at that spastic to see what happens when you go looking for money you're not owed.'

Teabag goes to intervene but Ger waves a hand. His face is red.

'Let me tell you about Donna and Marie, hah? They came up here a few nights ago. Hadn't seen either of them in fuck knows how long. Me own flesh and blood. Only ever come here when they're looking for money. And me already bled to death by their mother.'

Flecks of spit on his lip.

'But they're not looking for money,' he says. 'They're asking me about the fucking Lananns, of all people. All sorts of questions. I say to them, *Who's been filling your heads with this muck?* They won't tell me. And d'you know, by now I've half a mind to think it's probably that handicap out in the barn, cos he's the one who—'

'*Christ*, Ger,' Teabag says. He's glaring. A warning in his voice, hands raised. 'Take it easy now.'

Uncle Ger's breathing heavily through his nose. He's like a dog in a cage.

'Yesterday evening meself and Teabag hung about at the end of the yard, watching the house. Waiting for the cunt to show up again for more of his window-smashing bullshit. So what's he do? Gomey fucker comes scarpering up to the house. And this time he sneaks in, thinking he's the brave man. Starts tearing the place up. Like a rat that doesn't even know it's in a trap.'

He sneers at Teabag. Then he looks at me. 'Know where we caught him? In the twins' room. You should see the state of the place.'

'I have,' I say. I think of the knifed mattresses. The puke and the blood smudges on the ground. 'That's the whole reason I came up here, like. I thought this is where the twins would be hiding out.'

Uncle Ger and Teabag stare me out of it.

'What d'you mean, *hiding out*?' Uncle Ger says.

'Donna and Marie,' I say. 'No one's seen them in days.'

A quick look between Uncle Ger and Teabag.

'Since when?' Teabag says.

'Friday.' I wave my phone. 'They've been sending weird WhatsApps.' I pass them the phone and they scroll through the messages from Marie. The picture of me and Dudley. **NO POLICE**. The photo of Kala with the twins on her lap. 'The twins put on a big front,' I say, 'but they're pure sweet, like. Why would they send around stuff like this?'

Another look between Uncle Ger and Teabag. There's this whole other conversation happening between them, in their eyes.

'He wouldn't dare,' Uncle Ger mutters.

'Maybe he would,' Teabag says.

'Me daughters?' Uncle Ger says. 'Me fucking *daughters*?'

I go to ask them what the hell's going on but they're already rushing out the back of the house, towards the barn. I grab my phone and message Joe:

get out of there

now

It's only then that I realize. I still have his phone. He gave it to me, to show me a photo from the other night. A picture of a hooded man, standing tall between the twins.

Joe

THE GRASS TOWERS over you. Slosh through it and it sounds wet, though it can't be wet, cos it hasn't rained yet, but it's going to, soon. Sky's dark with it. Thick and heavy with clouds like giant bruises and you're running away from the farm. You were too afraid to budge at first. So frightened in that barn you couldn't move.

Mush had put a hand to your arm when Teabag called out. He told you to stay put. As if you needed to be told. You stayed where you were, hidden, safe, removed. Couldn't hear what Teabag and Mush were saying. Blood was too loud in your ears. Sat on the ground, face in your hands, tried to imagine you were elsewhere. This wasn't happening if you didn't see it happening. Covered your ears at the sound of the man shrieking. Tried not to piss yourself.

And then it was quiet. Just you, the silence, and the ruined man crumpled against the pillar.

Dad would come and fix this. Dad would save you. Wanted to call Dad. But Mush still had your phone.

You knew you'd have to rush behind the barn, into the long grass.

That's where you are now. Finding your way back to the Warren. The safety of the car. Mush will be there, waiting for you. Safety of him. The bag of cans. It'll all be fine. Nothing bad can happen, you're Joe Br—

Screams begin to peal across the sky, from the barn. You've never heard anything like them. You run, stumble, grunt, get

264

up, whimper, thrash your arms at the long grass and stamp it down, anything to get the fuck out of here. Want Dad. Want Theresa. Want someone to cradle you. Want a drink. Want to hit Mush for bringing you here.

You'd always thought of yourself as the hero of your own life. But as you walked out of that barn, you weren't heroic. Shoulders hunched to make yourself smaller. Heard the man stirring against the pillar. 'Please,' he said. His voice all clotted with snot, blood, who the fuck knows. 'Help me.'

You looked at him.

One of his eyes was sealed shut with a welt. The other was open, swimming with redness. It blinked. That was all it took. You saw it happen in his face, like you've seen it happen in thousands of faces. The recognition dawning. Who you were. His eyes rolled upwards and he moaned, 'Oh God. Oh God.' Then he began to roar, his voice echoing, 'I'm gonna die here. I'm gonna die.'

You ran. You're still running. Away from the barn. Away from the man. Away from anything that reminded you how, inside every person, beneath all the faces they prepare for the world, there's a mewling animal, trembling and alone.

Your whole body was ringing. A hot-cold rush of anger and fear and other ugly feelings you'd never had to feel before, feelings you were having more and more, all because of Kala. She was doing this to you. Aoife'd told you that Kala was going on secret fucking trips out of Kinlough with Helen. She mentioned this like it was no big deal, but the thought of it – of Kala thinking and doing things that hadn't first passed through you – made you want to fucking break things. You didn't know why. You hated feeling this way. Why was she doing this to you? You were heroic but she made you feel weak. Look weak. Sometimes in your head you called her a bitch, and you hated how she could make you do that. Fuck sake. You wanted her to be everything. To know what you wanted before you wanted it. You wanted her to be just as you wanted her. Her hair like that. Her clothes like this. But you hated whenever she was *just* as you wanted her, too, cos she was supposed to be of the Other Place, beyond you, elevating you. Wanted her to carry you beyond everything you knew. Couldn't fucking *stand* when she knew things beyond what you knew. All these stupid in-jokes between her and Helen. A new one every weekend. Wanted her to be mysterious. Hated any aspect of her that was a mystery. Kept thinking about what Teabag had said, that day in Hogan's Square: *You know how many lads this wan's had in and out her cunt?* She was your first shift, but you knew you weren't hers. She was too good a kisser. The thought of her as some sort of experienced slut, her skin, her mouth and smell, her body begging to be ruined by other guys, crushed into nothing. Made you get hard. Made you furious. Couldn't stand this power she had over you. Wanted her ruined and exalted. All for you. Couldn't stand when she was all for you.

How she texted every day, asking to meet up. She didn't get that you couldn't hang out on weeknights. Being number one in school didn't just *happen*, you had to work for it. You told her ye could only see each other on weekends, each Friday evening a frenzied drama of reunion, tongues and teeth, attacking each other down dark laneways. But she agreed to this a bit too easily. What did she get up to during the week? You pictured strangers' eyes lingering on her body on Fox Street, and you wanted this, wanted them to want her, to envy you. But you couldn't stand the thought she might want it too. Might invite it. You wondered who she was when she was alone in the dark, in her room, without you there, to make her what she was to you. Who was that stranger? What were her thoughts?

The day Aoife told you about Kala's secret little trips, you decided to test Kala when she arrived at the Arch. Went into a sulk and ignored her, talking to everyone but her all afternoon. Said goodbye to the gang and went home for your dinner without even acknowledging her. Waited for her to call to your door, wearing that look on her face like she was sorry, even though she didn't know what she had to be sorry for. Like a dog coming back for another kick.

As ye walked to Lough Caille, she took your hand. Her skin was warm and soft. You let yours go limp. At the jetty, she said, 'What's up, babe?'

You shrugged. Let her figure it out.

'Where've you been all day?' She opened and closed her hand, like a toddler asking for a toy. 'I miss you.'

'I'm right fucking here.'

A different sort of quiet then. In the distance, birds were churning in great wheels against the sink of the sun. The evenings were coming in quicker now. Autumn now. Summer, fucking over.

You know how many lads this wan's had in and out her cunt?

In Teabag's words, you heard the shadows of other words, said by other voices, unknown faces, people who knew things about Kala that you didn't. People laughing at you all over Kinlough.

'What was Teabag talking about that time at Hogan's Square?' You hesitated. Then pushed further. 'Made it sound like you were some sort of slut.'

A wrinkle between Kala's eyes. 'What?'

'Said you've been with loads of lads.'

'Does it matter what Teabag Lyons says? Everyone knows he's a cunt.'

Your breath was tight in your chest. Everything inside cranking up.

'Girls aren't supposed to say *cunt*,' you said.

Kala gave a joyless laugh. She tucked her hair behind her ears. 'This conversation's stupid.'

'So you're calling me stupid.'

'Joe,' she said. 'You're after calling me a slut.'

'You're not denying it.' A new sort of feeling in you. A coiling poison. 'How many lads have you shifted before me?'

She was quiet.

'It's a simple question, Kala.'

'Come on,' she said. Her face was going red. 'I'm with you. We're together, like.'

'Go on. How many lads have you let in your mouth before me?'

She said nothing for a long time. Her eyes were glassy. Fuck sake. How could she belong to the Other Place if she was going to be this pathetic? Her lip trembled. Some part of you, you were surprised, felt pleasure at this. Shame.

The others were approaching on their bikes, loud and laughing. Helen's stupid dog running around them.

'How are the lovers?!' Aoife called.

'Fuck sake,' Kala muttered, turning away.

You raised a hand to the others. 'We'll catch up with ye in a bit, right?'

Helen looked from you to Kala. 'Is everything okay?'

'Yeah, all good,' you grinned. It was mad, how you could switch faces.

Helen lingered a moment longer, staring at you. This suspicious fucking bitch.

When they fucked off, Kala's face was all flushed. 'I don't want you to think badly of me,' she said.

You could apologize. Part of you knew you should. Even wanted to. But fuck sake. She'd made you feel weak enough today. You were Joe Brennan.

'I feel terrible,' she said. 'You've made me feel really terrible.' Then she cried.

'Hey,' you said. The sight of her tears immediately softened you. 'It's all right. It's okay.'

She leaned in to you. 'I'm not a monster. I'm not a freak.'

It was a weird choice of words. You didn't know what she meant.

But that didn't matter. What mattered was she was looking to you for comfort, even though you were the one hurting her. The feeling was pale and still. The sense of something being securely fixed in place, even if that meant it first had to be broken.

You're walking the Warren, back to Kinlough. The cans are rushing through you. You got them from Mush's car. One after another, a relief to each cough-spit they make when you crack a new one open. You're no longer climbing into fields to piss. Fuck that, no need for that. Just go on the side of the road. No one here to see you. You're loud inside yourself. Moaning.

Sound of a car coming around the corner. Pulling to a stop behind you.

You've barely closed the passenger door when Mush takes off, racing back to Kinlough.

Your vision's gone wonky. Gotta squint to keep Mush in focus. His face is tight, glaring at the road.

'Fuck was that back there?' you slur. Drain the current can, reach for another one. 'We need to go to the Guards.'

Mush shakes his head. 'No. Teabag and Uncle Ger reckon he's—'

'I don't wanna know!' you shout. 'Don't tell me any of this. I can't be involved in—'

'You're already involved,' Mush says. 'Blinkie Roche. That name mean anything to you? Put down the fucking can and *think*, man. Never heard that name before?'

He shoves a hand in his pocket and hands you your phone.

'Send me that photo you took the other night. The one of the twins with the lad in the hood.'

'You think that's the guy in the shed?'

Mush rubs at his forehead.

The relief of having your phone. A tether to the world. A protective wall. Phone's full of notifications. Message from Theresa apologizing for the argument earlier. She's sent you a childish drawing of a cute creature holding a sign that says, 'I believe in you.'

'Why can't we go to my dad?'

'Fuck sake,' Mush snaps. 'I said *no*. Not yet. I need to think.'

'What's there to think about? We can't just *pretend* not to have seen what we saw.'

Tap-tap-tap. Mush's fingers on the wheel. It's only now you notice his knuckles are swollen, discoloured. Bruises. Blood.

He catches you looking at them.

'Don't ask,' he says. This nervousness in his voice.

'Jesus, man, I've a reputation to lose,' you shout. 'I'm not about to implicate myself in—'

'You're as fucking self-involved. Did you see what was happening in that shed?'

'Did *you*?'

'I swear, man, if you go to the Guards about this—'

'But—'

'I've forgiven you plenty,' Mush says. 'But you fuck this up and I'll never—' He catches himself. Shakes his head.

'Go on,' you say.

'Whatever. Nothing.'

'Don't play the quiet dope with me, man. Fuck sake, I *know* you, remember? Can't you say what you think, for once? Think I can't feel it off you? This stubborn, sulky—'

'You're hammered.'

'Who the fuck are you to *forgive* me for anything? It's not my fault your life's shit. No one made you stay in Kinlough. Just because I—'

'Joe,' he groans. 'Peel your eyeballs off your navel for five fucking seconds, would you? No one thinks about you as much as you do.'

Fuck him. Trying to make you feel bad. You already feel bad.

'Pull over. I'm sick of this. Fucking... passive-aggressive shit.'

Mush stops the car and sighs, like he's a parent indulging a toddler screaming and punching the floor. You're not a fucking toddler.

'Look,' you say. 'I know you think I abandoned you. I know you think I should've come back for Aidan's funeral. I—'

Mush raises his hands like a preacher and shouts, 'Joe! Jesus fucking Christ! It's *not. About. You.* None of this is about you. I've enough on me plate and the last thing I need is you making it worse, okay? I'm asking you – *begging* you – to forget what you saw tonight. Don't call the Guards. Don't tell your dad. Go back to your own little world. Let me take care of this.'

And there it is. Your oldest friend. The distance between ye.

You squint at Mush. 'When I look at you, man... I feel this... like, guilt all the time, and... I want to get rid of this feeling and I need you to... I want—'

Mush's eyes soften, then he looks away. 'I don't have time for this, Joe. I need to take care of the twins.'

'But... I can help, man. I can take care of things.'

He glances at the empties in your lap. An expression on his face that you're going to remember.

'Christ, man,' he says. 'You can barely take care of yourself.'

Helen

I PUSH THE bed aside and check the loose floorboard in the corner of the room. Evening light, like gold on the wood. Donna's dress for the wedding hangs in its plastic cover from the wardrobe door. Pauline must have left it there for her. I still have not met Donna and Marie. When Dudley dropped me home, I found Theresa and Pauline in the back garden, talking about them. But my mind was churning with everything – Mulkerns at the school, Aoife in Carthy, Dudley and the investigation – so I excused myself and came up here to Donna's room. My room.

Donna has not found my secret spot. My things are where I left them, beneath the floorboard in a large Tupperware container. I go through the objects methodically, an ugly throb in my chest. The bracelet Kala made for me, red and green twine, frayed. Magazines I do not remember reading, postcards, knick-knacks kept for obscure, incoherent reasons that must have mattered at the time. A stuffed packet of photos from different disposable cameras. I remember one specific camera. Something in it was broken, so when the counter went to zero, the machine reset to the beginning and allowed us to take photos on top of the existing pictures. It was only later, when we got the film developed, that we realized. Each photograph was now two different pictures, mapped on to one another. Most of these pictures are chaos, but several achieve an uncanny juxtaposition. There is one of Joe playing guitar while Kala sits against the wall, knees tucked in to herself, watching. Hovering over them are three sets of eyes, three mouths. Kala, Aoife, me. One of us is holding the camera. We are laughing. Aidan is behind the neck of Joe's guitar, petting Misty, looking at the lens.

I find a collection of tapes. A bootleg PJ Harvey concert, the cover a cheap photocopy print-off with a handwritten setlist. But the cassette inside is labelled 'Midnite Jams 30 Oct 2003.' The night before the Halloween party. I remember this. I was sleeping over at Kala's. We were sleepy, but wired with excitement for the boys' gig the next day. It was just Kala and me, sitting cross-legged in the centre of her room, with the lights off. Three tealights purled the dark. Aidan's drum kit glinted in the candlelight. A tape recorder was on the floor between us. Threads of smoke poured upwards from a stick of incense. Kala had her guitar in her lap and I had Joe's in mine. I was playing a single chord, over and over, changing the cadence of my strumming every minute or so. The drone thickened in the room. Kala was playing simple progressions. She closed her eyes and began to sing. Long, held breaths. She rocked her weight back and forth. When she did not stop, I closed my eyes. The candlelight was a blur of hot reds. I began to harmonize. I heard the smile in Kala's voice. There was no eye watching us, judging us. There was only us. Our voices moving in and out of one another. I thought about what the Mammy had once said: in an earlier time, they would have burned us as witches.

The next morning I lay in the rumpled mess of her bed listening to the recording, the sheets still drowsy with the tang of sleep, watching Kala as she kneeled before her mirror, preparing herself for the day. This was something I recognized as essential to girlhood: the endless act of getting ready, as though some inevitable something would deliver us into life. But with Kala, it was different. Life was already happening. We were happening to it. In my mind, she was not applying make-up: it was warpaint.

She bunched her hair between her fists to pineapple it at the top of her head. The movement raised her cheesecloth shirt over her hips. She pinched at her stretch marks. Forks of lightning across her softest parts. 'Gross,' she said. This was a dance we did often. Kala made efforts to hide things I loved about her body and I reassured her they did not exist. I liked the shadow of stubble under her arms. The lip of belly fat when she bent over, cursing after a dropped contact lens. These fractures in her perfection were fissures through which I could slip and be with her, behind the curtain of herself, sharing parts of her she would never allow Joe to see. I loved her concentrated look as she adjusted her fringe to veil her crooked eye, the focus with which she tried out different earrings, layers of necklaces and bracelets. These moments were for me.

'This music's as good as anything the boys do,' I said. 'We should play this for them and not say it's us. I guarantee they'd be into it.'

Kala smiled in the mirror at me. A faint sprinkle of glitter on her cheeks.

'We should make our *own* band,' I said, leaning up from the mattress.

Kala scoffed. 'Can you imagine? They'd never stop taking the piss out of us.'

'We wouldn't be doing it for them.'

Kala's voice had a faraway note as she continued to apply her eyeliner. 'Yeah, but they wouldn't look at it like that. Joe wouldn't like it.'

'Pity about him.'

Her eyes fixed on me in the mirror. I had violated some sort of threshold. There was a moment, then Kala smiled. 'Babe, you're beginning to sound like you're from Kinlough.'

I want to hear this tape. I look about the room to see if there is anything that plays a cassette. That's when I see Dad standing in the door, watching me.

'How long have you been there?'

'Are you okay?' he says.

'I'm fine.'

I ignore him and open my laptop and read through all of Mrs Mulkerns and Dudley Brennan's information. I have organized a coherent set of timelines, questions that require answers.

September 1988

Fiona Lanann (13) is taken out of school. Clear evidence of pregnancy.

October/November??? 1988

Mulkerns visits the Lanann house to check on Fiona. Turned away from the door.

Fiona gives birth to Kala. Where, when, how? Hospital records? Kinlough or elsewhere? (how to access...?)

- Father: aware of Kala? still in Kinlough?
- Fiona: sent to relatives? mother & baby home? Magdalen Laundry?
- Fiona now: aware of Kala?

Dad begins looking through my box of things. 'I didn't want to throw anything away,' he says. 'I didn't know what stuff was of value, or...'

'What about Mam's clothes? There used to be bags of Mam's clothes. They had value.'

Dad frowns. 'Sure they were eaten alive with moths.'

'They weren't yours to throw away.'

Dad shifts uncomfortably. My words came out too fast, too sharp. I did not mean it that way, but I do not know how to tell him that.

Dad rubs at the back of his neck.

'Yeah, no... it's... eh... yeah like, with everything going on with, eh, with Kala and that... and ah... I thought... I don't know like. Yeah. If you need a shoulder to cry on, or—'

I blink and look back at the screen. I do not know how to have this conversation with him.

September 2001

- Kala enrolled in St Anne's.
- Teachers are notified not to mention Fiona – possible question of neglect of care on part of school (school should have followed up on Fiona's well-being)?
- Find out more on this (Mulkerns to provide contacts w. retired staff)

October 2003

- Kala comes to Mulkerns with information from school mags
- Mulkerns: Fiona was taken out of school while still pregnant. Not seen since. No further information.
- Kala v. distressed. Notable absences from school prior to Halloween break.
- Did Kala talk to the Mammy about Fiona? (need to speak to the Mammy)

I asked Mrs Mulkerns if she thought that there was some sort of connection between Kala's investigations into Fiona and her subsequent disappearance. Mrs Mulkerns said she did not know, she did not have enough information, but that her gut told her: yes.

November 2003

- Incident at St Anne's. Kala absconds from school.
- Hyundai incident: car belongs to a Seamus Roche (?) – Worked as a handyman for the Mammy. Dudley says he was a 'person of interest'. Interviewed but never charged. Who is Roche? Where is Roche now?

The dark begins to gather around the laptop. The screen throws blue shadow about the walls.

Dad is about to leave the room when I say, 'You ever heard of a man named Seamus Roche? Local guy, about your age.'

Dad frowns. 'You mean Blinkie? Sure you'd know him. Himself and his brother Dodo used to call over here, back in the Ger days. Why d'you ask?'

Blinkie. I remember – one of Ger's men, the twitching face, the squinting eyes. I remember Aoife impersonating the handyman working for the Mammy. I remember Kala laughing.

'Nothing. Just curious. Are you still in touch?'

Dad scratches his head. 'Nah, them bridges are long burned. Why – you didn't run into him last night in town, did you?'

'No,' I say. 'What was he like?'

Dad pauses. 'What's this about?'

'Nothing. But how would you describe him?'

'...He was unpredictable, y'know? If he got it into his head that someone was taking the piss he could turn very nasty.'

The doorbell rings downstairs.

Dad is frowning. 'What exactly is this about, Helen?'

Sudden, unfamiliar voices enter the house. Dad goes out to the landing to see who is at the door. When he does so, he rushes down the stairs. I go to the top step to see what is happening. An ugly heartcatch to the sight of two Guards shuffling down the hall after Dad and Pauline, following them to the kitchen. An echo of the days after Kala went missing. I take a moment to get my head together. The Guards have finally come to ask about Kala. I do not know what I will say to them. Dudley rattled me earlier, with his talk about sloppy investigative work, leads that were not followed up. I know from Canada – cops range from incompetent blowhards to complicit enforcers of entrenched power.

I go downstairs, ready to size the Guards up, figure their angle.

But when I enter the kitchen, it only takes a moment to realize the situation is different.

The Guards are sitting opposite Dad and Pauline. One of them is writing while the other speaks. Theresa is standing behind Pauline, one hand on Pauline's shoulder while the other worries at her mouth. This is not about Kala. It's about the twins. I am trying to meet Theresa's eyes when Pauline suddenly bursts into tears.

'Ah, love,' Dad goes to comfort her and Pauline shouts, 'If *one more person* tells me everything will be all right!'

She sniffs.

'I can feel it, Rossie. Right here, under me ribs. It was the same when we couldn't find Aidan. I knew it'd be bad. I knew it'd be so bad.'

Joe

IN TOWN, BY the canal. Vodka buzz. Birds perched on wires like ink silhouettes. Etchings against the sky. Used to stop and linger over sights like this. Used to look at them and not think anything, just let the image look into you. Sights like this, this small gap between Kinlough rooftops threading birds on a wire, how these moments imprinted themselves on you as a kid, when you were young enough that the rain on the cobblestones with the music in your headphones and a few dark birds on a wire would re-map your imagination, how moments like this conjured the coordinates between which your dreams still ping back and forth, the burning points from which your life's lived, the walls against which your heart hammers when you're alone and fucked in the dark.

You remember here, this spot, one of the first times ever being stoned. You were with Mush and Aidan. Seventeen years old. You don't know why, or how, this could've happened, because in your mind there's clean lines drawn between the childhood days of friendship, the Kala days when you all touched the Other Place, and the aftermath days of silence, disintegration, avoidance. Your brain's a static thing, stodgy, old, and you need to hold everything in distinct linear blocks. But life isn't like this – it doesn't come in neat episodes, it leaks and twists and knots and coils. Drink from the bottle. Put a hand on the canal railing. The metal's cool, like it was back then with Aidan and Mush, cos it was a wintry sort of night. One of those nights at the end of secondary school when yourself and Mush went to the cinema every Friday. It might have been the *Lost in Translation* night. You had to go to the bathroom during the film because 'Sometimes' by My Bloody Valentine came roaring like a tsunami out the walls in the middle of the film, a feeling like Kala was suddenly sitting in the row behind you. Barely saw the rest of the film, you were looking through the screen, to the blank darkness behind it. Yourself and Mush walking home that night and ye came across Aidan, sitting here, on the railings by the water. He was almost always alone now. By then the changes had already happened. Aoife's family moving to Carthy. Helen drifting into herself. Mush disappearing from life. And Aidan, leaving school at fifteen, to become whatever he was now becoming. You still spotted him the odd time around town, lingering around the winos and crusties down the Arch. You'd pretend not to see him. You heard the odd thing here or there – he was doing loads of pills, someone had seen him with his shirt off one lunchtime at Hogan's Square, trying to get lads from school to mosh with him. There was no clear point where you made the decision to let your lives unbraid themselves from one another. You just stood back and didn't intervene as it happened. 'The world doesn't hold itself together,' Dad once said. 'People make decisions. That's what keeps things intact.'

Somewhere along the way you'd let Aidan slide from your life, and now he was there in front of ye, perched on the railings behind the Cineplex.

'Well,' he said. 'How are the lads?'

Mush did most of the talking. Yourself and Aidan pretended not to see each other. Then he looked at you, still in your school uniform at nine o'clock on a Friday night. He made a lame joke about how hard you must be studying for the Leaving. You laughed, but it was a polite sort of laughter, and he knew it. Aidan took out a huge joint and lit it like it was a pure normal thing to do. He offered it to Mush and Mush said no, he was heading home and needed a clear head. When he offered it to you, he already had a look of triumph on his face, like he knew you wouldn't be up to it. So you took it. He smiled, a sort of 'Is that how it is?' smile. And it surprised you, but you couldn't help but smile back at him. And it wasn't cos you could always play Aidan on his terms and win, and that that was what made him Aidan and you Joe Brennan. It was something else. Like something you didn't realize you'd been missing was suddenly alive and in the world again, some part of yourself waking up after a long silence.

Ye dropped Mush off at the caf and kept walking together. Aidan asked you what you were thinking of doing after school. The hash was strong. You felt weak in your legs. A sort of rising in your chest. The floor falling out of every thought into a billion other thoughts whose floors were collapsing into even more thoughts.

Aidan was talking and you tried to focus, but the sky was wild.

'You should get the fuck out of this town, man,' he said. 'It's a dead end. Nothing here for you. Whole place is diseased.'

You didn't answer, you were too baked. Neither of ye spoke for a while. Which was fine. Ye were enjoying each other's company.

At one point Aidan started to walk slower, so you slowed down. Then he began to walk faster, so you walked faster. It became a silent game. One of ye would gradually modulate the speed, and the other would follow, and counteract it. Neither of ye acknowledged it. Ye just kept slowing down. Speeding up. Faster. Slower. You could feel him grinning. You grinning.

It made you feel good, which made you feel bad, because in that moment of being in his company, and seeing his face, the dark half-moons under his eyes, the surprising softness of his hands when he grabbed yours and pulled you into a quick hug goodbye, saying yeah yeah, goodbye goodbye goodbye, you knew then, in the face-to-face, that it had been wrong to think of Aidan as a lost cause, that no one is the simple playing card you reduce them to, that the versions of people you shuffle in your head while going from one moment to the next are just that, playing cards, flat and one-dimensional, that there's this whole animal being to everyone and that in this animal being there's a point where you and everyone else in the world can meet, but sure, what sort of a way would that be to go through the world? constantly crushed by the humanity of others? what would that mean for you, Joe Brennan, and the Other Place, a safe place beyond such frailty? so you pulled back from Aidan even before pulling back from the hug, because it was easier that way, to make him another card you could return to the deck, and walked home, and you wrote about that moment years later, when he died, in a song that might've meant something to you in its genesis but is now one of your encore anthems, a tune that rhymes the word 'sky' with 'wonder why', a song that soundtracks redemption arcs in reality shows, where real people are themselves reduced to playing cards shuffled in the deck, their lives flattened into something more digestible, and yours is the music the world chooses to accompany such false moments, because the people who engineer such moments recognize your music as being fit for this, and you sold them your music for this, and this is who you are, and how you will be remembered, if you are remembered, till you are forgotten, like all things are forgotten, like Aidan on this canal bank is forgotten, but you remember, and you drink.

Mush

FOX STREET IS quiet out the window, in the blue dark. The last dregs of Sunday night staggering against the shopfronts, heels in hand. Can't sleep, thinking about the twins. What Uncle Ger told me about them coming up the farm, asking about the Lananns. What Blinkie said about them. He must've been fucking with my head, like. He must've. Cos Uncle Ger and Teabag went at him in the barn, knocked the shit out of him, like, and he didn't say a word about the twins. Not to them.

My knuckles are aching. All bruising. Cuts and dried blood. What I done.

My head's full of my stomach and my stomach's one thick knot. Mam's at Rossie's with Auntie Pauline. Awake, too. Worried sick. Tomorrow was meant to be the wedding. I should be worrying about the twins getting me to sneak them drinks at the reception. Marie trying to get me to dance.

I FaceTimed Mam after the farm. Told her the twins weren't there. She said Pauline had been on to the Guards. Two officers came out to the house, took a report and all that. Mam looked old, on the phone. Maybe it was just the light. Last time I saw her like that was after I got my face. I remember. Whenever she thought I wasn't looking, she was gone elsewhere, in her head. At first I thought she was worried about the caf, if we were gonna go under. That was her usual fear. But I knew we were better off since my scars, cash-wise, cos Uncle Ger had stopped asking us for rent. He'd made me the offer in the hospital. Told me he wanted to help out. Felt a duty to make sure I was looked after. So I agreed not to say anything about what had happened my face if he left Mam alone, and that was that: Teabag and the lads never called in to the caf again. In my head, Mam thought of this as an act of kindness from Uncle Ger. Kids always think parents are fucking naive. As the years went by, I realized she must've known. Maybe not in detail, but... she knew. Some sort of bargain had been made between Uncle Ger and me, and she knew she was benefiting from it. She never asked, and I never told, cos why bother? The things that make life comfortable are always unacceptable, if you look at them square on. Someone, somewhere, is always suffering so you can be happy. Which is why most people spend their time looking the other direction.

I dunno what to do.

I scroll a while to disconnect, feel myself sliding down the surface of the world, when I realize I don't want that. I've lived too many evenings of that. The world's not gonna reset to normal after this. It'll have changed, and so will I. Something's getting lost, or has been lost already.

I dunno.

I don't fucking know.

I keep hearing Blinkie's voice in the barn, after Uncle Ger and Teabag ran out to the shed and got at him. The screams.

I walk down Fox Street with my hood up, even though there's no one about to look at me. The River Purr's galloping past the Arch into the Atlantic. There's a cold wind running over the water. I'm the only person around. Kinlough's humming, all its edges blurred in the half-light. This is where we came, Kala and me, the night of the first-ever sneak-out. I'd been all nervous about hanging out with her, one on one without Joe, and she'd rolled her eyes and rode ahead on her bike, smiling over her shoulder. 'Be nice to me,' she'd said. We cycled into town. Kala pulled up her bike across the river from the Arch, and stood looking at the town like it was about to reveal something.

'It's amazing, right?'

At first I thought she was taking the piss. I went to say, 'Sure it's only Kinlough,' but I didn't want to sound like a fool. There might be something she could see that I couldn't.

So I looked, and looked. How the light from Toner's Bridge ran over the river, pure warm and bright with street lamps, and taxis were zipping across the bridge into town. From where we were, even with the noise of the Purr, you could hear the hum coming from the pubs, the people. All this life in the night.

For the first time I looked at Kinlough and thought, it could be a film. Kala was smiling, and I'd this mad notion for a moment that she knew what I was thinking.

'It could almost be a real place,' she said. She had her Polaroid in her hands. She took a few steps back and told me to turn myself, so I'd be looking at the town in profile. Normally I'd have been squirming, but something felt loose with Kala, so I did what I was told.

'Turn your jaw more towards town,' she said. 'I wanna catch your bone structure.'

The night flashed and Kala's camera wheezed as it made the photo. 'Now do me,' she said. We swapped places, and I waited a moment while Kala threw her head forward and back, her hair fanning in the air then landing back on her head where she put a hand through it. She turned at an angle and I saw how she'd wanted me to hold myself. Girls knew how to do stuff like that, like they could always see themselves how a camera would see them. This look of concentration on her face, holding one arm with the other. She looked like a rock queen.

When I took the photo, her look broke and she gave me a big smile, and stood close as we waited for the photos to develop. We both looked cool – our skin ghostly in the flash, a mystery of murky lights behind us.

'If Teabag or any of the lads saw me looking like that, they'd murder me.'

'You're not like them, babe,' she said. 'You're better than that.'

There's water trickling down my neck, inside my collar. It's cold, so I pull my hood tight. I've always reminded myself of what Kala said, that I wasn't like the Lyons, I was better than them.

But it's not true. My knuckles are in bits, like. I betrayed myself tonight, up at the farm. Betrayed the person Kala thought I was. Betrayed her.

In the barn, I flinched every time Teabag or Uncle Ger hit Blinkie. It was awful. They'd hit him first, then ask a question about the twins. Blinkie kept saying he didn't know what they were talking about, but every time he spoke his voice was quieter and his mouth was bloodier. Then they kept hitting him, over and over. His face was in bits and he wasn't making proper words any more, just mouthing to himself. Uncle Ger and Teabag stood back to rest, breathing heavily, opening and closing their fingers. I saw that they were just enjoying it. Hurting someone. I told myself I wasn't part of this. I was better than this, outside this.

That was when Blinkie whispered up at me. 'They were asleep,' he said.

My guts froze.

'What?' I crouched down in front of him. His face was such a mess. 'What?'

He was looking me right in the eyes. He wouldn't speak. But I swear he was smiling.

I hit him. I dunno how many times. 'That's it,' Teabag called from behind me. 'Good man,' Uncle Ger said. I stepped back to stop myself, but when I saw the red pulp of his nose and mouth I felt this mad rage at him for the guilt he was making me feel, rage at myself for the way Donna had looked at me through the window of the caf, her eyes, my favourite eyes, and how I hadn't just got off my arse and gone after her, and I grabbed Blinkie by the head with my thumbs on his cheek-bones, didn't even know what I was doing, and said, 'Where are they?' and his eyes rolled and he was still smiling under all that blood so I sank a thumb against one of his eyeballs and he shouted, 'No!' and I relaxed my thumb as he breathed out the words, 'I was only being friendly,' and Teabag yanked me back and Uncle Ger took Blinkie by the neck and went, 'The fuck you just say?' and slammed him in the stomach with all his force and said, 'The fuck you just say?' and I was gonna be sick, my fingers all bloody and hurt and I couldn't stand the sound of the hitting, the yelling, and I went out of the barn with everything in me all shaking and I leaned against one of the sheds and heard Ger shouting, hitting, my hands pure bloody, I felt carsick, dizzy, walked around the back of a shed when—

It was Kala. I could swear it. Looking just like she did the night of the Crawley House. This startled look on her face, staring at me. I thought I was losing the plot. 'Is it really you? It can't be.'

But I blinked and there was no one there.

I puked. My phone was full of messages from Mam and Theresa, saying that the Guards were out at the house taking a report. When I tried to message them back, my hands were shaking. I had to grip the steering wheel tight as I drove from the farm, just to stop them shaking asunder, and I was still gripping the wheel when I picked up Joe in the Warren.

The rain's louder and faster on my hood now. A dazzle of pinpricks in the puddles already forming at my feet. It's beginning to lash. Somewhere, Kala's out there in all that rain, inside a world that's lost and drowning, begging to get washed clean.

I take out my phone. For the first time in years I know exactly what I have to do.

Helen

MUSH CALLS TO ask if I am free. He has something to show me. He will not tell me what it is, or where we need to go, only that we need to go there by car, and it is important. Everyone in the house is still awake, waiting for word from the twins. Dad has gone for a drive about town, just to check if there has been any sight of them anywhere. As I take a quick shower to wake myself up, I work through who I need to speak to next about Kala and Fiona. The Mammy, of course. I will return to her house first thing tomorrow and ask her about what Mrs Mulkerns told me. But there are others.

When I go back to the bedroom, towelling my hair, Mush's mam is sitting on the bed looking through my old photographs.

'No word on the twins?' I say.

Lydia shakes her head. A picture of Mush and Kala in her hands. 'All that potential, hah? Ye were all so gorgeous.' She sniffs. 'You heading out somewhere?'

'Yeah. Me and Mush.'

'Doing what?'

I hesitate. 'Just... things.'

'I heard you've been going about asking questions. I hope you're not getting him involved in something.'

When I do not answer, she holds up the photo of Mush and Kala. 'They went out looking for trouble. And look where it got them.'

A sudden movement down at the front door. Weight shifting about in the dark. A groan of floorboards. Dad shouting out. I hear Pauline and Theresa rush out to the hall, calling the twins' names.

When I look down from the top of the stairs, my stomach sinks. I have a déjà vu of the night I found Dad slumped at the front door, at the feet of Ger and his men. Only, no. It is not Dad on the floor. Dad is standing, holding someone beneath the arms. The rest of the body is sliding into a thick puddle of itself.

It's Joe. Dad says he found him slumped against a wall outside the estate.

Joe's head falls back like a baby's. Theresa is grabbing his ankles. She and Dad carry him into the sitting room. They gather around him, putting him on the sofa.

'He's after pissing himself,' Dad says.

Pauline says she'll get pyjamas for him. She rushes past me, up the stairs.

Theresa is on her knees by the sofa, unbuckling Joe's belt and unzipping his jeans. Joe flails at her with his hands and she brushes them back.

'It's okay, it's okay.'

Joe's eyes roll back in his head.

She peels the soaking denim down his thighs. The dark stain covers half his underwear. I look away.

'Get your friend a glass of water, love,' Dad says.

But I do not move. I do not know why. Pauline is back with pyjama pants and she hands them to Dad, who has already removed Joe's boxers. Dad gathers up the legs of the pyjamas, takes one of Joe's feet and snugs it into the ankle sleeve, then does the same with the other foot. He carefully pulls the waist up, lifting Joe's hips. The gentleness confuses me. Some memory of him doing the same for me, after my bath, as a kid.

He looks at me. 'The water?'

Joe lurches up and vomits all over his own clothes. He groans.

'Don't worry about it,' Dad says. 'We'll get you cleaned up.'

'I'll get a bucket for the night,' Theresa says.

'I'm sorry,' Joe slurs.

'Helen,' Dad says. 'The water.'

Joe is crying. 'Please don't tell my dad.'

'You're all right,' Dad says.

Theresa comes back with a bucket.

'Help me,' Joe says. His face is all twisted up. 'Help me.'

Theresa breathes heavily. She pauses and pinches the skin between her eyebrows. She glares at me. 'Are you going to do something or what?'

I open my mouth.

Theresa shoves past me and mutters, 'You're as useless.'

I follow her into the kitchen where she stands at the sink, filling up a glass of water.

'He told me he was serious about being off the drink,' she says. 'I believed him.'

I put a hand on her arm. 'Joe Brennan's not worth getting upset over.'

'Oh, take a fucking day off, Helen, will you? Do you even care about people?'

'Excuse me?'

'Oh yeah, I forgot. You care about *humanity*. The *idea* of people. You just can't stand actual flesh-and-blood human beings. You swan about, looking down the length of your nose at us—'

'Where's this coming from?'

'Forget it.'

She makes to leave, when I say, 'Jesus, I don't look down on you. I *envy* you. You have a life, people who love you, a home town you—'

'Don't patronize me. I live in Kinlough cos I can't afford to live anywhere else. I'm twenty-six years old and Dad still has to give me a dig-out every few months, like. I'll never have a life of my own unless I can bring my work to where it needs to be, and I can't do that unless I meet the right people, and I can't do *that* cos they all live in cities, and – guess what? – every single fucking city in this country is too expensive to live in, and I'm completely suffocating and—'

'I didn't know.'

'How could you? You haven't bothered to talk to me for more than thirty seconds since you got here. I've been bending over backwards to include you in things and all you do is come out with condescending bullshit about how much of a shithole Kinlough is and how people I care about don't deserve my help. I mean, Jesus, why did you even come back?'

I stammer, like Dad. 'The... the wedding, obviously.'

'As if you give a *shit* about the wedding,' Theresa says. 'Every chance you've got, you've run a mile from anything to do with it. With us.'

'I—'

'I know you're dealing with the Kala thing. I get it. But, like, we're freaking out down here about the twins and you spend the whole evening up in your room? You're as fucking cold, like. Jesus, it's like all you do is upset people.'

I want to be mocking, but my voice is shaking. 'If you don't want me here I'd rather you just come out and say it.'

'Oh my God,' Theresa laughs. 'That'd make your life so much easier, wouldn't it? If you could tell yourself *we* were the ones rejecting *you*, instead of the other way around. How can someone so smart be so thick? I don't *hate* you, you stupid cow. I love you. We all love you.'

'Then why are you so angry?'

'Because you *left* us!' she shouts. The words reverberate around the kitchen. 'You left *me*.'

Her eyes are wet.

'Do you know what it was like, growing up here, alone, with Dad? He was a fucking mess.'

'I couldn't have looked after you.'

She groans loudly. 'I didn't want *you* to look after *me*. We're *sisters*. We could have looked after *each other*.'

'Girls.'

Dad and Mush are standing in the hall doorway. I do not know how much of this they have heard.

'It's nothing, Dad,' Theresa says.

Mush looks nervous. Car keys in his hand.

I look at Theresa. She looks at me.

'Oh, just go,' she says. She turns her back to me. 'It's what you're good at.'

Mush

THE BARN IS cold. They've taken Blinkie's shoes. The blood coming out of his ear's after drying into a brown streak. He's trembling in his sleep. Soaking wet, I don't know if it's sweat or what.

Took me and Helen ages to work up the balls to run from the long grass to the barn. She'd stormed out the house without even saying hello and was on an absolute rant the second we sat into the car, spieling on the way she always does when something's upset her – all these words out of a thesaurus. Which is half the reason I wanted her with me, to be honest, cos she's smart. She'd be able to figure out what Blinkie was saying, sort the truth from bullshit. She'd know what to do about him, better than I would anyway. But maybe that was all just crap I was telling myself. Maybe I just wanted her with me cos I feel safer with Helen. Cos I can't do anything on my own.

But when I finally got a word in edgeways and told her about Blinkie and the barn, all of it, Helen just stared at me, like she couldn't believe what I was saying, and I realized, fuck. Maybe I shouldn't have told her. Maybe this was a mistake. Maybe she was gonna say I was fucking nuts, that I should have called the Guards right off.

But instead she just said, 'Blinkie Roche?'

'Yeah.'

She said she wanted to see.

*

Now her hand's over her mouth at the sight of him. It's pure quiet in the barn. I'm edgy as fuck. Half expecting Uncle Ger or Teabag to come rushing out at us. But they don't. It's too late into one day and too early into tomorrow.

I lay my hand on Blinkie's shoulder and he jerks awake with a shout. His breath's foul. I whisper at him to be quiet.

'We won't hurt you.'

He asks for water. A hoarse moan. There are sawn-off barrels full of rain. I find a rusty trowel and sink it into a barrel and water climbs my wrist and I feel like someone's watching this happen. Like I've seen this before.

Helen's got this stricken face. 'We have to help him.'

Blinkie's lips are all raw, pure swollen. I tip the trowel to them and he whimpers, pursing his mouth. One eye is still bashed shut, but his open eye's fixed on me, like he's waiting for me to hurt him. The water dribbles about his mouth. He swallows and grunts like a calf at a bottle, and for a weird moment I feel safe in the knowledge that I'm doing something good. Then Blinkie begins to choke. He gurgles and retches and water trickles down his chin.

'That water's fucking bad,' he moans loudly.

'Keep your voice down.'

'Hose,' he says, looking behind me.

There's a hose on the floor, coiled up like one of the roads out the Warren. I get it, now. Why he's soaked. They sprayed him, then left him to the dark, knowing the night would bring a chill. That's why he's shuddering so badly. That's why he has no shoes.

'I know you,' he says, squinting at Helen. 'You're Rossie's girl.'

I want Helen to take charge of the situation – to give it her attitude, like. Use her skills. Find out what he knows about the twins.

'Helen,' I say. 'Ask him some questions.'

But she just looks freaked out.

'Cut me loose,' Blinkie says. 'Please.'

I creak the handle on the hose and water begins to piddle at the stone floor. Blinkie's tongue curls on his bottom lip, eager for it.

I need to seem in control. I dip my head and swallow spit.

'You spoke about the twins. Before.' I meet his eyes. 'What'd you mean?'

We stare at each other. His tongue slides slow across his bashed-up lips.

'Nothing,' he says. 'I dunno... I just said it, like.'

'We're not going to hurt you,' I say. 'Just... just tell me if you know anything about—'

'I don't know anything about anything, right? Just let me fucking go. I haven't done nothing wrong.'

'Why would Uncle Ger and Teabag tie you up like this,' I say, 'if you've done nothing wrong?'

It's hard to tell what he's thinking, his face is that bashed up. But I can hear the smile in his voice. 'They told me you were smart,' he says. Then something happens. His voice changes.

'*Mush is like a fuzzy TV*,' he says, doing Donna's drawl. It's surprisingly accurate. He changes to Marie's voice. '*Sometimes you need to slap him to make sure he's working.*' He switches voice again. '*But he always works in the end.*'

He waits a moment, watching how this lands on me.

'You know how they do that,' he says. 'Finish each other's sentences. Good kids. Sure you wouldn't wish a bit of harm on them.'

This battered fuck is taunting me. I look at Helen. I don't know what to do.

'Give him some water,' Helen says.

I bring the nozzle close to Blinkie's chin. His neck strains against the cable tie. When I stop short of giving him a drink, his open eye darkens.

'What you mean by all that?' I say. I tap him with my toe. 'Hey.'

Blinkie stares at the ground. He squints, his eye darting about, like it pains him to think.

'Don't act the hard man,' he mutters. 'Doesn't suit you.'

I can't work out if he's fucking with me or what.

'Blinkie,' I say. 'Have you spoken to Donna and Marie?'

He smiles at my feet. 'Oh, now and then.'

I step back, take the water away. 'Why?'

'They ask me things. I told them some stuff here and there. Few breadcrumbs, like.'

The little bird. The girls said a little bird told them things. About Aidan. And Kala. And my scars.

'Are you the little bird?' I say.

Blinkie grins at me like I'm stupid. 'Am I what?'

On my phone, I pull up Joe's photo of the twins and the hooded figure. My hand's shaking.

'That you?'

He looks at the photo for a long moment. A slight nod. This acid taste in my mouth.

'You gave them those photos of Kala?'

Another nod. 'Good kids,' he says. 'Nice kids.'

'Stop fucking around with me,' I hiss. 'Have you done something with them?'

'Well... I couldn't possibly say now, Mush.'

'How about I go up the house right now and get Uncle Ger? Maybe I'll get him to make you say.'

Blinkie scoffs. 'D'you even know who your fucking uncle is? The minute you involve him I'm as good as dead. And what good does a dead Blinkie do for you? Without Blinkie, how do you ever find them girls?'

I step forward. 'What?'

He snorts and bows his head, muttering to himself.

'What the fuck d'you just say?' I say.

He laughs. 'You've no idea what you're getting into. Why don't you run back home to your mammy and her fucking cappucc—'

I whip the nozzle down on his mouth. Once, twice. I've done it before I even realize. Helen grabs my arm to stop me and I step back, heart doing ninety, and Blinkie sucks his gums, breathing hard through his nose. His lips are bleeding again. He spits and glares. It's a weird feeling, not avoiding his look. I've been turning my eyes from people for years.

His eyes flit about from side to side. He's thinking.

'They showed up at me caravan, like. Weeks ago. They'd photos of Aidan with them. Wanted to know if I could make contact with him.'

'What the fuck's that mean?' I say.

'Sure I didn't know what they were on about either. It took me a while to cop – they'd got their wires crossed. I've been living in me caravan for months, like. Ever since the brother Dodo died. Been parked out the front of me sister's house. That's who the twins were looking for, her. Me sister, Moira. Calls herself a shaman, says she has the gift. "The sight". Daft fucking bitch. All that hippie shit your auntie Pauline's into. The twins came out to Moira's looking for a psychic, but I'm what they found. Sure I was well wide to who they were. Talking about their mother getting married, how they wanted to know more about their big brother, how no one in the family would talk about him. I thought to meself, fuck it. I'll go along with this. Cause Ger a bit of grief. Cos I know *plenty* about Aidan, like. I was there after he was born, y'know? I was there when we cut him down from the rafters of the Crawley House.'

He grins and I want to knock his face in.

'Yeah, I told them all about that,' Blinkie says. 'Pretended I was receiving word from *the other place.*'

The worst is, I can see it: the twins, asking around, fumbling in the dark for information we've kept hidden from them. Knowing about Auntie Pauline's faith in all that woo-woo horse shit. Even believing in it themselves. They're only kids. Innocent, like. They'd believe anything.

'Christ,' I say. 'Why?'

'*Why?*' he says. 'Fuck you is why. Gimme some water.'

I hold the dribbling nozzle to his mouth and let him drink, then tell him he'll get more if he talks more.

'Kinlough Associates,' he says, water dripping off his bottom lip.

I shake my head. 'What's that?'

'Fucking everything,' he says. 'Kinlough Associates owns your mother's café. The roof over your head.'

I don't know the first thing about this shit. All I know's how to serve punters.

'Never heard of them,' I say. 'But you're wrong. Uncle Ger's always been our landlord.'

Blinkie sneers. 'Ger's only fucking middle management. A cog in the big machine. Kinlough Associates owns most of Fox Street. All the venues for the Festival, like.'

Helen touches my sleeve. 'The site in the woods,' she says. 'Where Kala's remains were found.'

He nods. 'The Lanann wan, yeah. Made a real mess of things for Ger, don't you think? Them bones showing up on a KA building site like that? Might raise a lot of awkward questions.'

He smirks at us, like he expects us to smirk back.

'You know something about all that?' Helen says, stepping forward. 'About Kala?'

'D'you know I was supposed to be a partner in that site?' Blinkie says. 'When Dodo died, I'd got this huge fuck-off payload. I was flush, like. Ger and Teabag said it was time I struck out on my own. Get on the ladder. They got me to put everything I had into that site. Had me signing one piece of paper after another. Then what happens? The cunts dilute me share till it's next to nothing. I sign a few bits of paper, next thing I know I'm left holding me fucking lad in me hand. I haven't a fucking penny. Living in a caravan. You know what that feels like? All the things I've done for the Lyons down the years? And Blinkie's left twisting in the wind?'

'What's this got to do with the twins?' I say.

He spits.

'Christ. There's a sea of fucking sharks swimming all about ye and the pair of ye don't even see it. Ye're going to be eaten alive.'

There's the hint of a smile in his eyes.

'And I'm the only one who can help ye. So stop the play-acting. Let me go. I can help ye.'

Helen and me look at each other.

'You said it yourself,' Blinkie says. 'There's a reason they haven't reported Blinkie to the Guards. Last thing they want's auld Blinkie talking to some pig about Kinlough Associates. You know why? Cos Blinkie knows too much.' He lowers his voice to a whisper. 'Blinkie knows... exactly how your friend's bones ended up on that building site.'

The pigeons above us stir in the dark. There's soft rain on the roof.

'How?' Helen says.

Blinkie's eye searches her face.

'I'll tell you what I know,' he says. 'If you don't tell the Guards.'

'How did Kala's bones get to the building site?' Helen says.

Blinkie pauses. 'Because,' he whispers. 'Sure wasn't it my job to bury her body in the first place?'

An icy jolt to the heart. Hot shivers of blood through my arms, down my back.

The air's gone thick, heavy. I look to Helen, eyes wide.

She steps towards Blinkie. Pure focus on her now.

'What?' she whispers.

Blinkie fidgets his legs.

'You won't call the Guards,' he says, 'if I tell you what I know?'

Helen takes out her phone. 'I'll call the Guards right fucking now if you don't.'

'No! No.'

He pauses. Comes to some sort of decision in himself. 'Meself and Dodo. We were called up here the night she died. The Lanann girl, she was laid out on the ground. Right there.'

Blinkie's staring at the ground behind me. I follow his gaze, half-expecting Kala to be lying there, staring up at us.

But the ground is blank. Silent dirt and pebble grit, tatters of rubbish, dark puddles from the hose.

A flash of Kala's face, the way she looked at me for the last time. The fear.

Blinkie speaks pure blunt. 'Lot of blood, like. Back of the head. Already dead a while, so she was.'

'Wait,' Helen says in a hoarse whisper. 'Ger killed her?'

'I don't fucking know,' Blinkie says.

'What do you mean you don't know?' Helen says. 'If she was here—'

'Fuck sake, that's not how things *worked*. It was all spaghetti. Me and Dodo were just told to get rid of her. We got our orders, we did them. No explanations asked or—'

'Why would Kala be *here*?' Helen says. 'After everything that—'

'Ach,' Blinkie snaps. 'It probably didn't even *happen* here. You ask me, Ger was only tidying up the mess for someone else.'

'Fuck this, I'm calling the Guards,' I say.

'No!' Blinkie shouts. 'Fuck sake. Ye don't know what ye're dealing with here. You can't trust the cops. You can't trust anybody.'

'But you're going to help us figure it all out,' Helen says in a flat voice. 'Why should we believe you?'

'Stupid pair of fucking... If ye go and talk to the cops, I'm as good as fucking dead. That's a fact. Ask the Mammy Lanann. She knows.'

'*What?*' Helen says.

'Fucking cut me loose!' he screams. 'Cut me loose! I'm the only one who can help ye!'

I shout-whisper at him to keep his voice down but Helen's already speaking over me, asking what he meant about the Mammy.

'It's all the one fucking thing,' Blinkie hisses. 'And Donna and Marie are after getting awful close to it. The *Lananns*. The *Lyons*. It's the one fucking murder hole.'

Himself and Helen begin to jabber over each other. My head's blitzed with questions like what the fuck's he got the twins tangled up in and how the fuck am I going to fix this and Helen's on about the Mammy, Kala, Kala's mother, and my heart's thumping in my ears and it takes a second for me to realize what I'm hearing. Sounds outside. Voices.

Blinkie and Helen are still talking over each other when I peek out the barn door and nearly fucking shit myself. Uncle Ger's outside the house at the far end of the yard. He's chatting with two fellas in hoods. From the way they're standing, they're having serious words.

But Blinkie's making too much noise.

In the distance, one of the hoods turns to look over at the barn.

I rush to the others. Blinkie's after telling Helen something that's made her face drain of colour. No time to find out what. I grab her arm.

'We gotta go right fucking now.'

'No, wait,' Helen says.

'We gotta go!' I say.

'There's another door out the back,' Blinkie says. 'Cut these ties off me, please. Take me with ye.'

'There's no fucking time,' I say.

'Please,' Blinkie cries out. 'I'll tell ye everything I know. Don't leave me here.'

But we do.

Monday

Helen

TODAY WAS MEANT to be the wedding. That is not going to happen now. The house has that unnatural feel that comes with sleeplessness, with things being out of joint. The parents are all gone, driving around to the houses of the twins' friends. But they were still up last night when Mush and I returned from Blinkie and the barn. We found Pauline, Lydia and Dad all sitting grey-eyed at the kitchen table. A look of tired hope in their faces as we came through the door.

Mush put his hands behind his back to hide the cuts and bruises on his knuckles and I asked if they had heard anything yet. Pauline said the Guards had called asking for details on the girls' social media accounts and whether or not they used any medications. Apart from that, nothing.

The cup of tea clutched in Pauline's hands looked cold. She had been doing all the things I remember us doing with Kala. Calling Marie's phone, leaving voicemails. 'Just let us know you're okay.' I remember that feeling – like Kala was somehow everywhere but absent; that the world had closed over her like a veil, but if we just reached out enough, we would find her there, waiting.

Dad said they were going to postpone the wedding. Lydia looked at Mush with her angry face and he looked back, some intricate conversation happening in the silence between them, and when her eyes softened to reveal her real feeling – fear – she looked away.

Just before Mush had grabbed me in the barn, I was asking Blinkie if Kala's death had anything to do with Fiona.

Blinkie looked at me like I was a fool. 'The Lanann girl didn't die cos of her mother,' he said as Mush started to rush at me, saying we had to go. 'You should be asking after her father.'

Mush was pulling me. 'Wait,' I said. 'Wait.' But there was no time.

Eventually we went up to Donna's room and sat on the bed. We looked at my notes – all the dates, timelines, questions that needed to be answered – and tried to piece things together with everything Blinkie had said. Mush admitted it was impossible to know whether Blinkie was telling the truth about the twins. He knew Blinkie might just have been saying what he knew Mush needed to hear, to secure his escape. Mush asked if I thought we should call the Guards, regardless – but Blinkie had seemed to be as afraid of the police as he was of Ger and Teabag. I told Mush about what Dudley had said – that the Garda investigation into Kala's disappearance had been questionable from the start. Now Blinkie was insinuating the same. Perhaps, I said, the Guards were not to be trusted on this. Neither of us knew what to believe. But whenever I pictured Kala lying on the floor of the barn, I got a terrible feeling, like icy fingers opening inside me, that Blinkie was not lying. He was showing us something hidden. And I wanted to see.

Mush is pale and agitated now, making coffee in the kitchen. The daylight is thin, stretched. Pauline's wedding bouquet lies on the table, forlorn and abandoned. It arrived a few moments ago. I put the bouquet in a vase while Mush puts the coffee in a flask. I pull at my face and try to get my head together. It is after midday. We are running late. We were meant to be out the door first thing in the morning, but as the light had begun to turn outside my bedroom window, the churn of blue milk pouring the dark, our energy guttered out and I woke up with my head on Mush's chest. His boy smell, like the days after Kala went missing, holding on to one another. We had both fallen asleep. I shook him awake. 'Fuck,' he said. '*Fuck!* What time is it?'

Before we leave, I quietly click the door into the sitting room to check on Theresa and Joe. Joe is still on the sofa. I can smell him from the hall. Theresa has passed out on an armchair. She was in and out of the kitchen from time to time in the night, drinking glasses of water, ignoring me.

Mush's hands have a tiny shake in them in the car. Plum-coloured cuts on his knuckles as he grips the wheel, bruise-like shadows under his eyes. He mutters non-stop under his breath as we drive.

Mush

I CAN'T THINK straight. Like, if Blinkie knows where the twins are, we should just call the cops. But Helen's adamant: cops can't be trusted. She's experienced too much in Canada, and heard too much about the Guards here. So I said, right, if she doesn't want the Guards, why don't we just go up the farm and get Blinkie ourselves? But Helen wants to verify what Blinkie's said with the Mammy first. 'Just give me an hour with her,' she said. I said no, we don't have time for this. But she insisted. One hour, max.

Christ, I could puke. My guts are fucking slurry.

Donna. Marie.

'Mush,' Helen says. The Coast Road blurs behind her in the passenger seat. 'You all right? You're shaking.'

'Don't be minding me.'

Feels like my body's made of fucking bumblebees. Can't believe I fell asleep. My vision's spotting, like. And it's beginning to rain.

Kala's house rises up through the windscreen wipers.

'This is going to be delicate,' Helen says. 'Just getting the Mammy to open the door will be a challenge. We need to get her talking first, before we ask anything about last night.'

I'm clearing my throat over and over in this mad way. When I rub my eyes, my hand's fucking fluttering, like.

'Hey,' Helen says softly. 'You okay?'

We pull up outside.

Helen touches my arm. 'I can do this alone, if you want to wait here in the car.'

I'd actually love to let her do this. Fucking coward. I undo my seat belt. 'You'll do most of the talking?'

Helen touches my cheek. 'Of course, pet.'

We get out of the car, into the rain. I hesitate, then follow Helen onto Kala's empty porch.

The Mammy was on the porch, waiting for me and the lads to arrive. She saw us on the Coast Road and shouted, 'Here they are. Kinlough's answer to fecking U2. Have ye butterflies?'

I smiled but I was on the verge of shitting myself. It was Halloween. Night of the gig. We'd had to practise in Joe's room earlier cos the girls wanted to get Kala's room ready by themselves. Joe'd convinced himself he'd a sore throat. He kept drinking milk to protect his voice, till Aidan said that milk isn't good for the voice cos it gets you all phlegmy.

'No use telling me that when I'm after drinking three fecking pints of it,' Joe snapped.

Aidan smirked, pretending he wasn't nervous. His bruises from Uncle Ger had mostly faded, just a green tinge to his cheeks now. I'd meant to talk to him in the days after that had happened, to say I'd heard Ger hitting him. But it was like the moment had passed and now it was weeks later, too late to be bringing it up. I didn't realize then that the moments when you can say something are just that – moments – and once they're gone, they're gone, and you've added another brick to the wall.

That night I was too busy worrying if I'd fuck up the bass solo in 'Welcome to Paradise'.

Misty was tied up outside Kala's house, next to the Mammy. Her tail was going mad when she saw us approach.

'What's Helen's dog doing here?' Joe said, but me and Aidan crouched down and patted her for luck. She was a good buzz, this dark little bullet of energy.

Kala's room looked class. The bed was shoved into the corner, fairy lights and fake cobwebs all over the ceiling.

Kala was Winona Ryder from *Beetlejuice*. She'd grey rings painted under her eyes and her hair piled on top of her head like a giant spider, her fringe in these black triangles stuck to her forehead. 'How'd you do that?' I said, and she muttered, 'Enough hairspray to fuck the ozone layer for ever.'

Helen looked amazing. I'd been there when she and Kala were discussing their costumes. Helen had said she was going to dress as Wednesday Addams, all severe pigtails and old-woman pinafore. But Kala said, 'Fuck that, babe. Why be Wednesday when you could be Morticia?' And there she was. Helen had her hair straightened and her face pure pale, with dangerous red lipstick. Even Aidan was staring.

Aoife had straightened her hair too, and was wearing a beret and a striped tank top.

'Who are you meant to be?' Aidan said. '*Where's* fucking *Wally?*'

'Gwen Stefani,' she said. I saw it now. And I remembered Joe and Aidan talking about how much of a ride Gwen was in the video of 'Let Me Blow Ya Mind'.

'Lame,' Aidan said. 'It's Halloween, like.'

Aoife's face fell, and I saw her notice a quiet smile pass between Helen and Kala. I didn't get what had happened, but I knew Aoife'd fucked up big time. Misread the codes and got the night wrong. Her face flushed red.

Kala kissed Joe softly so as not to mess up her make-up. She held her arms around his neck and leaned back to look at him, her belly against his.

'Are you nervous?' she said.

'Bit, yeah.'

'You're going to be so good,' she said, and he nodded, and they stood like that with their foreheads touching. I remember that.

The girls had made a flag for us – a huge black flag with all these trees tangling inside each other in the shape of a big heart, and in the middle it said, 'Jungle Heart'.

'Who made this?' Joe said.

'We all did,' Kala said. 'It was Helen's idea.'

Joe nodded at Helen and she nodded back. A peace treaty.

'That your dog tied up outside?' Joe said.

'Yeah,' Kala said. 'Helen's dad's out trick-or-treating with Theresa.'

'Is she gonna be here the whole time?' Aidan said.

'What's it to you?' Helen said.

'Just asking, Jesus. Don't have your period,' Aidan said.

I let Kala paint my nails and Helen put some eyeliner on me, and some dark eyeshadow too, to make me look a bit ghoulish. Kala took a picture of me on the camera-phone Joe had bought her.

The Mammy laughed when she saw me. 'You're like what's-his-face,' she said.

People were already arriving. Lads from St Simon's. Girls from St Anne's. Most of the lads weren't wearing costumes, cos dressing up wasn't for boys, but the girls looked class. Vampires, witches, all that sexy stuff. I was sweeping about the place, filming with Mam's camcorder. I wanted to get Joe on video before the gig, cos he was the main man, but he was keeping himself apart from everyone. I filmed him in the corner of Kala's room, pacing back and forth, doing la-la-la vocal warm-ups. Aidan stood in front of the camera and nodded at Joe and pretended to wank himself off.

The Mammy had snacks on a table upstairs, cocktail sausages, bowls of sweets and fun-sized chocolate bars. She was smoking away, watching her house fill with kids.

At first people were sneaking sips from naggins, but once they realized that there were no adults in Kala's room, they began to drink openly. There was this wild feeling, like the world was a playground with no parents and we could all go proper fucking mental. The room was heaving and suddenly it was time for us to play and I was up there, my arms pure weak as I put the strap over my shoulder and double-checked I was in tune. Aidan was doing warm-up fills on his kit. I looked over at Joe and he was somewhere way off inside himself, and for a sec I thought he'd be too nervous to sing. But then, the weirdest thing, he turned to the crowd and it was like he'd flicked a switch inside himself and become someone else completely. He made some joke into the mic and the crowd laughed and he smiled at them and I realized – Fuck me. He's it – and then he winked at Aidan and me, and Aidan clicked his sticks together, and we hit the room like a bomb.

Lads moshing. Girls moshing. Girls dancing. Silhouettes swaying as we played 'A Forest'. Some lad from the year above us being hoisted in the air and licking the condensation off the ceiling. Everyone screaming. People transfixed by Joe. Aidan nailing the drum solos in 'Burnout'. Lads I barely knew frowning with furious approval, giving me the Satan sign with their fingers, screaming, 'Fuck, yeah.'

It was amazing.

Kala and Helen were jumping into each other and laughing, screaming. I didn't see Aoife – I found out later that she'd left in a sulk – and I didn't see Teabag and the Lyons come into the room and shoulder their way through the crowd, but suddenly they were there, standing in front of us, watching us with their arms folded. Big smirks.

We kept playing and Joe kept singing but I looked back at Aidan and his eyes were serious. Between songs me and the lads huddled at Aidan's kit. Teabag was calling out to Joe, trying to goad him. Joe looked at us and said, 'Let's play "Killing in the Name" right at them.' Boomerang was standing at the edges of the moshpit, shoving people into the whir and daring them to shove back. The vibe in the room was changing. Kala came to the front, shouting at Teabag over the music. I could read her lips. 'This is my house. You're not welcome.' Teabag reached out to touch her pointy fringe and Kala pulled her head back, pure disgusted. The crowd wasn't dancing any more, not even listening to us, just watching the drama. Teabag looked at Joe for a second and raised his hands, like he was about to leave. Then he grabbed Kala's

wrist and yanked her hand to his crotch and held it there.
Teabag made his eyes wide, letting his tongue poke over his
bottom lip, leering at Kala even as she hit him with her free
hand, even as Joe stopped playing and threw his guitar off and
rammed into Teabag. People began to shout. Teabag stumbled
and let go of Kala's wrist. Then he came at Joe fast. He took
Joe by the throat and marched him backwards, right into
Aidan's drum kit. The kit toppled over and I saw Joe's feet fly
up as Teabag shoved him into the sounds of cymbals crash-
ing, and the crowd were all shouting and jeering and I saw
Teabag hit Joe, hard. I was frozen, pure dumbfounded, like.
Kala jumped onto Teabag's back and I saw him straighten
up and twist around and Kala was digging her nails into his
face and he threw her off him and she fell over and suddenly
Helen was in Teabag's face, shoving him in the chest, shouting
at him, and he was laughing her off as Boomerang began to
pull him away. Then I saw it happen. Helen leaned back and
spat in Teabag's face. His eyes went wide and I saw the shock
darken in them as Helen shook her hair back and stared right
at him, just like she'd stared down the bouncer in town during
the summer. He slapped her, proper fucking slapped like, and
she stepped back holding her cheek, and the room was roaring
as Boomerang dragged Teabag back and people hounded the
Lyons out the room and up the stairs. The place was a frenzy,
some faces laughing and others pure serious. Joe was still
tangled up in the kit on the floor and Aidan tried to help him
up but Joe told him to fuck off. His nose was bleeding and he
kept tapping at the blood and looking at his fingers, blinking,
as if he couldn't believe it was real. Kala was touching Helen's
cheek where Teabag had slapped her, whispering something in
her ear. Then she stood over Joe and saw his watery eyes and
bloody nose and got furious. 'That fucker!' she said. She ran
upstairs and didn't come back.

The party cleared out quicker than I would've thought
possible. People were outside Kala's house, a drunk flood. I

couldn't find Kala. When I went back downstairs Aidan was crouched over his kit.

'Me snare's fucked.'

'Where's Joe?' I said.

Aidan shrugged. 'Probably after running home. He was crying like a—'

I looked around for Helen. Helen would know what to do. She wasn't there.

Myself and Aidan went upstairs. The Mammy was telling people the party was over, they should be ashamed of themselves.

Me and Aidan went outside. The crowd was already thinning out and I saw Helen and Kala, searching frantically.

'What's the matter?' I said.

'Misty,' Helen said. 'I can't find Misty.'

I looked to where she'd been tied up. Misty was gone. The leash was gone.

'Anyone seen a dog?' Aidan shouted. He cupped his hands. 'Hey, listen up, you fuckers. We're looking for a black dog.'

Some girl dressed like the Bride of Frankenstein said they'd seen the Lyons walk with a dog into the woods.

We ran into the trees. It was dark. Helen was shouting for Misty.

'Misty!'

'Here, girl!'

None of us had torches.

'It'll be okay,' Kala said.

But I knew it wouldn't be okay, and we found Misty in a clearing, silent in the moonlight, like a shadow hanging from a tree.

Joe

YOU'RE ON A sofa. Under a blanket. Curtains drawn. Sounds of daylight outside. The room beyond the sofa is unfamiliar. The pounding in your skull's not. Can't remember anything of last night.

Rise slowly. Acid churn of your guts.

Fuck.

Dad's silhouette is in the armchair in the corner. He stirs to your movements.

Fuck.

Fuck. Fuck. Fuck.

Think of an excuse for this that he'll accept. A joke. He clicks on a lamp next to his chair. The light's warm but still makes you wince.

'You're awake,' he says.

It's not your dad. It's Theresa's dad. You're in Rossie and Pauline's house.

Memory flashes: someone undressing you, a blitz of concerned faces turning over you in a bright light, hands tucked under your armpits, pulling upwards, wet grass against your face.

Fuck.

Paw at yourself. You're wearing another man's pyjamas. Must've pissed yourself. Not the first time. Put the shame in a box. Save it for later. Not the first time you've done that either.

'That happen often?' Rossie says.

Your mouth. Must've puked too. Close your eyes. Slowly press your eyelids. Head's splitting. Try and hold it intact.

Your elbow is killing you. Must have landed on your hand. Should never have taken off the cast.

'Nothing like the morning after,' Rossie says, opening the curtains. Here we go. The spiel, the wisdom every sober fucker's so eager to share. Sentences worn clean from repetition. Every narrative turn, sculpted to fit. But he doesn't rattle off a speech. 'Your clothes are in the dryer upstairs. Go up and have a puke. Take a shower. Always helps.'

You nod.

'Got any friends that help you out?' he says. 'A sponsor you can call?'

Shake your head. Apologize.

'It's not me you need to say sorry to,' he says. He clears his throat. 'Theresa must be fond of you, like. Stayed up with you, all night.'

'Does my dad know about this?'

'No,' Rossie says. 'You were fairly adamant about that last night.'

Vague relief. Dad still thinks you're Joe Brennan. You won't let him down, not again. Muscle memory, a hot shard of the anxiety you felt seeing Dad's outline stirring down the hall to the click of your key in the front door when you rushed home from Kala's Halloween party, knowing in a few seconds' time he'd see you weren't his idea of Joe Brennan, you were just a boy, with a boy's tears, a boy's bloody nose. He was in the kitchen, leaning in his usual spot by the window, turning with a surprised smile on his face, about to ask why you were back so soon, how the gig went, and it was this – Dad just wanting you to do well and have a good night, the innocent approval of it, the shock at the mess of you – that made your lip tremble again *fuck* crying again *fuck* and his face dropped and he said, 'What's after happening?' and Mam was on the stairs and, 'Jesus, Dudley, what's he done to his nose?' and Dad said, 'Who did this to you?' and you said it didn't matter, you wanted to go to bed, but Dad was already grabbing his keys – 'Get in the car' – and he took you by the arm and steered you out the house and you realized the neighbours could see you, had probably seen you gulping back tears as the blood came from your nose with your eyes already bruising in the reflection that floated across the metal of the car door as you opened it and sat inside and cried harder and Dad had already started the engine and begun to pull out by the time you'd closed the door and now on the road, roaring out the estate, he said, 'Who was it, Joe? I need a name,' and you begged him not to drive you back to Kala's, told him they wouldn't even be there any more, and he said, '*They?* More than one fella? How many? Would you know them if you saw them?' and you half nodded and the car was going faster than you'd ever felt, and you said, 'Everyone was laughing at me, Dad,' and his jaw went tight and for a moment you thought he might be disgusted with you for crying like a girl but his voice was quiet as he said, 'Their names, Joe,' and you said it so quiet that maybe he couldn't hear you and he looked over at you for a second with the street lights over his face marking a look that frightened you and he said, 'The Lyons?' and stared back at the road as he bulled the car into the Warren taking turns at wild speeds, dangerous speeds, kamikaze approaches to bends about a maze of roads you'd never seen before and next thing you knew he was driving down a narrow trail, over a cattle grid, through an open gate, roaring up a yard to a farmhouse where *fuck* the Lyons were all there, Teabag, Boomerang, Lee, all their cronies, some auld lads you'd never seen before, all of them hanging about and straightening up at the sight of this car flying towards them and Dad asked, 'Which ones hit you? Point them out to me,' and his voice was calm like a bomb is calm and you said, 'It was Teabag,' and Teabag was standing by the house frowning at the car and Dad drove at him, straight on, like he was going to mow him down, and Teabag was frozen in the glare of the lights and Dad stopped the car so sudden that the seat belt ate at your neck and Dad was already out of the car, 'Come here to me,' already rushing at Teabag who had his hands up and was saying, 'Dudley, naw,' and Dad had a baton in his hand and he brought it down on Teabag's forearm and then his shoulder and Teabag let out one scream then another and Dad already had Teabag's arm twisted behind his back and was slamming Teabag's chest onto the hood of the car in front of you and you could hear Teabag grunt through the glass as Dad said, 'You touch my fucking son?' and the others were all hanging back like they were afraid to approach and Dad grabbed Teabag by the ear and closed his fist over it like he was going to tear the ear off and he yanked upwards so Teabag's face came away from the hood and for a moment Teabag's stare met yours, saw yours, recognized you sitting there in front of him but you had no time to see anything in his eyes – fear, hate, rage – because Dad had clapped Teabag's head into the bonnet of the car and yanked him up by the ear again and cracked his head into the metal again and now he was holding his skull down, shoving it into the metal like he was trying to mash Teabag's head into the car and Teabag was screaming and Dad shouted out to all of them, 'If I hear of *anyone* going near my son again, *ever*,' and then he peeled Teabag off the hood of the car, still holding him by the ear, and twisted as he threw Teabag off balance into the dirt and Dad stepped forward and opened his arms shouting, 'Any questions? Anyone got anything to say?' and then he was in the car with you, slamming the door, driving back into the Warren, and he said nothing all the way home.

Mam was waiting when ye arrived, but Dad told her to go upstairs, it was taken care of. In the kitchen, he told you to sit at the table. He took a bottle of whiskey and two glasses. One for him, and one for you. His hand was trembling as he poured but he acted like he was totally fine. He asked if you were all right. He poured you half of what he gave to himself, but still. Ye had never had a drink together. Your heart was going mad. You kept seeing Teabag's face – the way he'd looked at you through the windscreen.

'What if he comes after me?' you said.

Dad shook his head. 'You'll never hear from that fool again. He wouldn't dare.'

You sipped at the whiskey. It tasted like smoke and metal.

'There's people in this world, son, who can't stand greatness. Resentful pricks. They'll always try to drag great men down to their level. I don't like the word, but' – he lowered his voice – 'there's a lot of *sad cunts*. And you'll need to be able to handle them, cos they're going to come at you. They always do.'

You knew there'd be some sort of revenge for this. The Lyons wouldn't just let it go. They'd find a way to hurt you.

'How'd you do that?'

Dad looked distracted. 'Hm?'

'The way you handled Teabag. I didn't know you could do that.'

Dad stood. 'Come here to me.'

You thought he was going to hug you. But he didn't. He said, 'Come at me. Like you're going to attack me. Do it slowly.'

You raised your hands and stepped to him and swiftly, gently, so fast you didn't even know it was happening till it had happened, you were facing the opposite direction and Dad was right behind you, one arm around your neck and a hand against the back of your skull. He wasn't holding tight, but you were already powerless.

'That's a chokehold,' he said. He let you go. 'You ever need to overpower someone, that's the move. You can do it safely, securely. Take control of a situation in less than twenty seconds. Want to learn it?'

You went through the motions like a slow dance. Pull your opponent close. Get your dominant forearm around his neck. Your opponent will raise his arms to his neck, to try and protect it. This is your opening. Place your non-dominant hand behind his head. Wrap your arm tightly around his neck and grab his shoulder with your dominant hand to stabilize your grip. Good man. Slide your non-dominant hand behind his head, in between the neck and the centre of the skull. Wrap your fingers around your elbow. Lock your dominant arm in place. Squeeze. That's it.

You repeated this sequence many times. Eventually you could hear Dad smiling.

'Good man,' he said. The whiskey was warm in you now. Dad's cheeks were reddening. 'Now lean back. Spread your feet out there to brace for resistance. Very good.'

He struggled against your grip and you were able to keep him in place.

'That's it, son.' His voice was restricted, tight. You saw how difficult it'd be for him to fight back.

Ye practised this several times, getting faster each time. You saw your reflections in the patio glass of the extension.

Dad poured you another glass. This time, he poured the same amount of whiskey for you as for himself. He handed it to you and ye sat together, sipping. Leaning back in your chairs, legs spread. Real men. The whiskey rippled through you, a delicious heat.

'Don't be worrying about Teabag, or any of them,' Dad said. 'A place like Kinlough is too small for a man like you. This town will try and get its claws into you. Drag you into a pit. Don't let it. Remember: who are you?'

'I'm Joe Brennan.'

Dad raised his glass and ye clinked them. You felt like a grown man, doing what grown men did. Having a drink, putting the world to right.

Your clothes are warm from the dryer. Some childhood memory to this feeling against your skin. Hair wet from the shower. Stomach purged.

Enter Theresa's kitchen and all the faces turn and clock you. Rossie. Pauline. Lydia. Theresa. The shame of it.

'How's Joe?' Lydia says.

'Sorry,' you say. 'Won't happen again.'

Theresa won't meet your eyes. This brittle energy. Pauline looks terrible. Whole face sunken, like you can see the skull beneath the skin. Everyone looks drawn. There's more on their minds than Joe Brennan. *Peel your eyes off your fucking navel*. That's what Mush said to you in the car.

'Is Mush around?'

'He's with Helen,' Theresa mutters. 'Gone again.'

Rossie is offering to make toast when a mobile rattles on the table and Lydia grabs it. 'Well,' she says, 'speak of the—'

She stops. Her eyes go wide. She stands. 'Slow down, Mush. Slow—'

Her face drains – '*What?*' – and her eyes flit to Pauline.

Helen

THE PORCH IS speckling with rain. I knock again.

'Mrs Lanann? It's Helen Laughlin. Did you get my note yesterday?'

Mush is agitated, walking to and fro. Rubbing the back of his neck.

'Mrs Lanann?' I say. 'Could you give us five minutes of your time?'

Mush cups his hands around his eyes, looks through the windows.

'This isn't right,' he says. 'If—'

'Shh.' I lean against the front door and listen for the sound of a floorboard creaking under wheelchair wheels. Nothing.

'We understand that you don't want to see people,' I say. 'We're not here to—'

Mush knocks on the door. 'Mrs Lanann!' He knocks again, hard.

'Mush—'

'We're wasting time here. Blinkie knows where the twins are. If we go back to the—'

'Mrs Lanann,' I say. 'I'm going to be totally honest with you, okay? Cards on the table. We want to speak to you about some things which might be upsetting. But Kala was our friend. We want what you want. We want to know what happened to her. We want to find the person responsible.'

Mush goes to speak again and I hold up a hand.

'I spoke to Valerie Mulkerns,' I say. 'Mrs Lanann... I know about Fiona. I know you sent her away. I can only imagine how difficult that must have been for you. I know how few choices you must have had.'

Silence. I hesitate. Then I take a risk.

'And I know that you and Kala fought about that, right before she went missing. Did she confront you about her mother? Her father?'

Mush suddenly begins to hammer on the door. 'Fucking open up. Jesus,' he says.

'Mush,' I hiss. 'You'll frighten her.'

But his eyes are wild. He shouts. 'We spoke to Blinkie Roche. He told us to come see you.' He mutters that we don't have time for this bullshit, then begins to shout – 'Are you in there? Fuck sake' – and starts pounding on the door – 'Are you even fucking there?'

He goes to force a way in. But when he grips the handle it immediately gives. The door opens into the hall.

'...Mrs Lanann?'

No reply.

We step inside.

Kala's house. The familiar smell, curdling with the tang of rot. We round the corner to the sitting room. Light shines through holes in the curtains. Everything about the living room reveals itself in glimpses, details emerging then sinking back into darkness. The moth-eaten sofa is still the same; the dusty lamps and knick-knacks are the same; the TV is the same clunky box that Mush and I struggled to carry down to Kala's room to watch *Romeo + Juliet*. It is all the same, but ragged. An armchair with visible ribs. As though the place is made of echoes. We are inside a photograph that is fading.

'Mrs Lanann?'

No sound but the rain on the roof, and the creak of Mush going through the other rooms. In the Mammy's bedroom, the bed is unmade. Old sheets, thick and frayed. Photos by the bed of Kala as a little girl, on Santa's lap. Another photo of

Kala, probably about eight years old, her front teeth missing, an arm over the Mammy's shoulders. The Mammy, smiling. They look alike.

I return to the living room.

'Where's—'

Mush raises a hand. He nods to the door to Kala's room. I had seen it before, but my brain is so scrambled with tiredness that it is only now that it all registers: the door leading downstairs is open. The Mammy's wheelchair is empty beside it.

'Mrs Lanann?' Mush calls down. 'You all right?'

'Blinkie?' a cracked voice calls from below. 'Blinkie?'

Mush goes down the steps slowly, hands against the cold walls.

I take out my phone. The torch lights up Mush's shoulders. My mind runs through all the scenarios. The Mammy, desperate to be in Kala's room again. She fell. Or, no. The slow wheeze as she lowered herself out of the wheelchair, to the floor. Sliding her weight along the floor, to the top of the stairs. Lowering herself, step by slow step, beneath the house. And then, upon finding herself down there, realizing she was too tired and weak to hoist herself up.

'Mrs Lanann?' Mush says. His voice echoes off the brick.

At the bottom of the steps, the heavy door into Kala's room is open. Pale light hovers at the threshold.

Mush goes through and stops short.

I put my sleeve to my nose. The smell of shit.

The Mammy is lying on the floor, crumpled on her side. A shock of white hair against the red carpet.

We run to her, crouch down. Her hair is long, burning white, but it has thinned at the roots. She is tiny. I put a hand on her shoulder and feel thin bones.

'Mrs Lanann.'

She is whimpering. It is like she does not even see us.

I turn to Mush – 'Call an ambulance' – and push the Mammy's hair back from her cheek. Her face is a shock. One of her eyes is closed tight, a half-moon of vicious purple beneath it. The papery skin of her thin neck, cobwebbed with lines, is wildly discoloured. Someone has had their hands around her throat.

'What happened?' I say. 'Who did this to you?'

Mush has his phone – 'There's no fucking signal down here' – and she looks up at him, and becomes alert, as though rising up to us from some depth inside herself.

'Good Lord,' she says, reaching with pale fingers. 'What did they do to your face?'

'I'll call the ambulance,' he says, and ducks out the door, up the stairs.

The smell – it is not the Mammy. My eyes dart about Kala's room. So much of it is unchanged that I feel the room beginning to rush in on me.

The Mammy's eyes are tearful, frightened. She clutches my sleeve. 'I don't know what's after happening.'

'It's going to be okay.'

She shakes her head. 'Blinkie said he'd be back soon. He promised me.'

She is looking over my shoulder.

'They won't wake up,' she says. I follow her eyes. 'They won't wake up.'

I see them in the corner, lying silent like two shadows.

Mush

THEY'D BEEN WITHOUT food and water for three days. At first I was glad to get a concrete reason why they wouldn't wake up, why their skin looked almost grey-blue. Then the doctor began to list all the potential effects of three days' dehydration – hunger and headaches by day one, joint ache and fainting by day two, and everything that could happen once you hit day three: brain shrinkage, kidney failure, cardiac arrest. Rossie had to hold Auntie Pauline upright.

Both of them hooked up to IV drips now. Their beds are next to each other. They haven't woken up.

None of us has a notion what was going on in that fucking house. What they were doing there, how all the pieces fit. The Mammy won't say. Even when we were waiting for the ambulance, trying to help her, she just kept crying to herself, mumbling incoherent shit. She's in another part of the hospital, being treated for dehydration and shock.

Auntie Pauline and Rossie are sitting on the foot of Donna's bed, and I'm on Marie's. Her little hands, still a kid's hands. Bruises on her wrists from cable ties. This feeling in my guts, a burning, like I'd do anything to be in their place for them. Split myself in two and lie there for ever if it meant they'd be all right. I look over at Mam and I know she knows what I'm thinking. I'm experiencing what happened to Mam, after what happened to me.

We were still in our Halloween get-up, me and Kala. We must've looked like ghouls pushing through the long grass. I remember the sound of the dogs barking like mad in their cages when we entered the barn. I'd been full of anger for Helen, for Misty, right up to this moment. Helen had been in bits when me and Kala had dropped her home. Insisted on carrying Misty's body all the way herself. Had to keep stopping to adjust Misty's weight in her arms. Her eyes all bubbling with tears but it was like she refused to let herself cry. Told us to leave her to go into the house alone, to face her dad. She kept saying, 'Theresa's never going to forgive me.' It was Kala's idea to do this, now. Sneak up the farm, set Uncle Ger's dogs free.

But I was beginning to see this was a bad idea. Bad fucking idea.

It started with one dog barking as we entered the barn. Then they all joined in. Must've thought they were getting fed. Some were muscular, but most were smaller than I'd expected. They all had scars. Patches of fur missing, lumpy caves in their flesh. Kala ran down the row of cages, the latches shrieking as she slid them open.

The dogs were hammering against the iron meshes and Kala was deep in the back of the barn. I was at the door, looking back at the farmhouse in case the Lyons suddenly came out charging. The cloud was peeling itself back off the moon. The yard was beginning to glow bright.

I shouted inside, 'Kala, let's go,' when the dogs crashed out their cages and began to nose at the air and snap at each other.

Kala's face dropped. She was at the back of the barn, and the dogs were between her and me.

More dogs, coming out their cages. They were shouldering about one another in the middle of the barn. A river of muscle. Low snarling.

'Mush!' Kala cried.

They started to growl at Kala. She clambered into one of the cages and pulled the door behind her, holding it shut with her hands.

People were coming out the farmhouse now, looking across the yard. I darted around the barn to hide. The sound of dogs leaving the barn, now in the yard, yapping. Voices coming. Teabag, Boomerang, Lee, a few others. 'Grab that one.' 'You fucking grab it.' 'Don't let them off.' 'I'm not going near them, you mad?'

A scatter of dogs thundered past where I was hiding, into the long grass. Some lads ran half-heartedly after them, but gave up quickly. It'd be too dangerous to try and catch them. I stayed quiet, hunched between pallet heaps, as they turned back to the yard.

That's when the voices raised in the barn. Kala's voice among them. A rush of excitement amongst the lads.

The Lyons were in there with her.

I climbed a stack of pallets next to the barn. I looked through the gap between the wall and the ceiling. Boomerang and Lee were dragging Kala out of the cage where she'd hidden. She struggled to break free and the other lads laughed. Boomerang and Lee slammed her arms against one of the cages and held her there. The others watching.

Teabag was limping back and forth in front of Kala, ranting about the dogs being loose. He'd all these cuts and bruises on his face. Later, Joe would tell me how Dudley had clattered Teabag about earlier, humiliated him in front of the lads. Much later, I'd try and use that information to explain to myself what ended up happening.

'Hold her by the wrists there, lads.'

Boomerang and Lee did what he said.

'Piglet thinks he's untouchable. Thinks Teabag can't get to him.'

It wasn't clear if he was talking to Kala, or the lads, or himself. He was all over the place.

'But I know well how to get to Joe fucking Brennan.'

He touched Kala's cheek and she jerked her head back.

'Fuck you,' she shouted. But she was scared.

'What do ye reckon, lads? How many of us do ye think she'd manage?'

Murmurs. Shuffling feet.

Teabag began to rub at his crotch. 'What if we spread her right open?'

Kala screamed.

'All right now, Teabag,' Boomerang said. He looked nervous. 'Relax.'

'I am relaxed!' he shouted. His eyes were wild. Everything in him short-circuiting.

He grabbed a plastic container from the ground and marched up to Kala.

'Know what this is?' he said.

He unscrewed the cap carefully and jerked the container at the cage beside Kala. A slug of thick liquid hit the cage and hissed. Snakes of smoke twisted up from the metal. A chemical smell.

'This shit'll dissolve a dog in no time,' he said. He waved the bottle in front of Kala.

'Think Piglet would still be keen on you?' he said. 'If I give you a taste of this?' He held the bottle before her face. 'How 'bout if I melted those tits? Think Joe Brennan would want you then?'

Kala screamed and Teabag put his hand over her mouth. 'Shut the fuck up,' he said, and I jumped down off the pallets and ran around to the door of the barn and ran in yelling and Teabag turned to me and Kala bit down on the hand he had over her mouth so hard that Teabag shouted and Kala wrenched her arms free and made to run to me but Teabag shoved her back, and he was turning to face me, container still in his hand, when Kala kicked him hard against the back of the leg and he yelled and started forward and spun around whipping the plastic container in a wide swing that sent a snake of thick liquid through the air where it hung for what felt like for ever, suspended in front of all their wide-eyed faces, before roaring through mine.

It starts with a flicker of the eyelids, barely a pulse. Then Marie begins to murmur. We're swarmed round her and the nurse shows up and gets us to make space. Auntie Pauline's crying, holding Marie's hand. Even Mam's wet-eyed. It's this mad whir of feelings – relief, joy, fear of relief and joy – and we're all swept up in it, all except Helen, whose smile can't cover up the agitation in her eyes.

She comes close to me and whispers, 'Has anyone told Ger and Teabag the twins have been found?'

Who gives a flying fuck? I take out my phone. 'I'll call them now.'

'No,' Helen says. She pulls me back from the others and whispers, 'Mush, we have to go to the farm.'

I give her this incredulous face. 'I'm not leaving now, like.'

The others are flocked about Marie, who's blinking out of somewhere way deep, completely disoriented.

Helen leans up and whispers in my ear, 'What happens to Blinkie the moment Ger and Teabag get word the twins are safe in hospital?'

I want to turn away from her, say, fuck this, it's not my problem, the twins are safe, that's all I care about.

Helen whispers, 'Blinkie's the only one who can tie all the pieces together – the twins, the Mammy, what happened to Kala. He *told* us to go to the Mammy. We can't just leave him. The truth is right fucking there with him. We need to hear it from him ourselves.'

'We can report it to the cops,' I say.

'*Fuck* the cops,' she hisses. Frustration on Helen's face but her eyes are pleading at me. 'You heard Blinkie last night. Nothing about the investigation into Kala added up. Jesus,

Mush, I've seen this kind of thing before, in Canada, and if there's one thing I've lear—'

'Helen Laughlin?' an official voice says.

It's a uniformed Guard. She's young, tired. A yellow note-book in her hand.

'Yes?' Helen says.

The Guard consults her notebook. 'Joe Brennan here, too?'

Joe looks over at us. He raises a hesitant hand.

I catch the Guard looking at my scars. Her eyes linger. 'You must be Mush. Can the three of ye come with me for a minute?'

Mam gives me this concerned look. I just wanna stay with her, with the twins.

The Guard turns back to us as she walks away. 'Now, please.'

Helen

THEY'VE FOUND BLINKIE at the farm. That must be it. They've found him, just in time, and he's told them how Mush and Joe discovered him, how me and Mush abandoned him. They will charge us for obstruction, at the very least. Aiding and abetting false imprisonment.

Mush and Joe look to me, anxiously, as though I know what is about to happen. We follow the Guard towards a private room, where a detective stands outside the door. He straightens up and glances between the three of us. His smile is friendly.

He will be the good cop. But Bad Cop turns to us, and she's the one who speaks. 'Mrs Lanann won't cooperate with us. She's been insisting on seeing the three of ye since we got her here. Wants to explain herself. She's... she's very tired.'

'Five minutes,' Good Cop says. 'That's all we'd need. Help us get the ball rolling with her.'

I know not to pay attention to his friendly smile. They are not really asking us to help. Their eyes are hard, and they are already shepherding us into the Mammy's room.

She is tiny in the hospital bed. The bruise shimmers beneath her right eye – her neck is bruise-stained like a birthmark.

The Gardaí indicate chairs for the three of us to sit. Mush stands back, holding his arms. He looks afraid, like a little boy.

The Mammy's eyes are glassy. She does not look up from her sheets.

'I'm not a monster,' she says. 'I want ye to know that.'

'What was going on in your house?' Mush says.

I give Mush a quick look; let me. I lean forward in my seat. 'Help us understand.'

'Blinkie Roche,' the Mammy says. She looks at Joe. 'He showed up at the house after you left me on Saturday. He had them poor girls in the back of his caravan. They were both unconscious. Flat out.'

I blink. I was *there*. I saw this, after I left Lough Caille. The mobile home, parked before the porch. I was standing outside the house when this was happening.

Bad Cop is scribbling in a notebook. 'You knew he was going to endanger them?' she says.

The Mammy looks at Mush and me. Desperate eyes.

'I'm not a monster. I knew he'd been talking to the girls. I knew he had them involved in things, telling them all sorts about their brother and Kala. He'd asked me for some of Kala's old photos. Said he'd give them to the twins, stir things up with their fa—'

'But you knew he would endanger them girls?' Bad Cop says.

The Mammy cries out, 'He told me he'd find out what happened me granddaughter. I... I just wanted—' She stops. '...I wanted...'

Good Cop speaks up. 'You got a proper name for this Blinkie fella?'

The Mammy ignores her. She is still talking to Mush and me. 'Blinkie kept saying it'd all be over in a matter of hours. I only needed to wait a bit longer. I told him this was all out of control. I even threatened to call the Guards. He... he slapped me. Held me by the throat. He promised me he'd be back in a couple of hours. I never wanted them girls hurt like this. Ye have to believe me, I wouldn't—'

'What's Blinkie's actual name?' Good Cop says.

The Mammy sniffs. She withdraws completely.

The cops are fucking botching this. I give Good Cop a look. *Just let me do this.*

'Mrs Lanann,' I say quietly. She looks at me. We hold each other's stare.

'Seamus Roche,' the Mammy whispers. Good Cop nods at Bad Cop and Bad Cop immediately leaves the room, tucking her walkie-talkie to her mouth. Putting the search on. Mush looks at me and I look away, keeping my face neutral.

'Why didn't you call us?' Good Cop says.

The Mammy glares at him. 'Try living my life and see if you have any faith in the Guards,' she spits. 'Blinkie showed up at the house weeks ago. Looking for work. I hadn't seen him in years. He'd been our handyman after me husband Mick died. Called about every month or so. Any odd job, for a few quid. Cup of tea and a sambo. He was... only Blinkie. But he stopped calling around after Kala went missing. I put that down to the usual. This town, shutting the book on us. And me left for years, alone in that house with the place falling asunder about me.'

She stops for so long that I think she has lost her train of thought. Good Cop makes to speak, and I glare at him. *Just let her talk.*

'So he comes knocking at me door in a lather, talking about how his brother went and died on him and someone's after conning him out of his money, he needs the cash, all this craic. He starts calling around every day, doing bits and pieces about the house for a few bob. I ask him to go downstairs and have a root around, try and find Kala's old photo album for me. I hadn't been down them stairs in years, like. But Blinkie starts asking about Kala. About what I thought had happened her. He said he knew things.'

The Mammy hesitates.

'What things?' I say.

'He says the person who done for my girl was still out there. He told me Kala would be found on that Kinlough Associates site. I didn't know what to think. The following week, there it was on the radio: human remains found in Caille Woods. You spend years knowing you're being lied to. And someone finally tells you a bit of truth. He knew about Kala. About her father, about Fiona, everything. He *knew*.'

The Mammy breathes heavily through her nose. One hand worries at the other. No one speaks. I flex my fingers towards Good Cop. *Don't interrupt this.*

My voice is quiet, soft. 'Mrs Lanann? What did Blinkie know about Kala?'

The room feels smaller. The air thicker. The Mammy is having a silent argument with herself, and we are gathered, waiting. Her mouth makes word shapes, like someone in prayer.

Then something changes in her face. Her eyes meet mine. They are burning.

'I'd grounded Kala. After that fiasco at Halloween. *There'll be no more sleepovers with your friends, little missie. No more hanging about town all hours.* Christ, the roars out of her. And she just bulldozed me. Everything she'd cobbled together about Fiona, thanks to that fool Mulkerns. How Fiona had been so young. How I'd let her believe for years that her mother had abandoned her, when we'd obviously sent Fiona away. You lied to me about this, you lied to me about that. Jesus, sometimes a lie can be the right thing. The only thing. Kids never understand that. It's always so bloody simple.'

She shakes her head.

'You know what's the worst of it? When you get caught in a lie that awful? The relief. Just for a moment. Even if everything after that moment's a horror, there's... it's a release. Kala thought she wanted the truth, right up until she knew it. And then, the way she looked at me—'

Her face is flushed. She shakes her head.

I touch the frame of her bed.

'No one is judging you for sending Fiona away. I can only imagine how heartbreaking that choice must have—'

'*Choice*,' the Mammy says. 'If you think I'd any choice... I never *sent* Fiona anywhere. Took her out of school and I looked after her myself, at home, for the final weeks. Then one morning I get up. Fiona's bed is empty. I can't get a hold of Mick. This is before mobile phones, like. I'm panicking. I can't go anywhere by meself with the bloody chair. I tell meself: Mick's with her. Maybe he's taken her to a doctor. The bloody lies you'll tell yourself, sitting by the phone. But Mick came home for his dinner and I realized – he didn't know where she was. And the lashings of rain, the cold outside. We were out of our minds with worry. He figured she couldn't have gone far, in her state. There was a search party. He'd a whole bunch of his fellas trawling the woods for her. Mick Lanann was a high-ranking Guard, like. He ran Kinlough. The man didn't answer to anyone.'

'And there'll be a record of this?' Good Cop says. 'A Garda search for—'

'Ach,' the Mammy says. 'This was all done on the quiet, like. Fellas Mick could trust to keep their mouths shut. There were probably a few of your lot involved. There always is. But it was mostly his other crew. That whole miserable lot out the Warren. Ger Lyons.'

'Kala's granddad knew Uncle Ger?' Mush says.

'How d'you think the Lyons never get fingered for anything?' the Mammy says. 'Ye think a crew like that operates in a town like this without someone like Mick Lanann? There's always a Mick. He's in everything.'

Her mouth is tight over her teeth.

'They found Fiona that evening. By then it was too late. Too much blood. And the exposure. Blinkie told me she was amongst the trees. She was holding the baba to her chest. Wrapped up in her duffel coat to keep the child warm. When I think of what must have been going through her mind.'

The Garda's pen has stopped scribbling. A heavy quiet in the room.

The Mammy seems lost. Unaware of us.

'Mick arrived home, with Kala in his arms. Ger Lyons and his lot did what they do. Disappeared everything. Like my daughter had never even happened. Do you know, not one person in Kinlough ever asked after her. Not one.'

Her eyes are far from all of us, staring at some inner thing.

'It was just Kala and me, against all of it. There's no way she should have survived the night she was born, you know. But she did. My little fighter. And when Mick passed away a few years later, it was only us. Me and Kala. Just us.'

I swallow. '...And Kala's father? Was he aware—'

'Jesus Christ, girl,' the Mammy says. 'Do I've to spell it out? Are you going to make me say it?'

She breathes hard through her nose.

'Mick Lanann didn't answer to anyone.'

Joe

YOU DON'T UNDERSTAND. Your thoughts stutter, rearrange themselves. Helen's whole body has tensed. Her eyes are wide. You look at Mush, but he's like you, confused. Ye don't under—

'*Mick?*' Helen says. 'Kala's grandfather?'

'What'd you've done in my place?' the Mammy says. 'You think any Guard would move against Mick Lanann? No one was going to help me and Fiona, even if they wanted to. But try explaining that to a fifteen-year-old girl.'

Her lip quivers. She bites down on a nail.

'When I told Kala about her father... Jesus, her face—'

The Mammy puts her hands to her mouth. Her chest rises and falls.

The Gardaí shuffle on their feet.

Someone should say something.

Someone should say *something*.

'Fiona was all I had. And they took her from me.'

Her mouth trembles. Her hands tremble. She jabs herself in the chest with a finger.

'Because I *let* them. And when Kala was all I had, they *took* her from me.' Her voice breaks. She jabs herself again. 'Because *I let them*.'

Her eyes flash about the room. She glares at you.

'What are you supposed to do with that? Ask for forgiveness? Sure no one forgives anyone. My girls are dead. Nothing's going to fix that.'

338

She points at Helen.

'And don't tell me ye're any better. Where were ye when Kala needed you most? Hah? The dogs in the street knew something was wrong with her. So what did ye do? Hah?'

Heart's thundering in your ears. Because you know that she's right.

The days right after Mush's accident were a fog. There were phone calls. Lots. Not just between you and the gang, between the parents, too. Mostly the parents. Ye were all grounded. You had to beg Mam and Dad just to hold on to your phone. You spent most of the time sitting next to the fire in the sitting room, heat on your back, strumming pointlessly on the guitar. Mam made snacks and left them next to you. You wished you could go back to knowing nothing about anything, to just living towards the Other Place. Found yourself turning from the Other Place in this moment, huddling closer to normal lights. Fuckhead comforts. Watching dumb shit on TV, football, the usual crap.

There were text photos doing the rounds. Grainy phone pictures of a field of sheep out in Carthy. The sheep were all dead. Wool smeared with blood, pink cords bulging out their sides. People were saying it was the work of Devil worshippers, but you knew better. Ger's dogs were out there, a wild pack of them loose in the back roads and fields of the Warren. More animals would be torn up in the coming days.

'Only a matter of time before some poor person gets mauled,' you heard Dad mutter on the phone to a colleague.

It got so bad it was even on the TV news. They interviewed a farmer, an auld lad in a cap. He was talking about his sheep and his voice broke off and he turned away from the camera and waved a hand, shook his head. You shifted in your seat. Mam and Dad were in the room with you. You were convinced they knew your thoughts. You knew they blamed Kala for all of it. Your bloody nose. Helen's dog. Mush's face.

Texts from Kala started at eight every night, cos that's when the Mammy let her have her phone. Her messages had been getting weird. Between all her

Miss u xxx

and

wish u wer here wit me x

there'd be something like

whis Id never bin born :-(

On the Saturday before she went missing, she said, **I rlly need 2 c u.** You'd pretended you needed to borrow a T-square from someone, to get a head start on a tech drawing project that would begin at school next week. That pleased Mam and Dad. As you cycled to Caille Woods, you visualized Kala there, waiting for you. How she'd run to you, and you'd step off your bike, and ye'd kiss and the camera would swoop around ye, music swelling.

But Kala wasn't there. She made you wait. And when she arrived, she wasn't the girl from the Other Place. She hadn't made an effort for you. She was grey-faced and thin. Didn't even kiss you properly, or ask about your nose. Just sank into your chest and held you tight.

'Come on,' she said. She took your hand and ye walked into the woods.

She was talking fast. Interrupting herself every few sentences. She said she'd tried to visit Mush in the hospital but Lydia had told her she wasn't welcome. She tugged at your arm. You wished she'd calm down. You didn't have much time – Mam and Dad would be expecting you back. But she kept asking about Mush.

You'd been to visit him only once so far, with your parents. Mush was asleep the entire time. You didn't even recognize him at first. Would've walked right past his bed if Lydia hadn't been sitting there. Your mam gave Lydia flowers, like that'd help.

Half his face was just gone.

Nurses stopped by to gently apply some sticky goo to the places that used to be skin. He didn't even flinch. He was hooked up to a morphine drip, a load of bleeping machines.

The sight of him made you want to cry. Made you want to run away.

'Don't tell me that,' Kala said. 'Please don't say that. I can't bear it.'

She was freaking you out, the way she was acting. Her eyes bouncing off the trees. Like she was manic.

'What's wrong with you?'

'Nothing. I'm just... I had this huge fight with Nana, and...' Her face was all crumpled. She seemed confused. 'It's like everything's sliding apart. I can't hold everything, I...'

She was slurring.

'I should never have been born. Joe, I'm a freak.'

'You sound drunk. Are you drunk?'

This was not what she wanted you to say. A darkness flitted over her face. Then she held herself against you. 'I just, I really need to be close to you.' She slid her hand down your waist and over your crotch.

You stepped back. 'Jesus, Kala. What the fuck?'

'Don't you want to?' she said. She began to cry.

It was frightening. Too much voltage going in too many directions.

'Be fucking normal,' you said.

'I'm sorry for not being *normal* enough for you, Joe. You're such a...'

'What?'

'You pretend you're cool but... you need to read the instructions before doing anything.'

You wanted to hit her. Can't hit a girl. 'What does that even mean?'

'It means I don't need you to fucking tell me I'm not normal. It means fuck off.'

'I'm going home. I'm already late. Sort your head out, would you?'

'Oh, piss off, Joe.' She gave a bitter laugh. 'You're not my father.'

You turned and looked at her. 'Maybe if you had a father you wouldn't be the way you are.'

You left her standing alone amongst the trees.

Hours went by. Sitting in your room, strumming directionless chords. That night she sent you a photo. It was a picture of herself, kneeling before her foggy mirror. She was naked from the waist down.

I love you

Plaese dont dump me

You didn't reply.

She stopped texting you after that.

On Sunday the night was swimming outside your window. You longed to hear from her again. You just couldn't be the one to make the first move.

You were willing the phone to buzz on your bedside table when the doorbell rang.

'Joe,' Mam called from downstairs. 'Some girl for you.'

'Who is it?'

'I didn't realize I was your secretary,' Mam said.

Downstairs, the cold of the night was blowing into the hall.

'Heya Joe.' It was Aoife. 'What you up to?'

'Nothing.'

'I know, fucking boring right? You grounded? I'm grounded. I told my parents I was going over to Helen's to get a fucking book.'

'You been chatting to Helen?'

'Uh, *no*,' she said. 'We're not exactly seeing eye to eye these days. I suppose you're in the same boat. All that secret stuff she's been up to lately. With Kala.'

You knew Aoife well enough by now. She'd dangle things and wait for you to reach for them. You knew you should resist.

'Want to come in for a minute?'

She sat on your bed while you stood.

'Just wanted to see how you're doing,' she said. 'Like, poor Mush. It's awful, isn't it? I guess Kala will be acting even weirder now. You know how she always is about Mush. He's like her teddy bear, you know? She always wanted him next to her in the bed whenever we had our sleepovers.'

A cold feeling in you at this. Aoife, watching your face. 'Wait, you didn't know about the sleepovers? I could tell you some stories. Believe me. Buh-lieve me.'

Heart beating.

'Like what?'

'Oh, nothing,' she said. 'I guess Kala can just be a bit slutty. You know the way.'

Your mind racing. For the first time you asked yourself, why had Kala been alone at the farm with Mush?

'You know she sent me phone pictures of herself,' you said. 'Dirty pictures.'

Something flashed in Aoife's eyes and she looked over at your phone on the table.

'No way,' she said. 'See? This is what I mean... like, what kind of girl would do something like that?'

Mam called you from downstairs. You went out to the landing.

'What?'

'Wrap it up there,' she said. 'Don't forget you're grounded.'

Aoife hugged you as she left. 'Mind yourself, Joe. Kala can be, like, so careless with people.'

You went back to sitting with your guitar. Head ringing. It was a while till you looked over at your phone. Only, it wasn't where you always left it, on the bedside next to the photo of Kala. It was on your bed, where Aoife had been sitting.

In the hospital corridor, outside the Mammy's room. Helen's asking the Guards why they haven't interviewed any of ye about Kala yet, and the cops exchange a strange look you can't decipher. Head's gone pure cloudy. You should have a drink.

They ask ye to stay nearby. The moment they leave, Helen and Mush stand close to each other, whispering rapidly. You can't follow what they're saying.

'What's going on?'

'Me and Helen gotta go,' Mush says. 'We don't have time to explain.'

'But... can't I help?'

Mush pauses. Ye look at each other. Even in his frustration, his face softens. He's still Mush. You're still Joe Brennan. He's never been able to stay pissed off with you for long.

He takes you aside and puts a hand on your shoulder. There's something weirdly paternal about it. 'If you want to help, man, just sit tight here with the twins. It'd mean a lot to them to have you there. It'd mean a lot to me too.'

'...It would?'

'Yeah, man.'

Before you can say anything else, he's clapped you on the arm and himself and Helen are gone.

Mush

THE RAIN STARTS with slow thick drops on the windscreen. Sky's seething out there. All bloodpurple, ready to let rip. We're in the Warren, near Uncle Ger's place. Engine running. I've checked out the house. Uncle Ger's up there all right, but he's alone. Teabag's car is gone. I wanted to call Uncle Ger and tell him that the twins are at the hospital – that way, he'd go visit them and the coast would be clear for me and Helen to get Blinkie. But Helen vetoed that, reminding me that once Ger knows the twins have been found, Blinkie's as good as dead. So now the plan's for Helen to call up to the house and keep Uncle Ger out front for a few minutes, while I get Blinkie out the barn and into the long grass.

'You're one hundred per cent about this?' I say. 'What if Uncle Ger tries something weird with you?'

Helen shows me the can of Canadian bear spray in her handbag, then goes back to leaning her forehead against her window, staring out.

I'm hoping Blinkie can walk. I don't know if I can carry him all by myself. Plan is to get him to the car and bring him to Dudley, but only when he's answered all Helen's questions. We just need to wait till it gets fully dark. Not long now.

The radio's on quietly in the car. It's the only light. Everything else is growing darkness, the sound of rain. Helen exhales heavily. Her face is pure sad, fragile.

'You all right?'

'Just thinking,' she says.

345

We'd been trying to work out who had any motive to hurt Kala. What threat Kala might have presented. Fucking mess, like. Maybe Kala was going to expose the cover-up around what happened to her mother. Or the dogfighting. Or what really happened to my face. Any one of those things might have been enough. The only common thread was Uncle Ger, which meant that people working for him could also be involved. Even Teabag. Fuck sake, Teabag might've gone after Kala randomly, just to spite Joe. Or to teach her a lesson after what had happened to me. Or to get back at Joe after Dudley slapped him about, the night of the gig. Teabag was always fixated on Joe, like. I could see it happening. The Lyons hovering around her, intimidating her. A punch thrown. Kala falling the wrong way, her head clapping against the ground. The Lyons panicking. Bringing Kala to the farm. Uncle Ger saying he'll make it disappear, calling up Blinkie.

I don't know.

I look over at Helen and she's frowning. Something delicate about her.

'What's up?'

Her voice is pure quiet. 'Just thinking of Kala.'

Her eyes are shining, her cheeks all flushed.

'The Mammy's right,' Helen says. 'What she said. There's no forgiveness for this.'

'What d'you mean?'

'We don't deserve it. People like me. Cold. Uncaring.'

'Who the fuck says you're uncaring?'

'Theresa, last night. Joe, all the time.'

She is quiet in herself.

'I know I can be tough on people,' she says. 'I know I can be... hard.'

The rain on the windscreen makes spotty shadows on her face. It's like something's tugging down on her mouth.

'You're not *hard*,' I say. 'You're just...'

She looks right at me. Big vulnerable eyes on her. 'I dunno. You don't want to be taken for a ride by people, is all. You're no bullshit, like. It's one of the things I love most about you. Jesus, I wish I could be more like that.'

'You don't want to be like me, Mush.'

Silence for a bit. I'm trying to think of the word for how Helen is. What's the fucking word?

Withhold.

'You just withhold yourself a bit. That's all.'

Suddenly she begins to cry. I've never seen Helen cry. Ever.

'Oh,' I say. 'Hey, hey. That's no bad thing, like.'

'Yes, it is,' she says. There's a tremor in her. Her face is as raw, like. And then she tells me about the last time she saw Kala.

Helen

WE WERE WALKING to school. One earbud each. A brittle sulk hung through the earbud cord between us. Dad and Theresa were both furious with me because of Misty. Ger had been over to the house and spoken with Dad, and they had had a shouting argument about Misty. About Teabag slapping me. Ger left the house in a rage and Dad sat for a long time at the kitchen table, looking at job listings, staring at the walls, drinking one glass of beer after another.

Theresa sat out in the garden the whole weekend, near where Dad had buried Misty. Every time I tried to joke with her, or made her a sandwich, she would not look at me.

I had been texting Kala about Mush, trying to find out exactly what had happened. I wanted us to make each other feel better. But every time I texted her, it took her ages to text back. Sometimes, she did not reply at all. I didn't realize then what I know now. What she had learned that weekend. The way the world must have been turning itself through her over those hours.

That final morning, we met at the entrance to the estate. 'Hello, you,' Kala said, sadly, and I said, 'Hey,' and it felt like Mush was there between us, and we held each other in a hug for a long time. I remember that. I remember that.

The schoolyard felt wrong, the moment we entered. Girls cupping hands to their mouths, whispering to each other, tugging on each other's sleeves at the sight of us. Energy coursing like electric current. A laughter of anticipation.

In the yard I saw several teachers standing about, looking flustered. The principal, Sister Irene, giving sharp instructions to Willy, the caretaker.

Then I saw it. It was sprayed over the wall in giant letters: KALA LANANN IS A SLUT

The entire classroom was full of chatter about it, all morning. People were rabid. Teachers had a strain to their faces – 'Settle down, girls. Settle down now' – as they tried to act like everything was normal.

But it was not normal.

In the break between classes, girls gathered at my desk. One of the popular girls, Ailbhe Hynes, asked if the rumours were true.

'What rumours?'

She looked at the other girls, her eyes wide.

'Uh, oh my God? About you and Kala Lanann, shifting each other on Halloween. A little lesbian show for the Lyons.'

The other girls all giggled. Nervous hunger.

'What?'

'Oh my God, she's blushing,' Ailbhe said. 'You guys, she's totally blushing.'

'It's just some stupid graffiti.'

'Um, hello?' Ailbhe said. She handed me her phone. 'What's this?'

On her phone there was a photo of Kala. She had taken it herself, in her foggy mirror. My stomach lurched. She was naked from the waist down.

'That's not just graffiti,' Ailbhe said.

I realized now, why there was such a fever going around the room.

'Why do you have this?'

'God, like, ten people must have sent it to me already,' Ailbhe said. 'Basically anyone with a camera on their phone. I've already got it from, like, five lads at St Simon's.'

*

I looked for Kala in the yard at breaktime. She was the only thing people were talking about. Aoife appeared out of the crowd. She was agitated. Anxious.

'Is Kala okay?' she said. 'Sister Irene came and took her from maths this morning. I think—'

A jeer rushed through the yard, like a breeze moving through long grass. Kala was walking into the yard alone. Girls parted around her, like they were afraid of contagion.

We made eye contact from a distance. I knew I should rush to her. And I was going to do that, but it was like I couldn't. It was just a moment, a moment where I looked away. A withheld kindness, a deferred compassion. When I looked back, Kala was no longer there. My eyes flitted across the bodies in the school yard. I glimpsed her, hunched and walking out of the school gates. The flux of bodies passed over her. Later I would tell myself how I would have gone to her if I had been able to see her in time. I would have.

But I didn't.

The wipers slosh the rain about Mush's windscreen. Walls of water. I am afraid to look at Mush. To see the disgust in his face.

'Ah, Helen,' he says softly.

'What if I'd just gone to her?' My voice is clotted. 'What if she hadn't left like that?'

'You couldn't have known,' Mush says.

I take a deep breath and hold it in, trying to calm down. My hands are all shivers. I almost tell Mush the facts of my life. Soon I will be older than my mam ever was. I do not have anything or anyone. I live alone, above a shitty pizza place in a miserable town an hour outside Montreal. No career to speak of. Instead, I say, 'Sometimes I think of who we were back then, you know? When Kala was with us? We were such a *force*. What happened to us?'

'Hey,' Mush says. His voice is deep, gentle. 'Don't be thinking like that.'

'Kala was always there for me. And when she needed me...
The Mammy's right. There's no forgiveness for this.'

'Ah, here,' Mush says. 'Sure what sort of world would it be
if people don't forgive? A fucking madhouse. And forgiveness
isn't some one-way thing anyway. Cos... when you forgive
someone, it doesn't just release them, does it? And, like... Ah
fuck this, Helen, it's cheesy to say this sort of shite out loud.'

Mush hesitates.

'You know that whole spiel about how you can't step in the
same river twice? I sit at my window at the caf most evenings,
yeah? Fox Street is like the river. It's got all these faces and
lives, with all their memories, plans, whatever. And it's always
changing. Sometimes I think that's what life is, you know?
Rivers inside rivers within rivers.'

He stops. I do not know what he is trying to say.

'Go on.' I want him to keep talking. I want to know what
Mush thinks. I want to be for him the way he is with everyone. Expansive.

Mush hesitates. Then he turns in his seat to face me, and
his face is boyish. Scars and all.

'Like, you see a smile ripple through a group of people on
Fox Street, or two lads fuck up a handshake, whatever, and
you see it happen, like. The knock-on effect. How we influence things. Cos we're all affecting each other all the time. So
maybe life is just a load of flows affecting each other, in all
directions. And holding grudges or, like... say you get caught
inside one fixed idea of things, and you're always clinging
to it or whatever... that shit puts a block inside you. So now
the river's gotta move around this big fuck-off rock, and the
more rocks you add to it, the more it starts flowing in weird
ways, awkward diversions and stuff. And now you're blocked
up inside yourself, so you start to put blocks outside yourself
too, in the world. Y'know? But even if you're putting all your
energy into saying no to life, making sure nothing new ever

happens, holding the world at bay, it doesn't matter. Cos, basically, life doesn't give a fuck. The rivers flow on regardless, inside you, and outside you, and... em... I don't fucking know, I sound like a pure stoner. That's what the twins always tell me.'

I look at him for a moment.

'Jesus, Mush, why didn't you ever just *leave*?'

Mush laughs. 'Cos I'm a fucking hypocrite. I shite on about rivers and flows but sure I'm the most landlocked fucker you've ever met. I spend me whole life holding the world at bay. Watching it go by.'

'Did you never dream about leaving?'

'Ara, I can out-dream any fucker, Helen. I dream me hole off. Day and night. But it doesn't matter, does it? Dreaming. Thinking. You're only what you do, in the end. And I do fuck-all. I'm useless, like.'

I begin to protest. 'How can you say that? You were always the bravest. Remember the night Kala cycled down the big hill, into the road? You were the only one brave enou—'

Mush waves a hand.

'Fucking coward is what I am. I was the last person to chat to Kala, like. And I was no use to her. She came to the hospital, the evening when the photo of her was going around town. Uncle Ger had fed Mam this whole story that me and Kala had been together, messing about on a building site where Ger was running security. 'An act of high jinks gone wrong.' That's how he described it to Mam. Like we were up to Halloween vandalism or something. Such fucking bullshit. But he'd been there when I woke up in the hospital, and he told me that Mam could have the caf rent-free if I stuck to the story he'd spun. He said Teabag and Boomerang had already got Kala in line too; they'd made her swear on it before they even brought me to the hospital. The lads were all with Uncle Ger, like, standing next to my bed. Aidan too, looking at me face, pure scared. The drip had me knocked out half the time, so I was out of it, but even so, I was afraid. Just wanted to retreat from everything, like. Switch off.

And I'm drifting that evening, pure spaced in the morphine thing, when I heard Mam, giving out to Kala. She blamed her for me face, like. I managed to get a word in, tell her I wanted to see Kala. So Mam tells Kala we could have five minutes to chat. *Not a second more.* Then Kala came to the bed. She got such a fright in her eyes when she saw me, I turned away. I was already beginning to do that, like. Turning from people. Pure reflex now, sure. But Kala was staring at me, her mouth trembling like crazy, eyes pure glossy. Face gone all red. She was all, *I'm sorry I'm sorry* and I just wanted her to stop. I was like, *Sure it's not your fault, is it?* But she said it was. *Everything's my fault,* she said. She was as fragile, that night. One wrong word and she'd fall into a million pieces. I tried giving her the spiel I was giving everyone else. *It was an accident. Doctors said I was lucky not to go blind in this eye. And the hair here will grow back.* But Kala had been there, like. She knew what had really happened. She looked at me like I was mad. *Mush, it wasn't some accident.* And I... I just looked at her and said, *Yes, it was.* I said it pure hard, like that'd make it true. But Kala was on a mission, like. She was saying we should tell the cops it was all Teabag. She'd tell them about the dogs, and the dogfighting, all of it. But I told her, *No, Kala. No,* I said. And I remember her face when I said that. Like she thought maybe, deep down, I really did blame her for everything. But I *didn't*, like. I just... I just wanted to forget everything. Wanted to go to sleep for ever, y'know? Then Kala asked if she could hug me. If it'd hurt me, like. We went to hug but then Mam came back, telling Kala to clear off. *Okay, bye,* Kala said.'

Mush clears his throat. He looks out the windscreen, and scrunches his face up.

'I *saw* her, Helen. That night. I saw who Kala was. Joe could never see that, and... to be honest, I don't think you could either. Ye had such ideas about her. She was some kind of icon to ye. More than a person, like. Which meant she was less than a person. But I *saw* her. Flesh and blood, all the way through. All the feelings in there, all them Kalas, on the surface of her face, changing by the second. Flows. Soft. Fierce. Lovely. Afraid. She was a person. She was me friend. And I didn't even hug her.'

He tucks his chin in for a moment. The rain is beginning to hammer on the car. I have to strain to hear him.

'The twins are pretty much the only people I have at this point,' he says, 'and look at the fucking state of me. Few hours ago I didn't know if they were okay, where they were, or what the fuck. But there was a time I could tell what Donna and Marie thought about something before they even thought it themselves, like. I know it's lame but... they gave me days direction. And I just fucking let that all slide as they got older, telling meself all this bullshit about how everything's like rivers, only going to trickle away from you, between your fingers, and sure there's no use trying to hold on to rivers cos you'll only end up drowned, and why bother, maybe life's all just drowning anyway, and blahdy fucking blah, like... You know what's appealing about floaty hippie ideas like that? They let you pretend the world isn't made by decisions and consequences. No one's responsible for anything, we all just float along. Load of fucking bollocks. I didn't help Kala when she needed me. I didn't help Aidan when he needed me. Every thought I have's a fucking dead end. All these walls piling up in me skull. And most nights I just have another can, blow past those thoughts, and pretend... but like, I've let so many people down. I *have to* believe that people forgive each other. Cos what's the alternative?'

He stops. Clears his throat. Bites the side of his mouth.

'You're here now,' I say.

I take his hand and squeeze it. He squeezes back. This is what I love most about Mush. About us. Sometimes he is the strong one, sometimes it is me. We can do that, flow between one another.

'Right,' he says, turning the key in the ignition. 'Fuck all this whingeing. Let's get this over with.'

Joe

Jesus

yeah

they going to be ok?

Theresa and Pauline are dozing against one another, by the twins' beds. Donna still hasn't woken up. Marie was awake for a little while, but she wasn't herself. The doctor said this was normal, not a bad sign. Didn't make it any easier to see how frightened she looked, how confused. Eventually she started to moan, long and loud, tears streaming down her cheeks, face all bunched up like a child's. She began to shout out. Then she started screaming. *Screaming.* Fucking terrifying. A nurse came and did something with her drip, and she sank into sleep after that.

Don't know how to answer Dad. Don't know if they're going to be okay.

hope so

Rossie comes back with two coffees in plastic cups. He sighs as he sits next to you, hands you a coffee.

keep me posted
look after them

will do

'Any craic?' Rossie says.
'Just updating the parents.'
Rossie pauses. 'They know about you, last night?'

Shake your head. Roll up your sleeves. Rossie winces when he sees the corsage of bruising, still unhealed around your elbow. Colours like rotting fruit.

'What happened there?'

'I had a fall a few weeks ago. Dislocated the elbow.'

'Feck sake. Sports, was it?'

You hesitate. Fuck it. 'No. I was alone, actually. In my house.'

Rossie nods. 'Ah.'

It's a strange feeling, being honest. But you're too tired to pretend. When the Guards speak to you later, you'll tell them the truth of the night Kala disappeared. You've never told the others this – the truth about where you were. November in Kinlough. Darkness, rain. You'd called to Kala's house that evening only for the Mammy to say you'd missed her by half an hour. You needed to see her, to make things right. So you huddled under some trees on the Coast Road, waiting for Kala to come home. Leaves dripping with rain as you shivered, trying to ignore the dread. Kala wasn't answering your texts. Every time a set of headlights approached in the rain, you hoped Kala would be there, warm and safe in a stranger's car.

Later, when it was clear something was truly wrong, Dad and Mam sat you down and asked, repeatedly, where you'd been in the hours after Kala was last seen. You told them the truth: you'd been alone, waiting for Kala on the Coast Road. Mam and Dad exchanged worried looks. 'Jesus Christ, Dudley,' Mam said. 'If anything's happened to her, that's a big target all over his back.' You didn't understand. 'You're the bloody boyfriend, Joe. They always blame the fella. And you have no alibi.' This was the beginning of endless hours with the same acidic taste in your mouth. Pure panic as you said, 'But I love her, like.' Dad raised his hands. 'Right. Right... Here's what we say. Joe was here. He... he spoke to the Mammy, but came straight back home. We watched a film together, all three of us. All night. Okay, chief? What film?'

You told that lie to every officer who questioned you. Heart motoring in your chest each time, wondering what Kala would say if she could see you. Something getting lost in those moments. Something you were giving away.

Thoughts like this swarm the silence as you sit with Rossie.

'The morning after's always gonna be there,' Rossie says. 'You gotta be a friend to yourself, like.'

'What if you don't particularly like yourself? What if that's exactly what you want to get away from?'

Rossie takes a deep breath. 'Pauline and T are mighty women for the big questions. Stuff makes my head spin, to be honest. But there's a thing they once said that clicked with me. Your *self* isn't some "deep down" thing that exists, away in some other place, separate from your day-to-day. Like, there is no other place. You're always here. Becoming what you are.'

'You a Buddhist or something?'

Quiet smile on him. 'Maybe I've picked up some lingo, I dunno.'

He nods at Pauline and Theresa, and whispers fondly, 'They talk the ear off each other, pair of them. It's lovely to see it like. Theresa didn't have that. Growing up. And...'

He shuffles his weight next to you. His eyes are distracted.

'Helen's more like her mam. She's strong, but fierce defensive. Shuts down whenever she feels vulnerable. Lashes out. And I get that. I've earned that from her.'

He rubs at the back of his neck.

'But she came back for the wedding so I thought... I'd half hoped, her and me, we could maybe begin something different. If she wanted. But now, all this, with Kala... I don't know.'

There's a long moment where he stares at the ceiling. 'I don't fucking know.'

'She did come all this way,' you say. 'That probably means something.'

His eyes brighten. 'You think?'

You nod, and he smiles like you've done him some great service. 'Good man,' he says. 'Good man.'

There's a moan from Donna's bed. She's stirring. She's waking up.

Rossie stands, calls to Pauline, who bolts upright, waking Theresa, calling out, and suddenly it's a totally different moment – the bedside now alive with nervousness, excitement – and Rossie goes for a nurse, and Pauline's tearful, stroking Donna's cheek, 'That's it. That's it, love,' and you call Mush's phone, but it rings out, so you stand next to Theresa – 'Oh, thank God, Joe,' she hugs you – and you try Mush again. No joy.

'Call Helen,' Theresa says. 'They're together.'

You're smiling down the phone, ready to give them the good news. But when Helen answers, your blood freezes. Her voice is wordless, breathless, all language torn apart in a shrieking. A screaming.

Helen

GER'S DOORBELL DOES not work, so I knock. I squint against the rain. Chipped paint on the door. Veined glass. The tinny cacophony of a TV inside. I need to be calm, but I am vibrating with feeling. Theresa's words, in the kitchen last night. The Mammy. Kala. The conversation in the car with Mush. Something has cracked inside me and things are beginning to bleed to the surface. Things that will make me soft. Heart pain. Real heart pain.

The rain is pouring. I ball my fist and bang the door again. Hard.

'Ger,' I call. My voice reverberates around me, like I am calling to myself from the bottom of a well. 'Ger? It's Helen Laughlin.'

I check my phone: 22:24. Mush will already be on his way to the barn. All I have to do is keep Ger at the front of the house. Wait till Mush has untied Blinkie and gotten him into the long grass. From there Mush will call me and I will make my excuses. I will rush to the back road nearby, where Mush parked the car. 'If I don't call you by ten-thirty,' he said, 'make an excuse and get out of there.'

Six minutes left.

The house creaks on the other side of the door.

Everything sharp and tingling. I feel for the bear spray in my bag, in case I need it later.

The latch clicks. The door opens a little. Inside, the lights are off. The cavities of Ger's skull sinking back in the dark, deeper blacks inside the blackness. He drinks me in with blinks.

'I wondered if we could talk,' I say.

He sticks his head out, peers into the rain. Looks around me. An animal alertness. 'You can't be here now,' he says.

He goes to close the door and I say, 'Wait – I wanted to ask you some—'

'Fuck off. I'm busy.'

My mind flits. I need to keep Ger at the front of the house. That is all I need to do. By now Mush is running in the open. He is probably in the barn. I picture Ger seeing him. Finding him. Hurting him.

I just need to keep him engaged. 'The twins,' I say. 'I have news about the twins.'

He should snap to attention at this. Surprise. Delight. A burst of emotion and questions, eager to learn more. But he does not. His face is blank, staring at me. Like he already knows.

He lights a cigarette.

'You better make yourself scarce, Helen.'

I toss my hair and smile. Turn my leg in, shift my weight to one side. I hate myself for resorting to this. 'You gonna leave me in the rain?'

He pauses. Squints over the smoke as he takes a drag, eyes blank.

I nod to his cigarette. 'You got one of those for me?'

It works. He steps aside.

I walk past him into the house, tightness in my throat, feeling his eyes on my body, his hand now on the small of my back, steering me into the dark.

The air is stale. Old takeaway. Salt, grease. The only light comes from jagged blue shapes thrown about by the wide-screen TV as it barks in the corner. The speaker must have some sort of loose connection; it buzzes and rattles as tanks zoom across the screen to a cacophony of orchestral strings.

Mush told me he would need ten minutes, maximum. I check my phone: 22:26. Two minutes have already gone by.

When Ger leads me to the kitchen, I freeze. The cracked window above the sink gives a view across the yard, to the barn. Ger is staring through it as he takes a packet of cigarettes from the countertop.

'Spark that.'

I thank him. Nearly 22:27.

Ger is looking back out the window again. I need to get him away from the window. He frowns back at me, mouth open to speak, when a sudden burst of light erupts in the yard. It blows through the rain on the window, surrounds Ger's silhouette like a halo.

Behind him, I can make out the shape of a van in the yard. It is outside the barn.

Shit. There is someone else out there.

Ger catches me staring behind him. Something in his expression changes and I look at my phone again. Still 22:27.

Call me, Mush. Call me now.

'You're fooling no one,' Ger says. 'Running around playing detective. Trying to piece things together. That's your mother's shape under that jumper. She had notions about herself. Just like you.'

There is a sudden screech of tyres from the yard. Ger turns back to the window. He squints against the glare of the headlights. I know I should distract him. Call out to him. But the van is already rushing back from the barn, towards the house. The lights blare the rain. Mush and Blinkie should already be in the long grass. Mush should already be calling me.

Then something strange happens.

Ger goes out to the yard to meet the van, muttering to himself. But the van does not stop for Ger. It speeds right past him, by the house, and away from the farm. Ger follows it, running to the front of the house. I hear him shout, 'Where you fucking going?' I take my chance and run out the back. I cross the yard, running in the direction of the barn. My bag bounces under my arm. My phone is in my hand. I can hear my breath, my feet. I hear the distant shouts of Ger. Too late to stop. I keep running. I shout for Mush. There is no answer. I run into the barn to make sure he is no longer there. My feet echo off the stone floor. The sound bounces at me around the walls as I catch my breath. My body knows what is happening before my mind can catch it. It takes a long moment for my eyes to see to what I am seeing. And then I scream.

Mush

BIG FAT DROPS fall warm and thick on my face as I watch Helen walk towards Uncle Ger's.

Here we go.

I hear the bell. Check my phone. Less than ten minutes to get in and out. It's getting darker.

Keep to the hedges. Keep low to the ground. Keep quiet.

It's real. I'm real. This is happening. I'm really doing this. I can be brave. I remember the evening Helen brought up in the car, the one when we wheeled our bikes up the hill. Kala was right, the sky was amazing up there. Kinlough all twinkly. I was late realizing the plan was to cycle down the hill and cross the road, through the traffic, to the park on the other side. Kala said she wanted to be the first to go, like we were all gonna take turns or something suicidal like that. But I knew we'd all go down together. I looked to where the hill fell away, down, down, rushing through the small gap into the cars flashing about the road. I knew we'd all stop before we reached it. That'd be the real challenge – slamming the brakes in time without flipping over the handlebars.

But Kala's eyes met mine for a second as she steadied herself on her bike, and I saw. She was for real. I flexed my knuckles on the handlebars and went to tell her that it wasn't gonna be safe, but she was already pedalling off the top of the hill and next thing I knew I was rushing after her, chasing her, rushing in a roar of rattling bike-chains with Kala leaning deep into her handlebars and pedalling hard as she reached the gap, screaming, and then she was through, and in the road, and so was I, and time dilated and stretched around us, and I didn't look to the left or the right, cos we were gliding, safe from everything, braver than anything, and it was suddenly super-clear, all the mud on my brain blown away, eyes clean, and we didn't stop even when we were over the kerb racing deep into the park, not checking to see if the others had followed us, we just kept cycling, harder and harder, as if we could outrun everything, both of us screaming wild laughter and surging forward, forward, like escape was always that bit further out of sight but we'd reach it if we never stopped going.

I'm at the barn before I know it.

The rain's loud on the roof's metal sheeting. My shoulders all hunched up but I still crouch low, even though I'm inside. Even though no one can see me. Time's ticking by, gotta get Blinkie untied and out of here now, just hoping he's not gonna be too heavy, and—

There's a kerosene lamp on the go. Someone else is in the barn with me. I can see tall shadows flickering up the wall, behind Blinkie.

I peer around the corner to see. There's someone crouched over Blinkie. His back's to me. Elbows out, arms tensed. The rain's like nails rattling off the roof, but I can hear the strained breathing. Grunts. Held breath. Blinkie's legs are still bound but he's kicking them wildly, scraping his heels off the ground. They're strangling him. Whoever it is – they're killing him.

It's like I can't move. I should do something.

But I'm just standing there, legs on me like pure lead.

I should *do* something, like.

There's a sudden buzz in my pocket and my phone rings out. The ringtone's loud in the barn, despite the rain. I fumble for my phone, to cancel the call. It's Joe.

I look up, almost bowing, like, ready to give my excuses to Teabag, or Ger, to tell them I saw nothing, to act like I saw nothing, to just turn and run.

But I can't move, like.

Cos it's not Teabag. It's not Uncle Ger.

I have to squint for a second to make out his face, standing upright before Blinkie, facing me now. The skin all about his eyes, pure taut with concern.

It's Dudley.

'Oh Jesus,' he says.

'Dudley,' I say. I open my mouth but there's nothing there to say.

'What the hell's going on?' he says. He steps towards me. 'What are you doing here?'

'Dudley,' I say. My breath's gone all short.

'Does Joe know about this?' Dudley says.

'What? No,' I lie. 'Just Helen Laughlin and meself.'

My phone starts to ring again. Joe, again.

'Sorry,' I say. The phone's shaking in my hands. I try to cancel the call, but my thumbs are all jittery. 'It's just, like, me and Helen—'

There's a loud crack inside my skull and a white flash and the room's rushing in at me so fast filling my head so the shed's tilting and tumbling and the floor's climbing up as my head hits the ground so hard the room rattles and the light's going mad and Blinkie's voice is high-pitched in his gag and my eyes busy with blotches like bats dazzling and I scrabble on the ground, stone cold on my hands, a feeling of something hitting my leg hard and something bursting in my knee, bone crunching into the ground like a sinkhole and I let out a high-pitched gasp and cry and roll on my back and Dudley's above me and I reach up to him for help but he doesn't reach down and take my hand cos he's standing above me, one foot either side of me looking at his face and his face is there, where it should be, but Dudley isn't there, I don't see Dudley in his face, and he has one arm reaching up above him, arcing so high it seems to hit the roof, and his arm looks longer than possible cos he's holding a baton high above me, and it seems to arc back from me through the roof with all the blotchy bat shapes in my eyes in my skull and a voice saying I'm sorry, I'm sorry and I don't know if it's Dudley or me saying it when the baton comes down

crack

and Mam in the caf in the flat in a playground with Aidan on a bike with Kala and all of us running like a rope through the long grass with the twins under a duvet stretched between two beds like a fort the way Donna looked at me through the window the last time I saw Kala with the baton rushing down at my

sorry I'm sorry

I'm so

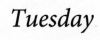

Tuesday

Helen

I AM IN the Crawley House. I cannot breathe. My neck is being crushed by someone I cannot see. Mush is sitting on the floor, head between his knees, because Aidan has fed him a rag covered in blood. A shadow hangs on the wall. A baby is crying. I try to help Mush. But I cannot reach him.

This is when I wake up. My body feels like murky water. It takes a moment for me to see Mam standing at the foot of the bed, watching me. I know I am not dreaming. I am eerily calm. The numbness of Pauline's sleeping pills, still purring in my body. The sun catches the fuzz around Mam's hair. Her sad smile in the split of light coming through the curtain.

'What are you doing here?' I say.

'It's late,' she says. 'After four, I guess.'

It is not Mam. I push myself up from the pillows. Theresa sits on the bed. She is still in her pyjamas. 'You were out cold. Thought you needed it.'

I rub my eyes. 'I was in the Crawley House.'

'Sorry?'

'The place in the woods. Near where we found Misty.'

Theresa sniffs. 'I know where the Crawley House is, Helen.'

Irritation flits across her face – she has never quite forgiven me for Misty – but immediately her softness returns. Her kind eyes, searching for me.

'I was just dreaming,' I say.

My blood feels like sludge. The blank sleep of medication, like the vacant tingle when you plug out a TV.

Last night is a bundle of snapshots. The bright lights of the police station. Doors opening, closing. People constantly telling me to sit. Voices in corridors. Laughter and shouting. Guards with suspicious faces. Guards with kind faces. Guards with no faces. On the barn floor, Mush's face. Just blood and meat.

Good Cop and Bad Cop tried to get me to speak. I was not able to answer their questions coherently. I did not ramble, or rant. I just shook, like jelly.

There was kindness and patience in the room, even when they were asking about Blinkie. 'The deceased.' That is what they called him.

Then they asked if I had ever been interviewed in the immediate wake of Kala's disappearance. The question was so bizarre it grounded me.

'Of course. Loads of times.'

The Guards shared wary looks. They said there's no record of any of us being interviewed. Me, Mush, Joe. Nothing. They said the file on Kala's disappearance is almost empty. Everywhere they turn, there have been obstacles to their investigation. All items of physical evidence taken from Kala's house in 2003 were missing from the evidence storage facility.

A quick knock on the door and Dudley entered. I was grateful to see him. He gently told the other Guards they could resume the interview tomorrow, I was clearly in too much shock. He steered me through the maze of corridors and offered to drive me home. I wanted to sit in his clean car and disappear.

But Dad and Theresa were waiting for me in the foyer. Dad had been drinking one cheap coffee after another. A clutter of tiny plastic cups next to him. He waved his hands before the automatic doors as Theresa steered me out of the station. The sky was swollen with white-blue morning light. Everything in me hurt.

In the kitchen Dad made me a cup of warm milk and gave me two of Pauline's pills. He said Pauline was with Joe and Lydia at the hospital, waiting for news on Mush. The thought of Lydia was too much to bear. I pictured her learning about Mush and felt something inside me devour itself, like the crumple of paper over a candle. I was shaking as Theresa brought me upstairs and helped me undress. She spoke in quiet whispers. Arms up. That's it. Wait till I open your laces. She helped me into a long T-shirt. Put the duvet over me. Touched my hair. When I began to sob into the pillow, she did not leave. Eventually, as the world began to darken and slip, I felt her weight in the bed behind me. Her arm over my chest, like when she was small and used to sneak into my room. Her hand, hot over my heart. It was in her warmth that I fell asleep.

She squeezes my foot through the blanket. 'I had to put your phone on silent hours ago,' she says. 'It was ringing non-stop. Unknown number.'

'Any word on Mush?'

She shakes her head. 'Joe's just arrived downstairs. He's been getting updates from his dad on everything.'

I look for a hairclip and when Theresa passes one into my palm, she takes my hand for a moment. She makes to let go but I hold on.

'I'm sorry, Theresa.'

'No one thinks it's your fault.'

'I'm sorry. I'm sorry.'

We look at each other for a moment. Then she leans in and kisses me between my eyes. She runs a quick fingertip through the kiss, her finger trailing down the bridge of my nose.

I sink my face into her neck and let out a long breath. We stay against one another for a long time, each of us absorbing the juddering heat of the other.

Joe

THERE'S A SHRINE of Aidan in Rossie and Pauline's sitting room. Picture of him and Mush on their first day of primary school. First day you met them. Mush sat next to you and offered you some of his Maltesers. Said he liked your Turtles schoolbag.

Make tea. Make coffee. Do something useful. That's what Dad told you earlier. 'You'll need to be solid for that family today, because they can't be solid for themselves.'

He'd called in to see you at the hospital. You were still sitting up with the twins while Pauline went home to shower. The twins were both asleep. Dad was staring at them thoughtfully.

'They said much?'

You shook your head.

'Been talking to Helen?' he said.

'No. Theresa messaged me there, says they're all just awake. Was gonna head over there, maybe. Make myself useful.'

'Good man,' he said. 'It's moments like this where you see a fella's character.'

One of the last things Mush said to you was that you could barely take care of yourself. You felt your throat clot up. Swallowed the feeling back.

'Mush and I had this big blowout, couple of nights ago. I was thinking to myself, what if he doesn't pull through? What if that argument is the door I always walk through, whenever I remember him? Like... this stupid fight will colour every memory.'

Your face creased and Dad turned away and cleared his throat. He didn't need to see this. You were Joe fucking Brennan.

'The doctors will do the best they can, son. There'll be time for being upset. But this is his family's time.'

He was right. You held your breath. Counted to thirty. Waited for the feelings to sink back into the pit of your stomach.

'All we ever have is each other, eh?' Dad said.

You try to channel some of his stoicism now, as Helen and Theresa come downstairs. Helen looks destroyed.

'Hey,' she whispers.

You touch her arm and, to your surprise, she puts a hand over yours and holds it for a moment.

Tell them everything you know. Ger's still in police custody. The two Guards from yesterday are working him, but he isn't cooperating. They're treating his entire farm as a crime scene. The Guards found Blinkie's caravan in the Warren, by the long grass. Blinkie had no fixed address – he lived in a caravan outside his sister Moira's. Moira Roche was questioned at length last night, but isn't suspected of any wrongdoing. Blinkie had been absent for days and she couldn't get in touch with him. Phone records all check out. Forensics are at the caravan taking samples, but the twins were definitely there. Signs of a physical struggle. They found Marie's iPhone in the caravan, alongside an old photo album that belonged to Kala and dozens of Polaroids Kala had taken. The photos were all defaced. It was him sending all those weird messages on Marie's phone.

'Listen,' you say. 'I'm not supposed to know any of this, but Dad told me what they think happened. The Guards examined the scene last night. They found a weapon on Blinkie. A baton. He must have attacked Mush with it.'

'And what?' Helen says. 'Spontaneously fucking died afterwards? Be serious. I was *there*. I told the Guards – I saw a white van leave the barn while Mush—'

You wave your hands. 'Look, I don't know all the details yet. But according to Dad—'

'I'm telling you, Joe,' Helen says. 'That's not possible. You didn't see how they looked on the barn floor. Both of them. Their faces—'

'Oh, there she is now.'

It's Lydia, in the kitchen doorway. Herself and Rossie. Lydia's glaring at Helen.

Helen steps towards her. 'Lydia, I—'

Lydia slaps her in the face. It is clumsy, and connects badly. A dull thud.

'I *told* ye.' Lydia's mouth trembles. 'I *told* ye not to go looking for trouble.' Her hand flies at Helen's face again. Helen doesn't even try to avoid it. Lydia stops herself. Her fingers flutter in mid-air. 'I can't even bloody look at you.'

Her fingermarks are red on Helen's cheek.

She throws herself into a chair by the kitchen table, puts her head in her hands, rubs at her face, and searches her handbag. She takes out a packet of cigarettes and a lighter, muttering, 'What did he think he was doing? Hah? What was going through his mind?'

You look at Helen, wait for her to respond. But she just opens and closes her mouth, eyes all glassy, like a lost kid.

Say something.

'Mush was just trying to do good,' you say. 'You know Mush. All heart.'

'And no brain,' Lydia snaps. She tries three times to light her cigarette, but her hands are shaking so much she keeps missing the tip. 'Fucking *Christ*,' she roars, slamming the lighter down. She dips her head to her chest. 'What am I going to do without him?'

She begins to shake. Theresa puts an arm around her.

No one moves. Just the sound of the clock ticking, and Lydia's choked breaths. Whole room feels like it's spiralling. You want a drink.

When your phone rings it's a relief. Duck out to the hall. It's home.

'Dad,' you say. 'What's up?'

But it's Mam. 'There's someone here for you, Joe,' she says. 'I told him you were busy but he shoved past me into the house. Joe, he won't leave.'

'What?'

'Your father's not here. This fella's walking about the place like—'

Her voice cuts off. She speaks to someone, saying calm down, she's talking to me right now.

A man's voice says, 'Tell him he'd want to get over here sharpish before I lose me patience.'

'My son is a very busy man,' Mam says. 'Perhaps you should—'

'He's not too busy to see me,' the voice says. 'Tell him it's his old pal Teabag.'

Helen

I STAND ALONE in the garden. My jaw is throbbing. The heel of Lydia's hand made me bite my tongue. The feeling of chopped meat in my mouth. The taste lingers. Copper coins.

I am in the same spot I stood with Lydia when we were hiding from all the other women at the hen party. I remember how she hunched her shoulders and put on a deep voice, imitating Mush – *'I'm grand, leave me alone, would ya'* – and I spontaneously want to call Mush, for comfort. This has already happened several times now. Dumb instinct. He is part of some constellation through which I navigate the world.

I take my phone off mute. Anything to slip out of where I am. Theresa was right. Over thirty missed calls. All from an unknown number. The most recent was only five minutes ago.

Joe has been gone half an hour, maybe. Time is all woozy.

I chew on my cheeks. I keep chewing till I draw more blood.

A hand on my back, and I startle.

It is Dad, offering tea. He lingers, as though unsure if he should leave. Eventually he clears his throat. 'Don't be taking what Lydia said to heart,' he says. 'She didn't mean it.'

'Yes, she did.'

'Well,' he says, 'she's wrong.'

'No, she's not. Mush would never have been there if it wasn't for me.'

Dad rubs between his eyes. 'Mush knew what he was doing. Everyone underestimates that lad. He was trying to do right. So were you.' Dad goes to put a hand on my arm, then takes it away, as though afraid of my response. 'Mush would be glad you're okay, love. I know I am.'

He clears his throat again, noisily. Rubs the back of his neck.

'I'm s-so glad you're here. It's—'

My mobile rings. Dad immediately defers to it. Retreats into himself, steps back. 'You go and answer that now.'

'No,' I say, turning to him. I want to hear what he was going to say. 'It's fine.'

'Ah, no, it might be something important. Sure we've all the time in the world to be chatting.'

I hesitate, then answer. It is an unknown number, again.

'Who is this?'

'Helen. Finally. It's Dudley Brennan. This a bad time?'

'You're grand. What is it?'

'Can we meet?'

I look back into the kitchen, where Dad has gone to boil the kettle again, just for something to do. 'Can it wait?'

'There's something you need to see. I can't tell you over the phone – it's something I have to show you. It's relevant to what happened to Mush.'

When I do not answer, he says, 'We'll be done in no time. Just tell them you're going for a walk to clear your head. Don't mention me at all. I won't keep you for long. You remember where Cotter's shop used to be? There's a bookie's there now. I'll collect you.'

I take a moment.

'When can you be there?' I say.

'I'm there already.'

I tell Dad I'm going for a walk. As I open the front door, Theresa steps out into the hall.

'Where you off to?' she says.

Despite Dudley's request, I tell her the truth. For a moment I think she is going to try to stop me. 'Okay,' she says. 'But... be gentle with yourself.'

Outside, the air is prickled with hot static. Clouds like black jellyfish hover overhead. I hold my arms as I walk to the bookie's. Rain is patterning the ground, sparks of it catching in the hazard lights of passing cars. It looks later than it really is, as though night is arriving early.

In the distance, by the bookie's, there is a van parked at the kerb. Its lights flash at me three times. I think of Kala and her torch, out my back window. One. Two. Three. I see the shape of Dudley in the driver's seat. I wave to him. He waves back.

Joe

THIS FEELING, SEEING Teabag Lyons, standing in your parents'
sitting room. Mam normally insists all visitors remove their
shoes upon entering the house. But Teabag isn't a visitor. This
is a violation. His boots have already marked the cream carpet.

Mam's in the back garden. She told you when you arrived,
'I don't want a man like that here.'

He hasn't changed much over the years – hairline higher,
waist and neck thicker. He has his back to you, moving
about the room restlessly, fidgeting, sniffing, looking at the
Jungle Heart albums framed on the wall. The awards on the
mantelpiece.

'Always used to wonder what your house was like,' Teabag
says. He looks back at you in the mirror over the fireplace.
'Let me guess. Ye'd all sit in here together and watch the telly.
The big happy family, living the happy life.' He points to Dad's
armchair. 'That where your auld lad sits, is it? King fucking
Dudley, on his throne.'

Teabag examines a framed photo. You and Dad on the
Brooklyn Bridge, both giving the thumbs-up. He clicks his
tongue and sneers. 'Dudley Brennan claps and everyone
jumps. That's how it works.'

You're not the kid Teabag used to hound. You're Joe
fucking Brennan.

'What do you want?'

'I was looking for your auld lad,' he says. 'But he's not
answering my calls today. Reckon he might be in a bit of a

lather. Uncle Ger's keeping quiet, for now. But he knows your auld lad's like a cornered animal. Acting rash.'

He's talking gibberish. Fold your arms. No, that looks defensive. Step to the side. 'Yeah, I think you should leave.'

Teabag snorts. 'You're going to make me, are you? With them wall-climber arms on you? Think a few fucking tattoos and deadlifts mean fuck all to me? You wouldn't know what to do with me, even if you tried. Your whole life's been plain cruising.'

'You don't know anything about my life.'

'I know more about you than you know about yourself. Even when you were just a scrawny little shit, running around town with your tongue in Tits Lanann.'

He throws an eye at you, waits for you to react.

'Oh, there he is,' he smiles. 'The nice polite boy, holding back. Wouldn't stoop to my level, would you? Feels good, turning up your nose at cunts like me? Thinking your shit doesn't stink?'

You fold your arms. 'I was in the hospital with the twins all night. They're your actual family, right? Cos I've been taking care of them while you're—'

'Oh yeah. That's what you're doing. The Brennans, taking care of everyone. Well, aren't ye fucking great. Where would we all be without the Brennans? Where'd Mush be, if not for your auld lad? And the Lanann wan, too.'

His eyes linger on you.

'Jesus, you really have no idea.' He laughs. 'Well, fair play, like. Meself and the lads used to wonder why you never used your bit of fame to draw attention to her. Even though it's pure obvious all your early tunes are about her. I thought to meself, is Joe Brennan really that fucked up? Then I realized. It'd never *occur* to you to draw any attention to Kala Lanann. Not cos it'd dunk your auld lad in it. Oh no. You wouldn't talk about her cos it'd mean talking about anyone besides yourself. That's the secret, isn't it? This whole world was built for posh lads like you to be centre-stage while the rest of us slink about in the background, cleaning up after you.'

You scoff, but it feels weak. 'Is any of that supposed to mean something? Or am I meant to guess?'

He's getting irritated. The inky darkness of his eyes. They stare at you, shark-like, before he says, 'Kinlough Associates. Dudley ever talk to you about that? The little property consortium. Our nice fucking laundry for everything.'

When you're silent, he gestures about the room.

'D'you never ask yourself, growing up, where all this came from? How come your house is the biggest one on the road? Where'd that big fuck-off extension come from? The new car every year. Who pays for all that?'

'My Dad takes care of—'

'First smartphone I ever saw was one your dad got for you. The little fucking prince. He had it shipped over from fuck knows where. Falling into one pot of gold after another. All this crap, on one Guard's salary. Almost hard to believe.'

He sneers at your awards. 'All this fake shit.'

'I've worked for every—'

'You've walked through doors that were fucking open for you. Where'd the money come from? Who the fuck paid for all the time it took you to become Joe Brennan? All your gear, your music lessons? All those years paying London rent, without a fucking job? Yeah, I know all about that. Who paid for it? Your mam? Never worked a day in her life, leathery bitch. Too much time to be spending on the sunbed.'

'I don't—'

'Use. Your fucking. Brain. Where'd your dad get all that money from? Bet you've never even asked, have you? Let me guess. You've never cared about money. That's what loaded fuckers always say. Cunts who can afford not to give a fuck just *love* talking about it. Patting yourself on the back. But whose work was funding your dad's little bank? Whose spines he had to keep standing on to give his piglet the life of fucking Riley?'

'You want to know about my dad, ask him. I've never—'

'This isn't a fucking charade, like you and your auld lad. This is real. I'm real. My family's real.'

He steps towards you.

'You know, it was her who went to Dudley. The night she went missing. Oh yeah. Telling him all about her mother. Her fucked-up auld lad. The dogs. Mush's face. Like Dudley wasn't up to his neck in all of it. Like he wasn't part of it, every step of the way. Like he didn't inherit everything Mick Lanann had built with my family. Dudley brought her out for a spin that night. In the Warren. Told her he'd be taking an official statement. She got into your dad's car. I wonder when it dawned on her, what she'd gotten herself into. What was about to happen.'

He stands right before you. Too close.

'Still want me to leave?' he says. 'Push me. Go on. If you can make me move one step, I'll go.'

He shoves you.

'I said push me, cunt. Go on.'

You try to push him. But it's like you have no strength. Your arms are hollow.

Teabag laughs. 'There's nothing there, is there? Nothing but surface. You're Dudley's son, all right. Ah, don't look so frightened, Piglet. I'm only going to tell you about reality. Think of it as a gift, like. From me to you.'

He sniffs.

'D'you know,' he says, leaning close, 'I think today's going to be the first real day of your fucking life.'

Helen

THE COAST ROAD rushes beneath us. It is so dark with cloud that Dudley has the headlights on. He sings along quietly to the radio. He does not ask any questions about last night, and I am grateful. When I ask where we are driving, he tells me not far.

He asks, again, if I told anyone where I was going. My phone rings. It is Joe. I cancel the call. Dudley asks who it was.

'No one.'

'Looking for you back at home already, are they?' he says.

'No,' I say. 'It was no one.'

But my phone rings again. Joe, again. I put it on silent.

'They must be very confused,' he says. 'With everything that's after happening. Jumping to all sorts of conclusions.'

I lean against the window. I am so tired.

'Do you think Mush will wake up?' I say.

'I wouldn't imagine so.'

I look over at Dudley. For a moment, I find myself feeling the way others must feel when they look to me for a consoling lie. The cruelty of truth.

Dudley waves a hand. He is wearing ridiculous leather gloves. He goes on, 'His head injuries were so severe, by rights he should be dead' – and I wish he would shut up.

Joe keeps ringing me, over and over.

We pass Kala's house. Pass the entrance to Caille Woods. Dudley turns us in to the Warren. For an insane moment I wonder if he is taking me back to Ger's farm.

I begin to tell Dudley what the Guards told me, about the case records. He had already warned me about leads that weren't followed up back in 2003. The only explanation behind disappearing evidence, interference with files, is some sort of Garda involvement. The Mammy said as much last night: *Where there's a crew like the Lyons, there's always a Mick.*

Dudley keeps his eyes on the road.

My phone rings again. This time it is Theresa.

I answer, 'Jesus, what?'

'Helen!' It is Joe. He sounds breathless, panicked. 'Helen, where are you? Theresa said you were meeting my dad.'

'Yeah.'

'Don't meet him, Helen. Where are you? Theresa and I will get you. You're not safe.'

'What are you talking about?'

On the other end of the line I hear him and Theresa mutter to each other. Theresa comes on the phone. 'Helen. Act completely normally, okay? Give me simple answers. Are you with Dudley right now?'

'Yes?'

'Helen,' she says. Her voice is tight. 'Helen, you need to get away from him. He's not safe.'

I frown. Theresa is speaking rapidly at the end of the line. She is talking about Kala. About Kala's mother. About Mush, last night. This sour thrum of the heart as she talks, a strange sensation of pieces slowly clicking into place. Garda involvement. Missing evidence. Cops who helped Mick Lanann. On Sunday when I met Aoife – Dudley and Ger, both in the same Carthy coffeehouse at the same time.

Dudley is watching me. He is wearing gloves. He is steering us down a narrow slip road of the Warren, next to Caille Woods. The road is getting darker, stone walls hemming us in, trees bunched over the van.

I keep my voice calm. 'Next week,' I say. 'I'll be taking over the morning group from Stefan.'

'What?' Theresa says. 'Helen, you— What? Helen, where are you?'

'That's right,' I say. 'I'll head over to that place where Misty ran her last group. You remember where that is? Misty? Yeah. All right... Byeeee.'

I hang up.

Dudley glances over at me. His eyes are busy. Suddenly he pulls the van over, the tyres shriek and I lurch forward and the seat belt cuts into my skin and he is already out of his door, rushing around the front of the van as I struggle out of my seat belt and try to crawl across his seat to get out his door but it is too late, I hear my door open and suddenly his fingers are in the waist of my jeans, tugging me back, the strap of my handbag tight around my throat, jerking me upwards. I gag and reach behind me but my nails catch only air and he slams my head hard into the dashboard, a huge clapping sound, my eyes watering and I am bleeding from somewhere in my face while everything echoes slow and fast as I levitate backwards out of the van – he is dragging me outside – and I try to get my footing but the ground thuds into my back and knocks the air from me and I groan, fumbling into my handbag while Dudley opens the side door of the van.

Inside it there is nothing. Darkness.

This is where he will put me.

In the distance I hear a voice shout, 'No,' and I think someone is coming to help me. But no. It is just my voice. 'No-no-no-no-no—'

My hands scramble through my bag. Fingertips close around the canister of bear spray, hook into the pin. As Dudley's footsteps crunch the grit on the road he says, *Stop that*, and kicks my arm and I drop the canister and he is standing on my wrist saying, *Calm yourself*, and he kneels over me, *Stop fighting, it's okay*, holds me by the throat squeezing as my hand beats about the ground next to me trying to find the cool metal of the canister at my fingertips but I cannot grip it and it feels like my neck is going to cave in my eyes bursting I feel the canister in my hand and swing it upwards and squeeze the trigger and there is a great burst between us, strong enough to make both of us choke and he falls off me, retching on all fours as I stagger to my feet coughing with eyes blurred face crackling raw rash as I run my head ringing with the rush of the grass around me because I am racing to the wall of trees, to the edge of Caille Woods, screaming, 'Help!' screaming, 'Help me!' but it is beginning to rain harder now and the sound swallows my voice as I reach the edges of the trees and I look back and see a light beam splitting the dark in the road—

He has a torch. He is already following me. I hear my name in the rain.

I run into the trees.

Branches tear at me and I grab them, break them, hold my hands before me as I run squinting, half blind, stumbling over knots in the earth, slipping in fresh muck, the rain stinging my spray-burned skin, the sky boiling, and I am moaning, I am weak, I am not going fast enough.

'Helen!'

I see the glow of his torchlight bounce off the trees about me and realize that, by tearing all the branches, I have been clearing an easy path for him to follow, to catch up. I am running out of distance. I am running out of time.

The Crawley House. I can see it up above. Its shadow slouches behind the trees, waiting for me. My chest feels like it is bursting.

When I reach the clearing at the top of the hill, the rain is ferocious. It punches the earth. 'Help!' I scream. But there is no one there. I go to the Crawley House. I do not go inside. I am not a fool, I will not trap myself.

But I have trapped myself. I am alone in this, now. Alone with Dudley.

I round the corner of the Crawley House and lean against the wall. My lungs ache. My throat is shredded with the spray. My legs and arms feel weak. A stabbing pain in my side, below my ribs.

I take my phone and try to call Theresa. No signal. I almost cry.

When I peer around the corner I see Dudley's torch beam lop through the trees, coming closer.

But suddenly the torch stops. It hovers in the trees, then slowly sinks to the ground.

The rain squalls. I am squinting at the trees, trying to see movement. But the rain is too thick. The torchlight is on the ground, and still.

What is he doing? Is he waiting for something? Has he seen me?

It takes a moment to realize what is happening. He has seen me. And he is not where the torch lies. He has left it down there to distract me. He has—

A fist closes tight on my hair and yanks me back. The pain shoots up my neck and I shout but he has me off balance and is pulling me by the hair. My heels dig at the ground but I am stumbling. He is dragging me inside the Crawley House.

I am screaming.

'Shut up.' His voice echoes off the walls. 'Just fucking shut up.'

He sounds like he is on the verge of tears. This frightens me even more.

He knocks me to the ground and I reach for one of the stones that lie scattered about the floor. I take one in my fist but he is too fast and he is on top of me, knocking it from my hand, turning me over on my back and holding me by the neck, and I reach to scratch at his face because Mam always told me to do that, get the DNA under your nails, that's the best most women can hope for, and I realize I am one of those women, I am another one of those women, and I do not know if it is this thought or the way my head lifts and claps off the ground that suddenly makes all the strength leave me, nothing above me now but a closing sort of dark and Dudley's wild eyes and the sound of my name, my name

Joe

'HELEN!' THERESA SCREAMS. 'Helen!'

She's faster than you, running ahead of you, up the hill to the Crawley House.

'Helen!'

Follow Theresa inside, see her hunched over someone, something. The freakish sight of Theresa on your dad's back and, underneath both of them, Helen's legs, juddering. A nightmare vision, this screeching six-legged monster, it's so outlandish that you freeze.

Theresa's head snaps up and she falls backwards, flailing. Blood is pouring from her nose. Dad turns from Helen and goes after Theresa. He doesn't even see you standing there.

The look in his eyes.

He is choking Theresa. Hitting her.

'Stop!' you shout. Get your dominant forearm around his neck. Place your non-dominant hand behind his head. Wrap your arm tightly around his neck and grab his shoulder, stabilize your grip. Slide your non-dominant hand behind his head, wrap your fingers around your elbow, lock your arm in pla—

But he's a fucking bull under you. He surges up onto his feet, and walks you backwards with such speed you almost loosen your grip on him. He slams you into the wall, but you don't let go. 'Stop it,' you gasp. He slams back into you, again. Again.

You're squeezing tighter on your elbow when it happens. The sharp shooting pain, like white light coursing through your arm. Your injury. The bruising, all that weak tissue, pulling apart. The pain is so intense your vision blotches and your grip slackens and Dad shakes himself out of the grip and turns to grab your throat and glares at you with such hate it frightens you and you realize that yes, you would let him destroy you, yes, you—

And then he recognizes you.

It all happens very slowly, the following microseconds. A rush of things over Dad's face – confusion, a childlike lostness, a regaining of control, a frowning as he opens his mouth to speak – when there's an almighty scream and a crack and Dad's eyes roll and his legs buckle and he hits the ground.

Theresa is standing behind him, eyes wide, a large stone in her fist.

'Dad!' you say.

He's on his back. One of his legs kicks wildly, full of current.

Theresa is crouching over Helen. 'Please wake up, please wake up.'

'Dad!' you shout.

Theresa tells you to call an ambulance. But there's no fucking coverage.

You run down the hill, through the woods, trying to get signal. The rain is relentless. No bright-coated walkers, no joggers. The light is jangled in the trees, a horrible flashing feeling in your chest, your belly, shouting down the phone at the operator, alone on the Coast Road, hoping for headlights in the rain.

To Here Knows When

Helen

SHARDS OF LIGHT spark off her back as we cycle beneath the trees. She is more confident on a bike than me – I have not cycled since I was a teenager. But rituals are a way of holding the world intact, and Theresa and I have been making this journey every day. We eat breakfast together, make a flask of coffee to bring to Dad, and cycle under the trees of Blake's Road, across Toner's Bridge and through the Widow's Arch, past the street cleaners and keg-changers on Fox Street, then up the hill, pedalling hard against the slope, till we reach the side door of the hospital.

They brought me here in an ambulance, on a stretcher. I kept trying to sit up and they kept insisting I lie down. At one point I tried to get off the stretcher, and the ambulance began to blot and spin. The paramedics were patient, and it was their matter-of-fact kindness, the idea that care for other people could be formalized in such a way, that whole professions and disciplines and rituals could cultivate themselves around the simple goal of taking care of people, which made me begin to cry on the stretcher. The paramedic was a gruff man with a Birmingham accent. 'Don't worry, love, you'll be fine.' He thought I was just in pain, in shock. Perhaps I was. He made me inhale something in a plastic mask and my head began to warp. The light in the ambulance suddenly spangled. Part of me was convinced the paramedic was secretly Mush. I wanted to hug him.

Theresa and I were discharged within a few hours. My neck was discoloured ugliness, like the Mammy's. Theresa's nose was broken, but there was little they could do about that besides painkillers. The bruising under her eyes was vivid, like the shadows on peaches, but she was upbeat, commenting every hour or two about how she thought the swelling was going down. Before, I would have dismissed this as a pathological commitment to cheerfulness. But people cope differently. This is her way. We both sleep in my bed because we are afraid to sleep alone, and we both wake up often, feeling drowned. We take turns calming each other in the night. There is something solid and grounding in the repetition. It makes the world seem like it can be relied upon.

This morning I checked the news on my phone, waiting for the coffee to brew. I have been avoiding most media and online commentary since the press discovered the Joe Brennan angle. Initially, at least, they had focused entirely on the Garda aspect of the story: Dudley Brennan, the legacy of Mick Lanann, a history of Garda-sanctioned illegal operations in Kinlough. All of it funnelled through Kinlough Associates, who have been laundering their illegal activities since the eighties by helping to found and bankroll the Races, the Festival, and more. Kinlough's economy, both legal and illegal, has been structured to ensure that everyone, local or tourist, knowingly or not, has been putting money into Kinlough Associates for years.

I learned most of this from Good Cop and Bad Cop. Caille Cottages, the holiday homes by the lake, was only the latest major Kinlough Associates project. But Ger and Teabag had grown dissatisfied with the share of the profits Dudley had been allocating them. They were attempting to expand their margin, not by disputing with Dudley, but by scamming multiple other partners out of their share in the property deal. Blinkie was just one of those who lost out financially. The Lyons had expected no significant blowback from this. That was a mistake.

The media are all peddling the line that it was Dudley Brennan alone who ensured no Garda interference with the organization's activities, expanding on a foundation Mick Lanann had put in place. The idea that one man could do this, that there was not a broader system of corruption within the Gardaí, a network of which Dudley was just a leading part, was grotesque.

But then it came out that Joe Brennan was Dudley's son, and that he had been Kala's boyfriend, and the press got far worse. All questions of systemic corruption and collusion forgotten. Everything reduced to persona. Social media was like plunging into sewage. I scrolled through the comments. The ones that claimed to speak for Kala were the worst. Her name, reduced to a rhetorical device, fresh meat for likes and Retweets. Our lived experience being used as the opening paragraph for clickbait op-eds making facile points.

So much noise, and Kala is nowhere to be found inside any of it. It is like they are erasing her all over again.

The night she went missing, after she had left Mush at the hospital, she called Dudley and arranged to meet him. He collected her in an unmarked Hyundai. When I met him out in Carthy, Dudley had told me the Hyundai had belonged to Seamus Roche; in reality, the car was never traced to anyone. Kala told Dudley about everything she knew. The dogfighting, the disfiguring of Mush, the abuse and rape of Fiona by her father, the Garda-aided cover-up of Fiona's death. She had no idea she was speaking to someone implicated in all of those crimes.

I see this often, in my mind's eye: the CCTV footage of Kala crossing Toner's Bridge, vulnerable but defiant, refusing to be beaten by Kinlough. I picture her stepping into Dudley Brennan's car, believing he was going to help her.

Mush is in the intensive care unit, on the fifth floor. He remains in an induced coma. Lydia refuses to let me visit his bedside. Still, I go to the hospital every day to be close to where he is, to sit with the twins. Every day, Theresa and I cut through the waiting area of the hospital. We are familiar with the antiseptic smell, the blank surfaces, the familiar faces wearing brave smiles. The old man who makes his lost walk down the ground-floor corridor every hour, saluting us in his chequered dressing gown. All the burning points of life – birth and death, loss and recovery – cradled in an impersonal space. The hot core of the world, raging beneath a calm surface.

Dad is usually asleep in the chair by Donna's bed when we arrive. Pauline, holding Marie's hand, her head dipping low, then jerking up.

It took Donna much longer than Marie to come around. The first person she asked for was Mush. We needed to explain everything to her several times, and each time I could see she did not understand, and we would soon have to tell her again. She has barely spoken a word since waking up. It is like all her language has been snatched away. Almost everything she has to say, she whispers first in Marie's ear.

'Oh, Donna's getting back to herself now,' Pauline insists every morning, squeezing Donna's hand, and we all agree loudly, as though that will make it true. But she moans and sweats in her sleep, and she wakes up yelling, every time. It takes ages to calm her down. Another ritual.

Marie is usually awake whenever Theresa and I arrive at the hospital. Theresa passes Dad the flask of coffee and he knocks it back before he leaves us to do the morning shift in the bike shop. I see that Dad and Marie have in-jokes. He always gives her the first cup of coffee from the flask, and when he leaves for work, they do a fist-bump and make slow explosion sounds with their mouths. It looks like something they might have done when she was a few years younger, but experiences like what she has been through tend to make people older and more childlike at the same time. Time goes crooked, folds itself inside the body.

My thoughts are like this a lot these days. Slants of light crossing through one another. Glimpses. I am not quite in the world. I see the same sort of in-between space swimming in the twins' eyes. They are very far from us. We are all far, together.

*

Yesterday, I came back from the toilet and saw Marie leaning over Donna's bed as Donna slept, whispering in her ear. I hung back for a while. I did not want to intrude. Marie kissed Donna's hand. When I eventually approached them, Marie's eyes were pooled. She did not cover up her tears, she just sat in a chair next to Donna and quietly cried.

I sat beside her and we stayed like that for a while, saying nothing, watching the slow rise and fall of Donna's chest. The bleeps and hisses of machinery on the ward. Marie began to speak about what had happened. She does this every day. I understand it – the compulsion to repeat the story, wrangle the shapelessness of experience into some form, contain it in language. Each time, her sentences became clearer, more concise.

'Blinkie'd been acting all weird for a good while. He'd given us all these photos of Aidan and Kala. Told us there was plenty more where that came from, if we could pay him what he wanted. He'd started asking us for crazy money, like. Way more than we'd been paying him for the psychic readings. I was up for trying to get it. I thought we could squeeze a few quid out of Mush, maybe. But Donna was pure suspicious, like. Where'd Blinkie get these pictures from? Why's he looking for so much cash? I was like, *whatever, Donna.* That night we'd arranged to meet Blinkie at Hogan's Square. We took a bus out with him to where his caravan was. But out at the caravan, Donna started going *off,* like. Asking Blinkie all about the photos. *Why d'you have them, where'd you get them?* The whole time he's been going through these drawers in the caravan, looking for something. He kept saying he was our friend. I was getting a bit freaked out, I just wanted to go. But Donna just kept going at him. Goading him, like. And he turns around and just lunges at her, grabs her by the neck and holds this rag up to her face. And she's kicking and scratching and I'm hitting him and yanking his hair but he's so much stronger and he doesn't let go of Donna till she just, like, drops onto the floor of the caravan. I thought she was dead, like. And I go down to help her when I feel his arm around me neck and this stinky rag over me face, and then I'm gone too.'

When they woke up, they were locked in Kala's room. They had no idea where they were. Blinkie had left them there, to go up to Ger's farm. I have discussed, with Good Cop and Bad Cop, what Blinkie had been planning to do there; he had already been waging a campaign against the Lyons for a while. It began with attacking their property, and escalated to poisoning Ger's dogs. He had planted Kala's remains on the building site by the time he began to drip-feed information to the twins about Aidan, making promises to the Mammy that he would help her find out the truth of what happened to Kala. Kidnapping the twins was a calculated tactic to extort money from Ger. During the examination of Blinkie's remains, the Guards found several defaced photographs – pictures of Kala, and of the twins – in his pockets. They believe his plan was to trash the twins' room and leave the photos on the bed as tokens of ransom. This plan went out the window when Ger and Teabag caught him tearing up the house. Blinkie would have known the Lyons would never let him leave the farm alive if he admitted to endangering the twins. So Ger and Teabag put him in the barn, and the twins were left downstairs without water, with the Mammy unable to reach them. That is when the slow horrors began in Kala's basement. Their bodies gradually shutting down.

'It was awful,' Marie said. 'You've no idea how awful it was.'

She is right. I do not. But I do not pretend to understand. She just needs to be listened to.

Every couple of hours, I ask the twins if they want to go outside for some air. I tell them the sunshine will do them good. They always say no. They will not step outside the hospital until Mush has woken up.

But there is still no sign of Mush waking up.

*

Some afternoons, Marie and I share Mush stories, making each other laugh. Donna seems more responsive to conversations like this. She smiles. Yesterday, Marie was saying how they used to upload videos of themselves pulling pranks on Mush. She pulled up a video of them, probably about twelve years old, sneaking behind Mush as he slept on the sofa, setting up speakers by his head and blasting him with a song by Cannibal Corpse.

Marie scoffed. She smirked at Donna, and Donna put on a deep Mush-like voice that startled me. '*Me fuckin' ears*,' she said. '*Oh noooo.*'

They laughed at each other and, for a moment, I saw it – a flash between them, Aidan's eyes, a flare of mischief, and it was like Mush was there, nudging me, saying, 'See? The twins!' But he was not.

I smiled at them, trying to hide the quivering tenderness in my stomach, like my insides were made of light and the light was threatening to burn brighter than I could handle. This feeling of too-much is always there these days. It happens whenever Marie scoots next to Donna on her bed and plays videos off her phone, talking to Donna like she is back to normal. There is a video in which Donna is playing tunes with Dad. They are in the Crannóg, part of a large group of musicians on a session. The music is ferocious, racing along. Dad is on the guitar and Donna is playing the box, frowning with concentration, staring down. She looks so much like Aidan in this clip, it startles me. There is a moment where she looks up at Dad and he smiles at her with his eyes and you can see Donna biting back a smile of her own, knowing that she is playing well.

I watched Marie whispering to Donna about the video, and thought of the night I spent at the Crannóg with Mush and Joe, of Mush getting me in a headlock when I was giving out about trad – '*Helen*,' he'd said. '*Heleeeeen*' – and I had to go to the hospital bathroom and sit in a cubicle for a long time, holding my arms.

I have seen Joe in the hospital once, but I did not approach. He was in a private room, next to Dudley's bed. I stood in the hall and watched him sitting, elbows in his lap, staring at his dad. A shaft of light from outside had broken around his chair. His eyes were like hollows. There was something dreamlike about it. He saw me and hesitated. He looked utterly lost. Then he slowly raised his hand, and I raised mine.

Theresa invites him to join us in the garden every evening. He is too ashamed to come. Theresa keeps inviting him, regardless. There is a strange sort of power in how she consciously lays her heart bare to the world. It makes me think of something Mush said to me while we were parked in the Warren, something like: *It takes strength to be open to life, to the possibility things will change for the better.* I did not believe him when he told me that those words were not his, but something Dad had once said about Pauline. I have been thinking about those words a lot, over the past few days. They remind me of Mam's notebooks, and what she wrote about how everything always happens in the present, but the present can echo forwards and backwards in time to itself.

Last night I said this to Theresa as we sat in the back garden, before a fire she had built in a small iron pit. She stretched her arms behind her in a slow, feline movement. 'Well, there's that whole mystical messianic idea about redemption in time, no? I think that's what Mam was getting at. Kind of Talmudic thing she was into, I guess.'

She said this in an offhand way, like she was talking about the weather. I had no idea what she meant. I asked her to go on.

Theresa was staring into the curling heat. 'Basically, it's this idea of how all suffering people project their ideas of something better into the future. So by being alive now, we all carry this redemptive promise that was dreamed into time by the suffering people of the past. And, like, every present generation has the potential to honour that promise. What we do now can echo back and redeem what was lost. Every present moment is the gate through which the Messiah can pass. Something like that. Long story short, you gotta believe in the world if you want to save it.'

She added wood to the fire.

'I think you should write something about Kala,' she said. 'Something that's real.'

In the firelight, she looked like Mam.

My stomach was swimming with the too-much feeling again. Normally I would pull back from feeling such vertigo, but I am trying hard to stay true to this jangled whir of the guts. This is the real reason I am staying offline. The internet smothers me with thoughts that are too easy to think, feelings that are too easy to feel. Whatever the too-much feeling is, I am curious.

But this morning it really is too much. In the hospital ward, before we even arrive at the twins' beds, I can feel a flutter of energy. Dad is holding a wheelchair in place while a nurse guides Donna out of her bed. Marie is pacing back and forth excitedly and Pauline is telling her to calm down, she'll only exhaust herself.

'What's happening?' Theresa asks.

'Auntie Lydia,' Marie says. 'She thinks she felt an actual pulse in Mush's hand. Like maybe he kind of squeezed it.'

Dad looks at me, a cautious expression on his face.

'Let's not get overexcited,' he says. 'We don't know what the doctor's said. And we need to be calm, Marie, when we go upstairs.'

'Yeah, yeah, sure,' Marie says. She licks her finger and rubs at a smudge on Donna's face and Donna grumbles. Marie takes Pauline's phone and points it at Donna in the wheelchair. 'Donna, like, I just have to Snapchat this. Stephen Hawking here.'

'Fuck off,' Donna says.

I linger behind as they leave for the elevator.

Marie looks back. 'What are you doing?'

'Lydia wouldn't want me up there,' I say.

'Fuck *that*,' Donna says.

'Donna!' Pauline says.

'Mush would want you there,' Donna says. 'We want you up there. Come up to fuck, would ya.'

'Donna, the language,' Pauline says. But I can see she is happy. It is the most Donna has said in days.

Things move very quickly then. Marie links her arm in mine and marches to the elevators. The doors glide shut behind us. Donna and Marie look at themselves in the mirror and make rapid adjustments to their hair.

'State of your eyes,' Marie says.

'Your whole actual face,' Donna says.

We go past the rows of beds. Mush's eyes are closed. He is in a hospital gown, arms limp at his sides. From his mouth, a tube coils to a machine next to the bed. The tube is held in place by a mesh of bandages all over his lower jaw. At the edge of his curls, there is a shadow of discoloured skin where his bruises are still changing.

Lydia's smile drops when she sees me with the others.

'Can I hold his hand?' Donna says to her.

Lydia nods, still looking at me. Dad wheels Donna to Mush's side. She takes his left hand, while Marie goes to the other side of the bed to hold his right.

'I thought you said he was waking up,' Marie says.

'I thought I felt a squeeze,' Lydia says. 'Maybe I was only imagining it, I don't know. Me head's addled. Doctor said that waking up from something like this isn't the same as switching on a light.'

'But he *will* wake up,' Marie says. 'Won't he?'

My body feels like it is under siege, looking at him there. It is the too-much feeling, again. Donna has noticed my agitation.

'Helen,' she says.

The others look at me. I do not want them to see me upset. I do not want them to ask if I am okay. I bite down on my cheeks.

'D'you wanna hold Mush's hand?' Donna says.

I blink.

Lydia breathes heavily through her nose. She looks me in the eyes. 'He'd probably like that,' she says. As I pass her, she stops me and squeezes my shoulder quickly.

Mush's hand is large in mine. I touch his pulse. I close my eyes till it feels like there is fire beneath my eyelids, and I am alone in this moment with him.

I open my eyes and look back at the others gathered around the bed, staring at Mush with open faces, all wanting him to be okay. At first I think it is their suffering that makes my belly ache. Then I realize, it is not their suffering that frightens me, but their hope. I feel my stomach being pierced by it and instinctively want to retreat.

I ask the twins if they want to go outside for some air. They decline, as I knew they would.

'Not till Mush wakes up,' Marie says.

'Exactly,' Donna says. 'We'll follow you out once he starts waking up.'

This sort of magical thinking makes my belly rev further. Heart pain, cleansing, violent.

I nod and make to leave, but Theresa has noticed I am upset and she follows.

We go to where we parked our bikes, at the top of the hill. I lean against mine and try to roll a cigarette. But my hands cannot do it this morning, so I give up.

Theresa does not comment. She knows me.

She taps at her phone. 'We'll see if Joe wants to join us,' she says.

Down the hill, Kinlough is quivering in the light. Ropes of heat turn in the distance, and it looks like a tide from which one thing rises to the surface, now another. The sunflash of distant cars. The sounds of nearby laughter. The birds changing formation in the soaring quiet. There's a turning melt of sky above us. The town glittering below. This is where I saw Mush and Kala pedalling towards the roar of the road, for ever ahead. We are perched on our bikes at the top of the hill. And they are not.

I am about to say this to Theresa when there is a crunch of footsteps on the gravel behind us. Theresa looks up from her phone and turns on her bike to see who is coming. Her face brightens, her eyes flare, her mouth opens wide.

'Hello, *you*,' she says.

She wobbles on her bike and I reach out to catch her, in case she falls.

Acknowledgments

Thanks to my brilliant agent, Lucy Luck. Without you, none of this would exist. I can't thank you enough. Thanks to all at C&W, especially Saida Azizova, Kate Burton, César Castañeda Gámez and Matilda Ayris. Thanks to Anna Weguelin and Theo Roberts at Curtis Brown.

Huge thanks to my editors, James Roxburgh at Atlantic and Lee Boudreaux at Doubleday. Your intelligence, sense of the craic, generosity of spirit, and commitment to the Kinlough crew has been incredible.

It takes loads of people to transform a Word document on a laptop into a physical book that exists in the world. In London, thanks to everyone at Atlantic Books, in particular the following folk and their teams: Joanna Lee; Felice McKeown; Kirsty Doole and Kate Straker; Dave Woodhouse and Gemma Davis; Niccolò De Bianchi; and Emma Heyworth-Dunn. Thank you to Helen Crawford-White for the gorgeous UK cover design. In New York, thanks to everyone at Doubleday: to Cara Reilly for her help on all things, big and small; and to the following people and their teams: Lindsay Mandel; Jillian Briglia; Vimi Santokhi, Romeo Enriquez, Amy Brosey and Anna Knighton. A special thank you to Kathy Hourigan, and to Bill Thomas. Thank you to Emily Mahon for the wonderful US cover design, and to my sister Sarah for all her Lynchian magic. Finally, thanks to Mary Chamberlain for her careful copy-editing.

I couldn't have written this book without the time afforded by getting a literature bursary from the Arts Council. I'll always be grateful for this. A special thank you to Lisa Coen, Sarah Davis-Goff, and Sara Baume for their support and advice. One reason there's so much good writing coming out of Ireland is because of Arts Council-supported literary journals and organisations like the Irish Writers Centre, all of whom actively nurture Ireland's literary ecosystem and strive to make it accessible to as many people as possible. Thanks to Sean O'Reilly, Declan Meade and everyone behind the Stinging Fly Summer School; to Sarah Moore Fitzgerald and the Doolin Writers' Winter School team; and to Belinda McKeon for her 'Finding Fiction's Shape' workshop.

Thanks to the good people of Cultuurloket, especially Tobias Van Royen.

Thanks to all at 190 – Colette, Brendan, Ciara, Graham, and Sara; thanks to Veerle Staepels and Karel de Vos; Earthsong and the field; Galway friends, especially Andrew White, Brendan Jones and Patrick O'Toole; college crew back home and abroad; Tom and Susie Besant; Neasa Malone and Ruth McAuliffe; Rosanne Claes, Marie Claes, Margo Van Herreweghen, Ignace Wouters, and Vera Tylzanowski; a special thanks to Rein De Wilde for his photographic magic. Thanks to Sammy and Nuala for the vibes.

A very special thank you to Daniel Leufer and G.P. Parhar for taking me aside and telling me I needed to start. Ye're true friends. Ye changed the direction of my life.

Thank you to my sister Sarah, and Joe Loftus, two beautiful people and fighters of the good fight. Thanks to my parents. We'd be here for another hundred pages if I got into all the reasons why. I love ye so much.

Most of all, thank you to Chloë, het kleine aapje x

Note on the Author

Colin Walsh's short stories have won several awards including the RTE Francis MacManus Short Story Prize and the Hennessy Literary Award. In 2019 he was named Hennessy New Irish Writer of the Year. His writing has been published in the *Stinging Fly*, the *Irish Times* and broadcast on RTE Radio 1 and BBC Radio 4. *Kala* is his first novel. He is from Galway and lives in Belgium.